Warren Sparks is the owner of the local mill providing employment to most of the residents of the quiet forestry Town of Lakedge. When he suddenly dies, the search for his heirs unveils a load of issues for the employees and the town. Greed is at the heart of the conflict that could spell the end for Lakedge.

Once again, Joshua Stuart, the town manager, has to devote all his energy and ingeniousness to save the town. But he is caught in the middle of a scandal. With suspicion of foul play hanging over him, his way of life, even his family is in jeopardy. Having survived many disasters before, will Josh and Lakedge finally perish to the demon of greed?

Table of Contents

Acknowledgements

I wish to thank Jay N. Rosenblatt for the legal advice that came at the most appropriate time while I was envisioning options to get Lakedge through their predicament.

Having encountered some difficulties in the editing of my previous books, I decided to expand my editing team and asked a few more people to help me, each with their own specialty.

So I want to thank all members of my review team:

Brian Reid, a fan from Merrickville in Ontario, who was a bit disappointed with my previous editions, and decided that helping out was a constructive form of critique.

Joan Crouse, a neighbour who was so enthralled in the story that she kept forgetting to correct the text; just the fact that she enjoyed the book so much is enough for me.

Angie Cedrone, an English Literature teacher in High School, who had several hours on her hands to help me out; he mastery of the language add tremendous value.

Nicole Normand, my roommate for life, my biggest fan, supporter and critic, who gets annoyed when I forget to put question marks and other punctuation.

Special Salute

I started planning this book in mid-2006 as I was finishing *The Curse of El Niño*. I wanted to show the risk that small towns faced particularly if they were heavily dependent on one industry. Then in February 2007, with this book already well underway, the Town of Nipigon, Ontario, Canada, faced exactly the situation I was describing. A major fire destroyed the MultiPly lumber mill, one of the major employers in the small town; Nipigon had 2000 citizens at the time, MultiPly employed 175 of them.

For a short time, as I followed through the various media including the town's website regarding the struggles Nipigon was facing, I wondered if I should continue with this book as per my original plan. I kept reading news, council decisions, and comments on the web regarding Nipigon. What I noticed was how the community pulled together to regroup, console each other, and rebuild. This convinced me that what I was writing needed to be said. As I have tried to express in the two previous books in the series, small communities are often more resilient than larger ones because everyone knows everyone else, and everyone cares for each other. When a disaster hits one of its members, the community as a whole works to find a solution. Although the characters and the situations in my book are fictitious, I was inspired by the commitment of the citizens of Nipigon to transcend their ordeal and survive as a thriving community again.

Prologue

Brent quietly pushed the door open and wheeled in the breakfast cart. He left it in the middle of the room so he could draw open the curtains. It had been his daily routine for almost ten years now. Since his accident, Brent was no longer able to chop down trees. So Warren Sparks, the owner of the mill and the richest resident of Lakedge, had taken him in as his personal valet.

Pulling the curtains aside, he let in the first rays of sunshine peaking through the branches of the nearby forest. With unstained snow on the ground, the effect was brilliant. Each snowflake reflected the sunshine creating an illumination in heavy contrast with the darkness of the bedroom.

Warren's bedroom was furnished with a dark brown stain. The wood panelling and the floors were of exotic hardwoods of different shades, intricately carved with elegant designs. The oil paintings were mostly native, depicting majestic animals and birds surrounded by peaceful landscapes. Warren Sparks lived in the forest, and was a part of it in every way.

Brent went back to the cart for Warren's breakfast, kept warm in a chafing dish. He rolled the cart closer to the bed. Usually Warren would sit up as soon as the curtains were opened. This morning he hadn't moved yet so Brent came closer.

"Mr. Sparks. Good morning. It's almost seven o'clock."

He waited. No answer came. He tried again.

"Good morning Mr. Sparks. I have your breakfast." Hesitantly, he added, "Would you prefer I came back later?"

Again, no response came from the bed. The man was turned on his side, almost in a foetal position. Brent took a chance and tapped him on the shoulder, repeating his greeting with less assurance. He started to worry and leaned in. Warren was too still. Something was wrong. Brent then began to gently pull Warren on the shoulder towards him. Warren gave no resistance. He rolled over in Brent's direction, his eyes open, but looking nowhere.

Brent gasped. He grabbed Warren's hand. It felt cold. Although he wasn't experienced at this, he started searching for a pulse. He couldn't find one and feared the worst. He looked closely at Warren's chest and could see no expansion. The man wasn't breathing.

Brent didn't know CPR. He suddenly regretted never having taken the course. He took the phone on the night table and dialled 9-1-1. He explained the situation. The operator assured him an emergency crew was on the way.

Brent looked at his boss again. His face was a bit constricted. Warren Sparks was wrinkled, as most people close to eighty years old would be. This morning it held an additional appearance, an expression of pain and surprise. Brent couldn't bear to watch this. He turned away, trying to find something else to look at while waiting.

He remembered the cart and went to turn off the burners. This was one breakfast nobody would enjoy. He decided it would be better for him to leave the room. He closed the door and went downstairs to wait for the emergency crew.

As he sat on the sofa in the lobby, a shiver ran through him. This man was like family to him. Warren had taken him in when he was most vulnerable. Was he really gone? Although Warren was his boss, they had developed camaraderie. They told jokes together, they shared difficulties, they discussed issues, and they knew almost everything about each other.

The chime rang in the lobby from an old grandfather clock. Seven metal gongs. Brent started to get up. His routine required that he bring up Warren's coffee. He felt ridiculous. There would be no more coffee served. He looked at the clock, through a veil of tears in his eyes.

He sat again expecting to hear the door chime every second. Being so distant from most services also meant the wait was longer. In a situation like his, the wait was agony. If his diagnosis was confirmed, Warren's death was unexpected at best, possibly a mystery. The man had been active, working at least half days even at his age.

Questions swirled in Brent's head. How he wished the ambulance were here. If he had to answer the paramedics' questions he wouldn't have time for his personal soul searching.

This day would be the most difficult of all so far in his life. What would the coming days hold?

Tuesday February 14

In terms of greeting cards sent, Valentine's Day ranks second only to Christmas. But how did we come to put aside a day for love and romance?

It started as a pagan festival. On the eve of February 15, in honour of the goddess of marriage, Juno, young women would put slips of paper with their name on it in an urn that young men would draw the names out of. Each couple, thus associated, would be partners for the duration of the festival. Sometimes the pairing would last one year, and they would fall in love and would later marry.

Pope Gelasius I (492-496) wanted to stop this custom. So he decided that the lottery should be both for men and women. The name they would draw would be of a saint; they would then try to be like him/her for a year. The name of the festival was changed to Valentine's Day. But Roman men continued to seek women's company in the old way, and it became tradition to give out handwritten love letters that included Valentine's name. Where did the name come from?

Some say that the bishop of Interamna, called Valentine, was a priest in the Roman Empire during the reign of Claudius II (268-270). He helped persecuted Christians escape harsh Roman prisons where they were often beaten and tortured. Claudius had Valentine seized and thrown in prison. While in prison, it is believed that Valentine cured a jailer's daughter of blindness. She visited him during his confinement. Claudius heard about it, became enraged and had Valentine clubbed and beheaded around February 14, 269 A.D. Before his death, it is alleged that he wrote her a farewell message, which he signed "from your Valentine", an expression still in use today.

1. Coroner

Brent had discussed the situation with the paramedics. They had simply confirmed his guesses. They were not allowed to give a definite diagnosis but both of them believed Warren Sparks had died of a heart attack. The coroner was on his way and only he could give the official diagnosis. Lakedge was too small to have a coroner, so when there was a death, one had to drive the sixty kilometres that separated the town from the nearest city of Greenmeadows. It took almost forty-five minutes to drive the distance so the paramedics had to sit and wait.

Brent prepared a fresh pot of coffee and they chatted. It felt eerie to Brent to have a friendly discussion just a few feet away from Warren's body. He tried to focus on happier things but it was a struggle. The paramedics tried to help steer his mind away from Warren by talking about sports, weather, and even politics but to no avail.

The doorbell rang.

Brent left the paramedics to answer. A man introduced himself as Gene Suffolk, the coroner from Greenmeadows. Brent explained his finding, the paramedics now behind him confirming what they had seen upon arrival. The coroner asked to see the victim and Brent led him to the room. The coroner did a quick examination and came to the same conclusion as the paramedics and Brent.

"It all points to a heart attack. At his age though, you shouldn't be surprised. I am sorry for your loss."

Brent felt his chest seize. His breathing was shallow and he was fighting tears. The coroner looked around the room. Finding nothing suspicious, he went to Warren's desk and scribbled something on a form. He continued with a couple of other forms. He gave one to the paramedics and gave them permission to remove the body.

He turned to Brent and asked if they could sit somewhere to talk. Brent led him to the dining room and offered him some coffee. The coroner refused saying he couldn't stay very long.

"So what time did you find Mr. Sparks this way?"

Brent searched his mind for the answer. "It must have been about seven o'clock. Yes, because that's when I usually serve him his breakfast. But this morning he didn't wake up when I came in the room."

"You live in this house Brent?"

"Yes I do," Brent said.

"Did you hear anything last night?"

"No I didn't. I sleep in the opposite part of the house and I don't really hear anything from that side. When Mr. Sparks is in his bedroom and he needs anything, he has a bell that rings in a number of the other rooms. I know it's him so I go and enquire what he needs."

"I see," said the coroner. He stayed silent for a few seconds.

"What happens now?" Brent asked.

"Well, I don't see any signs of violence. To me it's a natural death but because he died at home I am obligated to do an autopsy. In the meantime, I have here a death certificate that you need to give to his next-of-kin." He paused to look straight at Brent, "You're not related, are you?"

Brent suppressed a sigh. "No, I'm not." He felt he was probably the closest thing to a relative that Warren had. In the decade he had been working for Sparks, no family member ever showed up or even called.

"Very well, then you need to give this to his executor. They will need it for the estate." He got up to leave.

Brent stopped him almost in a panic. "Wait. I... I don't know who his executor is. I don't know where his family is. I know he was married and he had a daughter but he hasn't seen or heard from either since I arrived, and that's almost ten years. Where would I find this..." he struggled with the word "...executor?"

The coroner sat back down. "Oh my. That is a problem." He looked at Brent noticing the anxiety in his eyes. "I'll tell you what. After the autopsy, I'll give instructions for the body to be brought to the Ridgeway funeral home. They will maintain the body until you find the family. They usually prefer to have the funeral over within a week, preferably all arrangements within 72 hours, but I can have them hold on for a while."

Brent sat there, his eyes transfixed. He was a valet, a helper, and an ex-lumberjack. He had no experience with matters related to wills, and estates, or searching for lost families.

The coroner continued trying to give him a few hints. "You could do a search through his papers. Maybe something will come up that he kept for a long time."

The coroner hesitated but he had to move on. He put his hand on Brent's shoulder and then handed him a business card. "Brent, I have to go, but here is my phone number. If you find something but you need assistance for the next step, call me. I will do my best to help you."

Brent heard the reassurance expressed in the coroner's tone but he had a hard time taking hold of the comfort. It seemed as if his whole world was scattered and that he had to try and find the pieces.

The coroner walked back to the exit with Brent following. They walked down the stairs in the fresh snow to the car. Brent remained there as the car turned in the circular entrance to the Sparks' mansion. He kept his eyes fixed on it until it disappeared amongst the rows of trees lining the alleyway. His feet felt the cold before the rest of his body. He looked down and noticed the inch of snow on the steps.

He went back in, put on his coat and his boots, grabbed the shovel in the storage cabinet, and went out to clear the steps. His body did the chore as it had so many times before. His mind was stuck in another dimension. A gulf had just opened under him. He couldn't see the bottom of the pit and was scared.

He finished the shovelling and walked back inside. For a while he went on with his usual routine of household chores but as he approached the study, he hesitated. His only access to that room had been to make sure it stayed clean. Never had he dared to look at any of Warren's papers. He had never opened a book, never peaked in a drawer. This room had an aura about it that was utterly private to Warren Sparks. Brent had never defiled its sanctity.

The instructions to do a search still resonated in his mind, his inner being struggled. Finding Warren's family, getting them to clean up this mess, unloading the burden of responsibility now piling on his shoulders, was essential. Yet, he couldn't force himself to open the door to the study.

He went on to find more things to do, more chores, more cleaning. The house was silent. Not that it was unusual; Warren Sparks was absent at least half of each day, insisting on running the mill alone. Brent wasn't an avid music enthusiast either; he preferred opening windows and listening to sounds of the forest. The multitude of birds was much more musical to him than any concert.

Today, however, the silence was bothering him. It was a different type of emptiness. He fought to keep his mind on other things. The clock in the kitchen kept ticking, inexorably sending him the message that he was getting closer to the time when he couldn't put it off anymore. Every second was a step closer to being forced to action. He went by the study time and time again, his heart pounding more rapidly as he neared the door then passing by at the last instant still unable to comply with the coroner's instructions.

Exhausted from the struggle, he sat on the living room sofa and finally burst into an abundant flow of tears. He cried loudly, feeling that every sound was releasing an ache trapped inside. He let the tears fall not wanting them to be imprisoned in the way he felt trapped by the situation. He wept like never before in his life. Brent, the rugged outdoorsman, the lumberjack, the toughened shell creating a carapace to surround him and isolate the threats, had finally broken down.

Finally, he recovered and felt he was now ready to go in the study. He had started the grieving process and was ready for the next step. He walked in.

The room was small in comparison to the other rooms in the house. It had enough space for a large desk, a leather chair resembling a sofa, a couple of wooden filing cabinets and two large bookshelves. The shelves had only a few books on them, supporting many pictures, trophies, awards, and objects that didn't mean anything to Brent but must have been important to Warren Sparks.

Two carved lamps, depicting rafters on the river driving logs down to the mill, sat on the desk. Everything surrounding Warren Sparks had a link to his way of life.

Brent went around the desk. He sat in Warren's chair, feeling awkward, but now reassured of his duty to search for Warren's heirs. From this point he could see the whole room. His eye spotted some of the pictures. They were all positioned in a way so that they could be seen from behind the desk. There were pictures of Warren receiving awards; some where he was shaking hands with prominent political figures of the last four decades, others with groups of people that he didn't recognise. One seemed to stand out, right at eye-level and in the centre of the whole display, a picture of a much younger Warren with a very beautiful lady and a young girl.

He rose and picked it up. He turned it around. On the back was a date, November 15, 1982. Beside it were three names Warren, Teresa and Joy. He remembered the names. Teresa was Warren's ex-wife and Joy was his daughter. Joy seemed about twelve years old in the photo.

At least it was a start. He had names. He guessed that Joy was now in her late thirties; Teresa would be in her sixties.

What it didn't tell him is where they would be located. He looked at the other pictures, turning them over. They all had dates and names, but no other leads.

He went back to the desk and opened the file drawer. It contained a lot of papers mostly dealing with the mansion but unable to shed any light on his dilemma. He continued with the other drawers, then the filing cabinets but these were all related either to Warren's home or to his business.

He definitely needed help on this. Someone had to direct him to find Warren's family. He started going through the people he knew. Then he remembered one person that might have the answers.

*****

Speed on the roads was the main reason for having police in the area. With the exception of the multiple homicide of the previous summer, crime was almost unknown in Lakedge. Sure, there was occasional mischief by local teens; the occasional family quarrel that led to police intervention; but most of the police work was linked to the highway, cutting through town, splitting it in two. The signs at the entrance of town ordered vehicles to slow down to 50 kilometres an hour. Drivers unfortunately often ignored the signs and tore right through at dangerous speeds.

For this task, Sergeant Mark Dexter, the senior Provincial Police officer of the Lakedge detachment, could count on four junior officers taking turns to watch the road. They used the latest radar technology and could time a vehicle from almost five kilometres away. It gave them enough time to react and stop offenders before they came into town.

When the sergeant received Brent's call for help, it was something new for him. Change was both welcomed and feared. It meant a break in the routine but going into unknown territory. In remote areas like Lakedge, it was difficult to get support. The senior officer of the detachment was generally left to his own resources to take care of issues that arose.

With all the required training and keeping up with new police methods and procedures, Mark was a good policeman. In small towns, however, it was difficult to apply the new methods. Psychology and criminology didn't always work the same way as in urban communities. Most of the research and development of modern policing was based on the needs of large cities. Mark often felt left to himself to find solutions to new problems, which was the reason for his hesitation when something different popped up.

He hurried over to the Sparks residence. Brent invited him to visit Warren's room. Warren's clothes were neatly folded on the bench at the foot of his bed. Nothing seemed out of order. The door opposite the one he used to come in was closed. There was no blood, no sign of struggle that he could make out. Brent recalled how Warren had seemed fine last night when he left him. Mark went to the window. There were no traces in the snow although they could have been covered by the light snowfall overnight. The windows were locked and there was no sign of forced entry.

They went downstairs and sat in the dining room. Brent had made a fresh pot of coffee and they sipped the hot brew. After the initial explanations from Brent, there were long moments of silence. Mark wanted to let Brent express what he was feeling. He knew that in such situations people needed to be heard. So Mark listened, resisting the temptation to offer what would amount to a lot of empty words.

"So you see, I just don't know where to turn next. We never spoke of either Teresa or Joy in all the time since I moved in with Warren. It was as if that part of his life had been erased. I only remembered it because of the picture in his office. I vaguely remember seeing the lady and the little girl once when I was still working at the mill. But that was at least twenty years ago."

Mark nodded. "I don't remember ever meeting her. You're right; Warren never spoke to me of his marriage either."

The room remained quiet as if the walls themselves were mourning. Another silent pause gave Brent time to ponder.

"I don't get it. I know he was getting old but I never suspected he had any kind of heart condition. Why didn't he say anything? At least I would have been able to prepare for it."

He took a small sip of his coffee.

"I mean prepare emotionally. Maybe I would have been able to ask him. 'Where is this Teresa?' and 'Where is your daughter Joy?'" He continued loudly, but sadly rambling, "How do I let her know if something happens to you? Is there anybody else in your family I can reach? Who is going to get all of this?" He pointed around the room, indicating the mansion's full content.

Mark looked at the luxury surrounding him; the long dark table with intricate designs, the hutch full of delicate china and glassware, and the chandeliers hooked up to a ceiling with elaborate arches, curves and decorative mouldings. The estate was worth a lot of money. Someone out there, who didn't know it yet, was going to suddenly become very wealthy.

"I should have thought about it. I guess I was too scared and I never asked. I couldn't bear to see him die. I knew he was getting old so I should have known. How stupid could I be?"

Mark had to react. "Brent, you can't blame yourself. You were his valet; you weren't a family member. You had no responsibility in this."

Brent looked at him and raised his voice. "Maybe I wasn't officially a member of his family, but I feel I was the closest thing to it. Nobody else ever came to see him other than to ask for money. He took me on almost like a son and I cared for him. I should have done more. Maybe if I had seen it coming I would have stayed closer to his room. I could have called for help and saved him. I should have learned CPR. Maybe

I could have done something. Don't you see? I failed him when he needed me the most."

Mark didn't dare reply. He let Brent pour out his frustration, waiting for it to blow over before trying to bring the conversation back to the topic of the estate.

Brent stopped and calmed down somewhat.

Mark gathered his thoughts. "Can I make a suggestion?" he asked in a gentle tone.

Brent took some time to face him. "I guess. I don't have any avenues. That's why I called you."

"Would you be okay if I called one of the attorneys I know in Greenmeadows? I know we could call on someone here in Lakedge, but this man knows a lot of people, he may be able to help me in finding out if Warren ever had a will."

"Sure. I don't have anything to lose."

Mark took out a notebook from his pocket. He flipped through a few pages. He stopped and pointed his finger at one of the entries in the address book. "Here we are. Let me make a phone call."

He walked to the lobby. He was on the phone for about fifteen minutes. Brent didn't move.

"I was lucky. I reached him at his office. He is actually rarely there. He told me he would ask one of his apprentices to do a search through the archives. He has access to a few resources that some of the other attorneys don't and he may come up with something. Even if there isn't a will, he will try to see if there were some divorce papers or something like that."

Brent thought about this for a few seconds. "I don't know if that's going to work. Warren kept his wedding band until the end. I don't even know if he was divorced. He may have still been married."

Mark hesitated. "You may be right. Although, I know in some cases where there was a divorce, one of the two didn't really want the separation so they kept the ring as if it didn't happen. They tried to keep the dream alive. Maybe she left him and he didn't want her to leave."

"It could be. Hopefully your friend will be able to find something."

"He said to give him a few days. All we can really do is wait."

Brent poured more coffee in both cups. Mark wanted to get back to the precinct but didn't have the courage to stop him.

The furnace came on, pushing heat into the room and breaking up the stillness. The soft rumbling covered the delicate ticking of the clock.

Mark asked. "How about you Brent? Do you have any family?"

Brent came out of his thoughts. "My family sort of gave up on me. I was too rough for them. I have a brother out West somewhere but my parents passed away a long time ago." He stopped and sighed.

"I never did get married because I was always out there in the woods. I preferred the freedom. Then when I got hurt, I thought no woman would ever want a cripple for a husband so I closed myself in here and hardly ever went out."

Mark pursued this a bit. "But what are you going to do now?"

"I haven't had any time to really think about it. I guess I have to wait until we find out who owns the place now. Maybe they'll keep me on as the valet. That's really all I can hope. If it doesn't work out, then I guess I'll have to find something else."

"Waiting sounds good," Mark agreed, "in the meantime, if you need anything, you just have to call me. I'll do whatever I can."

Brent looked up at him with a bit of moisture in his eyes, and then quickly turned his face away hoping Mark hadn't noticed. In a quiet, trembling voice he barely let out a thank you.

"I know my way out," Mark said, not wanting to get caught up in the emotion, "you don't need to move. Take care of yourself Brent."

He left without waiting for the answer that was choked in Brent's throat.

2. Mill

Jim Stone drove his pickup truck into the huge parking lot. Being one of the first employees to show up at the mill, he usually took one of the spots closest to the yard.

A light snow fell overnight, not quite enough to warrant ploughing. The contractor usually waited until there was a worthwhile accumulation. They had received so much snow this year that there was no room left to put the stuff. At the end of the lot lay a huge greyish mountain. It had gradually spilled over and took away six parking spots, consigning them in a blanket of snow until spring.

Jim pulled the huge lunch box from the passenger side along with his hardhat. He would wait until he was at the gate to trade his beaver cap and earmuffs for it; safety was important but the hardhat rule didn't apply to the parking and this morning was cold enough to freeze your ears off.

He closed the truck door and walked to the locked fence. The yard smelled of cut wood, fresh sap and snow. This was the true smell of nature. He felt in communion with the earth every time he came in this yard. This place was better than home.

He walked to his office at the edge of the lumberyard. He dropped his lunch box in the corner of the room, picked up a binder and started flipping through the pages. Each page was an order sheet. He reviewed the orders planned for pick-up today and started scheduling.

As shipping yard superintendent, he was responsible for all stocks going out. With a just-in-time approach to maximize revenues, it was important to verify all outgoing shipments so he could keep the inventory as low as possible but never too low to risk running out.

Satisfied he had the day all mapped out in his mind, he walked out to inspect the inventory.

For three decades Jim had been coming to work at Sparks Mill; almost every weekday, and even sometimes on weekends when a very special order came in. He rarely missed a day except to fulfill his obligations as a volunteer firefighter.

The morning crew started trickling in. He kept an eye out on the employees walking through the door. Occasionally he let out a holler to someone to put the hardhat on. Jim always ensured that the rules were being followed once past the gate. Safety was important to this company and Jim did his best to ensure it stayed that way.

At the other end, the main gate opened. Fully loaded trucks had been parked in a line near the receiving entrance. They revved up and drove into the yard going to the inspection station. They were directed to a temporary parking spot where each load was evaluated for species, size and quality. While the inspection team did their job, the drivers would wait, grabbing a coffee and warming up from the cold morning air.

Each log was checked. The inspector spray painted the size of the log, and stapled a tag with the species and quality rating of the log. He would also wax the ends of each log to help them retain their moisture, thereby preventing splitting and cracking of the wood.

The trucks would then move on to their designated piles, and large cranes would throw the huge logs onto a conveyer belt as if they were matchsticks. The ramp rose a hundred feet in the air carrying the logs and dumping them onto piles already three or four stories high. There were a number of such piles from one end of the yard to the other, covering over twenty hectares of land. Each pile held one single species and a range of closely related sizes. Sprinklers constantly rained on the piles to keep them moist.

In these parts, the main species they worked with were jack pine, white and black spruce. They also had smaller piles of balsam and tamarack. These were all softwoods. That was the bulk of the Sparks Mill business. Once in a while they would get an order for hardwood, used for more delicate carpentry such as furniture and millwork. They used aspen for those shipments. The rest of the wood went into what was referred to as dimensional lumber, a term meaning wood that had predetermined dimensions for use in house building.

Sparks had developed a reputation for quality over the years, rejecting products that were substandard and turning the lower grade of wood into chips for plywood. All his employees followed this rule with pride. The reputation of the mill was such that some builders would only use Sparks Mill products.

Once through the extensive process of debarking, steaming, canting, edging, trimming, drying and planning, the lumber ended in Jim's section ready for shipping. In contrast to the mass of logs that were piled in a somewhat disorderly fashion at the receiving end, the lumber in this part of the yard was stacked in neat arrays on pallets ready to forklift onto trucks going to lumber yards and hardware stores across the country or to specific developers working on construction sites.

Jim removed his mitten from one hand and having safely tucked it under his arm, he pulled a bar code reader from his pocket to register the tag at the end of each piece of lumber.

Trucks backed up to take delivery. Jim would discuss the details of the order with the driver. Once sure he had the right truck and the proper destination, he would give the order to load. The teams would lift, balance, restrain and carefully tighten the restraining straps on the lumber stacks. Once all the wood was loaded on the truck, Jim did a visual recheck of the load along with the driver and signed the packing slip.

The equipment was more modern than when Warren Sparks had built his fist mill. The technology had evolved. For a long time, axes were used to chop down trees. This took down only one tree at a time in a slow methodical way, and left huge waist-high stumps, wasting a lot of lumber. Today they used feller-bunchers. Those machines could grab one large tree or a bunch of small trees and saw them off at the ground level in a few seconds. This would leave no stumps and no waste. The machine would then pick up fallen trees and bunch them to be picked up by another machine, the grappler, which brought them to the side of the road and loaded them up on the trucks.

A typical winter day at the mill brought in twenty trucks with logs, and sent out ten trucks with lumber. The balance of the wood was discarded in the treatment process and the waste was reused to heat the steamers and create electricity for the saws to operate.

The same routine had applied at the mill for at least the last decade since the technology had been introduced. Occasionally a new machine was brought in, people were trained to use it and it became part of the landscape. The product, although prepared differently, was still high quality, the wood treated with the same love for nature and strict attention to safety.

That was the legacy of Sparks Mill, the only life Jim had ever known.

It was close to midday when the loudspeaker buzzed and a female voice called out. "Jim Stone, telephone on line two."

Jim wasn't sure he heard his name over the noise of the mill and the idling trucks. He listened more intently as the message was repeated. He swore. Jim didn't like being interrupted while he was counting. He told the driver to wait a moment while he answered this page. Usually people would leave a voice mail and he would return the call in between shipments. If someone had him paged, it must be important, so he reluctantly headed for the yard office. He picked up the receiver.

"Hello, this is Jim."

At the other end the voice sounded a bit distraught. "Jim, it's Brent. I... I don't know how to tell you this."

Jim read the anxiety in his tone, recognised Brent and knew something must be wrong. Brent wasn't the type of person to get anxious over small disturbances.

"What's the matter, Brent?"

"It's Warren. I mean Mr. Sparks. He's dead...of a heart attack."

"Sparks. Dead." It was Jim's turn to be dumbfounded. He had known Warren Sparks almost all his life. He heard the words but couldn't grasp the meaning. "When?" Jim asked.

"Last night. He died in his sleep." Brent was talking in short sentences broken up by lengthy pauses.

"He... he's dead? No." Jim uttered as he sat in his chair. He said the words more to give himself time to think and let Brent know that he was still there.

Brent needed help. "I don't know what to do. The coroner came and he signed some papers, then they took his body to the morgue."

Jim was distraught himself but, used to dealing with crises he quickly realised Brent needed help in this matter. "What can I do to help?"

"I'm not really sure. I need to find his exec... executor. I don't even know what that is. I also need to find his family but I don't know anything about them and I don't know where they are. Would you know anything about his family?"

Jim thought a few seconds. This was not his area of expertise.

"Brent, I'm not sure." He tried to come up with something quickly, so that Brent wouldn't be left on his own. "Maybe the funeral home will know."

Then he seemed to click on something, his mind racing rapidly to find answer for Brent, and for himself. "Didn't Sparks have a daughter?"

"Yes, he did. Her name is Joy. I also know her mother's name. Warren's ex-wife is Teresa. What I don't know is where either of them are. I don't even know if they kept the same last name. I think they left Lakedge when the girl was about twelve or so. They haven't come back since and that's a long time ago. How am I going to find them?"

Jim wished he had an answer. "Let me think about this and I will call you back a little later."

Brent felt unsure but agreed. Jim felt the pain in his voice. "Brent, how are you holding up?"

He took some time to answer. "I guess I'll be okay. I just don't know what I'm going to do."

"Me neither, but we will work on that. Hang on, buddy. Okay?"

"Sure Jim. Thanks." They hung up.

Jim leaned back in his chair. The weight of the news started to sink in. Then the questions popped in his mind. What about the mill? Who would manage it? Warren Sparks had always run the mill on his own, only delegating the operational decisions to his superintendent. The strategic positioning of the company, the pricing, marketing strategies and the negotiations with vendors and customers, as well as all relations with government organisations had always been left up to Sparks.

Without him at the helm, how would his company be steered? He looked up. Through the window he could see the yard, the trucks, and the workers. He remembered he was in the middle of a shipment when he received the call. The driver was still waiting.

He stepped out of the office. He knew he would have to tell the others but didn't know how to say it. For now, life had to go on, so this shipment needed to be completed.

He went back to work but his mind was elsewhere. He quickly finished the shipment then called on one of his helpers to take over the next one. Finally, he headed for the main office. Others had to be told of the tragedy.

3. York U

Mike sat in front of the blank screen. The term paper was due in two days. Yet he couldn't get beyond the title. *"The six o'clock news; information or entertainment?"*

He had done the research. He knew the message he wanted to convey. As always, the first sentence was the most difficult. It had to grab the reader, at the same time giving a glimpse as to the nature of the rest of the document.

Michael Stuart had left Lakedge in September to start his Communication degree at York University in Toronto. After spending all his life in a small community, the transfer to Toronto had been brutal. Lakedge didn't even have one traffic light, just stop signs. In his new environment, traffic lights were at every corner, some even at the exits of shopping malls. Around Lakedge, the largest highway had two large lanes, and an occasional passing lane on one side; in Toronto, most streets and avenues were larger than those highways.

He lived in residence, sharing a small room simply containing two beds, two desks, two chairs, two dressers, and two closets. The twelve young men in the north end of the floor shared a common washroom and a common kitchen. His roommate was a quiet biology student from China, currently in Canada on a visa. His English was difficult for Mike to comprehend and he spent most of his time in the library with his friends, all Chinese. Mike ended up alone in the room most of the time.

He had made a few friends since his arrival, but he found it difficult to relate to them. Most of them were from large urban areas, or at least in the vicinity of major metropolitan cities. Mike had never gone any farther than Greenmeadows, which was tiny in comparison.

Leaving behind his girlfriend, his family, his friends and his home had taken a toll on him. He tried to keep a good front for his floor mates, but there was a void inside him that he longed to fill. Every evening he would be on the computer chatting with Ashley, sharing his daily routine, but mostly hinting at his loneliness, letting her know he was missing her yet never saying it in so many words.

He called home every weekend and spoke to his mom, dad, sister Amanda, and grandmother. He had gone home for the Thanksgiving long weekend and then again for almost three weeks to spend Christmas and New Years.

He got up to look out the window. At this time in Lakedge the snow would be everywhere; here, all he could see was wet pavement with a few small piles of greyish matter where the snow had been ploughed and hadn't fully melted yet. Here, people had no idea what winter was really about. He longed for trees with bright green needles. All he saw were dull oak and birch trees without leaves, with a few scrawny little brownish fir trees, here and there, not even fit to use for decorating at Christmas.

He sat at the computer again.

Mike had opted for a communications degree. Back home, an English teacher had noticed his skill at writing and provided much encouragement. He had volunteered as the editor of his high school newsletter. He also had a good sense of the important issues in his community. Now, he had doubts. The world was far different outside of Lakedge. He felt unprotected and vulnerable.

His community had shielded him from the issues and concerns that politics and economy yielded. Here he was surrounded with homelessness, unemployment, and poverty. In Lakedge, everyone had a home, everyone had a job, and everyone had enough to eat. Whenever one member of the community was in trouble, the whole community pulled together to help. Here the concept of community didn't exist. It was a world where every person was on their own.

The culture shock had overwhelmed Mike. He had quickly developed a very critical mind, seeing selfishness and greed at every turn. He now tended to doubt everything. Such attitude had pushed him to be cynical even of his own studies. He had dreamed of being a news reporter, telling the world about what went on. Somewhat idealist as a teenager, he was going to find the good stories and report only on those. Now he struggled to see any good in the stories surrounding him.

He had watched news reporters in action for the first few months, trying to understand what made them different, how they used their skills, where they went for stories. It took him a while to understand how this observation exercise also had the effect of pushing him into an even more depressive mood, beyond the impact of longing for loved ones.

All this had led to the title of this essay on the role of media. It wasn't about providing news to the public. It wasn't educational. News was simply another form of entertainment. Whoever got the most gruesome pictures, the most horrific story, the most sensational video was the entertainer of the day. It was about being there first and sending back those clips before anybody else.

As sugar cubes in hot tea, Mike's dreams were slowly being dissolved. The intent, like the sweetness, was still there, but it had blended within the pungent taste of the tea. It had also lost its original shape.

He knew he had to go on. Mike had worked part-time for years at the grocery store and all summer at the mill to get enough funding for this. His father had also invested a lot of money to send him here. Everyone was counting on him to come back with a degree. The motivation had changed.

It made it even more difficult to go on.

He saw the calendar on his desk. He had highlighted the third week of February in yellow; Reading Week. In a few days he would be able to go home for a full week. He realised he was now living almost from one holiday to the next, struggling to get by until the next occasion when he could go back to Lakedge. Summer was still eons away but at least there would be a few pit stops.

His MSN popped open. Ashley had come online. His heart fluttered slightly; a chance to put aside his gloominess for a while. She was on lunch break so it would be quick. Ashley had finished high school and went to work for the Cosy Retreat motel and cottages. She was a maid there, cleaning rooms and helping out with the meals. She was also taking some online secretarial college courses.

Mike clicked on the logo.

Her first sentence was. "hpy V day luv u" On MSN, most of the text was abridged to save time and space. Ashley and Mike, like most youth of their age, knew the codes. You never included any punctuation, you used the sounds rather than the full spelling, and you omitted pronouns. For a communications student like Mike, it was quite a conundrum.

He replied: "luv u 2 wts up"

Being far from each other on a day like this was especially difficult but emotions were not something easily expressed online.

The next half hour went by quickly, and then Ashley had to get back to work. She promised to call him that evening and they logged off.

Mike went back to staring at the blank screen.

4. Riviera

Émilie took her time to reach just the perfect spot on the beach. It wasn't the angle of the sun. It wasn't the consistency of the sand. It wasn't the shade. It wasn't the wind blowing the cool air of the Mediterranean. None of these really mattered since every spot between the mansion and the sea was basically the same.

What made the difference was who was already on the beach. Winter is the time when hundreds of students from the universities in the North of France, Belgium, and Germany would come South to relish the sun they couldn't find back home. For Émilie it meant potential new admirers and she intended to make the most of it, even in the cold air of February.

Her very dark sunglasses hid the direction of her stare. She kept her head straight towards the water, but her eyes were really scanning the area to and fro. She noticed a couple of young men kicking around a football. She scoped their muscles, their faces and their physique, and then made her decision; they would be her next targets.

She was an expert at this game now. She pointed without a word to a place about fifteen feet away from the two. She had to be close enough for them to see her but not so close as to make her intentions too obvious. Gilbert knew the routine. Already starting to sweat in his black valet suit, he put the long chair in the exact spot, opened the parasol, unfolded the small table, opened the basket, took out the champagne bottle and the glass, and set them on the table. Then he stepped back.

She feigned checking the sun. She pointed to the parasol. Gilbert rearranged the angle and moved back. Seemingly satisfied she started to undo the bra of her bikini. Actually, there wasn't much material on the contraption to start with, more like strings with a few square millimetres of fabric in the appropriate areas. But here, on the French Riviera, this was the norm. For Émilie, being topless, even in the cooler weather of February, was only a great occasion to flaunt some of her best attributes. As the absence of suntan marks demonstrated, this was the only way she ever exposed herself on the beach. Her golden brown skin glistened in the sun.

She slowly sat in the long chair. Gilbert knew it was the signal for him to leave. She pulled out her suntan lotion from her bag and started to squirt the white cream over herself. She started with her long gaunt legs, rubbing the lotion gently on every inch of skin. She moved on to her arms, then her front.

All this time she continued observing the two young men. Their football game was less concentrated; they had noticed her and the hormones were starting to awaken. They regularly peaked at the vision that had appeared next to them. This woman seemed to come right out of a girlie magazine. Already sweating from the sun and the activity, this new surge of adrenaline increased their body heat.

Now that she had their attention she moved to her breasts and started applying the lotion very carefully. Her nipples became erect and firm. She looked up. The two had almost forgotten the football.

She waved at them and pointed to her back. They came over immediately, leaving the ball behind. The first one, a six foot, blond, athletic man in his early twenties seemed to have a German accent when he greeted her in French. He took the bottle of lotion and started to rub it on her back. She moaned lightly as he applied it. She took her long tan-coloured hair and raised it so he could add the cream to her neck.

The second man, with darker hair and brown eyes, was slightly younger, just out of his teenage years, and had a clear French accent. He started a conversation, introducing himself.

Émilie spoke French very well, but had not quite mastered hiding her English background. There was a slight remnant in her speech that made her origins known.

She pulled out a couple more champagne glasses from the basket Gilbert had left behind and started pouring as they chatted innocently about the weather, why they were in Cannes, how long she had been here, and all sorts of other nonchalant discussion themes.

Inside the mansion, Gilbert had now removed his coat, and changed his completely soaked shirt. From his room on the second floor, Gilbert watched. He observed the beach with his binoculars. He knew the darkness of the room made him invisible to the outside.

Inside him raged a constant battle. Yes, he was jealous. He deplored how she repeatedly exposed herself this way to total strangers. She was so beautiful; she could have any man she wanted. So many already had told her they would give anything to spend the rest of their life with her. But he also knew she was insatiable. She would never be content with just one man. She wanted them all.

He hated her and he loved her. He hated how she treated him as though he was invisible. She went along frolicking shamelessly with a different man almost every other day, right in front of him. She walked around the house almost naked all the time without any concern for the servants. She ordered him around without ever a thank you or a kind word of appreciation.

Yet, he couldn't leave. He couldn't bear not to see her anymore. As much as he despised what she did, he always remembered that one night of passion he had shared with her. On her bed, in embrace, he had confessed his love for her more than a dozen times on that night. But the next morning, it was over as if nothing had ever happened. He had only been another sex partner. There was no emotion, no attachment, no commitment; nothing left from their encounter.

He was the servant; she was the master. She owned him. She had used the one night to strengthen her ownership. She knew Gilbert could never leave her now. Since then, she used him even more than before.

Today, like most days for the last year or so, Gilbert was planning his revenge. He would someday make her see what he was really worth. He would make her see how she should have chosen him. He would demonstrate how he could bring to her more than just one night of passion, more than just a servant's daily chores. She would find out. Soon.

As Émilie and her two new conquests drank the champagne, time went by. Then Émilie decided they were ready. She told them it was getting too cold. She invited them to finish their champagne at the mansion. They didn't hesitate. She restrung her bra, got off her chair, and they quickly folded all of her equipment ready to follow her. The younger one went to get the towels and the football they had left behind while Émilie led the way back to the house.

Gilbert saw it and put his uniform back on. He went down to the kitchen, ready for her to call.

From the beach, it was only a few hundred feet. The house was a large structure hiding twelve rooms. The orange roof shingles covered white granular walls, with orange shutters framing every window. In the back laid an in-ground swimming pool. The hedges and gardens were well maintained and trimmed. Everything was spotless.

They followed Émilie in the living room where the three continued to sip champagne. When the first bottle was emptied, she rang Gilbert for more. At the third bottle, they moved from the living room to her bedroom.

Gilbert went to his room and turned on the small monitor on his desk. He saw her undress. He watched the three in silence. He raged and cursed, at the same time aroused himself from what he was seeing.

Émilie had just added two more prizes to her trophy case. Gilbert had just added more footage to his video collection.

Wednesday, February 15

Reading Week

York University classes will not be held from February 20 to 24 for the annual Reading Week. Libraries and all university services however, will remain open. Students are reminded that Reading Week is an opportunity to work on assignments in order to complete all requirements for the semester.

York University hopes all students will benefit from this week and wishes you a safe Reading Week.

The Chancellor.

5. Winter

Frank Ellis waited in the hallway. He had to see the town manager, Joshua Stuart. He had been going over the figures and they worried him.

Frank was the director of purchasing for the Town of Lakedge. He had worked in the municipal government almost all his life. He had started at the bottom of the ranks and moved up gradually, going back to school, then college part-time to help climb the corporate ladder. In his current position, he was one of the key employees of the town. Some said this was due in large part to his friendship with Josh, but Frank made sure he was worth his salary, often coming in before anyone and working much later than most staff. It reduced at least some of the gossip.

Josh had full confidence in Frank and often discussed subjects having no direct link with Frank's job. A town manager, the most senior official, needed someone to confide in and Frank was the right person. They had worked together for a long time and gone through some difficult periods in the history of Lakedge. Josh had counted on Frank's support when they established clinics to stop the spread of the influenza virus later known as the Lakedge Virus. He had been there when they had battled the fire almost destroying the town last summer. Then, while Lindsey and Margaret, Josh's wife and his mother, had been in the hospital following their terrible crash, Frank had been the acting town manager. In this position he had certainly shown his worth.

Winter had arrived early in November with a massive snowstorm causing schools to close and citizens to stay home for a couple of days. Since that time, two more heavy snowstorms had come through and dumped mounds of the white stuff on Lakedge and the surroundings.

After enduring one of the driest summers ever, creating drought conditions, engendering a number of disastrous forest-fires throughout the province, and hardening the crust of the earth to cement-like substance, the heavy rains had come but offered no relief, instead creating landslides in places weakened by the forest fires.

The snow was welcome because it would have all of spring to gradually seep into the ground, giving it the moisture desperately needed. Kids didn't mind a few "snow days" without school, and most people saw them as unplanned vacation days. In the country, everyone had tons of firewood, extra supplies of food, water, candles, battery operated radios and decks of cards to pass the time. While being snowed in for city folks could have catastrophic results, for Lakedge it was a minor slowdown.

The town had snowploughs enough to clear the majority of the roads within 24 hours following each snowstorm and would add salt or sand as needed. The Ministry of Transportation covered the provincial roads and their offices were in Greenmeadows, about 60 kilometres South of Lakedge.

But although the snow removal didn't worry the citizens of Lakedge, it worried Frank.

The door opened and Josh accompanied a gentleman out. Frank recognised the man as one of the developers interested in purchasing some land for future growth of Lakedge. Ever since the influenza virus, people had been interested in the town. The reputation of the town as a resilient community was something that some people liked. A few residents of Greenmeadows had already started enquiring about moving to Lakedge based on this reputation.

Frank greeted the man politely with a smile then resumed his previous frown. Josh looked at him and noticed the frown on his brow.

"What's up Frank? I don't like it when you give me that look."

"Josh, this is serious, you have to look at it."

Josh put his arm around Frank shoulder and brought him gently into his office. "All right Frank, I'm listening."

Josh was taller than Frank by at least six inches and much slimmer. Watching them together felt almost like an old Abbott and Costello movie.

"Well, here it is. This is our snow removal budget. I was speaking to Karl from Works about it and he confirmed my thoughts."

He put the papers on the small table in the middle of the room and sat on the small sofa in front of it. Josh sat beside him and bent over the documents.

"According to our figures, we have two weeks of snow removal left in our budget," Frank said, sounding pressed by the circumstances. "That will barely bring us to the middle of February. Then we have nothing for the rest of winter and spring. You know we need to have funds until the end of April, maybe even some salting and sanding during the melting season in May."

Josh respected Frank's insight and listened. He inspected the figures.

"So how did we get to this?" he asked.

"Remember after the second snowstorm, I told you we should pray not to get another one of those? Well, we got it anyway. So, now my predictions were right. We spent so much overtime on those storms that we used up the bulk of our budget. Then with the cost of fuel going up like there is no limit and our cost for sand and salt, we're basically busted," Frank said as he slumped backwards into the sofa rubbing his temples with his fingers.

Josh felt Frank's pain. His director of purchasing was responsible for managing all municipal contracts and he took it seriously. Frank was a bit of a perfectionist in some things.

"We are going to have to cut somewhere else, then. We can't just stop snow removal operations, can we?" Josh asked knowing the answer.

Somewhat disgusted about his response, Frank said loudly, almost in anger. "Of course we can't stop operations. Karl told me he could ask the guys to be careful when spreading the sand and salt; not to overdo it. Even that won't help us much."

"So where do we find more money?"

For the next half hour they pondered over different avenues for reshuffling budgets.

The phone interrupted them. Josh went to his desk to answer. "Yes, what is it?"

He listened. He confirmed he would be there in a minute and hung up. "Sorry, Frank, got to go. Mayor Hedgerow wants to see me. I think you're on the right track though. Keep at it and I'll give it some thought as well. Then we will bring it up at the directors' meeting next week."

He put on his vest and stepped out right behind Frank who had gathered all his documents and notes.

The walk over to the mayor's office took thirty seconds and when he walked into the reception area, the secretary told him to go right in.

Vivian Hedgerow was a huge woman in all directions. She sat behind a desk that had been fitted just for her. Her usually jovial face and her cheery mood had won her a number of elections. People kept choosing her as their mayor. She had captured the hearts of her citizens.

She looked up. "Josh, what do you think it's going to mean for Lakedge?"

Josh felt he had just walked into the latter half of a conversation. Did Frank tell Vivian about his concerns for the snow removal budget? He doubted it. Frank always informed him before he went to the mayor to discuss anything.

"I'm afraid I'm not sure what you are referring to Vivian." Josh had always been familiar with Vivian even though she was the mayor. She hated formalities when protocol didn't dictate it. In official meetings she was referred to as "Madam Mayor" and "Your Worship", but in private, she preferred to be called Vivian.

"Oh, it's all I've been thinking about since I heard. I'm referring to Warren Sparks. What do you think his death is going to mean for Lakedge?"

Josh felt like he'd been hit with a sledgehammer. He had rushed to work this morning and had been in meetings almost all day so he hadn't heard.

"Warren Sparks is dead?"

Vivian looked at him as if he had come down from Mars. "You mean you didn't know? Yes, he died in his sleep on Tuesday and I found out last night. That's all I've been thinking about all day."

Josh almost fell into the chair in front of her desk. Vivian realised he was getting the same shock as she had when she first heard. She gave him a minute to gather his thoughts.

"The man did so much for this community. It's going to be quite a loss for us."

Josh looked at her. "You can say that again. In a way, this town wouldn't exist if it weren't for Warren. But how?"

She gave him the few details she had about his death. She had called Brent in the morning to get more. She never liked hearing news second-hand.

"So the way I see it, we now have two things to determine. First, how do we make sure we pay homage to the man who built this town? Second, how does this town go on without the man?"

She let the thoughts float in the air as she realised Josh wasn't yet up to discuss this. His disbelief was evident.

Josh had worked for Warren Sparks at his mill as a young man before going to Ottawa to study. Warren Sparks had encouraged him to go, seeing in him a lot of qualities and skills that shouldn't be wasted in working as a warehouse clerk in a mill. Warren had provided Josh with the cash necessary to create the clinics during the influenza scare even though only a few people really believed in what Josh was trying to do.

He finally came out of his daze to address the mayor's questions. "Well, the first part is probably the easy one. We could have a plaque or a monument erected to commemorate his accomplishments."

She nodded. "Yes, that's what I thought. We'll have a monument built in front of the Town Hall in his honour and unveil it at a special ceremony where the whole town is invited. We'll also bring in his family and give them a plaque to go with it."

Josh had a moment of doubt. "His family? What family? I didn't even know he had a family."

Vivian stopped. "Come to think of it, I don't know either. I just assumed he had a family. Everyone's has one, don't they?"

"Maybe he does, but I don't recall him ever mentioning family or ever getting a visit from family."

Vivian pondered. "I'll have to ask Brent about this. Anyway. Do you agree about the monument?"

"Absolutely. I'll get Frank to look for an artist who could do this. I'll get Public Relations to look into holding a ceremony sometime in the spring, once the snow is melted."

This reminded him he had to mention the budget crisis to Vivian as well but it seemed less important at the moment.

"So what about the second part? How do we keep this town running with Sparks gone?" she repeated.

"I don't have any answers right now. I guess it all depends on what happens with the mill. One thing for sure, we need to stay connected with this in every way possible." Josh was thinking out loud. "Maybe, I should visit Brent to offer my help and make sure he keeps me informed at the same time."

"Good idea. Let me know if you need me to pitch in."

He got up and walked towards the door. He stopped and turned back. "By the way. I also wanted to let you know we are having a bit of difficulty with our snow removal budget. Frank and I are working on various options, but this is becoming a costly winter."

Vivian agreed. "I trust you Josh. Do whatever is needed."

6. Rumours

So far it had been one of those mornings. Lately the cold affected Lindsey's wrists. Since last summer's accident with the van, she felt intermittent pain. The wrist had snapped from the force of the impact and taken a long time to heal. Somehow the winter temperatures made it worse.

Lindsay was a dental hygienist. This morning she was struggling with the Stanford twins, each in turn and keeping either of the six-year old brats still on the chair was a feat in itself even without her sore wrists. Getting them to remain calm while she cleaned the tartar between their teeth was a challenge worthy of Samson himself. It made her late for Mrs. Tromboli's appointment and she had to skip her break.

Now the huge Italian-Canadian woman was slouched in the examining chair, going on about any and all gossip she could relay. Usually, Lindsey found her accent endearing, but this morning it annoyed her. She tried to keep the prong, the suction tube, and the mirror in her mouth as much of the time as possible to cut down on the amount of talk this woman's mouth would emit, but somehow the jumbled words kept coming at her.

This lady knew everything about everyone in town. She knew the history behind just about every family. She was familiar with every social, political and personal gossip and, of course, held an opinion on everything.

After the tenth garbled "Did you know that..." Lindsey phased her out. Her own thoughts were elsewhere. She was visualizing Michael, so far away in Toronto at the university. She had always known deep down that some day he would leave the nest and go out on his own. She couldn't quite cope with his absence yet. Michael was her first-born, her only son, her own flesh and blood. She wanted him to succeed, to become a man, a father, and an autonomous person but the separation was tearing away a small part of her heart each day.

He sent e-mails regularly, mostly just telling his parents he had nothing new to say and that he was doing fine. He had made a few friends since September and she was glad for him.

"What do you think?"

Lindsey just realised Mrs. Tromboli had asked her a question but she had no idea what the topic was. Now fully out of her daydreaming, she stuttered. "I'm sorry, I... I didn't quite understand what you said." She pulled out the suction tube to give the impression it was the reason for her confusion. Her conscience battled between lying to remain polite or admitting she wasn't listening. She maintained her initial position, faking misinterpretation.

"What do you think will happen now that Warren Sparks is dead?"

It hit her. "Warren Sparks is dead?"

She hadn't heard. Lindsey wasn't originally from Lakedge and somehow wasn't quite plugged into the local gossip networks and rumour mills. She knew Warren Sparks and what he represented to the town more because of her husband Joshua and his role as the town manager.

"You didn't know? It's all over town; everyone is talking about it. That's all I heard all night and all morning."

Lindsey's evening had been filled with household chores, reading, and coping with the pain in her wrist. Josh stayed home with her as well; for once, an evening he didn't spend at work. Her morning had been frantic.

"He died in his sleep on Tuesday night. It looks like he had a heart attack." Mrs. Tromboli continued.

"I'm sorry to hear that." Lindsey was a bit more attentive now. She kept the suction tube in her hand, determined to continue the treatment but not before she heard the whole story.

Mrs. Tromboli gave her all the details she had gleaned from various sources. Lindsey didn't know how much to trust the story. Rumours were always based on a bit of truth but could become so deformed by the time they spread from one person to the next. The shred of truth could be buried in depths of mistaken information.

Lindsey classified all of this in her mind and decided she would sort it out later. What did remain with her was the initial question. She pondered to herself. "What will happen to Lakedge now that Warren Sparks is dead?"

She finished the treatment and released Mrs. Tromboli. It was almost lunchtime and she had time to update the charts for her morning appointments. She snuck in the rear office where she found a bit of calm. She decided to call Josh.

She lucked out because for once he was in his office rather than one of those innumerable meetings he was always attending during office hours. She gave him the news but he had heard it already. He was considering the possible impact of this and talked a bit about his meeting with the mayor.

Josh reassured Lindsey that he would do whatever was required so this situation would not affect Lakedge negatively. He confided how right now the amount of snow and the prognosis for more winter woes was more concerning to him than Warren's death.

Environment Canada was calling for a wet winter with accumulations more extensive than they had seen in almost a decade and so far they had been right.

Lindsey hung up and tried to go back to her charts. She had grown to love Lakedge but there was much more snow here than what she was used to in her hometown of Ottawa. What had been blizzards during her youth would be considered mere flurries in these parts. You can always bring a city girl to the country but you can't take the city out of the city girl.

She finished Mrs. Tromboli's chart and felt the pain again in her right wrist. She tried to rub it out, and then the phone rang.

"Lindsey, your daughter on line one," the secretary told her.

She had a quick shiver. Amanda didn't usually call during the day. Lately, she had become more concerned and Joshua being so busy with his work wasn't really there to help. A father figure would have been nice around the house a little more often to deal with a teenage daughter looking for adventure.

Amanda was now sixteen and into boys. Lindsey frowned, she wasn't quite sure she liked such a stage for her daughter. She wanted to trust her, but Amanda wasn't as subdued as Mike had been. Her fear also had another source: Tim, Amanda's latest conquest. Tim was a bit of a character, known to play pranks, very much into motorcycles and snowmobiles. It frightened Lindsey.

She unhooked the handset. "Hi Amanda."

"Uh, Mom?" She asked in a questioning tone.

"Yes, what is it?"

"A few friends are going out after school. We are going for a snowmobile ride. Is it all right if I go with them?"

"I don't know Amanda. Your homework has been suffering lately. Your last report card wasn't too great. I think you need to come home to finish your homework first."

In an angry tone, yet just at the edge of what she knew would remain respectful enough to address her mother, she replied. "I knew you'd say no. I knew it was a waste of time to call. I can never do anything. All my friends can have fun, but I am not allowed. It's not fair."

"Amanda, you'll have lots of time to go with your friends on the weekend after all your homework are done."

"But Mom, Tim is picking me up and he wants to use his father's snowmobile. I won't stay out late, I promise."

Lindsey tried to stay firm. "Amanda, don't argue with me, I said no. Now I have to get back to work. I will see you when I get home and we can discuss it then. Okay?"

"Yeah, right." Amanda hung up.

Lindsey thought to herself. "Why doesn't Amanda ever call her father for this?" But then she knew too well that Joshua would have had even more trouble resisting his daughter than she had. In some way, like most men, Joshua had a hard time saying no to women. Lindsey herself had been able to get a lot out of him because of it, but now Amanda was also often using her charms to get her father to agree to her shenanigans.

The phone rang again. The secretary was letting Lindsey know her next appointment was in. She sighed and acknowledged. She prayed for a quick end to this day.

7. Bank

People were coming and going as usual. The line in front of the counters was small but steady. Most came to make small deposits, retrieve a bit of cash, or pay bills. Peter Cohen knew his branch would never beat records. While other branches competed for the most number of investors, or the largest return on dividends, Peter knew his bank struggled to remain open.

Now with the confirmation of his biggest client passing away, his chances of survival had just been reduced. He tried to keep his usual charming smile. He forced himself to give kind compliments to the customers. In his mind however, fear, uncertainty, and anxiety were battling for supremacy.

Every time the phone rang he jumped. Although cold air kept rushing in surrounding each customer walking in, he was sweating as if it were the middle of summer. Yesterday, he left a message for the regional director to call back and was still waiting. He debated many times whether he should call again. He didn't want to display his anxiety to the director but he needed to relay the message, to inform him of the situation.

Peter had already reviewed various scenarios hundreds of times in his mind. The death of Warren Sparks would cause a change in ownership. The change could mean many possibilities. The new owner could continue to run the mill as is, in which case he had no need to worry. The new owner could bring much change in the way the mill was run, which could mean some improvements and maybe a renewed prosperity for the town, with hopefully a new mortgage from the bank. However, Peter was more pessimistic. He knew what the forestry industry was like. He knew how many forestry operations had been closed in the last decade leaving ghost towns behind. This was the scenario he focused on. This was the scenario that scared him.

The phone rang again and he almost spilled the coffee he was sipping, his fifth of the day even though it was only eleven o'clock.

He waited for his secretary to answer. She gave the usual greeting then asked the caller to hold.

"Mr. Cohen, the regional director for you on line one."

He put his coffee down. His hand shook as he reached for the phone. He stopped midway. He had to compose himself. He wouldn't let the director wait too long, but he couldn't answer with the large lump blocking his throat. He took a deep breath and summoned himself to calm down. Then he picked up the handset.

"Reg, how are you?" he said trying to remain as casual as possible. He and Reginald Cromwell went back a long time and they knew each other well. Although they were on a first name basis, Peter had always retained a respectful attitude, a requirement when dealing with a superior in the banking industry.

"I'm fine Pete. What's up?"

Cromwell wasn't one to beat around the bush. His time was precious; production and profit were his middle names.

"Oh, I just wanted to give you a heads-up on a bit of a situation I became aware of yesterday."

"A situation. What kind of situation?" The interest level of the director had moved up a notch. Peter swallowed hard.

"Well, one of my customers passed away this week." Peter said trying to keep it as an item of interest, not the crisis his whole body was enduring.

"My condolences. Why are you calling me about this? I'm sure it's not the first time one of your customers has died. You know the drill."

"Yes, yes, I know the drill: we are holding his accounts until we get instructions from the next-of-kin." The harsh tone in Cromwell's voice had struck Peter. Although he had rehearsed his discussion hundreds of time over the last twelve hours, everything he had planned to say was now jumbled. "It's… it's that this wasn't just another customer. This was my biggest customer."

"Peter, spit it out, will you?" Cromwell said.

"Well, it's Warren Sparks, the owner of the mill. He passed away on Tuesday night."

"The mill. Is that the mill employing half the population of your little town?" Cromwell barked in the phone. "That's what you call a situation?"

"Well, it's not really half the population, it's only a few hundred people." Peter tried to offer sheepishly.

"Yeah, right. And those few hundred people live and shop in that little hole of yours which provides the revenues for half the population. Don't play me for a fool Pete. I wasn't born yesterday. What you should be telling me is that you could have a major crisis on your hands; people with no money to pay mortgages, loans, or credit card bills; people who will soon have to declare bankruptcy; suffer foreclosures on homes and cars, furniture and accounts. That's what this call is about."

Even though he knew his director was right, since he had foreseen all of this himself, he wanted desperately to disagree. He tried to be positive even against his own deductions. "It might not be that bad. We don't know yet what the next-of-kin will do with the mill. It's too early to speculate."

"It's never too early to reduce the risk, Peter. That's Banking 101. So what are you doing about it?" Cromwell's tone was now high pitched, denoting fury.

"I...I was waiting to speak to you first. I didn't take any action yet. I thought maybe we could wait to find out what the future of the mill would be." Peter stuttered.

"Don't kid me and don't kid yourself, Peter. Your little town is doomed and you know it. So since I have to hold your hand in this, here is what you are going to do. I want you to stop issuing loans and mortgages immediately. No new credit cards are to be issued. If there's any way you can block major purchases or uses of credit cards by locals, do it. Then, I want a report of the estimated potential loss for the bank by Friday morning. How many employees of the mill have mortgages, loans and credit cards? What are the amounts owed? How many businesses are directly linked to the mill? How many business loans do we own, and what is the potential loss there? I want to know what you are going to do for damage control. Don't call back unless it's to make sure my fax machine works so I can receive the report. Did you get that?"

"Sure, Reginald. I'll see what I can do." Peter started to feel a headache coming on.

"That's not an option, Cohen. I want the report on Friday morning. Even if you have to work 24 hours a day for the next two days, I will have it. Right?"

"Right. Yes. Uh... sure, Reginald."

"Good." Cromwell paused and then added. "Oh, and have a good day, Pete." The line went dead.

He dropped the receiver in its place and leaned back in his chair. He closed his eyes, squeezed his arms against his body and bent his head, his chin resting on his tie. He stayed there for a while. Shivers ran through him. He felt like crying.

Peter Cohen was born and raised in Lakedge. After University where he earned a degree in Commerce, he started working as a credit manager for a bank in a large community near Toronto. He did this for a number of years, regularly coming back to visit his family and friends in Lakedge. When the previous bank manager retired, he applied for the position. He was proud to be able to come back and do something for his community. He quickly gained respect from his customers as he showed attention to the needs of the people in his hometown. He had mingled in all sorts of events and today after twenty-two years in his position, he was considered a leader in Lakedge. As past president of the Lakedge Chamber of Commerce, and a contributor to many municipal initiatives, he had become famous.

Today, Peter wanted to crawl under a rock. He struggled to decide where his loyalty lied. He owed it to his employer. If it hadn't been for the bank providing him with this position, his career might have stagnated. If not for his job with the Lakedge branch, he would never have gained the attention and stature he had. He also felt that he owed the town. They had taken him back when he returned. They had gradually recognised his worth. They had trusted his advice for twenty-two years.

How would the people of his community feel if he started foreclosing on their mortgages? How would they feel if instead of being the provider of friendly advice on money management, he would become the enemy, trying to take away their belongings?

Maybe if he explained the situation to them. Maybe if he made them understand that he had no other option. This wasn't his money. He had no control. They would surely understand that. They couldn't blame him for the circumstances. He had to explain how he was forced to follow the rules.

Somehow, as he entertained these thoughts, he wasn't reassured. He didn't really believe they would see it this way. Maybe producing this report was actually a blessing in disguise. If he worked hard over the weekend, it might take his mind off the dilemma. Maybe also, he could find a solution out of the numbers he would be crunching away. Maybe the situation wasn't as bad as he envisioned.

He turned the computer screen on and logged in.

****

Jim drove out of the yard. His truck complained and moaned in protest. Jim didn't care. This was going to be the last ride this pile of metal would be doing with him at the wheel. Good luck to anyone who was going to buy this heap.

It was not that Jim didn't take care of the vehicle. He had followed all of the maintenance recommendations; he had oiled it and greased it regularly, he had kept it as clean as possible under the circumstances. Certainly the environment wasn't kind to vehicles at this latitude. Winters brought mountains of snow making the driving tricky, forcing motors under already cold and stressful conditions. In the summer, much of the unpaved roads meant tons of dirt and rocks would scrape the undercarriage, and dust would get into all parts of the engine. So after a couple of hundred thousand kilometres, it was time for Jim to lay his truck to rest.

He drove into town and went directly to the bank. He had discussed his loan with Peter Cohen, the manager, and everything should be ready for him. He and Peter had gone to high school together. When Peter had left for University, Jim had started to work at the mill and they lost track of each other until Peter came back almost eight years later with a degree and experience in a bank, making him the natural choice to take over the manager's position.

Jim himself had gone from a woodchopper to the yard superintendent at Sparks Mill.

He passed through the bank's doors, greeting the ladies behind the counter and the few people in the waiting line. He was careful not to seem too cheery. He didn't want to seem happy with the loss of his boss, yet a new truck was an event you couldn't ignore.

He noticed that the door to Peter's office was closed.

"Sylvia, is the boss in?" he asked Peter's secretary sitting at her desk adding up transactions.

She looked up. "Oh, hi Jim. Yes, he's in. He's just working on something. I'll tell him you're here."

She picked up the phone and dialled Peter. She was nodding and her face seemed to change. She hung up and turned to Jim.

"I'm sorry Jim, something's come up and he can't see you right now. He asked if you could come back next Monday instead." She asked apologetically.

"What do you mean he can't see me? I made all the arrangements. I'm supposed to pick up my truck this afternoon. I can't come back next

Monday. Let me speak to him." Jim walked around to the gate that gave access to the inner part of the counter.

Sylvia came closer. She spoke softly. "I don't think it's a good idea. He seemed to have something bothering him. I know Pete, and he doesn't sound like that usually."

"That's bull. I know Pete. Let me talk to him." Jim didn't give her a chance to reply. He pushed open the gate and walked directly to Peter's office. The door wasn't locked so he had no difficulty walking in.

Peter raised his head from the computer. "What the…" He stopped upon seeing Jim. "Sorry Jim. I have this urgent report I have to do for the head office and I don't have time now. Please understand and come back on Monday."

"No way Pete. We planned all of this. The paperwork is done. You said I would have the money today. My truck is waiting for me at the dealers. All you need is five minutes to give me my money."

Peter was white as a ghost. He was breathing heavily and didn't know how to answer. Sylvia was right behind Jim and she waited as well for instructions. She wasn't about to have Jim removed, she knew him too much and it just wasn't done in a small community like Lakedge.

So Peter was forced to give in. He hoped to delay this. He prayed to have the weekend to resolve this or at least to prepare for this encounter. Now, with Jim here, he had to confront reality. This was going to be the first in a series of difficult encounters to come over the next few months. It was most likely going to be the new norm unless a miracle happened.

He let out a heavy sigh. "Okay, Jim. Come and sit down. Sylvia, can you close the door, please?"

They both complied and Jim was now sitting looking at Peter expectantly.

Peter started. "Jim, I'm afraid I have some bad news."

Jim's face changed to a frown. "Bad news?"

"Yes, there was a change in your loan application and it was declined."

Jim jumped up. "What do you mean declined? You told me it was approved on Monday! You were ready to give it to me then but I knew the truck wouldn't be ready before today. I hope this is a joke. And if it is, I'm not laughing."

Peter unconsciously pressed against the back of his chair, trying to increase the distance between him and Jim. "It's not a joke Jim. It's just that… that… things have changed."

"What has changed, Pete? Explain this to me. Then give me my money."

"What has changed is… the bank isn't sure you will be able to pay back this loan." Peter said, hesitating.

Jim fell back in his chair. "Pete. I always paid all my debts in the past. I've never once been late in my mortgage. I pay my credit cards every month before the deadline. Why would this be any different?"

As he said it, Jim already had an inkling it was related to Warren Sparks' death but he wanted to hear it from Peter.

"It's different because Warren is dead. The bank knows about it and they are afraid the mill will close. If it does, then none of you will have jobs anymore. Without jobs you won't be able to pay your loans. So the bank has ordered a freeze on all loans until further notice."

Jim had his mouth open in disbelief. He didn't reply, feeling as if somebody had just shot him through the head.

Peter gave him a minute then added. "I'm truly sorry Jim, there's nothing I can do. I got my orders from the head office."

Jim looked at him. "Who's side are you on, Pete? I thought you were one of us. I thought you cared for Lakedge. Was it all for the trophies?" He pointed at the plaques on Peter's wall claiming the bank manager's contribution to the well being of the community. "Was it just for the glory? Is it normal that you give up on us the minute there's an indication of trouble?"

Peter reacted at that. "I didn't give up. I locked myself up to try and come up with a solution. I'm trying to find a way out of this. I have to convince my head office they are wrong about the situation. So don't hang me before I'm proven guilty."

Jim sat back. His anger was still vivid but he didn't know if he should continue to lash out at Peter. They both stayed there silent for a minute or two.

"Jim, let me see what I can come up with over the weekend. On Friday, I have to send a report to my boss. Then I intend to work towards a solution all weekend. If you come back after work on Monday, I might have some better news. Can you do that?" said Peter.

Jim was disgusted. He knew he had no choice. He was completely dependent on Peter. There was no other bank in Lakedge. The banks in Greenmeadows would probably adopt the same attitude towards him as Peter's bank had. The dealer would not accept delivering the truck without a loan agreement signed by the bank. There was nobody else in town to loan him any money. Ironically he thought of the only person who might have been ready to offer him such a loan; but Warren Sparks was dead.

Jim got up. He left the room without another word. The customers noticed how his mood had changed. No one dared to say anything. A dark cloud had just burst over Lakedge and Jim Stone was the first to receive the hit of the lightning bolts it carried.

8. Next-of-kin

"Guess what Brent? I'm on to something."

At the other end of the phone, Brent wasn't quite as enthusiastic as Mark. "Oh really?"

"Yeah. My lawyer friend called back. You were partly right. It seems that Warren and Teresa never divorced. That's why we couldn't find anything. But they did have a separation agreement. Teresa got the agreement drafted by a lawyer in Ottawa where she was living at the time. He traced the lawyer and confirmed she left the country. He remembered because he signed her passport and she told him she was going to Europe somewhere with her daughter."

Mark hardly took a breath. Brent still didn't respond.

"So my next step was for the passport office. It seems she has kept her Canadian nationality although she has been living for years in France. Since she wasn't divorced, she kept her married name and I was able to get an address and I'm waiting for someone to call back with a phone number. Isn't that good news?"

"I suppose it is." Brent didn't sound quite sure. "It could mean good news if our search is over. At the same time, I've been thinking how it could also spell the end of my career as the valet for the Warren estate."

Mark hadn't seen it this way, but didn't want to lose his line of thought. He continued. "We haven't found any will yet, which is certainly surprising from a man like Warren, but we know they had a separation agreement by which she kept custody of their daughter. He agreed to pay alimony until their daughter completed her studies. Apparently the amount of money he sent them was quite substantial."

Brent seemed to compose himself. "Do we know anything else about her? What about the daughter?"

"We know a bit. This lawyer said his wife was a fashion designer and wanted to start a boutique to sell her designs. With all the money she got from Warren it seems it was enough for her to start up a business and to take care of her daughter at the same time."

"Fashion design, eh. Well, from the picture in Warren's office, I can tell she was beautiful. This would have certainly helped her in a career as fashion designer. She might even be a successful entrepreneur like her husband; maybe some of his skills rubbed off on her. I get a picture of her as a model showing off her dresses to the haute society of France."

Mark smiled. "That's possible. So I'll wait for the call and get back to you."

They hung up.

Mark went on to other papers on his desk and kept at it for a while. Every time the phone rang he jumped, his heart skipping a beat. "Was this the call he was waiting for? Would he solve the mystery of the disappeared family members?"

Then finally, it came. An operator had located a number for him in Cannes on the French Riviera.

A renewed anticipation and anxiety swept over him. He had called families before to give news of a death, usually linked to a car accident, but this call had so much attached to it, he felt very different. Calling halfway across the world, to people he didn't know, to let them know a dear member of their family had passed away… But he stopped himself. Would they consider Warren Sparks in such a way? What if they didn't care? Under the circumstances, they probably forgot completely he existed. He never encountered anything like it before.

Taking a huge breath he dialled the number.

A man came on after a few rings. *"Résidence De L'Étincelle, qui dois-je annoncer?"*

Mark was taken off guard. He had forgotten that in France the person at the end of the phone would most likely speak French. His knowledge of French dated back to high school over a decade ago and had been minimal at best. He didn't even want to take a chance.

"I'm sorry, do you speak English?" He asked as slowly as possible. There was a slight pause at the other end, after which the man answered with a very strong accent. "One instant, please."

After a minute or so while Mark could feel his heart all the way to his throat, a woman answered the call. *"Allo, Émilie De L'Étincelle, j'écoute."*

He repeated the request. "Do you speak English?"

The lady changed immediately and replied in perfect English yet with an after tone of French. "I do. Who is calling, please?"

"My name is Mark Dexter. I am a Sergeant with the Provincial Police for the Lakedge Detachment. I am calling from Canada with an important call for Joy or Teresa Sparks."

There was a long silence and the same woman replied. She seemed annoyed. "Well Mister Sergeant. Mrs. Teresa Sparks is not here at this time. As for Joy Sparks, she no longer exists and I was hoping I would never hear that name again."

Mark didn't know what to reply. He stuttered a bit. "It's just, I...I... I have an important message to deliver."

"Since this is official police business, I suppose, I will have to accept this. I used to be called Joy Sparks. I changed my name many years ago. My name is Émilie De L'Étincelle."

"Emily." Mark had a bit of a shock but tried to recover.

She burst at the other end. "No! Not Emily. Émilie." She exaggerated the accent to try and convey how she wanted it pronounced. "With É, like hay, but without the h. Do you get it?"

"Oh, Eymeelee." He tried as best he could. He didn't dare try her last name. He had already forgotten half of it anyway!

"Yes, now, what is your news?"

Mark had almost forgotten why he had called in the first place. "Oh, yes. I wanted to confirm that you were related to Warren Sparks. Am I right?"

A long sigh came through. "I guess you could say I'm related. He is my progenitor." She said the last word almost as she was spitting.

Mark had heard all sorts of names for fathers –deadbeat dads, slouches, and drunks– but never heard anyone referred to as a progenitor. His image of Warren Sparks had never been one so low as to what Joy, or Emily, or Eymeelee, was trying to portrait.

"In that case, I am sorry to inform you, your father passed away on Tuesday."

There was no response. Mark always gave time to family members to take in the bad news. Émilie hardly took a few seconds.

"So? What am I supposed to do about it? Did you expect me to cry?"

Mark was starting to resent this conversation. He never liked announcing the passing away of family members, but this one was particularly brutal because of the ingrate attitude of Warren's alleged daughter. His tone went up a notch still trying to contain himself.

"Miss. I am not expecting anything from you. I just wanted to inform you. Now there will be a funeral. The man had assets and we are trying to locate a will. There will be paperwork to do and you just might get some of his inheritance. I don't care how you feel about it, but those are the facts."

She changed her manner immediately. "Now, if you put it that way, I might actually be interested. A will, you say? I hadn't thought of it. Very well, Mister… I'm sorry, I forgot your name."

"Sergeant Dexter." he replied firmly.

"Yes, Sergeant Dexter. What should I do, then?" Mark sighed and regrouped. He had a duty to accomplish, no matter who was at the other end.

"I will leave you my phone number just in case you need to reach me. If you are aware of any will Warr…" He stopped. He was going to call him by his first name, as he always had in the past. "Mr. Sparks would have written, you need to contact us immediately. The funeral home is delaying the service until Tuesday next week to give time for the family to be contacted and their wishes expressed. Since we were aware some of his family was in Europe, we wanted to make sure you had enough time, in case you wanted to attend the funeral."

Joy let out a laugh. "Attend the funeral? I don't think so. That's a good one! As for the will, I will do my own investigation. If I find something before you, I will call you."

He gave her his phone number and thanked her, although reluctantly.

Friday, February 17

Obituary

SPARKS, Warren Thomas

Passed away in his sleep on the night of February 14 at his home in Lakedge at the age of 79 years. Son of Richard Andrew and Laura Marie Sparks (nee Brighton), he leaves behind his wife Teresa and his daughter Joy, both currently living abroad. At the time of publication, no other family has been located.

Friends will be received at the Ridgeway Funeral Home, 1239 Main Street in Lakedge to pay their respects. Visiting hours will be Sunday February 19 from 2:00 p.m. to 9:00 p.m. and again on Monday February 20 from 10:00 a.m. to 9:00 p.m. The funeral will be held on Tuesday at the Lakedge Community Church at 2:00 p.m. and burial will follow at the Lakedge Memorial Cemetery.

In lieu of flowers, donations may be made to the Heart and Stroke Foundation or to the Greenmeadows/Lakedge United Way.

All those who knew him will remember Warren Sparks for his generosity and his goodwill. In particular, the employees of Sparks Mill wish to express their gratitude for the opportunities Warren Sparks offered them and the community of Lakedge.

9. Credit

"It's my faucet, John. The leak was driving me nuts but I tried to ignore it. Today, my wife called in a panic that it was squirting all over the room and she couldn't turn it off. I got her to turn off the main intake to the house and I rushed home. I tested it and I have to replace the whole system."

"I guess you do, Jim." John Fenster had a soft voice not quite fitting his burly rough looks. As the local hardware store owner for the second generation in Lakedge, he knew all about the ups and downs of the renovations and maintenance of the residents. He had advice for everyone and everything, and people usually followed his advice with success.

"What do you recommend? I want to do it myself if I can but I want it to last." Jim Stone said.

"I have just the right thing for you. The 'do it yourself' plumbing kit for changing faucets. Here." He pointed at the product on the shelf. Jim took it and examined the labels.

"As for the faucet itself, you have a couple of choices." He walked to the end of the isle and indicated a couple of samples that were adequate for kitchens. "You have the low end of the scale but I suggest you get something half-way. It will go far longer. I do have some upper-end stuff but it's mainly for show. The only one who would really go for this is Warren…" He stopped.

"Actually, now that Warren Sparks is dead, I don't think anyone will want to buy this stuff. Oh well, maybe I'll let it go for a rebate. It's taking up shelf space for nothing anyway. Here, why don't I let you have it at the same price as the middle scale one."

Jim felt a bit embarrassed. "It's just that I don't know if I can pay you. My credit at the bank isn't very good with the risk at the mill, and I don't have that kind of cash available just now."

John looked at him. His kind blue eyes were a source of comfort for many worried customers. Once again they would do the trick.

"Jim, your credit is always good with me. I'll just write it up, and whenever you can pay for it, you know where I am."

"I don't know if I can accept that John." Jim started to refuse and replaced the kit on the shelf.

"Nonsense." John accepted no excuse. "The way I see it Jim, if the mill closes, it not just you and the people working there who are going to be in trouble, it's everybody else in Lakedge. So you take this while I can still afford to give it away. If things get really bad, we may all have to declare bankruptcy. Once we get to that point, I won't be able to give anything away because it won't be mine anymore."

Jim didn't really know what to say. He stood there with a heavy heart knowing the whole community was starting to feel the loss.

"Someday I'll be the one needing help. I know you'll be there to help. Today, it's my turn. No more discussion." John placed the kit in Jim's hands and went to the back to get the faucet.

The front door opened and Ashley came in. It was a slow day and Jim was alone in the store. She noticed him.

"Oh, hi Mr. Stone. Have you seen my father?"

"Yes, Ashley, he went in the back to get something."

"Thanks." She said cheery.

"You seem in a good mood." Jim enquired.

"Yes, Mike is arriving tonight. He's here for a week." She said with a smile almost all the way to her ears.

"Ah, yes. The boyfriend is back in town. Where is he now?" Jim asked.

"He studies at York University in Toronto. But next week is Reading Week so he gets a week off and he's coming home for it. We are meeting him at the bus station in Greenmeadows tonight."

John came back with a box. He noticed Ashley with Jim. "Hello bright eyes. What brings you home so early?" John knew Ashley worked at the Cosy Retreat cottage until later and shouldn't have been back yet.

"Oh, Mr. Fleming let me go early. He knew I wanted to go pick-up Mike at the bus station." Ashley reminded him with a light hearted tone in her voice.

"Right, it's tonight. I had forgotten."

"That's why I came by. I wanted to remind you."

Fenster's Hardware store was located in Highway Mall, the only mall in town, and the Fensters lived a block away. "I'm just going to take a shower and change. Then I'm meeting with Mr. Stuart. He promised to bring me along to get Mike."

"Very well, run along then." John shooed her away playfully. "And say hi to Mike for me... if you can remember."

"I will Daddy. Thank you. Bye Mr. Stone." She said quickly as she left.

Jim turned to John. "Ah, love is in the air."

"It sure is. She's been talking about this evening all week. I guess we must have been like them at some point in our life."

"Yes, we probably were. It just seems so far away now." said Jim.

"So? Is there anything else I can do for you Jim?"

"You've done a lot more than I deserve. I'll remember that John. Thank you."

"Ah, go on. Get home and fix that faucet before your wife calls for you. You wouldn't want her to be mad because she can't have supper ready on time now."

Jim smiled and went for the door. "Thanks a lot. Bye."

John didn't answer. As the door closed he sighed. Jim was only the fourth of his customer expressing difficulty with the bank on the same day. How many more would he come upon in the next while? How long could he continue to offer charity before he started feeling the effects himself?

A lot of questions were coming up lately and there weren't many answers.

10. Local Hero

All the big brass of the Winnipeg Police were assembled. There were more gold bars in the council chamber than in the nearest bank. They came supposedly for him. Robert Cloutier, the veteran policeman and detective, was being hailed as a hero and offered an early retirement package for his being injured severely in the line of duty.

He should have been proud, honoured, yet his smiles were all for show. They were getting rid of him. It was a royal send off and the one with the largest smile was his boss, Inspector Moreno.

It had been brewing ever since the debacle of the Petroleum Producers Consortium. His mishandled arrest of Russell Dearbourne, the scapegoat for the consortium's plans to stop any research on alternative energy sources, had made Moreno suspicious of every action Cloutier undertook.

More recently, the operation that nearly cost the life of his partner Cliff Standish, had warranted the SIU being called in to review, which had ultimately led to this early retirement. As he stood at attention awaiting the start of the ceremony, he relived it once more. The scene was as vivid as when it occurred. He had probably seen it over and over again hundreds of times since that day. It was in his mind even when sleeping, haunting his dreams.

They had been staking out the place for two full days. Cliff and he had taken turns sleeping and going out to get food and coffee. They hadn't showered all this time and the car was starting to stink with body odour. They had cramps from sitting in the same position for so long. This was one takedown Robert didn't want to leave to anyone else. Even Moreno was unaware of the operation. Luckily for them the inspector was too busy with some new information that had come up on a cold case involving a prominent member of the Manitoba legislature.

Moreno wouldn't let any other detective be in charge of such a high-profile case, certainly not Cloutier. So it gave Cliff and him some room to manoeuvre.

At about two in the morning, all hell broke loose. Robert was on watch but had somehow dozed off and he couldn't tell for how long. When he came to, he noticed a light in the building. He nudged Cliff.

"We have something."

Cliff woke up quickly and looked where Robert was pointing. The building was an old brick house, with the front transformed into a showroom for motorcycles. The neighbourhood had once been residential but over time had changed into a business area so most of the houses had storefronts instead of verandas.

They got out of the car. As planned, Cliff went for the back, while Robert took care of the front. Robert felt the cramps in his legs, and the extra pounds on his belly. He wasn't in shape for walking, let alone running. He had hoped this would go down easily and he wouldn't need to exert himself.

He snuck past the first window and edged to the door. Crouching, he reached it and gently tried to pull it, but it was locked from the inside. For a moment he thought about calling for backup but this was *his* case, *he* would make the arrest. He needed this to his credit. His file wasn't glorious lately and a success here would bring it up a notch.

The man inside was considered armed and dangerous, and had been evading police for years now, but they had good evidence he was the suspect for at least one homicide. They just had to bring him in.

That's when he heard the blast. It came from the back; Cliff must be in trouble. To go around would take too much time, so Robert opted to smash the front window and rush in.

He ran across the showroom with his handgun in front and the safety off. He reached a hallway with doors leading to offices. He stopped an instant in front of each door to ensure nobody was inside. He had to move on to reach Cliff, so he couldn't afford a full search. When he got to the back, the fire was fully ablaze, an explosion had set it off. He called out to Cliff but no answer came back.

The heat was intense but he kept moving. Then he noticed Cliff lying on the ground. The flames were inching towards him. Robert started in his direction. Then he felt a push in his back and at the same time his feet were kicked out from under him. He fell with all his weight in the direction of the fire. He instinctively protected his face with his arms. His coat caught fire. He struggled and turned on his back, aiming his gun, trying to guess the position of his assailant. He aimed at a shadow and shot twice. Then he rolled over attempting to extinguish the fire. The shadow went down and didn't get back up.

Robert hadn't forgotten about Cliff. His hands and arms were aching from the burns. The smoke was strangling him. His eyes were watering, his mind starting to send messages of imminent shutdown. He had to get out, yet he couldn't leave Cliff there.

So he got up in extreme pain, struggling not to take in too much of the smoke, he started dragging Cliff's inert body away from the flames. It took all his adrenaline reserves to get out of the danger zone. Then he felt another presence. Someone was there and helping him pull Cliff. He had done it. They were safe. At that moment he blanked out.

"Attention"

The call to order shook him out of his thoughts. The ceremony was about to start. He was marched in with an honour guard composed of many of his colleagues in the division. His uniform hadn't been worn for a while and he felt the tightness of the extra pounds accumulated. There was no sense in asking for a new uniform on the day you retired, so he would have to suck in his breath for most of the ceremony.

Arriving at the front of the stage, the guard did a few manoeuvres and departed. Robert stood there alone facing the small crowd. In the front row, in all her beauty, was his wife Jasmine; her dark eyes, her silky long black hair, her small lips displaying a wide smile showing her pride for her husband, everything that had struck him the day he met her.

She didn't know half the story; he didn't let her in on it. She was so proud of him he couldn't dare break her illusion.

She only saw his maimed hands, riddled with burn marks. His muscles and tendons were damaged to such extend that he couldn't fully close his hands, and his fingers were almost locked in place.

She saw Cliff sitting beside her, alive only because of her husband's selfless determination to save his partner. Cliff had suffered burns to the right side of his face and had almost lost sight in one eye, but he would be able to resume his career after some cosmetic and eye surgery.

She saw all the officials assembled to give her husband the honour and recognition she truly felt he deserved.

Only he knew. He had messed up. He had recounted the story so many times to the Special Investigation Unit. It was standard protocol when an officer fired a gun. This time, however, Moreno had wanted to throw the book at him. Only through the intervention of the Deputy Chief who had known Robert for a long time, was he able to get some relief.

The shadow man was the suspect and Robert had shot him. He later died at the hospital. The deputy was grateful. By killing him, Robert had saved them the cost of a long court case and had rid the City of a dangerous criminal. So even though Robert was accused of a number of infractions based on his traditional disrespect for procedures –failing to call for back-up, endangering the life of a fellow officer, disobeying instructions from a superior, and the list went on– it was decided it would be a public relations success to make Robert a hero by recognising publicly his action in saving Cliff.

Robert had signed the agreement. He would get full pension and retire from the force immediately, in return for this ceremony and a promise of no further action –legal or otherwise– against the force. The police union saw it as a good deal and blessed the plan.

The Chief and the Deputy each said a few words. A medal was pinned to his chest. He couldn't shake hands because his were still heavily bandaged, so he received a number of pats of the shoulders from senior officers, most of whom he had never spoken to.

The media was there of course. As soon as the ceremony was over, a number of them rushed towards him asking for a statement, questioning him on how he felt. He felt scammed, was what he wanted to say, but he knew he couldn't. He was forced to leave against his will the only profession he had ever practised. He was trapped, cornered, but all he could say was he only did his duty.

They also asked him what had motivated him to run back to the fire to save his partner. That's how the story had been written for the media. The force wanted to show him as a hero combating an evil criminal. So the scenario was an investigation where they had stumbled onto a booby trap. Robert was supposedly outside waiting for back-up and covering the alley while Cliff was gathering evidence. When the explosion burst and Cliff was knocked out, Robert rushed in at the peril of his own life. He encountered the criminal, fought him, struggled and eventually fired the two shots that silenced him forever. Then he went right into the fire and extricated Cliff meanwhile getting badly burned. His burns were so extensive he could no longer fulfill his duties as a police officer. As he was close to retirement, the force had agreed to give him full honours for his heroism and a full pension. At least it was what the media would have in the papers on the next day.

Jasmine stood at his side. She received the same story as the media. She was proud of her husband, the hero.

Only, now Robert felt bitterness. No medal would ever give him back his pride. He had failed his last job. He had put his partner and best friend in danger. He had disobeyed orders and protocols. He was supposed to make an arrest but he killed the suspect instead. The families of the victims this criminal had murdered may never get closure since there would be no trial to prove he actually committed the crime.

This was not the way Robert had envisioned ending his career. He kept his fake smile as long as he could.

11. Competition

"We never had this conversation, right?"

"Don't worry, I know the drill. I'm not a beginner at this. Please, give me some credit."

"I can never be safe enough, that's all. So what have you got?"

"Here's the scoop: I heard from a reliable source that the owner of the mill up in Lakedge croaked a couple of nights ago. As far as we know he has no family. It's not clear who he left his estate to."

"Lakedge. Yeah. I know that mill. It's the Park mill or something like that."

"I think it's Sparks."

"Right, now I remember, Sparks Mill. The guy was a tough old lumberjack. He stole quite a few customers from us. He made a point of showing them his lumber was of better quality. He actually used a shotgun for his demonstration. He would take a piece of lumber from his production and a piece from us and shoot through both. Of course, his lumber was tighter so it resisted more than ours. Since he was selling it at the same price as us or lower, he'd get the contract."

"Sounds about right. From the stories I hear he was a tough negotiator so that would fit the description."

"So he died? Good riddance. May he rot in hell."

"So what do you want me to do? Are you interested?"

"Of course I am, what kind of question is that?"

"Just checking. Don't want to waste my time."

"I pay you enough that you can waste as much time as I tell you to. I want you on your way to Lakedge in the next five minutes to find out everything you can about this."

"I don't know if I'll get there tonight. There's a heavy snowstorm hitting all of the northern parts and I might be better to wait until Monday. I doubt much will happen on the weekend anyway."

"I don't give a hoot about a snowstorm. I want you up there sniffing around all weekend. You hear me? No excuses."

"Okay. I get you. It's just going to be a long slow ride, that's all. You're paying for the gas, remember?"

"If this works, we'll make up in lumber sales ten times what it's going to cost you in gas within the first two weeks alone. Let me worry about the money. You just get me the information I need to make this happen."

"All right boss."

"You got that part right. Now get going, I want that mill."

"You know this mill is quite a ways up north, don't you?"

"So?"

"Well, if you buy it, the transportation costs are going to be astronomical."

"I said I wanted to buy it, I didn't say I wanted to operate it. This is an opportunity to get rid of some of the competition. With this we can regain some of the customers we lost and probably get new ones. If we close our competition's plants, our own will do much better, right?"

"I guess."

"Well that's why I'm in charge here. I don't guess, I know. You just do what I tell you and everything will be fine. Call me when you have something."

The phone went dead.

12. Snow

The bus from Toronto was almost a half hour late. The road conditions on the way up deteriorated the closer they came to Greenmeadows. Even Mike, who was used to bad winter weather, had to hold his breath a few times fearing he wouldn't make the trip. The bus slipped here and there on the treacherous roads but the driver's experience kept them on track if not on time.

Josh, Lindsey, Margaret, Amanda and Ashley had been waiting inside the station. Josh got coffee and hot chocolate for everyone and they talked. A lot of the attention was on Ashley. Lindsey was curious to know more about her. Mothers always want every detail about the girl their son is likely to marry. Ashley was obliging and answered the inquiries with enthusiasm. She was in love with Mike, and anyone who cared for Mike was important to her now.

Margaret was observing the relationship building between them and could already see signs of bonding similar to those she had forged herself years ago with Lindsey.

Josh was quiet but attentive. His mind went from his son Mike's return, to Warren's death. He wondered how the roads were and prayed that Mike would be safe, occasionally slipping back to Lakedge and the path that lay ahead of it now that Warren Sparks was dead.

Finally, the Greyhound bus veered into the vast parking lot of the mall. Ashley had seated herself in a way she could talk to the family and watch the parking at the same time so she was the first to see the bus and jumped up as soon as it turned in. Lindsey and Josh got up with not quite as much anticipation as Ashley but glad the bus was finally here. There was relief in both their hearts. Amanda kept chatting on her cell phone hardly noticing the commotion around her.

Lindsey saw it and scolded. "That's enough. I told you to get rid of that thing. I know you're not happy to be with us, but you could at least fake it for your brother."

"All right. Who says I'm not happy to see my brother?" Amanda retorted.

"Watch how you speak to your mother, young lady." Josh told her abruptly.

"Sorry." she replied in a tone not quite fitting the word.

Lately, Amanda had been going through a phase of aggressiveness towards her parents. Both sensed a rebellion they had never experienced with Mike. He had always been the good son, not perfect, assuredly, but respectful and generally obedient. They were starting to wonder where they had gone wrong with Amanda.

From the sidewalk they waited for the bus to come to a full stop and let the passengers out. The wind was blowing the snow in their faces, twirling it around in spirals like little white tornadoes. It hit them and stung. Lindsey could only take so much. Passengers were only now getting up; there would be a waiting period before they started to stroll out. She couldn't see inside so she couldn't tell if Mike was near the front or the rear of the bus. She told Josh she would wait inside the mall. Margaret and Amanda followed her.

Ashley was too excited and wanted to wait outside. She didn't seem to mind the cold and the wind. Her anticipation was stronger than the frostbite. So Josh stayed with her, hoping Mike would come out quickly.

The driver walked down the stairs and went to the luggage compartments. He opened two on the main side then went to the opposite side.

The Greenmeadows stop wasn't the last on this route. There was a thirty minute stop to allow the bus to refuel. All passengers were asked to get off. As they filed out, they would run into the mall to the warmth, the washrooms and the coffee shop.

When Mike emerged in the alley between the two front seats, Ashley screeched with delight. "Mike, Mike, I'm here!" She waved at him as he took the stairs and then jumped in his arms, not even letting him get off the last steps. Other passengers were amused and allowed for the delay. A bit of distraction after a long trip was good for the soul.

Mike hugged her and gently dragged her out of the way, realising others were behind him. Ashley was oblivious to all this; she only had eyes for her boyfriend.

Josh was behind and after letting them have a long embrace, came closer. Mike saw him and slightly released Ashley who remained hanging on to his arm. "Hi Dad."

Josh almost had to yell above the howl of the wind. "Hi Mike! Glad to have you home!" he answered.

Mike had a backpack on but Josh doubted it would be all he brought along. "You have a suitcase, Mike?"

"Yes, just one and the backpack. I'm only here for a week."

They went towards the luggage compartments where other people were already sorting through to find their own baggage. Mike soon found his and Josh took it so Ashley could keep holding on to Mike. She hadn't let go of his arm.

They went into the mall, walking on either side of Mike. As soon as they crossed the doors, Lindsey grabbed him by the neck with both arms. Margaret waited patiently behind her. Amanda stood a few steps behind them both.

Once Lindsey had let go, Margaret got her turn, then Amanda went in for a hug. "Hey Bro" was all she said. Between adolescents, words were not abundant.

They started asking him about the trip. He had to tell them how long and painful it had been. Almost eighteen hours straight with only a few stops on the way for washrooms and snacks was difficult on many parts of the body, no matter how cushioned the seats were.

Josh went to get the van to bring it closer, so they chatted a bit more. Ashley clung tightly to Mike's arm, as if he would get away should she let go. Amanda stood back trying not to show how pathetic she felt the whole scene was. Ashley was about two years older but they seemed a generation apart and it hindered the relationship.

When Josh arrived, Mike took the suitcase and opened the rear hatch to lug it in. They embarked; Lindsey in the front passenger seat, and Amanda way at the back with her grandmother, leaving Mike and Ashley in the middle seat.

Even with the weight of all these passengers, the wind pushed the van sideways at every gust. They drove out of the parking area. At this hour and under these conditions, very few cars were on the road. As long as they were within the boundaries of the city and stayed on the main arteries, they could see where the road led. Once they reached the outskirts of Greenmeadows and drove into the forested area, the road became a large white trail ending at the tree line on each side. Josh had to measure where the road was located, based on the middle distance between the two edges of the forest. If he went too much to either side, he would meet a snow bank. Getting stuck in these conditions was not an option he wanted to envision.

Lindsey was holding on to the dashboard. She wanted to participate in the discussion coming from behind her, but last summer's accident was still fresh in her mind. Her wrist still hurt where it had snapped from the pressure of the airbags.

Mike and Ashley were chatting away, interrupted once in a while by one of the family members. Amanda stayed quiet in her back corner.

He started talking about his studies; how he learned a lot of theories about communications, but didn't feel he was becoming a better communicator. Josh told him to give it a bit of time; he was only in his first year.

The van slid occasionally and Josh kept the speed way below the limit. It was better to get there late than not at all. In some parts, the visibility became so poor that he had to go down to thirty kilometres an hour, squinting to see through the curtain of snow, with wipers at full speed.

The turns were the worst. They became visible at the last minute and Josh had to constantly steer to stay on track. They met oncoming traffic only a few times. The heavy trucks going by them would move the van sideways to the point they almost felt they would flip over.

It took them almost two hours to finally reach Lakedge. Margaret and Amanda had fallen asleep but Mike and Ashley were still happily chatting. Lindsey was nervously watching the road, trying to mentally help her husband. Josh felt his hands grip over the wheel. He was wondering if he would be able to open them again or if they would be welded to the steering wheel.

Lindsey sighed with relief when she saw the sign "Welcome to Lakedge". They were close. Up ahead there would be street lights, and people, and houses. All this spelled safety. They came to Trucker's Corner where the road widened to four lanes to allow for big trucks to turn into the parking without slowing the rest of the traffic down.

A couple of minutes later they were home. In the few hours that they had been gone, the snow had drifted into the driveway and they had to stop on the street because the van wouldn't get in. Lindsey went to the door, lifting her feet high in the air to get over the snow, now accumulated over her knees. She went in and started to prepare some hot cocoa.

They left Margaret and Amanda asleep in the van. Josh, Mike and Ashley got shovels and started digging a passage large enough to get the van off the street. It took them a while but they did it. They helped Margaret to the house and Josh took Amanda in his arms to carry her in. It reminded him of so many trips when his baby girl had gone to sleep in the car. She wasn't a baby anymore, but she was still his little girl.

Mike got his suitcase and they went in. Lindsey called out from the kitchen. "Ashley, I just got your mother on the phone. She said you could stay over for the night, with the roads being so bad and all. You'll sleep on the sofa in the family room. I'll get you some sheets, pillows and blankets when I am finished here."

Ashley didn't protest. She loved the idea. "Thanks a lot Mrs. Stuart."

After putting all the wet clothes in the bathtub to drip, they went to the table. Amanda guzzled her hot chocolate very quickly then headed to her room. Margaret retired soon after. Lindsey asked Ashley to come and help her make her bed.

That's when Mike and Josh had their first talk alone. They hadn't had such an occasion in a long time. Mike had heard a few things from Ashley, but he wanted to know more.

"So what does this mean, Mr. Sparks dying and all that?"

Josh was finding it unusual for his son to want to hear about it. Mike was older now but Josh still often felt he was a teenager and not necessarily interested in his father's affairs.

"Well Mike, we're not quite sure yet. That's what's disturbing. We don't know what the heirs to his estate will do. We hope they will want the mill to keep going because it means a lot for the economy of the town but until we hear from them, we won't know."

For the next half hour, they discussed the topic, reviewing various scenarios. Josh knew Mike had a very inquisitive mind, but he seemed to notice signs of new analytical skills and organisation of ideas not there before. Obviously, University education was already starting to have an impact. Josh enjoyed the talk and went more profoundly into the topic as the discussion progressed.

Ashley and Lindsey came back and interrupted the talk. Josh closed it. "We'll talk more later. We have the whole week."

"Sure dad, I'd love to."

A while later, with everyone tucked in, Josh and Lindsey went to their room. Before they turned the light off, Lindsey said a short prayer. "Thank you Lord for bringing Mike home safely. Thank you also for bringing us home safe. Amen."

"Amen." Josh said and turned the light off. "Good night Lindsey. I love you."

"I love you too Josh. Good night."

Sleep came quickly for both.

Tuesday February 21

Greed

A strong desire for more, an overwhelming desire to have more of something - such as money - than is actually needed

English Dictionary

Synonyms: gluttony, self-indulgence, avarice, materialism, craving, selfishness, stinginess

Thesaurus

Wealth is like seawater; the more we drink, the thirstier we become.

Arthur Schopenhauer, German philosopher (1788 - 1860)

And he that strives to touch the stars,

Oft stumbles at a straw.

Edmund Spenser, English Poet (1552 - 1599)

For the love of money is the root of all evil: which while some coveted after, they have erred from the faith, and pierced themselves through with many sorrows.

I Timothy 6:10, King James Bible

13. Retirement

"Large coffee, triple, triple." Robert ordered.

"Anything else with that?" The young girl in the brown uniform asked.

Robert eyed the donut display and selected two of them. The girl prepared the order, he paid and she turned to the next person in the long line behind him.

He struggled with the tray. His hands, still badly injured from the burns, were stiff; the weight of the coffee and donuts was putting enormous stress on them. He looked for a table. He had to put this down quickly. There were people at almost every table. He spotted an empty one in a corner of the restaurant and rushed towards it. Putting the tray down he sighed in relief raising his hands to bring back some of the normal blood flow to them.

Tim Horton's was always a busy place, no matter what time of the day. As he took his seat, he noticed the long line of cars going by at the drive-thru windows. Where did all these people come from? Didn't they have jobs to go to?

He had a good reason at least. The retired life gave him time to do whatever he pleased. Being retired however was just an abstract concept until Monday morning. The weekend had been business as usual. He'd done some work around the house. Not as much as he would have liked, his injuries putting a strain on his ability. Just getting dressed took him a lot longer than usual. Even the Monday wasn't much different from holiday long weekends, except for Jasmine being at work.

This morning had been the first real test. Jasmine got up early as usual to get ready. She hogged the bathroom, but for once he didn't mind.

He could shave later; or he could forego shaving altogether; in fact he may grow a beard now that his hands weren't as nimble as before. He had gone to the kitchen to prepare a lunch for Jasmine but he bumped into his mother-in-law who was already doing it. Ever since Jasmine's parents had moved in, both Robert and Jasmine had become spoiled. Mother took care of the house and a good part of the cooking, while Father took care of odd chores. There was little left for him to do.

This morning he would have liked to have something to do but he felt as though he were an intruder. Jasmine ate a quick breakfast then left the home with profuse kisses for everyone.

Robert took a shower, read the morning paper, then turned on the television but quickly realised he would have a menu similar to that of the previous day. He was somewhat disinterested with the meagre variety of daytime television. You had a choice between cartoons where characters constantly hit each other, talk shows where guests persisted in yelling at each other or soap operas where people repeatedly cheated on each other. If television was supposed to be a mirror of our society, we were definitely in trouble.

He turned it off. Looking at the clock he realised it was only 9:30 a.m. and he was already bored. He had a physiotherapy appointment in the afternoon but that left a lot of time to kill.

So he put on his coat, gloves and boots, hopped in his car and headed out the driveway. It seemed as if the car instinctively led him on his usual route. Soon he recognised the road; he was on his way to work.

"Why not?" he thought to himself "I'll get there for coffee break. The guys will be happy to see me."

He had to park in the visitor area; his parking privileges were revoked. He came in the station through the main entrance. He had also relinquished his employee access and identification card.

The sergeant at the desk recognised him. "Good morning Sir, can I help you?"

"Just going back to say hi to the guys, don't trouble yourself."

The sergeant hesitated just a moment. He looked at Robert with indecision. He peaked around and saw nobody else, so he pressed the button and the door unlocked.

"Thanks." Robert said. He walked to the back. A few of his colleagues crossed paths and saluted him with kind words, greetings and cheers but they all kept going. They were busy. No one stopped. He felt like a flea in an ant colony.

He reached the homicide division and went in the room. His old desk had a laptop with some piles of papers and folders beside it. They didn't waste time here; someone had already replaced him. Only a couple of his colleagues were in the room, either on the phone or busy at the computer searching leads or composing reports. He saluted them. They saluted back but went right on with the work.

He peaked towards Inspector Moreno's office and noticed that he wasn't in. After a few minutes, he understood. Everyone here underwent the same constraints as he had regularly been faced with. They were overworked and always under pressure. They wouldn't have time for him. They wouldn't be coming out for coffee. Come to think of it, he realised that coffee breaks were not a common occurrence for him when he was on the force. He had grabbed coffees on the go in so many places, almost never having the time to sit down for them.

He was about to leave when Inspector Moreno came in the room. The instant of surprise was almost as vivid for each of them. Then Moreno recuperated and said in his usual version of English coloured with a strong Spanish accent "Cloutier, what do you think you're doing here?"

The tone was unmistaken. Robert stuttered slightly. "I…I came to say hi to the guys, Inspector."

Moreno looked at him and was going to say something but stopped. His hands on his hips, he shook his head. He pointed to his office. "Step in here."

Robert followed his brisk walk as best he could. Now all the officers in the room were watching. Robert felt like a schoolboy going to the principal's office. He didn't know what he had done wrong.

"Close the door." Moreno instructed. Robert complied.

"Cloutier, you can't come here anymore. Let's make this clear right away. This place is full of confidential files, documents and data that you cannot access or even glance at. The people here have no time for you, they are too busy. You of all people should know that I really need another five or six officers just to handle the caseloads we have. I don't know who let you in but he shouldn't have. I won't pursue this for now because it was probably someone who felt he had to be kind to a …" he seemed to struggle with the word "a hero. What I need is for you to assure me is that you will never come back here."

Robert felt insignificant. He didn't expect a hero treatment; particularly not from Moreno. He would have liked just a bit of recognition for the good that he had tried to do. "Sir, I'm not here to look at files. I don't want to bother the guys, I know they're busy. I just wanted to say a quick hello."

"And that's why I will leave it be for this time. Now, go home, find yourself something else to do. Take care of those hands so they can heal."

He looked at him right in the eyes in a way that was clear. He had nothing else to say. He expected compliance. Robert got up slowly.

At the door he strained to turn the handle but eventually got it open. He walked out and then looked back towards Moreno.

"I've spent many years here. I thought I could leave with a few good memories, that's all. Thanks anyway."

Moreno didn't answer. He didn't care. To him, Cloutier had been a thorn pressed in his backside. He was finally rid of it, and no amount of emotional coaxing would change his mind.

Robert exited the office. A couple of the guys lifted their heads as he went by and gave him wishes and greetings. They didn't dare say more; they knew Moreno was watching them. Robert didn't put them on the spot. He left the station.

One of the restaurant employees came around his table with a mop and pulled him out of his daydreaming. The winter slush was making a constant mess and every fifteen minutes or so the floor had to be mopped up again.

Robert wondered how Cliff was doing. He had called him from home the day before and he was going to start cosmetic surgery today. He would undergo a number of interventions in the next few weeks and would have to stay home in convalescence for a while. His best friend and partner, Cliff would eventually go back to work.

For now, Robert felt useless. Everyone had something to keep them busy except him. He looked at the heavy bandages on his hands. He knew they would come off some day, but what would he do?

He and Jasmine had discussed retirement already a few times but it always seemed so far in the future. He was much too young for this. So now he was unprepared. He expected to have another ten to fifteen years to get ready for it. Instead, it came in a week. He had thought of starting a private investigation firm, or joining an existing one. To build such an enterprise took time. He had seen it as a long-term goal. He didn't really know where to start. He had a few contacts. He had the skills, but where do you get customers? How do you market yourself? Would he need an office? Should he work from home? How much would he charge? Who would do the accounting? He knew he was inadequate in all of the administrative functions. He hated math, he was a terrible salesman, and a disaster when it came to computers.

He had finished one of his doughnuts and taken only a few sips of his coffee, which was getting cold. He felt a tightening in his chest. After all these years of thinking only of others, never really taking personal time, how could he now turn his focus of attention to himself?

He looked at the white mess outside. The snow kept falling and accumulating. The roads were filled with snow and this made it difficult to manoeuvre. It seemed a reflection of his life.

A couple at the table beside him got up and left. A newspaper was on the table. He picked it up. He tried to read a few stories but they were mostly about the faltering economy, the inefficient government, or the corrupt business environment.

He reached the sports section. He knew a few of the teams that played but he had never really followed any of it. Ever since the Winnipeg Jets had been bought by another franchise, the city was without a hockey team. During the Stanley Cup Playoffs, he had to root for the closest team, even if it was in another province. It reminded him of his award. Jasmine had ensured the plaque would be prominently displayed in the dining room so she could remind all visitors of how her husband was a hero. It only served to remind him how much of a fraud all of his retirement was. It was supposed to lift him up, but it only deepened his depression.

He turned to the classified. There were a few jobs posted. He noticed a security company looking for experienced guards. Maybe he could qualify. He envisioned himself behind a desk in an apartment building, spending his nights watching surveillance monitors, walking the rounds to make sure doors were locked properly, occasionally letting in a tenant who had forgotten his keys. Somehow it didn't seem like the glorified plans he had for his retired life.

He folded the newspaper and put it back on the other table. He had no appetite for the second donut. The coffee was cold. He just picked up everything and threw it in the garbage bin.

He looked at his watch. He still had two hours to kill before his therapy appointment. He was used to never having enough hours in a day to get everything done. From now on, his time would be cut in half, but he would still get bored for the major part.

He went to his car. Maybe he could drive around for a while.

This was only the first week of retirement. He wasn't looking forward to the other weeks.

14. Eulogy

The church was filling up. There were additional chairs set-up at the back and on the sides leaving just enough room for one person to get by. Actually, a normal-sized person would fit. Vivian Hedgerow, on the other hand, had to go through the centre isle to get to one of the reserved seats at the front; she would never have made it otherwise.

Although the front pew was reserved for family as the usual protocol, today it was the only empty pew in the whole church. How ironic for a man who had done so much in his community to not even be remembered by his own family? In a way, the Lakedge community had become his real family, and they were there to pay homage.

The bells tolled and everyone took their seats. A hush fell over the assembly as the closed coffin rolled down the aisle. Jim Stone and five other workers from the mill were the pallbearers. Pastor Radcliffe, a small man with abundant energy followed them ceremoniously.

With the coffin in place the organ ceased. The pastor invited everyone to rise and offered an introductory prayer. He went through a few ritual readings and statements, let the choirmaster direct a couple of hymns, and went up to the pulpit to offer a sermon.

Margaret Stuart sat in the third pew from the front. Joshua, as the town manager, was sitting with Lindsey in the second pew right beside Vivian Hedgerow. Margaret was sitting behind her son Joshua. It seemed to her that lately she was attending too many funerals. Maybe it was due to the fact that most of her friends were about as old as her and at that age, death was something to be expected soon. It didn't do much to bring comfort but at least she could thank the Lord for her good fortune.

She looked around and recognised almost all of the people there. She pretty much knew everyone. It wasn't surprising in a small town like Lakedge. Then she noticed someone who wasn't familiar sitting in one of the additional chairs on the right side. The woman, in her sixties was elegantly dressed, showing much more refinement than most Lakedge residents would ever have. She kept her eyes low, as if she didn't want to meet anyone's gaze Margaret had seen this woman somewhere before but couldn't place her. She hated this. Now it would nag at her all during the ceremony. Her mind would focus on the woman instead of the funeral.

Pastor Radcliffe invited the mayor up to say a few words. Vivian, as eloquent as ever, recounted a number of stories about the benevolence of the great man Warren had been. She also used the occasion to announce how a local sculptor had been commissioned to prepare a monument in his name in front of the Town Hall. The local school board trustee went up next and announced the renaming of the Lakedge High School to the Warren Sparks High School.

Josh had his turn and then more speakers went up, not all as eloquent as Vivian. They all sang praises of the man Warren had been. The choir offered another hymn, the pastor said a last prayer, and the pallbearers came back to bring Warren Sparks' body to its final destination.

As they exited, Margaret couldn't keep her eyes off the mysterious woman. She had controlled her thoughts throughout the last hour or so of the ceremony. Then it came to her as a flash. Teresa Sparks, Warren's ex-wife, that's who she was.

Margaret now knew she had to speak to her. She followed the procession out and slid to the side of the main door to wait. She watched intently each person coming out. Finally, almost at the end, Teresa exited. Margaret went directly up to her.

"I'm so glad to see you here."

Teresa seemed a bit startled. "Ah, yes. Uh, Mrs. Stuart, right?"

"Yes, Margaret Stuart. How are you?" Margaret was cheery, almost a bit too much under the circumstances and a few people noticed.

Teresa spoke softly. "I'd rather not bring too much attention to myself, if you don't mind."

Margaret looked around and understood. She lowered her voice. "Sure. Where are you staying?"

"I don't know yet, I just got in and came directly to the funeral. I'll probably take a room in a hotel in Greenmeadows for the night."

"Nonsense" said Margaret. "You're coming with me. I can't let you stay in a hotel. You are part of this family." Her tone indicated she would accept no argument.

Teresa let out a tear. "You are so nice to say so. I don't deserve this attention."

Margaret looked at her with the kindest eyes she could muster. "You and I have a lot to catch up on. Let's get this ceremony over. Then you're coming with me for tea."

They had come in two cars. Josh and Lindsey went with the van to pick up the mayor and her husband, while Mike drove the car with Margaret, Ashley and Amanda on board. Margaret signalled to Mike. He came over.

"Teresa, this is Michael Stuart, my grandson. Michael, this is Teresa Sparks." Then she turned to Teresa. "I'm sorry, is it still Sparks or did you change your name?"

"No, it's Sparks. I never changed my name back."

Mike shook her hand. "Nice to meet you." He was examining her, not knowing what to say, so Margaret broke the stare.

"Michael, Teresa is going to come with us."

"I have a rented car." Teresa clarified.

"Then you can follow us. We are in the blue car." he pointed it.

Margaret suggested. "I'll ride with Teresa in her car then. How's that?" Teresa nodded in agreement.

They went to the cemetery. There was a hole dug in the ground with the mounds on the side already covered with an inch of snow. Everyone struggled to get to the site with dresses and snow boots.

The tombstone had trees sculpted in each corner, a symbol of Sparks' life. The inscription read "Warren Thomas Sparks, the man without whom Lakedge would never have been. May he find a tree in heaven to lean upon, sit back and watch over us."

Because of the cold, the ceremony was short and simple. There was nothing left to say.

They all returned to their vehicles, Margaret following Teresa. Soon after, they were at the Stuart home, Margaret had the tea brewing and they sat in the living room. Lindsey decided to make some cookies.

Mike was interested in knowing more about this lady. He was fascinated by her appearance, which was not your typical Lakedge dress. With only one clothing store in town, everyone basically bought the same clothes. Mike remembered days in class where half the boys would have exactly the same t-shirt, almost as if it were the school uniform. Teresa wore very distinctive clothes. Even Ashley was interested.

Joshua opened the conversation. "So Mrs. Sparks, I understand you now live in France?"

Teresa was a bit shy at first but she felt safe with the people in the room so she opened up to them. She explained how she got interested in the fashion business, her education, her apprenticeship, and eventually her move to France. She now owned a chain of five fashion stores in various cities on the South coast of France and was aiming to open another two in Paris within a few years.

Mike was the one to bring up the subject of Warren Sparks. "It seems to me you had to do a lot of extra work to get where you are today. You also had to raise your daughter on your own. So why didn't you stay with your husband? He would have helped you, don't you think?"

Teresa was taken back. She didn't expect such a direct question. Josh saw it and admonished Mike. "Mike, I think this is a bit private. Mrs. Sparks' decision isn't ours to discuss."

Teresa intervened. "Actually, it's quite an interesting question. I've been pondering this question myself all the way here, on the plane. I've been asking myself what life would have been if I had stayed here in Lakedge and raised my daughter alongside her father."

She turned to Mike, intending to answer him directly. "The only answer I could come up with, Mike, is that I was a proud and foolish young woman. I came from a big city and I wasn't used to the small town attitude. I felt that everyone wanted to put their nose in my affairs. So after a few years, I just packed up and left with my daughter in tow.

"I wasn't going to simply be the trophy wife of the richest man in town. I wanted to show the world I was more than just a pretty face. I worked hard to get the status I enjoy today.

"You see, I have to admit I was attracted to Warren Sparks by some of the same things everyone else was attracted to him at first; his money. I wanted him as a sugar daddy. He liked my looks and we sort of fell in love. It was a funny kind of love and not very deep at that but if I had given it more time, maybe it could have been stronger."

She paused, reflecting. "I know now he loved me a whole lot more than I ever loved him. I know he would never have left me. He agreed to take care of me even after the separation. He sent me a lot of money so I could continue to take care of our daughter and study at the same time. He always sent me more than what our separation agreement had required."

Josh tried to ease the tension. "Warren Sparks always was a generous man. He certainly did a lot for the community."

Teresa cut in as he was going to add more on Warren's accomplishments. "I was too young to see it. I was immature. All I saw was his money. It's almost as if I was rediscovering the man today. Hearing the testimonies at church this afternoon, reminded me of what he had done. He literally created Lakedge."

Mike's interest was stimulated. "How is that?"

Teresa smiled. "Margaret might be more of the historian here. She probably knows more stories about Lakedge than I do. What I do know is that Warren came north as a teenager when all there was of

Lakedge were a few hunting and fishing cottages. He started working as a lumberjack, cutting wood for a mill further south from here. He saved all his money and bought some land so that the wood he would cut would be his own. This way he got paid for both his work and for the wood he supplied."

Lindsey came in and placed a tray of steaming hot cookies on the table. She tried not to disrupt the flow of the conversation but the smell pulled everyone to the tray.

Teresa waited, taking a cookie herself.

"He quickly started to make a lot more money and hired a few people to work for him to cut the wood on his land. At the same time, he started making a clearing for what would eventually be the location of the mill itself. In a matter of a few years he had grown from a one-man operation to a mill employing a large number of people."

"So how did this turn out to create Lakedge?" Mike asked.

Margaret offered to help. "Maybe I can let Teresa breathe a bit. You see, Michael, there wasn't much in the northern parts at that time. The train had helped open up a lot of other regions and pushed the development of most of the cities and towns along the national railway line. You can read about this in the history of the development of Canada.

"However, in this area, we didn't have the train. Besides hunting and fishing, there was some trade with the natives, and there were a few mines, but the main industry had to come from the forest. With acres and acres of the finest pine trees in the world, this was the gold mine of the North. Also, because there were no trains, there had to be rivers to transport the logs to the mill. There were no roads, but the rivers were plentiful.

"That's how the North was developed. In many places, lumber mills were built to process the wood close to the mouth of rivers and then ship it by boat. Small towns started building around the mills to offer support to the workers. Families moved in and established themselves in the vicinity of the mills. Services of all kinds were created."

Teresa put her cup down and took over. "Lakedge had the advantage of being at the start of a long series of lakes enabling boats to bring the wood down south. So Warren established his mill at the mouth of Sawdust River, used up most of the land around by logging those trees first. Then he bought land further up the river and had the logs driven down to the mill by rafting. Rafters and loggers, that's what created Lakedge and that's what created most of Northern Canada."

Mike was interested. In his mind he could see himself writing an essay on the development of the North.

Josh liked the history lesson as well, but he was more interested in the future of Lakedge than its past. "So what happens now? Are you the owner of the mill?"

Teresa's face paled a bit. "Actually Josh, I'm not really sure. I think the authorities were looking for a will but I don't know if they found one."

She sighed. "I guess in principle, because I was separated and the agreement only refers to an alimony Warren faithfully provided, I don't have any rights to his belongings. It would seem everything will go to Émi... I mean Joy. That's our daughter. She was his only child and I know he had no other living relatives, at least none he knew about."

She stopped. Josh needed to know more. The town manager in him wanted to have insight on this situation. It could have dire impact on his community. "Have you had a chance to talk to Joy? Has she mentioned any of her intentions if she is the owner of the mill?"

Teresa struggled to find an answer. "No I didn't speak to Joy about this yet. You don't know Joy. She … she only has one interest in life." She searched for the right words. "I can guarantee you being a business woman isn't it."

She looked up at Josh. "I'm afraid I not only failed in my marriage, but I also failed in raising our child. I created a spoiled brat spending all I was receiving from her father on her. The more I gave, the more she wanted. I was weak and I didn't know how to say no to her. I felt guilty for taking her away from her father, so I tried to compensate by giving her all the material possessions I could obtain. Today, I know I created a monster. I am not proud."

Tears welled in her eyes. The room was silent. Margaret broke the silence. She wanted to find something positive in Teresa. "So what made you decide to come to Warren's funeral?"

Teresa wiped her eyes with her hand. Lindsey reached for a box of tissue and handed it to her. "Oh, thank you." She looked at Margaret. "When I got the news Warren had passed away, all I felt was guilt. I had robbed him of his money, of his love, of his daughter. I had always said that someday I would come back to ask his forgiveness. Every time I started planning the trip, something would come up and I postponed my intentions. In the end, I was too late. I waited too long and I missed my chance. So I decided I would at least come and say farewell to him. I just hope wherever he is, he will forgive me."

Margaret tried to console. "I think we all are ready to forgive people who recognise their mistakes. I'm just glad you came, Teresa."

She turned to Joshua. "I told Teresa she could stay with us tonight, it's ok with you isn't it?"

"Of course. Absolutely." Josh said without hesitation.

Lindsey added. "You can use Amanda's room. She can sleep on the sofa-bed in the family room."

Teresa objected. "I don't want to give you any trouble. I can book a room at the hotel."

The phone rang. Mike went to the kitchen to answer. He yelled from there. "Dad, it's for you! It sounds urgent!"

Josh excused himself. He left while the conversations turned to chitchat about the accommodation. The cookies were almost all gone and the teacups were empty.

Josh came back with a worried look on his face.

"There is trouble at the mill. It seems someone put a lock on the gate and there's a 'for sale' sign in front. Teresa, do you know anything about this?"

Teresa stuttered. "I… no… I don't know anything about this."

"Well, I'm going to take a look."

"Can I come with you?" Teresa asked.

"Sure. We'll take the van."

They grabbed their coats. Mike and Ashley tagged along. The four sped away, leaving Lindsey and Margaret to clean up.

15. Passion

Henri Montelierre had enjoyed the meal tremendously tonight. Either his cook had done a particularly good job, or was it just his mood? It made him find the taste and aroma of food and wine better than usual. The conversations with his wife and children were pleasant although he had found it difficult to stay focused on the talks. He had kissed them dearly before they retired to bed.

Between the children protesting to go to sleep and the seemingly longer hugs between them and their father, the nanny had to struggle to take them away.

Later, the valet offered Henri and his wife some coffee in the living room, but Henri said he wanted to review a few documents before going to bed so he went to his study, asking not to be disturbed.

He sat behind his desk. He found the envelope and stared at it. He felt a pit in his stomach. Suddenly, he franticly reopened the package and poured its contents on the desk. He slipped into a daze, with his left hand supporting his head and his elbow resting against the edge of the desk. He didn't move for ten minutes. Every single photograph showed him engrossed in adulterous passion. The note in the envelope was clear; tonight was the deadline. He had to reply or he would be in the French headlines by morning.

His popularity and his past accomplishments may sway the opinion of some of the people his way, but his reputation would be tarnished forever. He couldn't stand the publicity, the divorce his wife would most likely put him through, the risk of losing his children, the fear of being pointed at in the streets, and the horror of being talked about in the news for months and years to come.

This was the third demand for money in less than a year. He couldn't go to the authorities for fear that something would be leaked in the press. Yet he couldn't continue to drain his personal bank account.

This had to end here and now, he knew it.

He looked at the pictures. Seeing her reminded him of how he could lose his head. He had fallen over her like a puppy with a bone. He had jeopardized everything to get her. They had met while he was attending a conference in the South. He had spent the week with her. Then he went back under pretence of business trips. It had lasted a few months, until she asked him to choose between her or his wife.

He couldn't leave his wife. She would sue him for every penny he had. He would be in the streets. He would be disowned. His job was only the result of this arranged marriage, but he had never told anyone. Everyone in France who knew him believed the myth of his success being linked to his skills. He had become one of the highest executives in a large multinational corporation and had a high standing in the backrooms of the government because of it.

In reality he was a slave. He had to play the role to stay in the position. He had to perpetuate the myth. His wife would never let him have it any other way. So he had found passion, but he was tied to another. He never told his wife. He made the choice to stay with the power, the money, the prestige, rather than respond to his passion.

After their last night, she had said she didn't want to hear from him again unless he was ready to commit to her. Then the letters started to come. He had tried to talk to her about it, to ask where they came from but she refused to speak to him. She hung up every time she heard his voice on the phone and his letters returned unopened.

So he paid. Twice already.

Today, he would have to become accountable to all. He had played the role for long enough, now he was called to the bar and had to come clean.

He took out his favourite pen and started writing. He had thought of the words he would write over the past several days. Still he hesitated as he wrote and his hand shook a bit. He took a long, deep breath to regain control.

He laid it all out. He admitted how phoney he had been. He explained the deal. He confessed his passion. He asked forgiveness. He pleaded with his children not to be too harsh on him. He told them how much he truly loved them and never wished any harm to come to them. He included a few words for his wife. He regretted never having tried to really understand her. He recounted a few of the good times they had together.

Then he signed it.

The note lay there on top of the photos for a long time.

The clock struck ten o'clock and startled him a bit.

He put the pictures back in the envelope with the note. Maybe the police would be able to trace them back to the blackmailer.

He positioned everything in an orderly manner on top of the desk. He closed the pen and put it back in the drawer. Then he opened another drawer and pulled the gun out. He had bought this to protect his family from burglars after a scare a few years back. The gun was usually in the bedroom. Earlier today he had discreetly removed it and brought it to the study.

He had fired guns only during his military service and those were rifles, not pistols. He just hoped he wouldn't miss his shot.

The single gunshot resonated throughout the empty hallways and into each of the eight bedrooms of the manor.

The blackmailer would never get money from him again.

16. For sale

Industrial Avenue didn't have much industry. Besides a garage, a scrap yard, a carpenter's shop joined to a furniture store, and a couple of antiques shops – more like junk collections – the only real industry was Sparks Mill located at the end of the road.

The snow was packed more than ploughed under the heavy wheels of the logging trucks.

Josh rushed towards the mill. He had to suddenly stop almost a kilometre before arriving at the main gate. A caravan of trucks heavily loaded with timber was parked in the right hand lane. Nothing was moving; the motors on all the trucks were shut off.

Josh decided to go around them and cut into the left hand lane. There was no oncoming traffic. Arriving close to the mill's parking lot, they saw people standing in groups from three to ten. There must have been over a hundred people in all. Many were stamping the cold out of their feet, dancing in place. It seemed like school recess, everyone standing around, chatting.

He noticed the sign. It was huge, almost 12 feet high and the same width. In big letters it read "FOR SALE". It had a phone number, a web site, and a name. You could tell it had been put there quickly, nothing fancy.

Josh recognised the phone number as one for Greenmeadows. At least the real estate broker wasn't far; it might be possible to talk with him.

As he pulled in closer, some of the people recognised him and the word was passed along. He stopped, unable to go further. They all got out of the van and walked towards the gate.

People around them were asking Josh what he was going to do about this, some louder than others. Emotions were high so Josh tried to calm people. They walked slowly, pushing their way through the crowd now denser and pressing together even more since their arrival. Teresa was right behind Josh, Ashley followed with Mike closing the line.

They were almost at the gate when Josh noticed Jim Stone and came closer.

"Josh, I'm glad you're here." Jim said "When we came back from the funeral, we found the lock on the gate had been changed and the sign installed."

Josh looked at the gate. A heavy padlock restricted access. A sign had been added on the inside of the gate door reading "NO TRESPASSING".

Josh felt the anger and frustration all around him. For these people, someone was cutting their access to their livelihood. For years, they had come here, spent all their workweek on these premises, an average of eight hours a day, five days a week, and suddenly they are treated like intruders; outsiders without rights.

"So what can we do?" someone beside Jim asked. Josh was searching for a response when a large burly man interrupted him.

"We bash it in and we get back to work." Josh recognised Jeff Wallis, one of the mill workers, well known not only for his strength, but also for his violent tendencies.

"Now, Jeff, we don't want to do that. We have to keep calm. We need to think this through and find a peaceful solution."

Jeff didn't like the answer. "What is it to you anyway, Stuart? You still have a job. You're just one of those lazy town-government-people spending all our taxes. Me, if I can't get in there to work, I don't get paid. If I don't get paid, I can't feed my family. So who's going to take care of my children? Are you?"

Jeff had a lot of wrath in his words. Jim stepped in. "That's enough. This isn't Josh's fault. He's trying to help. So if you're not going to offer any useful solutions, go away and let us think."

Jeff stepped forward, aiming his fist at Jim and anybody else around. Instantly three strong men moved in and restrained him. Jim was somewhat shorter than most other guys but he had gained a lot of respect over the years and no one would allow Jeff to lay a hand on him. Jeff gave up, retreated and left the group, mumbling and groaning.

Jim turned to Josh again. "What do you think?"

"Well, definitely, we need to talk to the real estate agent about this sale. We have to find out why it came about so quickly. Warren isn't even buried yet and we need to know why they locked the place. To put it up for sale is one thing, but to lock it is quite another. I will make some calls to try and negotiate something."

At that moment, someone in the crowd behind them said "Hey I know who you are." Josh turned towards the voice. The man was one of the more senior workers at the mill and he was pointing to Teresa. "You're the Sparks woman. You're Sparks' wife, aren't you?"

The crowd stopped talking. There was complete silence save for the few birds still brave enough to sing in the cold.

Teresa answered sheepishly. "I am... I was Warren Sparks' wife, yes. We were separated a long time ago. I... I just came back to attend the funeral."

Jeff, who hadn't gone too far, heard this and pounced back into the group. "So you're responsible for this. You're the bitch who's locking us out of our work."

Josh quickly stepped in front of Jeff. "She had nothing to do with this. She didn't know about the closure. Leave her alone."

This time, however, the crowd wasn't defending Josh. Instead, they all started the mumbling again, some yelling in protest, a few demanding explanations, shouting questions.

Josh started fearing this could turn bad. "Jim, I'm going back to my office. Teresa and I will try to make some arrangements. I suggest everyone go home until we can come up with something."

Jim trusted Josh but was a bit uncertain following the shock of seeing Teresa Sparks there after so many years. He pulled on Josh's sleeve. "Are you sure about this?" he whispered, adding "What is she doing here?"

"Yes, I'm sure. Teresa just told us she wasn't even in the will. The whole estate went to Warren's only daughter. Teresa is only here to pay homage to Warren. She did spend at least twelve years with him."

Then speaking louder, more for the crowd than for Jim "I promise I will do everything I can to resolve this."

He started pushing his way through the crowd heading for the van. Teresa followed very closely now, scared for her safety. As they went through the large group, the infuriated people expressed discontent by shouting foul language.

They finally made it and jumped in the van. Josh let out a sigh of relief and Teresa melted into tears. The fear had been too much for her.

Josh tried to calm her down as he started the van. She regained some of her composure. Josh slowly and carefully backed out of the parking lot, trying to avoid hitting anyone. The crowd was still close to them, too close for Josh's liking.

He did make it to the road but stopped to write down the information from the *For Sale* sign before heading back.

"I'll drop you home and get back to my office." He said speaking mainly to Mike.

"Can I take the car? Ashley and I would like to go see friends." Mike asked in reply.

"Just make sure Mom doesn't need it first." Josh warned.

They remained silent for the rest of the trip. In his head, Josh was already planning the calls he had to make and what he would be saying. He prayed the negotiation skills he had acquired over years spent in the purchasing department would be sufficient to solve this issue.

Wednesday, February 22

Winter

In the bleak mid-winter
Frosty wind made moan,
Earth stood hard as iron,
Water like a stone;
Snow had fallen, snow on snow,
Snow on snow,
In the bleak mid-winter,
Long ago.

Christina Rossetti, British Poet (1830 - 1894)

Winter has famously had a history-making part to play in wars. At the height of his military powers in 1812, Napoleon marched on Moscow with an army of more than half a million men. The retreating Russian army had stripped the countryside bare of resources and so first of all the French army were starved of food, then winter arrived with a vengeance. A combination of poor and inadequate food prevented the soldiers generating sufficient heat from within, and 40 degrees of frost, merciless winds and ineffective insulation removing body heat from the outside, decimated the army. Less than 20,000 men eventually returned to France, over 480,000 had perished.

"The army was swathed in an immense winding sheet" - (of snow) - French survivor.

130 years later, Hitler made the same mistake as Napoleon, after gaining a series of victories over the Russian army he pressed on to Moscow at the start of winter. The result was that 100,000 German soldiers suffered cold injury (about 10% of the whole army) in November and December 1941 resulting in around 15,000 amputations, and the German advance was halted.

Paul Ward, CoolAntarctica.com

17. Blackmail

News crews were lined up outside the enclosure. Half a dozen French policemen called *brigadiers* were standing in front of the gate door to ensure nobody got through. More were stationed in the back. When word of a gunshot being fired in the mansion of one of the most prominent French executives was received, the paparazzi flocked to the place. A neighbour who heard the shot and saw the police and ambulance arrive probably tipped them off

Commandant Charles-Eugène Dumont had to push his way through. When he finally reached the front, he didn't even have to show his badge. The *brigadier* recognised him right away and opened the gate to let him through while the other *gendarmes* ensured no one followed him in.

The *commandant* had received a call from the *commissaire* himself. All he knew was that a violent death required a very delicate investigation. As the most senior *officier de police judiciaire* – the only police branch enabled to do investigations in France – all delicate matters ended up on his desk. Most other investigations went to a *lieutenant* from the *brigade criminelle*. The *commissaire* told him this had political ramifications and needed to be kept strictly confidential. He couldn't tell him more but the instructions came from someone higher up.

When he saw the mob in front of the house, Charles-Eugène knew this wouldn't be an ordinary case. Albeit, every violent death case was different, he had the feeling this one promised to be special and he didn't like it.

He walked up the marble stairs. This was an aristocrat's home. He somewhat despised people with a lot of money, but his personal feelings needed to be parked for a while.

He stepped into the main hall to find a large atrium with a spiralling staircase going to the upper floors. Hearing footsteps and talking coming from above, he climbed the stairs. On the second floor another brigadier saluted him.

"Where is the *lieutenant* in charge of this scene?" he asked.

"*Lieutenant* Leroy is in the study, *Commandant*. It's behind the last door on the right side of this hallway," he pointed.

Charles-Eugène didn't reply. He just headed in the direction he was given. He walked in the room with caution, not wanting to disturb a crime scene. A police employee in a white lab coat was taking pictures while another plain-clothes officer was scribbling in his notepad.

"*Lieutenant*, can I have a word with you?" he called quickly capturing the whole room in a glimpse. The body was slumped backwards on a chair near a desk, a towel over its head, and blood was splattered all around, most of it concentrated on the wall to the right of the victim. He noticed an envelope on the desk.

The *lieutenant* stopped his scribbling and came over. Charles-Eugène remembered him. He had worked on a few cases with *Lieutenant* Olivier Leroy before. A good cop, meticulous in his investigation, a bit too perfectionist at times, which meant he could be at this scene for two more days if nobody stepped in. With the mob outside, and the specific instructions from the *commissaire*, they didn't have two days.

"Leroy, I will be handling this case personally from here on. You will stay on to assist me. You need to know that I have orders from the *directeur* on this, so neither of us has a choice. Understood?"

Leroy looked at him perplexed but already resigned. When orders came from this far up, he was in no position to object.

"Understood." he replied.

"Good. So what do we have so far?"

Leroy explained how they found the victim just as he was. The valet had covered him with a towel to spare the other members of the household. The gun lay on the floor. Everything pointed to a suicide. That part seemed clear. Although he would want to wait until the forensic crew had finished their work to confirm it, he didn't see any indication of outside intervention. Henri Montelierre blew his brains out.

Charles-Eugène was inclined to think likewise. The reconstruction of the death would be easy enough. The coroner's job was fairly simple. The hard part might be determining what pushed this man to do it.

Leroy indicated that initial discussion with the wife and the employees produced no solid reason for the suicide. The man had a good meal the night before, was cheery with his family, went to the study and killed himself.

"What about the envelope?" Charles-Eugène enquired.

"I didn't touch it yet, I was waiting until forensic had all the fingerprints." Leroy explained.

"Good thinking. I have a feeling this envelope will be a strong clue to what caused this man to go to this extreme." As he said this, he took out a pair of plastic gloves from his coat pocket, put them on and took the envelope gently, then dropped the contents into his other hand.

Leroy was a bit disconcerted. "But, *Commandant*?" he started.

"We don't have a lot of time to deal with this, Leroy. So we are going to skip a few steps." He put the envelope back on the desk where he had taken it from and started going through the contents. There were black and white photographs showing a couple having sex. The camera shot from the same angle all the time but captured the couple in various positions. The man was clearly the target of the picture and on all of them the woman's face was hidden or only slightly visible. He turned to Leroy "Is this our victim by any chance?"

"Based on another picture I saw in the living room I would say it's very likely. You can't really tell from looking at him; there's not much of a face left."

With the picture was a piece of paper with a typewritten note. It read "I need one more deposit from you. Same amount 10,000€. Same place, same method. Deadline February 25."

"Blackmail. Not the first letter. I get the feeling Monsieur Montelierre couldn't see any other way out."

Leroy agreed. "I hope we find the other notes. If we can find out where the money is deposited, we might be in a position to get the blackmailer."

"Yes, possibly. Let's just make sure no one other than you and I know about this. What else did you find out so far?" the *commandant* continued.

"I questioned everyone. The kids are four and six so I don't think they can help us. The cook only comes in to prepare supper every night. She is in around three in the afternoon and leaves after nine when the dishes are done. She isn't very close to the family and doesn't seem to know much. It's somewhat the same for the nanny. She lives in and has her own room close to the children's bedrooms, but she spends all her time with the kids, doesn't really like the wife, and only occasionally spoke with the husband."

"Could be a front. Is she cute?"

"Nah. An old hag. Absolutely not the woman in the pictures." Leroy chuckled. "The valet told me the kids call her the witch. I doubt any man would be attracted to her. Certainly not with the wife he had."

"Oh. What about the wife?"

"She's actually good looking. Her character however is quite unattractive. She didn't even shed a tear. She said he was a coward. She seemed to despise him. She suspected him of having an affair. When I pressed her for more on that topic, she said it was private and she didn't want the news to get a hold of anything which is why she never confronted him. She comes from a rich aristocratic family, with a very strong attachment to tradition so divorce was out of the question."

"Those might be good reasons to push a man to suicide. Trapped on the inside and pursued from the outside. Like I said, no way out." The *commandant* said based on much experience. "Go on."

"Well, the valet on the other hand was very talkative. He liked the man but he also knew things weren't going right between the couple. He hates the woman but he is well paid and didn't want to leave. He's been with them ever since they got married about…"He pulled his notepad. "…eight years ago."

He checked a few more notes. "He was also aware that the man was having an affair. He thinks it started about a year ago. The man went down to the Riviera for a conference. When he came back, something had changed in his demeanour. He seemed much more jovial. He didn't let his wife win arguments as he had in the past."

"It was probably the woman in the picture." The *commandant* added. "Going from what is on these photographs, she would give any man some renewed energy."

Leroy smiled. "The valet also seemed to think that he went back a number of times over the next few months. He suddenly started going on more business trips than ever before. Although he claimed to go to different destination every time, the valet suspected from his darkening complexion that the south was his actual destination"

The lab technician completed his picture taking and left the room.

Leroy started again. "Another thing. The valet told me a package very similar to the one on the desk came in almost six months ago. It was marked "private and confidential" so he didn't open it. He says that when Montelierre opened the envelope he went almost white. He quickly fled to his study and didn't come out the whole evening. From that day on his mood changed and he went back to being the man he had been before the first trip."

"Interesting. We definitely need to find that envelope and any other that came after. If we can get a date stamp we could reconstruct the sequence of the events."

"Yes, the valet seems to recall that two more envelopes came in the same manner; one about two months ago, and the other last week."

Dumont scratched his chin. "Very well, so here is our plan of action. You need to find these envelopes quickly. If we get this on time we might catch our blackmailer. Find the deposit place and method. Get some marked bills and deliver them. Get a few people to help you snag this person."

"Sure. I'll get right on it. What if he doesn't show up?"

"It could be a she, don't forget. If nobody shows up then we will go to plan B. Try to reconstruct a face of the woman from a combination of the pictures. Try to find the origin of the letters; a postmark, information from the deposit location, anything. Find out exactly where the victim went for this conference. Then we go down there and with the picture we ask questions. In the meantime, I need to address the media."

"Yes sir." Leroy said. Dumont left him and headed outside to meet the mob. Leroy quickly went back to the room to initiate the search.

Dumont went out through the gate and indicated to the paparazzi that he would make a statement. They all pressed around him in anticipation.

"Here is what I can tell you. We have a male victim, which must remain unnamed for now until the family has been informed. Early indications are that the death was caused by a single self-inflicted gunshot wound to the head. Forensic evaluation is trying to determine if this was accidental. We are unable to reveal anything more because of risk of jeopardizing an ongoing investigation. We hope to be in a position to provide you with more within the next few days. In the meantime, we ask that you respect the privacy of the mourning family. Thank you. That will be all."

They started yelling questions left and right but he ignored them, cut a path through the crowd to get to his car about a block away.

That was enough for now but he knew he would have to face them again at some point in the future. Every day had its burden.

18. Recovery Plan

"This guy was a little too quick for my taste. He got the sign and everything ready for the sale done in one day. Can you believe this?"

Josh was in Vivian Hedgerow's office. The mayor wanted to be in the front line on this issue. Teresa had joined them.

"So what did he have to say?" Vivian asked.

"He just said he got the call from an attorney somewhere in France who gave him instructions from his client to lock everything up and to sell it."

Teresa looked depressed. "It's Émilie." Their looks remained blank. She explained "You would know her as Joy but she changed her name. We live in Cannes on the Mediterranean coast of France, on the French Riviera."

Vivian looked at her. "I can understand wanting to sell, but why would she lock the place up?"

Josh answered. "Apparently she told the real estate agent that she didn't trust anybody. She felt people here would pilfer everything and steal her property so she ordered the place locked up. Since she doesn't want to have anything to do with the mill and forestry industry, she ordered the sale."

"She doesn't seem to have a good impression of the people that work at the mill." Vivian added.

"Unfortunately Émilie doesn't have a good impression of anyone. Unless she can benefit from them, she has no interest in people." Teresa said with a sense of resignation.

"Can't we talk to her, try to reason with her? If she sees what this is doing to the whole community, don't you think maybe we can persuade her to reopen the mill?"

"You can certainly try but I wouldn't put my hopes up too much." Teresa answered.

"We need to come up with other options. We can't let this drag on for too long. The impact could be disastrous." Josh urged.

"I'm listening, what option do you think we have?" Vivian pursued.

Josh had been doing some thinking. "We need to divide the situation in a number of components. There is the sale of the mill itself, but even in the best of conditions, it will take a while before the transfer to a new owner is complete."

Vivian tried to remain optimistic. "It might be fast with this guy if he works on the closure of the deal as quickly as he worked on its initiation."

"True, but in the meantime, the real problem is that a lot of people are without work. They are soon going to run out of money. We need to find a way to reopen the mill or to find other work for these people."

"How do we do that?" asked Vivian.

Teresa remained quiet letting the two discuss the issue. Josh turned to her. "What if I went back with you and tried to talk to Joy... or Emily? Maybe I can explain the situation and negotiate an arrangement. If we provide her with enough assurance that we will protect her property, she might let the people go back."

Teresa wasn't convinced. "You don't know her. I doubt she will listen to you. She despises the people of Lakedge. She despised her father and she associates everyone here with him, so she despises them as well."

"Sounds like a great lady we have here." Vivian said abruptly. Then she realised what she had said. "I'm sorry; I didn't mean to offend you. I'm just outraged by such an attitude toward the citizens of Lakedge."

"You don't need to apologise, Vivian, I'm not proud of what I've done. Unfortunately, there's not much I can do now."

Josh wanted to get back to his idea. "Let me go there and try. We can't just sit here and hope things will change. Now to get back to the question of the sale, I was thinking. What if the town bought the mill and we operated it ourselves?"

There was silence in the room for a moment then Vivian said, "Can we afford such an investment?"

"Right now Lakedge is pretty much debt free. We could borrow to purchase the mill, and repay the loan directly from the revenues of the mill. This way we would preserve the jobs and keep the economy of the city going. In the long-term, we could consider reselling to a private industry but it would get us through the difficult time we are facing now."

"I like the idea." Vivian said. "How do we go about it?"

"First we need to find out how much the property and the business are evaluated at so we can make an offer. Then we need a council resolution to make the offer and another one to borrow the money. With those in hand we go to the real estate and present our offer."

"What if someone else beats us to it?"

"Well, I don't think it's a problem. Whether we buy it or someone else does, what is important is to get these people their jobs back." Josh replied.

"I guess. Although now that you've laid it all out, I would tend to prefer maintaining control of the place. This way we are sure the jobs are going to be protected. If someone else come and takes ownership, we don't know what they will do with the place. They may come in with their own people and fire all the other workers."

"True, I hadn't thought of it." Josh admitted. "So we need to take action quickly. I'll get to work on it right away. I'll get Carlotta to book me a flight to France. I want to meet with Joy as soon as possible. When are you leaving Teresa?"

"I'm actually here until next Tuesday. I wanted to take some time away from my usual routine to think. I also wanted to get a chance to visit the area a bit. I need to reconnect with Lakedge."

Josh though out loud. "Next Tuesday? It's a little far away but maybe it is better. It will give me time to prepare more adequately."

"Where are you staying Teresa?" Vivian asked.

"Margaret Stuart has generously taken me in but I feel I'm intruding on her and Josh's family. I was thinking of going to a hotel in Greenmeadows."

Vivian had another thought. "What about the mansion? Can't you stay there?"

"I…I don't think I can. I mean, I know I can't, it's not mine. It belongs to Émilie now."

"You mean to tell me she wouldn't let her own mother in her home? She's mean, but not that mean I should think."

"No probably not. Actually, it has more to do with me. It doesn't feel right for me to be going there. I left the place more than twenty years ago. I left in the worst conditions. I abandoned poor Warren. I don't feel I have any right going back now."

"On the contrary." Vivian insisted "Warren waited for your return. I'm sure he would be happy to have you."

"I don't know."

"I tell you what. While Josh takes care of the mill, you and I are going to pay a visit to the Sparks home." Vivian said as she got up. Teresa was going to protest but Vivian didn't give her time. "I'm the mayor around here so it gives me a few privileges. For now, you will have to follow orders. You're coming with me."

She picked up her keys and walked out the door. Teresa looked at Josh.

"She's the mayor." He said with a smile. Teresa followed Vivian.

As they got closer to the mansion, Teresa recognised some of the landscape. She had lived there for almost fifteen years. The nostalgia set in and she wiped a tear from the corner of her eyes.

They rounded the gate and went up the long alley. The house was just as she had left it. The reddish clay shingles on the roof of a beige stucco house. Ironically she realised it had the look of most houses you would find on the Riviera. Even the little imitation balconies on the windows enhanced the impression. In a way she knew moving to Cannes actually kept her close to this home. Every day she would see red shingles, black iron balconies, and beige stucco, reminding her of the house she lived in for all these years while in Lakedge. She had never made the connection before. Now it was clear: a part of her never wanted to leave.

Slowly they went up the steps Brent had maintained clear of snow. Vivian rang the doorbell. A few minutes later, Brent showed up in casual but well-groomed attire. When he saw the mayor, he immediately opened the door.

"Madam Mayor. Please come in. To what do I owe this pleasure?"

Vivian looked at him with a wide smile. Brent was initially a lumberjack but the years he had spent in this house had helped in creating a more refined person. Warren had entertained all sorts of people and Brent had learned a lot about etiquette and manners. He had become a gentlemen's butler.

"No need to be formal with me, Brent. Vivian will do."

"Very well Madam…" He stopped halfway "I mean Vivian. How can I help?"

She pointed to Teresa. "Brent, do you know this lady?"

Brent looked at her. "I can't say I do, I'm afraid. Your face does seem familiar but I can't recall where we've met. I'm sorry."

Teresa comforted him "Don't be sorry, Brent. I'm Teresa Sparks. I used to be Warren Sparks' wife. I left a long time ago before you came into Warren's service so you shouldn't expect to know me."

"Yes, that's it, the picture. That's why I seemed to know you. Mr. Sparks kept a picture of you in his study and I recognise you now."

Then he realised they were still halfway inside the door. "Where are my manners, please do come in. Let me get your coats."

Vivian wasn't quite as formal as your typical mayor. "Don't worry about the coats, let's just go into the living room to chat, we'll put the coats on a chair. You're not our valet, you know."

She took off her boots, Teresa did the same and they went in following Brent. Teresa looked at the atrium with the large chandelier. It gleamed and reflected the sunlight in every direction. Every part of the home sent shivers up her spine. Memories started pressing upon her. Brent had maintained the place with so much precision. Nothing had changed. Tears swelled up in her eyes again.

She followed and Vivian found a large sofa just right for her oversized frame. Teresa stayed standing a while looking around the room. With the exception of a few trophies and awards Warren had obtained after her departure, the rest was intact.

Brent offered coffee or tea. Vivian answered "Don't you worry. We're not here to give you work. If we need a coffee we will go to the kitchen and make it ourselves. Have a seat with us. We would like to talk to you."

Teresa sat in a small chair; a lump in her throat was hindering her speech. Vivian seemed to notice and led the conversation.

"Tell me Brent. Did the real estate agent contact you yet?"

"Yes, he did. He told me the owner wanted to sell the house but he felt there wouldn't be much chance of a buyer coming here. He said he was more likely to be able to make a deal with whoever would buy the mill to add the house in the mix."

"I guess that's why there's no sign in front of the house. He's probably right. Nobody in Lakedge can afford this place and I doubt anyone in Greenmeadows would be able to buy it either."

Vivian looked at Teresa who remained numb, overwhelmed by the mix of emotions. "So I guess, this means Teresa is the owner by association. Joy is the real landlord, but being her mother, she has to include you in this deal."

She turned to Brent. "Teresa is here until Tuesday. Instead of having her stay at the hotel, what would you say if she stayed here? It's still her home in a way"

Immediately Brent agreed. "Absolutely. There is no doubt about it. I will prepare everything for your stay, Mrs. Sparks." He moved as if he was going to go up and get working on preparing a room for her. She quickly protested. "No Brent, I don't want to give you any work. If I do stay here, I don't expect you to be my servant. I don't deserve this kind of treatment and you shouldn't have to do this."

"Nonsense. I would be honoured to have you stay here." He stopped and looked at her. "I have to be honest with you. The emptiness in this house is making it difficult for me. Your presence here would be a change for me. It would get my mind off the negative things I've been struggling with. I would love to have you, even if it's only for a few days."

Teresa smiled, a bit of strength coming back to her. "You are too kind. Oh, and please call me Teresa. I feel awkward with formalities."

"Very well… Teresa. Do you have any luggage?"

"I left everything at the Stuart's home but it's only a couple of suitcases. I knew I wouldn't be here for long so I didn't bring too much." Teresa said.

"You're better than me. I don't go anywhere without a whole caravan of suitcases. My husband always says we need two cars when we travel; one for us and one for the luggage!" Vivian laughed wholeheartedly and they all joined. It relieved some of the tension.

Brent offered. "I can go to the Stuart's later and get them if you want."

Teresa again protested. "Better yet, why don't we go together? That way we will have time to become better acquainted you and I."

"I think we may be on the verge of a new era here. I guess, I'll get back to the Town Hall and leave you two to make arrangements." Vivian said as she struggled to get out of the sofa.

They followed her back to the main entrance. When she had left, Teresa suggested. "Why don't you give me a tour? I remember most of this place but it has been more than twenty years since I left and things may have changed."

Brent agreed and they started walking slowly through the house. He explained some of the maintenance and renovations he had done over the years. A thought came to Teresa. "So how have you been surviving since Warren passed away? I mean, do you have enough food?"

"Oh, it's only been a week, so I still had a lot of reserves. Plus I haven't had much appetite lately. As for the bills they were all paid up to date so I don't have to worry for a while. I'm not sure how it works, but I think the rest will have to go through the real estate agent at some time."

Teresa pondered on this. "I'll have to verify this. I want to make sure you don't run into any difficulties."

"Can I be honest with you?" he stopped walking.

"I insist. You must." she answered.

"My only fear is being asked to leave the house. I have lived here for so long. I don't have any real skills. I can't go back to working in a mill because of my back injury. I wouldn't know where to go."

"Then I promise you, I will do everything I can for this not to happen."

In her mind, a few plans were already starting to merge. On their way to get the luggage, she would stop at the bank and get a large enough sum to ensure Brent wouldn't be in need until she was ready to send him more.

"For now, let's continue on our tour." She took his arm and he didn't resist. The company was as good for him as the memories were dear to her.

19. Cold

Ashley started grumbling soon after they left but now her grumbling was turning into cries for help. The initial "Are we there yet?" had turned to "I can't go on like this anymore."

Mike tried to encourage her although he was also starting to hope they would soon arrive at their destination. Their legs were sore already from having to lift their feet higher than normal with the weight of the snowshoes on them. It had taken them a while to get used to the method. The rear part of the snowshoe would drag on the ground and with the soft snow the front part would always sink a bit, obliging them to lift the heavy snowshoe before moving the foot forward. They tumbled a number of times until they learned the manoeuvre.

Andy was in front, leading the way. He was an expert on snowshoes and actually had to constantly slow down to give the pair a chance to catch up.

They had left the truck at the road almost three kilometres behind them. Mike trusted Andy to know where he was going. He said the cabin was only a few kilometres from the road. He had gone there many times to get out of the noise of the town, the nagging of grown-ups, or simply to get away.

Ashley yelled at him half angry, half scared. "Andy! I'm freezing! I can't feel my toes anymore! My whole body wants to shut down! I can't do this anymore!"

He simply yelled back. "Just a few more feet and we will see the cabin! Don't stop now!"

The trees were heavily laden with snow. The evergreens were more like everwhites. You could identify the type of tree only by the general shape under the weighty snow cover and from the bits of green branches peaking out at the edges. The sky was light blue with elongated streaks of white cloud. The wind was spreading the shape of each cloud into a thin line. Within the forest, the trees gave some protection from the wind, but the cold was still intense. Without a cloud cover to capture the little heat of the winter sun, it all dissipated quickly into the atmosphere and left only the cold at the surface.

Even Mike was starting to feel numb in his cheeks, his fingers and his toes. He'd known cold before but this feeling was more than he'd ever experienced. Although they were dressed as warmly as they could, he longed for the protection of four walls and the heat of a fire.

Then Andy called out. "Here it is! I told you I'd find it!"

Andy had been Mike's friend for a long time, and since Ashley had started dating Mike, she had become friend with him by association. Mike liked Andy because he always had interesting, often-fascinating, stories from his Ojibwa ancestry. Andy lived on the Ojibwa reserve but went to school in Lakedge.

Now that Mike was in Toronto, at York University, they didn't get to see each other as much, so Mike would make sure to spend at least one day during Reading Week with Andy. Of course, he also wanted to spend time with Ashley. As it turned out, she wouldn't let him go anywhere without her.

Ashley was told of their plan to go to this cabin. She had been warned it would be a cold trek, yet she insisted on tagging along.

As they rounded a patch of trees following the narrow path, stepping into Andy's snowshoe prints, they saw it too. The cabin was small and seemed to be falling to pieces, but it spelled protection from the wind, and Andy said they would be able to start a fire quickly.

When it came to survival in the woods, Mike trusted Andy. He had saved their lives the previous summer when they were surrounded by flames during the great forest fire. He had kept them afloat in the canoe while smoke and fire was trying to reach them from all sides of the lake.

Andy was not only an Ojibwa in name. His father had made sure he would keep the traditions, skills and pride of the Ojibwa nation alive within him. Andy was bright. He developed the skills readily and adhered to the principles his father and the other ancients of the reserve had instilled in him. Mike respected this in Andy. Although their cultures were worlds apart, Mike wanted to find out more on what made Andy and the rest of the Ojibwa the proud people they were.

They pushed the door open, sending much of the snow collected in front into the room. They tumbled in. With the snowshoes it was difficult to jump in and the ground of the cabin was much lower than where they stood. They had to bend their heads to get in, the snow being way above the middle of the height of the door.

Andy quickly looked around. Small windows on each side were letting in just enough sunlight for them to see. It took a few seconds for their eyes to adjust. Immediately, Andy went to work starting a fire. Ashley just slumped down on the ground, refusing to move any more. Mike stopped for a minute to catch his breath and regain some strength. He started by untying his snowshoes, then going to Ashley to free her from her bindings. She rubbed her legs and whined from the pain.

Mike went to help Andy who had already piled a number of logs in the fireplace and was working on getting a spark into the wood chips. It only took him a few attempts to get a small flame. He nurtured it, protected it from the winds seeping through cracks in the walls, and finally got it to ignite some of the dry branches laid around the logs. Soon the whole place was lighting up from the dancing flames. A bit of smoke seeped into the room carrying the smell of the burning wood. The heat would slowly travel and eventually create a protective barrier from the outside.

They sat for a while not talking, keeping their coats, ski masks and boots on. When the place started to warm up, they gradually removed a few of the layers. Within ten to fifteen minutes they were down to their normal clothing.

Andy opened his backpack and passed around a small container. "It's pemmican. Dried meat strips. This one is from a deer I caught last fall."

They both took a piece and tasted it. It was salty and a bit stiff but the taste was delicate. They enjoyed it. It helped them regain some of their energy.

Andy then took a small pail he had brought with him. He opened the door partly and reached out. From the sides of the cabin, he gathered snow being careful not to take it from where they had walked on. He brought the pail back in and laid it down near the fire. The snow melted quickly then he drank from it and passed the pail to Mike and Ashley who also drank some. It tasted a bit bitter and metallic. Mike felt the water soothing inside of him. He still ached a bit where the muscles of his legs did most of the work of lifting the snowshoes, but he was now feeling good about this. Once again, Andy had brought them through and now was making sure they would not only survive but would have some comfort as well.

They planned to spend the night there. Although Ashley didn't like the idea at first, Mike was looking forward to a diversion. His daily routine at the university was somewhat depressing. He had felt uprooted from his hometown, his friends, and his family while away. Melancholy had set in after a few weeks at York, never completely leaving him. This excursion was bringing back some of his spirit.

"When did you find out about this place?" he asked Andy.

"Oh my family has come here often. We come here when we go on hunting trips. I came here with my father when I was very young."

"Well, there's not much comfort here." Ashley intervened. "I don't know why anyone would want to live here."

Andy smiled. "The conditions in this cabin are actually like a luxury hotel for me."

"You got to be kidding, right?" Ashley snapped.

"When you compare this to some of the other places I've spent the night, this is luxury." he replied gently, still smiling.

"What do you mean?" she pressed on.

"This is luxury when I compare it to my vision quest, for example."

Mike was intrigued. "Your vision quest. What's that?" he asked. He knew this would be the start of an interesting story. It was one of the main reasons why he enjoyed Andy's company.

"You never heard of vision quests?" Andy asked extending the suspense for the story he was about to tell.

"No, never. Tell us more." Mike queried.

"It's a tradition of my people. The Anishinaabe, that's the name we call ourselves, although you call us Ojibwa. The Anishinaabe have been doing vision quests ever since Gitchie Manito created the earth. That's the great creator. He gave instructions to the Anishinaabe that when young boys were to come of age they had to go on a vision quest."

Although Mike believed in the Bible, he saw a lot of wisdom in the stories of the native people. He listened with attention as Andy continued to explain.

"This is only for the men. When we get to an age where we are ready, we know. I was twelve years old when I knew I had to do my vision quest. Not everyone does it at the same age. Most do it when they are a bit older. My father always told me I was a fast learner."

He spoke slowly. He had learned to tell stories from his grandfather and from his father. They would tell the traditions of their ancestors in a slow pace, with calmness in their voice that would create both anticipation and respect in the listener. Andy had studied their way and was now practicing it with his friends.

"The vision quest is where we find out who we are. That summer, my father brought me to the edge of a small river north of Lakedge and gave me a canoe, enough food for one day, and a knife. Then we sang a special song to ask for the protection of Mother Earth. We stayed silent together for a time, and he bid me farewell. I hopped in the canoe and I drifted down the river by myself."

"That's scary." Ashley said. "You were only a kid and your dad left you alone in the forest with just a knife?"

Andy didn't answer right away. He took time to maintain the pace.

"Yes, it could be seen as scary. Me, I was already prepared for this. I had learned all the lessons my grandfather and my father could teach me about living alone. I wasn't scared because I was in communion with Mother Earth. I knew she was there and she was all around me."

He paused again and took some of the dirt off the ground in front of him.

"Mother Earth cares for us. She has provided everything we need to survive. We only need to know where to look. I knew and I was able to survive."

Mike wanted to move on a bit. "So how long were you out there by yourself?"

"It's different for everyone. For me it took a bit less than a month."

"You were a whole month out there by yourself at twelve years old?" Ashley cried in disbelief.

Andy relished the effect. He knew women were more sensitive to the idea of a young boy being vulnerable. "Actually, I would have stayed longer but I knew I had to get back before my mother got too worried."

"I bet she was." Ashley continued.

"My vision quest was really finished after a couple of weeks but I stayed there because I found it so peaceful."

"So how did you survive?" Ashley was still worried about him. Mike wanted to understand why and how the quest itself was done, but he let Ashley's questions go first.

"I stopped at one place where I felt called to stay. I found a small clearing not far from the river and I started building a shelter. By the first nightfall, I had gathered enough wood to make a fire, I had the river for water, enough food to eat and I was protected. I stayed there for three days and nights, and then I moved to another place. By the time I got back, I had moved twice. In the third place I found my vision."

Now Mike intervened. "So why do your people do this vision quest?"

"We do it to find ourselves. We need to know why we are here and what our mission is. We get in touch with our inner person. You can't do that until you are completely separated from the rest of the people. We go away for this reason. Then we wait for it to come to us."

He paused. No one spoke. The fire crackled. The warmth surrounding them was now complete and restful.

"We also find our guide." Andy broke the silence.

"Your guide. What's that?" Ashley asked quickly.

"Our guide is the one sent by Mother Earth to show us the way we are to be. It is our model. It becomes part of our name."

Mike remembered. "Isn't your name Little Bear?"

"It is. I chose my name when I was on my vision quest."

"I'm afraid to ask why you chose Little Bear." Ashley enquired.

"When I reached the third place, I knew it was the site where I would find my vision. It had been visited by bears. The trees were full of scratches, there were tons of berries, and the river was jumping with fish. All of that meant the ideal place for bears."

"Are you crazy?" Ashley almost screamed at him. "You knew there were bears and you stayed there anyway?!"

"Yes. I did stop there. You see, my father is Nathan 'Standing Bear' Makwa. When he did his vision quest, his guide came as a bear. Every time the bear saw my father it would stand on its hind legs to greet him. My father took this as his guide name. He knew he would be one to stand for his people. He became a firefighter to protect his people from harm. That was his vision. Some of my vision had to come from his. Since he had been guided by a bear, there was a strong possibility my guide would be a bear as well. So I knew if I wanted to find this out, I had to stop where the bears lived."

"So how did you find this... Little Bear?" Mike asked.

"It was on the third day after I arrived at the last place. I woke up that morning and I looked to the river near my camp. There was a whole family of bears fishing in the river. I asked Mother Earth to protect me and tell me what to do. The bears were not interested in me, they just wanted to fish. Then the smallest one in the pack turned and looked at me. He saw I was awake and came to sit on the shore a short distance from where I was. He sat there and looked at me for a time, not moving. I knew then that he was my guide. He came back every day after. Some days he would be with the pack, on others he would be alone. We created a bond between us. He would be there in the morning, stay a few hours, fish a bit, then leave and come back again later in the day, as if to make sure I was fine."

He paused again so Mike asked "What do you think it meant? For your vision quest I mean."

"It took me a few days to answer this very question. I pondered on it every day until I knew why I was to be Little Bear. First, I was to be a bear because I followed in my father's path. The bear is intelligent, gentle when it doesn't feel threatened but powerful and strong when attacked or wanting to protect its young. It has wisdom to find the right places for food at any time of the year. I also knew it had to be Little Bear because I should not be greater than my father. I will be his companion but not his replacement. I will remain Little because I have the wisdom to counsel others but it's others who will take action."

"So you're sort of an advisor, not a leader, is that it?" Mike understood.

"Yes, that's right. I am to be there for help, not for leadership. I may be able to show the way, but the decision to go will come from someone else."

"And you found all that out by being alone in the woods?" Ashley was intrigued.

"That and a whole lot more. I found peace within myself. I learned to be satisfied with who I was meant to be. I understood what Mother Earth wanted from me. If I was to be happy, I had to accept my role and live to fulfill it."

He stopped and they didn't ask anything else. They were each lost in their own thoughts.

The afternoon wore on. They nibbled on pemmican, drank melted snow, watched the fire dance, rebuilt it with more logs once in a while, and shared stories.

By night time they were tired and lay down on their dried winter clothes. Ashley fell asleep quickly. Mike had questions for himself. He wondered if he should take up a vision quest of his own.

Andy got up a few times during the night to keep the fire going. They all had a good night. When sunlight drifted into the cabin, they gradually woke up. Andy gave them some fruit he had also brought along. They got dressed, put the fire out, strapped the snowshoes on and started the trek back to the truck. It seemed less cold than the day before and to Ashley in particular, the trip seemed easier. Maybe, she had a better sense of the distance they would be travelling back or maybe it was the anticipation of going back to civilization, but her pace was better than on the way over.

They soon reached the truck and headed home. Mike would have stayed on longer but he had to bring Ashley back. His parents would also get worried if he didn't come back when promised.

20. Tension

In most areas around Lakedge the snow was up to six feet high. Snow banks were actually nine feet high or more wherever ploughs and snow blowers had done their jobs. In the parking of Trucker's Corner however, the snow never had a chance to accumulate. Open twenty-four hours, seven days a week, there was always activity around the place. Being the last stop before reaching the more northern areas of the province or the long roundabout to get to Winnipeg, the coffee shop and restaurant was a popular place for heavy transport truck drivers.

The snow was crushed under the eighteen wheels, melted on top of the hot engines and cabs, or simply never reached the ground and got carried away to other destinations with the rest of the cargo. The owner of the place had a contract with a snow removal service but the work to be done with the plough was minimal.

Trucking is an industry that doesn't wait for the sun to rise, so this activity at all hours of the day and night was normal. Lately, there was even more activity at Trucker's Corner since the mill closed. In Lakedge you had very little choice of restaurants. With the exception of a couple of pizza or chicken take-outs, a small bakery and tea shop in the mall, and one somewhat more fancy restaurant near the Town Hall, you had to go to Greenmeadows, some sixty kilometres south, to get anything special. In addition, those places in Lakedge were only open until about nine in the evening.

Trucker's Corner was a full service gas station with a restaurant in a fifties décor including black and white ceramic tiles, green tables with metallic sides and red bucket seats. The waitresses were also dressed in the traditional pink suits with short skirts and little white-laced aprons. Of course the cute girls were an additional reason for truckers to want to stop in Lakedge.

Tonight, there were the usual teamsters, couples from Lakedge on dates, and families enjoying a break from the daily supper-making routine, but at one end of the huge room equipped to accommodate up to two hundred people, a group of mill workers and lumberjacks were talking with great emotion.

Near the centre of the table, Jim Stone was the focus of most of the conversation. Respected by his colleagues not only because of his supervisory position at the Sparks Mill but also because of his experience and extensive knowledge of the forestry industry, the group unconsciously made him the leader in replacement of Warren Sparks. His opinion counted more than any of the others around the table. Jim knew this and was careful to measure his words and to pace his thoughts. A large responsibility had ended up on his shoulders without his asking for it.

Across the table and two seats down, Frank Ellis had joined the discussion. Although he was a municipal employee now, and in a fairly high-ranking position in that organisation, Frank knew a lot about the mill. He had worked there for a long time before moving on to the town administration. He knew all the people at the table, and he clearly understood their anxieties. He also knew that because of his position, people saw him as a representative of government. Sometimes this was good, in that it brought some respect and attention, but often it was seen negatively as part of a bureaucratic scheme to drain citizens of their money through taxes.

Tonight some of the apprehension was turned to the town. As it is often the case in a crisis, people expect the government – the same one they complain about having to pay taxes to – to step in and bail them out. Often people in Lakedge had told Frank that they were paying his salary so he should give them the services. Frank occasionally replied that if he were to collect directly from all the people who said they were paying him, he would be rich and ready to retire.

Suggestions had been made that the town should appeal for help from the province. Frank explained that there were criteria to do this. The mill closure was temporary. In the meantime, people had access to existing governmental programs such as employment insurance and welfare payments. Jim was more worried about the business once the mill reopened.

"What we need to realise is that many of the mill's customers can't wait for weeks to get their deliveries. They are going to turn elsewhere to get what they need, if they haven't already done so. The competition will do everything possible to keep these customers as regular customers. If the service is good, and the products are acceptable, we will lose them as customers."

Frank, coming from a purchasing background, agreed. "It's a lot more difficult to regain customers after you lose them than it is to get them in the first place. In a way we are lucky it's winter because construction is slower; there are less orders to fill."

One of the workers interjected. "The wood is all there, already cut. Why don't we just go in, load it up and deliver it. That way we'll keep the customers. They can pay later when we re-open completely."

Frank disagreed. "Guys, you have to keep a cool head on your shoulders on this. Going in there now would be trespassing and you could end up with charges against you, fines, maybe even jail time. Even though these are tough times, you want to make sure they don't get any tougher."

"Frank's right" Jim added. "We didn't do anything wrong here and so far we should all be able to go back to our jobs at some time. We can't start doing anything illegal. We have to find other ways."

Grumbling and side conversations started again. One of them spoke louder. "I heard a couple of the guys went to get jobs at Woodland Mills, up near Kenora. Tom Henson is one of them; his wife told me he plans to stay at his sister's all week so he won't have to commute for an hour and a half every morning and every night. He plans to come back home only on weekends. There are others talking of doing the same thing."

"That's one option, I guess." Jim answered. "But even Woodland Mills will only be able to take so many new staff. After a while there won't be any jobs left there. We have to make sure that when we do reopen, we can keep the jobs that we had. That means we have to make sure the business can remain profitable."

More murmurs of concurrence resounded through the group.

Jeff Wallis hit the table with his fist. He was already on his fifth beer of the evening and the effects were starting to show. "All of this mumble-jumble isn't giving us our jobs back. I want to know what you're going to do about it." He was looking directly at Frank, implying that he was there as the municipality's ambassador and had to take the responsibility for the crisis.

Frank protested. "Hey, guys, easy. I just came here to have a beer or two. I wasn't sent here to negotiate anything. I sat down with you guys because I like you and I enjoy your presence. Don't lay any of this on my lap."

Jeff stood up, anger starting to swell. "Typical lazy government lackey. Won't lift a finger for you. You still have a job so you don't care. You get paid. You can pay your bills. So how I am going to pay for my house? How am I going to feed my children?"

Jim stepped in. "Drop it Jeff. We've heard you before. Frank is a friend. He's not responsible for what happens here. It's not his fault and there's nothing he can do about it. You have to find money on your own for now or make arrangements with the bank until you can get some."

Jeff stayed up and turned to Jim. "The bank…the bank. You want to know what the bank says. They say I have to pay for my house and my car even if I don't have a job. They say if I don't pay, when summer comes, they will take my house and my car away. That's what the bank says. Nobody wants to help. They're all hiding their heads in the sand. They're all passing the buck. It's nobody's fault. No one is ready to do anything. So screw you Frank. If you really were a friend, like Jim says, you'd do something."

"That's enough Jeff. Sit down or leave." Jim stood up to confront him. "Frank doesn't deserve this. I think you've had enough to drink for tonight. You should get back home before you're too drunk to drive."

Jeff looked at him almost ready to reach with his fist, but he saw everyone around him ready to stop him. He knew they wouldn't let him touch Jim. He probably wouldn't be able to get to Frank either. So he picked up his mug and downed the rest of the beer.

"The hell with all of you." He continued swearing at them as he headed for the door.

Jim sat down again. "I'm sorry about this Frank."

"Don't worry about it Jim. I've been called worse things in my life. I'll survive this. Thanks for sticking up for me."

"He was out of line. So… let's get back to our problem. How can we keep our customers?"

The discussion continued in a more subdued way.

Jeff was almost at the door when someone tapped him on the shoulder. "Hey friend. Can I buy you a beer?"

He turned around. A man in his mid-forties, smaller than him but with wide shoulders and bulky arms was looking at him with a huge smile.

Jeff was suspicious. "Why would you want to buy me a beer? I don't even know you."

The man smiled. "That's right, you don't know me. I'm not from around here. I'm actually just passing through. I'm Bernie, by the way. The reason I want to buy you a beer is because I heard some of what you said. You've got money problems. You seem to be out of a job. Maybe I can help you find some work and get some money."

Jeff was attracted. "What kind of work?"

Bernie's smile cut across his face almost from one side to the other. He rubbed his grey hair for a second trying to find how he would answer that question. There were a lot of people all around them.

"Why don't you come over to my table where we can talk a little more privately? I'll give you more details of what I am thinking."

Jeff still wasn't convinced but that money offer was difficult to turn down. He followed as Bernie went to his booth. On his way Bernie flagged down a waitress and got her to bring a pitcher of draft and an extra glass.

He sat on one side and Jeff sat across.

"Did I hear right, your name is Jeff?"

"Yeah that's right, Jeff. Jeff Wallis."

Bernie put his hand across the table. "Bernie Taylor. Nice to meet you."

They shook hands.

"So you see Jeff. My employer overheard that there were some problems in Lakedge and asked me to stop by on my next trip. I own a truck and I work for a forestry company. I haul wood products for hardware and lumber yards. So I came here to find out a bit more. I understand that the main mill here is closed for some reason but I didn't get why. Maybe you can tell me a bit more."

Jeff looked at him a bit disgusted. He had just been reminded of the source of all his anger. "What is it to you? You really think I want to talk about this?"

Jeff was signalling as if he wanted to leave again so Bernie quickly reacted. "What if I pay you to tell me?"

That struck the right chord with Jeff. He stopped. "I don't get it. You want to pay me to tell you what my problems are?"

"Well not just your problems but the problems everyone here is having. My employer may be able to help but he needs information."

Jeff was still leery. The waitress came with the pitcher. Bernie poured some in Jeff's glass. Jeff took a sip and started. He told of Sparks, his death, the closure of the mill, the waiting, the attitude of the bank, his anger at the town for not helping more, and anything else he could lash out at to relieve some of his inner frustration. Bernie listened attentively, encouraging Jeff for more along the way.

When he was finished, Jeff realised he had told everything he knew but had not received anything in return other than the glass of beer.

"Hey, just a sec here. You said you'd pay for this information. So how much, and where is the money."

"Right, I'm sorry." Bernie pulled his wallet out of his pocket and pulled out a one hundred dollar bill. "Would that do it for now?"

Jeff saw that there were more bills in the wallet. He hesitated a second, the beer helped in being more demanding. "Maybe you could hand over another one of those?"

Bernie got out one of his huge smiles again. "Oh definitely... a man who knows what he wants."

He handed over the two bills. Jeff reached for them. Bernie held on to one corner so that Jeff couldn't take the money yet. "Now, here's what I'd like to do." he said.

Jeff stopped with his hand in the air trying to pull on the bills and looked Bernie in the eyes. "What?"

"I'll call this a deposit. Let's say I give you this money for now as a down payment. There's a lot more where this came from." As he spoke he gently released his grip on the money so that Jeff could pull it. "I can offer you a couple of these every so often in exchange for information."

Jeff rolled up the bills in his hand, never leaving his eyes off Bernie. "What kind of information?"

"You see my employer is interested in helping the people of Lakedge but to do it, he needs to know what is going on here. Since I'm on the road all the time, I can't stay in Lakedge very long and I can't really tell him much. You've already told me a lot more than I gathered in listening to conversations all afternoon."

He took a sip of beer and Jeff did the same. "So what I would like is to have somebody local, like yourself, to call me once in a while when there is something new happening in Lakedge that could be of interest to my employer."

"Like what?" Jeff asked.

"Like: when will the mill reopen, what is happening with this succession, what is the town doing to help out, who are the people involved in negotiations, what is the bank doing about this. You see? Any development in this situation is of interest to my employer. Since you are on the inside, it's much easier for you to find these things out than it is for me. In the meantime, you will be making some money to help you pay your bills."

Jeff wanted this but was still a bit suspicious. "I don't get it. Why is this information so important to your employer?"

"Ah yes. I can understand why you would want to know. You're a smart man Jeff. I guess I can't really hide anything from you. Well then, I'll tell you. My employer may be interested in buying the mill and reopening it under a new name. But he knows that there will be others who want to buy it so he needs a bit of…how should I call it…an edge, if you see what I mean. You would be that edge."

Jeff looked a bit lost but the flattery was also working.

"We will pay you a bit right now, and as you provide us with more information we will send you more money. In the end if the deal works and my employer becomes owner of the mill, you can be assured of a job, probably with a promotion and a raise, and a sizeable bonus on top of everything."

Jeff was breathless. He raised his glass to his mouth but Bernie reached over and put his hand on top of his blocking him. "I do need one assurance from you, however."

Jeff stopped, wondering. "Assurance?"

"Yes. I need to keep this confidential. Nobody can find out about our deal. If this gets out and the purchase of the mill goes to someone else, then you can say goodbye to your bonus. Do I have your assurance?"

"Sure, sure. I won't tell anyone."

"Good, I could tell you were smart the minute I laid eyes on you." He let go of Jeff's hand so he could drink his beer. "I'm going to give you my cell phone number. Anytime you hear something, you call me, even if you're not sure it's useful. Then I can decide if it's needed. If it is, then I'll send you money. If it's not, I'll at least pay you the cost of the call. Do you have a cell phone Jeff?"

"I don't. I don't have any use for one. My son keeps bugging me to get one but I don't want to. I see all these people walking down the streets and in their cars with them and I get annoyed. What do all these people have to talk about all the time?"

Bernie gave him one of his charismatic smiles. "I get you. I tend to agree with you, but for business, sometimes cell phones are good to have. I'll tell you what. I'll be back in three days and I'll set-up a meeting. I'll bring you back a cell phone so you don't have to worry about paying for calls. We will pay for the phone and when we are finished, you can keep it. Maybe, you'll come to like it over time."

"Oh...okay... if you think I should." Jeff said.

Bernie took out a piece of paper and started scribbling on it. "Here is my phone number. As we discussed, anything you hear, you let me know right away. Deal?"

He kept holding on to the paper just as he had previously with the money. Jeff looked up at him. "Yeah…I mean deal."

Bernie let go of the paper. "Now tell me a bit more about you while we finish this pitcher."

They kept talking for a while, both now cheery. Jeff went on and on as if he was talking with an old buddy. In the other corner of the restaurant, the mood wasn't as joyful. Nobody could really see a way out. They had offered a number of suggestions but none seemed feasible. Frank had volunteered to make a few calls to find out more on a few initiatives they had discussed but they weren't going to find the answers tonight. The night grew on and gradually, one by one, they went home to their families until only the few single or divorced guys in the group remained.

In the restaurant the number of patrons diminished and the waitresses tried to close down some of the sections at the back to reduce the walk from the kitchen to the tables.

When Frank left with a couple of the guys, Jeff was already gone. In the corner of the parking was a long hauler with piles of two-by-fours covered with tarps and tied down. In the cab, Bernie was on the phone.

"I'm on to something. I found just the right guy. He desperately needs money and he is on the inside. He is also not happy about the way things are unfolding. He's not too smart so I can get him to do pretty much what I want. Call me when you get this message. You know who. Bye."

He hung up and lay down in the back for a snooze before heading out again.

Tuesday February 28

Deuteronomy chapter 30, verses 4 to 9, New King James version

4 If any of you are driven out to the farthest parts under heaven, from there the Lord your God will gather you and from there He will bring you.

5 Then the Lord your God will bring you to the land which your fathers possessed, and you shall possess it. He will prosper you and multiply you more than your fathers.

6 And the Lord your God will circumcise your heart and the heart of your descendants, to love the Lord your God with all your heart and with all your soul, that you may live.

7 Also the Lord your God will put all these curses on your enemies and on those who hate you, who persecuted you.

8 And you will again obey the voice of the Lord and do all His commandments which I command you today.

9 The Lord your God will make you abound in all the work of your hand, in the fruit of your body, in the increase of your livestock, and in the produce of your land for good. For the Lord will again rejoice over you for good as He rejoiced over your fathers.

Deuteronomy chapter 31, verses 7 to 8, New King James version

7 Then Moses called Joshua and said to him in the sight of all Israel, "Be strong and of good courage, for you must go with this people to the land which the Lord has sworn to their fathers to give them, and you shall cause them to inherit it.

8 And the Lord, He is the One who goes before you. He will be with you, He will not leave you nor forsake you; do not fear nor be dismayed."

21. Europe

The Lester B. Pearson airport is the largest in Canada. Although it's often referred to as the Toronto Airport, it actually resides in Mississauga, which is a neighbouring city to the West of Toronto. The airport has three terminals and welcomes over 40,000 people a day from all over the world. Over a year, this translates to more than 14 million travellers coming to the area. It also signifies thirty passengers a minute or one passenger going through the gate every two seconds. At the same time, there are a proportional number of people leaving the area.

On the tarmac, a plane arrives or leaves every two minutes. That's thirty planes an hour and over 700 planes a day. Looking out the huge windows, Joshua was becoming dizzy with the activity both on the ground and in the air.

Teresa and he had arrived early on the 6:00 a.m. flight from Winnipeg and were transferring to take the Air France flight to Nice, about twenty minutes away from Cannes.

Josh remembered the fate of another Air France flight at this particular airport a few years ago. The plane had come down during an intense summer storm and hit the runway too far down. The pilot had been unable to brake in time and the plane went off the runway, into a ditch where it burst in flame. All passengers exited the plane alive, thanks to the rapid intervention of the flight crew. The luggage was lost, a lot of the passengers ended up on one of the local highways where they were picked up by good Samaritans, and the plane itself was totally destroyed. Josh recalled the pictures and was a bit antsy about it but convinced himself that flying was still the safest mode of transportation and in this case, the fastest.

They had a four-hour layover. They had breakfast at the airport; the snack on the flight not enough to sustain much more than a mouse.

Now they were sitting in the waiting area, watching planes lift off and land, and chatting.

"Have you ever been to France before?" Teresa asked.

"No, I haven't. Actually, I've been to a few places in the states, a lot of places in Canada, but I've never travelled overseas. This will be a first."

"Well then, I'm glad we are doing this together."

Josh had another thought. "So why did you pick France to move to?"

Teresa smiled. "I've often asked myself that question as well. At the time, it was almost a flip of the coin. The deciding factor, in a way, was my impression that France was a better place to try my luck at fashion design. I felt if I could succeed in France, then my name would become famous around the world. I was a bit naïve at the time and ambitious as well."

"You didn't do so badly from what I gather?"

"You are very kind. It's true that I did fairly well, but my name never became a household icon. I am known only in a close-knit group. I owe my fame almost more to Émilie than to myself. If it wasn't for her looks and the way my garments look on her, the clothing itself may never have been discovered."

Every few minutes they were interrupted by an announcement reminding them to keep an eye on their luggage. They either spoke louder if they were in the middle of a sentence or stopped talking altogether if they were in between two ideas.

Then his cell phone rang. He picked it up and saw the name of the caller; it was Frank. He answered it.

Frank spoke quickly, almost not stopping between sentences. "Josh, I just found out. Someone made an offer to buy the mill. The real estate agent wouldn't tell me who. I was calling to find out more about the evaluation and the price in order to look into the purchase and that's when he told me. He wouldn't tell me the amount of the offer. What are we going to do?"

"Calm down Frank, you're going too fast for me."

"Sorry, it just that I don't know if we will have enough time to put an offer together. If they sell the mill to someone else, who knows what they will do with it?"

Josh tried to keep as calm a tone as he could. "I am well aware of that risk. It's exactly why I am going to France. I don't think they can close a deal that fast anyway. There are verifications they have to do."

"I guess you're right. So what do we do in the meantime?"

Josh paused a second to think. "I guess you need to continue trying to obtain an evaluation of the property and the business. Let the real estate agent know that the town wants to make an offer as well. He has to give you the information on the value of the property."

"He said he would send me the whole package by e-mail." Frank answered.

"Good. So let me see what I can get from my end. The first choice would be for Joy to operate the mill herself with some help. The second choice is for the town to buy the mill and operate it ourselves. Having another forestry firm buy the mill is the third option. If none of these work, then we will have to figure out something else."

Frank stayed mute on the other end for a few seconds.

"You got that Frank?" Josh asked.

"Yes, I did. I'll keep searching for more information." Then he remembered something else. "Oh, I also wanted to tell you. I spoke to one of the VPs of Woodland Mills this morning. That's a mill near Kenora. I asked if there was any way we could process some of the orders from the Sparks Mill there temporarily. He said he would have to think about it, but if there was a cut for them, he could arrange to create an extra shift. I suggested that we could send some of the staff from Sparks Mill to cover that shift."

"That's good work Frank. What does Jim Stone think of it?"

"Actually that's partly his idea. We came up with it yesterday while talking at Trucker's Corner. Jim remembers most of his regular customers and could recreate the list. With a few phone calls we could get them to resend the orders and process them at the Woodland mill. This way we keep the Sparks Mill's customers happy and we give work to some of our people."

Both of their spirits seemed raised by the prospect. Teresa looked on as Josh spoke and she saw his face light up.

"So when does the VP think he will get back with an answer?"

"He said he would get back to me either today or tomorrow. His only fear is the strain on the equipment. If they work the saws for too long and run the motors for more than usual, something may break and affect their regular business."

"Would there be any way we could find other equipment to supplement theirs temporarily?" Josh asked.

"That kind of equipment is hard to come by. If we could access the equipment inside Sparks Mill, we could maybe transport some of it over to Woodland and use it there."

"That might be something I could arrange on a short term basis if some of the other options don't work out. I'll put it on my list of things to ask for." Josh said.

They chatted a bit on some of the other items regarding the town management and Josh hung up. He explained the conversation and the Woodland deal to Teresa. She saw a bit of hope as well.

The call came for them to embark on their flight. Shivers ran through Josh's body. He couldn't tell if it was his slight fear of flying or the fear of what he would meet across the ocean.

22. Money

George Walgren had been crying. His face was puffed up, his eyes red and swollen. He sat in his car for a long time pondering his next steps. His conclusion was undeniable; he had nothing left to lose.

He stepped out of the car. The springs were so shot that even the relief from a heavy weight like George getting out didn't raise the car. He slammed the door with force – the only way to keep it shut – and went to the trunk. He picked up his Remington Magnum 175, the rifle he normally used for moose hunting.

George was a good hunter. Although he went moose hunting a few times, he preferred the deer-hunting season. He always brought his quota of venison when he came back. He didn't keep the head, otherwise all the walls in his house would be filled with them. He did keep that 12-year-old male he killed and had it stuffed. That "dust collector", as his wife called it, was his only trophy. A person of his size and his weight couldn't be involved in sports, and with his intelligence level, he couldn't win any Nobel prizes. He was, however, a patient man and a good shot, he knew the deer and the area.

For the first time, today he wasn't going hunting with the Remington. He crossed the parking lot and came in the bank. He was familiar with the place, doing business there regularly. He headed for Peter Cohen's office. The cashiers didn't notice him or if they did, they didn't notice the gun.

When he arrived in front of her desk, Sylvia looked up and saw him. First, she smiled and was going to greet him, and then she saw the gun.

"George, what are you doing with a gun?"

George didn't answer. He had no words left.

He pushed the door of Cohen's office. There was a woman sitting there but George didn't ever look at her. He raised the gun.

"I want my money."

Pete's face turned white instantly. "George… don't…don't do anything crazy."

George kept the gun lined up to Pete's chest. "I want my money."

"Okay, okay. Give me a minute. Maybe we can talk about this."

The lady managed to get up and run out of the office. Once outside, she started screaming. "He's got a gun!"

Sylvia was already on the phone calling 9-1-1. People ran out of the bank, scared for their lives. George stood still; Cohen was his only target. The banker had regained a bit of composure. His mind seemed to tell him if he wasn't dead yet, he may have a chance to survive this. So he started talking.

"George. Are you sure you want to do this?"

George's eyes started watering again.

"Why don't we talk about this?" Pete offered again. "Have a seat."

Peter Cohen knew George Walgren from grade school. The man had often been the butt of other kid's jokes. Being overweight and not very agile had made him a bit of an outcast. He was a high school dropout and began working for Sparks very early. He'd met his wife in town.

They married, and had two kids who were now adults and on their own.

Peter seemed to remember hearing that his wife had left him a short while ago. The banker also knew what George implied when he was talking about "his" money. George had applied for an extension on his credit card to do repairs on his car and had been refused. That was two days ago. He had left the bank discouraged and depressed, not angry. Even now, he wasn't yelling or exhibiting signs of violence. He gave more of a sense of resignation. This was the last option he felt he had.

Peter realised at that moment that George was probably not there to shoot him. He wondered however if George might attempt to take his own life if he didn't get what he was coming for.

"George. Let's find another way out of this." Peter said gently.

His mind started calculating, a skill he excelled at. "You need $3,000. You have accumulated some return on the value of your house. Maybe we can use that. Have a seat and I'll figure something out."

He was hoping George wouldn't tell him it's what he should have done two days ago instead of refusing him flat out. George backed up slowly, tears still trickling on his cheeks. He sat, keeping the gun at Peter's chest height.

"Good, good." Peter relaxed a bit. He may live to see another day. They both might.

"Talk to me George. We've known each other for so long, you know I want to help you." He felt somewhat hypocritical; he didn't try to help him when he came the last time without the gun.

Subconsciously, he hated what the bank had turned him into. He despised the pressure exerted by his avid superiors who considered money and success more important than people.

A light had just come on. Where were his true priorities? He took a deep breath. In an instant he knew he was most likely going to throw his whole career away. He started to smile. "George. You're right. Screw this bank."

George looked at him a bit perplexed. So the banker explained. "You see George, when the mill closed, I was ordered to stop loaning money to everyone in town, especially to the mill employees. I know you lost your job now that the mill is closed." He paused as George looked at him with red eyes.

"I also know your wife left you. Even though I'm very sorry about it, I can't really do anything in that regard.. I wish I could. But when it comes to the bank, I had orders. Up to now I had decided to follow those orders."

He stopped again. George frowned, waiting for more. The gun was now aiming much lower. They both had forgotten about it.

"You convinced me George. I say: Screw the bank and their orders. I was raised here, I've lived here all my life and I care for this town and the people in it. That's why I became a banker. I had forgotten this. I became a phony and I regret it."

He rubbed his aching temples, trying to think of how to explain his thoughts.

"The banking industry is a jungle. They make you believe they have your best interest at heart but the only interest they have is the one they make on your money. I had to struggle to get to my position. I worked long hours, I gave up a lot of evenings and weekends to the bank, and I never saw a penny in overtime. I was always measured in quotas and the profits I brought in. I was never evaluated based on who I was. Someday I will retire and nobody at the bank will care. They'll send someone else to take over and things will go on like I never existed."

George had stopped crying and was listening with surprise in his expression. He had never been a confessor before.

Peter went on. "So I ask myself: what is this all worth? Where are my principles?" He got up and went around the desk with his right hand extended.

"Thank you George."

George took the hand that Peter offered and shook it lightly, still uncertain of what was happening here.

"I know this may sound weird, but if you're crazy enough to come here with a gun, then I'm crazy enough to risk throwing my career away." He sat on the corner of the desk, very close to George. "I have authority to issue a cash loan to you here without needing anybody else's approval."

Sirens blasted coming from the parking garage, interrupting him. George seized and tightened the gun. Peter also jumped. He looked out the frosted windows. The flashing blue and red lights from the cruiser pierced through. He turned back to George who was now raising the gun. He had to think fast.

"No, no. Here's what we are going to do. If you give me your gun, I will go out there and tell them it was just a misunderstanding. You didn't mean any harm and you didn't know you couldn't come in the bank with a gun. You... You were heading to the hardware store to get your gun cleaned but you needed some money first. How's that?"

George didn't really grasp all of it. A bit of doubt remained in his mind. "How can I trust you? You just told me you were a phony."

Peter felt this as a shot through the heart. He sighed. "You are absolutely right. I was a phony; you can't trust me."

He looked him in the eyes intensely, hoping the police would give him a few more moments before taking any action. "I know deep down you don't want to hurt anyone. You're a kind man George. I am sorry you are in this situation but unfortunately you are going to have to trust me; you don't have many other choices. I swear to you I will not let anyone cause you any more hurt than you already have."

George waited a bit, pondering his options.

A loud speaker cried out. "George, this is Mark Dexter. Why don't you come out slowly now? Nothing will happen. You have my promise."

George cringed at another promise. Peter repeated the request. "Give me the gun. I will go out and explain everything to Mark. You can follow me."

More sirens arrived in the background. George turned the gun and handed it over to Peter who locked the safety and slowly opened the office door. The bank was deserted. From the windows he could see at least three provincial police cars blocking the access to the parking from all angles. Officers were crouching behind open doors of the cruisers. Peter walked to the main door holding the gun high in the air from the barrel.

He opened the door and yelled out. "Don't shoot, I'm coming out!"

He waited a few seconds and heard Mark over the loud speaker. "Hold your fire. Come on out Pete."

He did. The cold of the winter bit him but it was welcome. He didn't realise how hot he had been in the bank until then. Mark instructed: "Lay down the gun."

Peter followed the order slowly. Mark continued. "Does he have any other weapons?"

"No he doesn't." For just a second, Peter reviewed his position. He was safe. He could hold on to his career. Was George worth this? Quickly his heart felt a squeeze. It wasn't just George. It was the whole community. If he didn't do it for George, how many others would come at him? How many others would see how much of a phony he had become? He looked at Mark.

"It's all a misunderstanding." He told the lie they had agreed upon.

Mark asked a few questions, unconvinced. Peter continued. "Come on Mark, you know George. He wouldn't hurt a flea. It's just an accident."

Then George arrived at the door and another officer yelled. "Get down! Suspect in view." Guns were raised.

Peter rushed in front right away. "No, no, don't shoot. He's not armed." Mark kept his gun at his hand and went to the door slowly. He gradually opened it, keeping his eyes on George. "Okay, come on out George. Keep your hands where I can see them, alright?" Mark was trying to use as soft and calm a voice as he could. George spread his hands out in front of him. Mark holstered the gun. He reached out and took George's hand.

"Are you okay George? Pete tells me it's just a mistake. What do you say?"

George looked up through puffed eyes and sobbed. "Yes… It's… just a mistake. I'm sorry." Peter breathed a huge sigh of relief. For the first time in a long while, he started to feel good about himself.

"Good." Mark said. "Now, don't be afraid but I have to do this. Please don't move while I search you. Are you okay with this?"

George nodded. Mark gently padded over his clothing, searching for other weapons. Then he turned and yelled. "He's clean!" The other officers holstered their firearms and came closer.

Peter went to Mark. "Why don't we go back inside, you, George and I to talk about this?"

Mark had the rifle and handed it over to one of the officers. "Put that in the car and wait for me." He looked at the others. "I'll handle it from here. You can go back to your patrols. I'll take care of the paperwork."

He kept his eyes on George who hadn't moved. Then he turned to Peter. "If it's just a mistake Pete, then what is there to talk about?"

Peter smiled. He knew Mark was a good cop and did his duty. Mark was also from Lakedge. He cared for the people in his community. Peter pulled him a bit further and lowered his voice. "Mark, I'm actually worried for George. I think if we just let him go, he may harm himself. Do you see what I'm saying?"

Mark understood clearly. He squeezed his lips together, pondering. "So what do you suggest?"

Peter relaxed. "I can help him with his finances but that's not going to bring back his wife. It's not going to give him back his job... or his dignity. We need to work together on this."

Mark knew what Peter was saying. Lately, people in his town had grown anxious. Tempers were flaring, idleness bread restlessness, disputes turned to fights; he didn't have the staff to handle this.

"Very well, let's go in and talk." He said it loud enough for George to hear as well.

Pete added. "Good, let's go back to my office and we will finish our conversation." George nodded, his gaze still blank.

Peter opened the door and they walked in. He escorted them to his office and asked. "Can I get you a refreshment or a coffee?"

Mark answered. "Water would be good. How about you George?"

George nodded again. "Yes, water, good."

Peter stepped out and saw Sylvia still waiting in the parking lot with the other cashiers. Other people were huddled around them with coats and blankets to keep them warm. He went out, reassured them that everything was fine, and took out money from his wallet for Sylvia to get water. They all walked back in, handing over the coats and blankets to the good Samaritans who had offered them in the first place. Each went back to their work, most shaken by the experience. Peter knew he would have to hold a staff meeting before the end of the day to calm everyone down. Right now George was his priority.

He sat at his desk facing the two. "So, how much money did we say you needed for now?"

George hesitantly said. "$3,000 to get my car fixed."

Peter calculated. "$3,000 will only get your car fixed but it's not going to put any gas in it, right?"

"Right."

"So why don't we round this up to $5,000 to keep you going until the mill reopens?"

George's eyes grew a bit. "Sure."

"Now you have a bit of equity on your house, so we will use this as collateral. Do you agree with this?" George didn't quite grasp the concept of collateral, but he agreed.

Mark stayed silent. Normally, he should have been arresting George but nobody had been hurt, no shots had been fired, no charges were laid, and Peter had assured him it was a mistake. On what grounds could he arrest George? He had noticed the state that George was in, almost catatonic. He had to do something for his safety.

Peter continued. "Very well, give me a couple of minutes to get the paperwork done and I'll be back with your money." He stepped out.

Mark looked at George. "I'm willing to agree that this was a mistake George but I have to keep your gun for a while. I'll give it back to you before hunting season but for now I need to keep it. Do you understand?"

George agreed silently.

"Is there anyone from your family you could go to and spend some time with for a while? Maybe you could go visit your sons? What do you think?"

"They are too busy for me. They have jobs and their own families to take care of."

"Sure." Mark said. "But maybe they can have you over for just a short while until the mill opens again. Can't they?"

"Maybe. I'll have to call them."

"Here, I have a better idea. Why don't you give me their numbers and I'll call them myself while you finish the papers with Peter?"

"Okay." George reached in his wallet and pulled out a business card. He handed it to Mark. The card had the work number for one of his sons in Greenmeadows. Peter walked in with papers and some certified cheques.

"Pete, I need to make a phone call." Mark said. "I'll leave the two of you for a minute."

Peter started explaining to George how to use the cheques while Mark went to call. He came back a little later with a smile. He had explained the situation to George's son and the young man was on his way to pick up his father. Mark informed George.

Peter and Mark tried to make a bit of conversation to pass the time until George's son would arrive. After a while, Peter suggested to George. "Why don't you wait on one of the chairs in the lobby? I'm sure Mark has to get back to his work."

George got up. Mark asked. "What about your car? Do you want me to ask Danny to pick it up and start fixing it?" Danny was the mechanic.

"Okay, he knows what needs to be done." George replied.

"Good. I'll tell him to come and pick it up. Just leave me the keys."

George handed the keys and went to sit down, still sipping on the water bottle Sylvia had brought him.

"Thanks, Mark." Pete said. "I knew you and I could do something about this."

Mark smiled. "You're a good man Pete."

Peter frowned. "Not as good as I'd like, but thanks. I'm just glad of the way this all turned out."

Mark went back to his car and sat in it for a few minutes before turning the ignition. Pete watched him from the window. He shared some of the apprehension the policeman probably had. Everyone in town was stressed by the situation of the mill. How many more conflicts would have to be resolved? Would all of them end without violence?

23. Negotiation

Émilie sipped on her glass of fine Chablis especially selected by Gilbert to accompany the dessert of *profiterolles* they had just relished. Josh had opted for a cup of strong *cappuccino*. He wasn't really used to wine and two glasses with dinner was already enough to make his head lighter. He preferred to keep his mind in focus for the negotiation he wanted to get into.

They had moved to the parlour as Gilbert moved to the kitchen. The dinner was excellent but the conversation was all about France, the Riviera, and Émilie's environment. He tried to bring up Lakedge gently into the discussion a couple of times but she seemed to divert it each time to her own lifestyle. In essence, he hadn't accomplished anything yet and the evening was flying away, minute by minute.

She sat in the sofa across from him. Her one-piece white dress was designed to exhibit as much of her femininity as possible. Sleeveless, cut open in the middle from the top to almost her belly button, and cut on the sides to reveal much of her thighs, the leather seemed tight at the waist to enhance her curves. Josh tried not to look, but anywhere his eyes went, there was a part of her he preferred not to see.

She put down her glass and opened the conversation.

"So Joshua, tell me. I'm sure you didn't come all this way just to enjoy French cuisine." She spoke English very well, but with a forced French accent as if she wanted to renege on her origins. Josh was taken aback with her introduction into the topic but happy she helped him get started this way.

"That's right. I came here because we are having a difficult time right now in Lakedge and I'm hoping you can do something to help."

She smiled into a grin. "I like that. In fact, I always like when men need something from me."

He understood the real meaning behind the words. It didn't do anything to help enhance his level of comfort. He concentrated on his objective.

"As you know, your attorney has locked up the mill until the inheritance transfers have been completed. I understand this and we don't want to cause any problems for you. However, this has an impact on hundreds of employees at the mill who are presently without work until the situation is resolved. Not only does it affect the mill workers, but it also means that many of the woodcutters and lumber workers that bring the trees to the mill are also unemployed."

She was nodding, remaining silent to let him finish. Her eyes didn't express the concern he was trying to raise. She seemed to be looking at him with different intentions. He kept his train of thought.

"This also has an impact on the people who transport the finished products and the processed lumber to the lumber yards around the country, they are also without work. In turn, this means a lot of people from Lakedge without revenues and not buying anything. That leads to a lot of storeowners and services losing a large portion of their customers."

Her expression showed that she understood everything he was saying, but she didn't try to demonstrate any interest. Josh persisted.

"This is having a major impact on the economy of the town. Already, some people are talking about moving away. They can't pay their mortgage. Come spring, the bank will have to foreclose. They can't pay their taxes. If the population diminishes, the Town may have to lay off people as well. Can you see how the mill is central to the survival of my town?"

She looked at him and raised her glass for another sip. When she put the drink down, she said. "I do see it Joshua" and paused. He was sweating, but it had nothing to do with the weather of the Riviera. She seemed to enjoy his discomfort. In a way he was begging her and she liked to have men begging.

"What's in it for me, Joshua?"

He had rehearsed his answer many times on the plane, but now it seemed the answer was lame. Her attitude indicated to him that she didn't really care. He wanted to appeal to her sense of compassion but he couldn't even read a hint of it in her. He came up with plan B.

"The way I see it, every day the mill is closed, you lose a lot of money. There are orders unfilled, customers waiting, and expenses still need to be paid while there are no revenues. If you don't reopen soon, the customers will go elsewhere and you won't get them back. I guess that's what's really in it for you."

She laughed. "Joshua, *mon chéri*. I don't care about the money. I have all the money I want and more. If I sell the plant, it will pay for the debts and there will still be lots left."

Hearing this, Josh reverted to plan A.

"Then do it for the people of Lakedge. These people don't have the option of throwing away money as you do. I beg of you, let them go back to work."

She got up and came to sit right beside him, making sure her thigh would rub against his. She put her arm around his neck gently, caressing his hair. He could smell her perfume mixing with the aroma of the wine.

"Joshua *chéri*. You really think I care for the people of Lakedge?"

176

She paused for another sip; he remained silent. "Let me tell you what I think of those people. You see, I was always the rich girl. I went to school with everyone but I never fit in anywhere. I was short and chubby when I was young."

She let out a laugh. "I know that by looking at me now, you couldn't imagine that." Her tone changed and he noticed the sourness in her voice. "On my tenth birthday, I understood everything. My father thought it was a milestone to be celebrated so he organised a huge birthday party for me. He wanted a royal celebration for his little girl. He told me I could invite whomever I wanted and I asked to invite a hundred people. Ten times ten I told him, just like my birthday. When I told my classmates, they were fighting to get on the list. For the first time in my life, I felt important. I had something that people wanted. People wanted to be with me. I was on top of the world for about a month before the party."

She lowered her arm and laid her hand on his thigh.

"Then the day of the party came. We had a band, a huge cake, a sumptuous meal, and everyone showed up. They ate, they played games, they sang happy birthday, and they danced. Soon, everybody was busy and I found myself alone again. They all regrouped amongst their usual cliques. Meanwhile, me…" She stopped, almost snarling. "Me, I stayed alone in my corner. Even my parents were chatting with parents of children invited at the party."

They stayed silent for a minute then she started again. "They all left the party with gifts my dad had bought for each guest. The next day at school, it was as if nobody knew me."

She reached across the table for her glass, sipped at the wine.

"That was the turning point in my life. I decided that if people wanted something from me, they would have to grovel for it. I would bring people to my feet. In particular, the people of Lakedge."

The more she spoke, the less her French accent remained. "I started watching my weight. I made myself throw up; I became bulimic, just to change my appearance. Later I started exercising. When I reached my teens, I went for cosmetic surgery. I continued until I started having men crave for me."

Josh felt the anger and passion in her voice.

"When my mother separated, we moved away. I didn't mind; my father was never there anyway. It took us away from Lakedge, far from those ugly poor people I despised. Later we moved to France. My mother started designing dresses and she needed someone to model them. So with my new figure, I became the model. People loved me, men wanted me, women were jealous of me. And…I made money, lots of money. I soon became fully independent."

"I eventually forgot about my youth, about my father, and about Lakedge. If he hadn't left me a will, I might never have heard about Lakedge again. But now that I remember, it brings back the pain. It also brings back my desire for revenge. I told myself on my tenth birthday that someday I would have that kind of power; the power when you have something people really want and you are in total control of it. Do you understand Joshua?"

He had nothing to answer. He was sorry people were mean to each other. He was angry with those who had treated the young Joy this way. At the same time, he couldn't condone what she was saying. His upbringing had been about forgiving those who trespass against us. He looked at her in the eyes. He read a new determination and it scared him.

"It's a sad story Aymeelee." She had explained to him how her name wasn't Emily but had to be pronounced the French way with the accent on the E. So although he couldn't quite get the French tonality, he said it as close as possible. "What I think though, is that this is hurting you. You want to hurt others but in doing so you are causing yourself more pain." He sighed and paused a moment, internally asking for the right words to say.

"What if you repaid them for their meanness by giving them more than they could ever hope to get? What if you showed them what true strength of character you have by forgiving them and letting them know what you suffered and how you felt, then telling them that you are wiping the slate clean? Don't you think that would be better than revenge? It would make you a better human being. It would show them your superiority. It would help you heal instead of perpetuating the wound."

"Joshua, Joshua, Joshua." She said. "You're such a dreamer. I'm starting to fall for you. You are a nice, gentle, man; very good-looking I might add. However, you really don't know me."

Now her French accent had completely disappeared. "There are two main things that bring power in this world, Joshua. First, there is money. As I told you, I have plenty of money. I have so much I have to give a lot away to charity just to save me from paying extra taxes on it. Then, there is sex. You may have noticed I have somewhat of an advantage in this field as well. Which means I have the power to obtain anything I desire. I can buy anything I want, and I can use sex to get anything that can't be bought." She laughed. He knew he had lost this battle.

She sipped the wine again. He had his head down. She put her arm around his neck again. "There might be a way we can come to a compromise, Joshua *chéri*." She kissed him on the cheek. He jerked sideways slightly. "You are very attractive, Joshua. Maybe, there is another way you could convince me to change my mind. I might be able to let your mill reopen in exchange for something from you."

His heart was beating furiously. He was both aroused by her scent, and appalled at her demand. He saw her gradually coming on to him, but hoped it was just her normal personality. He had prayed nothing would come of it. Now he felt like a rat in a corner, caught between his own body's impulses, his love for his wife, the survival of the town, and his personal principles. He pushed himself away, truly afraid.

His head was spinning and it wasn't from the effects of the wine. "Excuse me. No."

"Joshua, you don't understand. I have needs too. I need to maintain this power I own. I need to nurture it, to feel it. In a way, I already feel the power of my money on the people of Lakedge; you've helped me realise it. If you now want to take it away from me, you have to replace it with something else. So, if you show me how I can use the power of sex in exchange over the power of money, then my needs will be satisfied. You have a choice to make here, Joshua."

He stood up. The struggle inside him was more intense than he had ever known any. "You can't do this. You can't ask me this. I'm a happily married man. I will not cheat on my wife."

"Joshua, who is going to know? It's just you and me here. I won't tell if you don't." She let out another small laugh. "I've had so many married men before; their wives never knew the difference. I'm actually very good friends with a lot of the wives of men I had sex with. Don't trouble yourself."

Josh just turned away heading out the room. "I won't do it." He left trying to find his way out to the main door. As he did he had the impression of driving the last nail in Lakedge's coffin.

He found a door that led to the outside. He needed the fresh air. He opened it and the cold struck him. He walked straight ahead at a quick pace never looking back. His head was still spinning. A lump blocked his throat.

He kept walking until he reached the ocean. The waves were light but steady, the tide was low and the sun fading in the West.

He stopped at the edge of the Mediterranean. He looked out over the water. The blue of the sea kept going until it merged with the blue of the sky. Not a cloud broke the scenery.

He regained his breathing. He stayed immobile for a long time pondering on what had just happened. When he came on this trip he had an image of the chubby little twelve year old that had left Lakedge long ago. He was coming to discuss arrangements with a businesswoman of thirty plus years of age expecting a larger version of the girl in the picture. Instead he met a mix between a goddess and a witch, a vision of paradise on the outside hiding a demon on the inside. He had come here expecting a bit of a challenge but he had just fought the worst battle of his existence.

And lost.

He heard footsteps behind him and tensed up. He turned quickly, expecting Joy/Émilie to be right there pursuing him, pushing some more to get her claws into him any way she could.

It wasn't Émilie. It was Teresa. He relaxed a bit and turned back towards the sea. She came beside him. For a while, they didn't speak, and then she started.

"I'm sorry Josh. I should have warned you. Now you know. I created a monster. I thought I was taking her away from a life without any hope, but all I did was make her into a being that takes hope away from others."

Josh didn't answer.

"I keep praying that she will change. I keep hoping as a mother that she will someday become the kind, gentle little girl I tried to raise. I keep seeing redeeming qualities in her. She is my flesh and blood; I can't deny it. Every time, I hope that this will be the occasion when she sees the light. Every time, I am deceived again."

The tide was rolling out and the waves weren't coming in as close anymore. The sand around them was drying. She sat. He looked at her and imitated her.

"I saw the signs as she grew up. I wanted to say something, I wanted to do something, but I didn't know how. I didn't want to confront her. I was afraid that she would go away and I would end up alone. I was afraid she would leave me and I would never see her again. So I gave in. I agreed to all her demands. She always got everything she wanted. Now, she can't take no for an answer. She has to have everything and she will get it no matter what the cost."

"At first, I thought she wouldn't care about the inheritance and the will. I was wrong again. I saw her hatred of Lakedge rise up. I tried to make her believe she had no interest in the mill, but she resisted my suggestions. She is waging a war and I don't think any of us have the ammunition to win it."

Her monologue was punctuated with sighs and pauses.

"I thought you might be able to convince her. I have seen you with your family. I saw how close you were. I saw your children and how you raised them. I know your mother and how strong a woman she is. I only wish I had been half as strong as her. Then I saw you run out of the house and I knew we had lost."

Josh turned to her. "I lost, you didn't."

"When I say we, I mean all of Lakedge. I was a coward twenty years ago when I left, but I want to be a part of that community again. When you say you lost the war, it's all of Lakedge who lost, and I want to think part of me lost with everyone else."

"You really think we lost the war, or did we only lose one battle?" he asked, now feeling the calm of the waves appeasing him.

"That's a good question. I'm not sure I have the answer. Certainly, if this wasn't the final battle, it was an important one. Do you have another idea in mind?"

"Actually, I was hoping you had one. You know your daughter better than I do. Is there any way we can convince her to change her mind?" He turned his body towards her, sitting with his legs crossed underneath him.

The night was quickly descending upon them. As they discussed options mixed with reminiscing of Lakedge and the raising of a monster, their forms became silhouettes and they finally had to get up and walk back to the house.

They arrived at the house and had the porch light upon them. She stopped.

"Josh, I think I will go back to Lakedge with you. I might be able to help over there. I can't do much here. I promise you I will do everything I can to save Lakedge."

She took his arm gently. "You're a good man Josh. I think your wife should be proud of you. It took a lot of courage to walk out of the house tonight. You're a brave man."

He didn't say anything. Leaving a conflict had never seemed to him like a demonstration of courage.

"Come, I'll show you to your room." She walked up the stairs. "And it locks from the inside." she added with a smile.

Once he was there she said. "Good night Josh. Try to get some sleep." He thanked her and she left. Sleep wasn't easy to come by.

24. Vision Quest

As soon as he had set foot on the bus back to Toronto, the depression had set in again. He was leaving Lakedge with everything he held dear in it. Ashley had run by the bus for as long as she could, blowing kisses and waving. His mom and dad had stayed on the platform but also waved and remained there until the bus was out of sight. The trip had seemed to be the longest in his life. Although he had done this a few times already, the cold outside seemed to penetrate his heart and he felt chills all the way to his soul.

He had tried very hard to get into his studies but it was as if his brain was freeze-dried. Two days later he was still moping around in his room. He didn't want to see anyone, didn't want to talk about anything. One of the few people he knew from his classes seemed to notice it and told him that he didn't look good. He suggested Mike go to the clinic and get checked out.

Now he was wondering if it wasn't good advice. Maybe he should see someone, although he was pretty sure that his condition wasn't physical. He thought of the University counselling service. He looked it up online and found out where it was located. So he put on his coat and walked over.

When he saw the desk, he backed out. He had no idea what to say. He couldn't find a way to express what he had. He turned away and walked aimlessly. He knew the campus by now but had no place to go.

He saw the Tim Horton's shop. A hot chocolate may help cheer him up. He checked his pockets and found a toonie, the Canadian two-dollar coin. It was enough for a hot chocolate and more. He ordered and went to sit in a corner. Students all around him were chatting, laughing, talking loudly.

He thought about the cabin with Andy. He recalled the story about Andy's vision quest in particular. His own religion was based on the Bible, but somehow this vision quest attracted him. Mike had been baptized at fourteen confirming his acceptance of the salvation message and his engagement to follow the doctrines of the Bible. That could be considered as a vision quest. He had studied for it and prepared for the ceremony but also prepared for its significance and the impact on his life. He had embarked on it willingly just as Andy had gone on his vision quest without fear.

Now, however, he felt he needed a vision quest of his own. He finished the hot chocolate and walked out. It was cold, but nothing compared to what he was used to in Lakedge. His winter coat was a lot warmer than what most Torontonians wore.

He saw the bus stop. A bus going downtown was idling. At that moment, Mike knew he needed to get away. It wouldn't be a canoe, it wouldn't be in the middle of the forest, and it wasn't likely to include bears. He took out his wallet and pulled his bus pass. Andy had a paddle; Mike had a card with his picture on it.

He boarded the bus and found a seat at the back. This was the first time Mike would ever visit downtown Toronto. The bus eventually drove off. As they got nearer, Mike recognised some of the structures he had seen in pictures; the Rogers Centre where the Blue Jays play baseball, the CBC building where the national radio and television stations broadcast, and of course the CN Tower, once considered the tallest free standing structure in the world. He had only heard of all these places but never seen them.

They arrived at a stop near Union station, the main train and bus terminal in Toronto. He stepped out. He immediately noticed people lying on the ground in sleeping bags and blankets. He had heard of the homeless situation in Toronto but he had never encountered it. An uneasy sensation came over him. He wanted to help but where would he start? There were so many of them. If the local services couldn't get them off the streets, how would he be able to do anything? He quickly realised that although his conscience was pushing him, in reality he couldn't do much.

He walked around. He came to a place with a sign: bed and breakfast, vacancy. Immediately, something stirred in him. Just as Andy had known the place where to stop for his vision quest, he now felt he had to stop there. He walked in. A lady was sitting behind a desk reading. She looked up.

"Hi, can I help you?" she asked with an East European accent.

"Uh… Yes, could I get a room for the night?" He hesitated as he said it.

"Sure, how will you be paying for this?" She seemed stern, not ready to make any arrangements until she was sure she would get paid.

Mike remembered the credit card his dad had given him when he left for Toronto in September. It was to be used in case of emergency. Mike wasn't sure if this qualified as an emergency but he felt sure this was given to him just as Andy's father had provided him with a strong knife. He handed her the card and she swiped it, then she printed the receipt, and he signed. She took a key from a hook and pointed to the stairs.

"Upstairs on the left, second room. There's a washroom at the end of the hallway. Curfew is at eleven, breakfast is down here from 6:30 to 9:00. Do you need anything else?"

"Eh… no thanks." Mike mumbled as he started up the stairs. He followed the instructions.

The room was small, just enough for a bed, a small dresser and a chair. There was a television on the dresser and a phone hooked up to the wall. A sign beside the phone read: *No long-distance from this phone.* A painting on the wall depicted a nature scene with trees, birds, a river, and white clouds in the sky. The bed cover was a patchwork of shapes and colours He sat on the bed. The springs squeaked but the mattress was comfortable.

"Now what?" he thought to himself. He hadn't really asked Andy much about what he did between the time he arrived at his selected site and the arrival of the bears. There wasn't much chance of him meeting a bear here, or any other animal for that matter. If he were to find a guide, where would he find it?

He reached for the dresser and opened the drawer. In it was an old Bible. It seemed to have been used a lot. Many of the pages were falling out. He opened it. There were markings, notes, and comments in the margins and between passages. The person to whom this belonged was an avid reader. He closed the Bible and wrapped it in his arms pressing it against his chest.

He stayed there for a long time, mulling over his feelings. His loneliness, his desire to go back home, his indecision as to where his life should go, and many more thoughts mingled in his mind. The exercise took some of his strength and eventually he fell asleep.

He woke up in a sweat. He had been dreaming. In his dreams he had seen big bears standing up and dancing with little bears. The bears then started chasing him. He ran away scared and that's what woke him up.

"I guess my guide is not going to be a bear after all." He thought in amusement once he was over his initial fear.

He noticed he was still clutching the Bible. He decided to read a bit. The pages opened to the story of Noah. Well, at least here he would find many animals; maybe it would inspire him. He read on.

Noah's family was in the ark. Mike felt a chill in his heart. Noah may have felt lonely not being with the rest of the people but at least his family was with him. The passage talked about how God remembered Noah and made the waters recede.

In the passage Noah sent out a raven to learn if the waters were completely receded and the raven travelled to and fro around the earth. Then he sent out a dove. The dove came back a first time without anything. When Noah sent the dove again after seven days, the dove returned with an olive leaf in its mouth.

Mike raised himself. He looked at the painting on the wall. There were trees and scenery, but coming closer he noticed a large bird on one of the trees. It was white. Maybe this was a dove as well.

That's when Mike knew. His guide would be the dove. The dove was a messenger. He was learning communications. He would be a messenger. A new feeling of joy started to fill him.

Andy had shown him a way to find himself. In his own way and with God's help through his word he had understood what his life was to be.

Now he could rest. He slept well without any more dreams of bears.

Wednesday March 1

Winnipeg, Cold Capital of the World?

Winnipeg is Manitoba's Capital, but it is often considered the Canadian capital of cold weather. Located in the southeast part of the province, it has the reputation of being the coldest and windiest place in Canada.

So how cold is it?

On February 5, 2007, the temperature in Winnipeg went down to −42.2°C or −44 °F, the coldest day in 31 years. With the wind creating a windchill factor, the temperature actually represented −50°C or −50°F. In such weather, it would take less than two minutes for exposed flesh to freeze and on that day hospitals treated numerous cases of frostbite and hypothermia.

In 1996, Winnipeg had an average winter weather of −28° C or −14°F. The thermometer stayed below −20°C or −4°F for 17 consecutive days and even below −30°C or −22°F for 12 consecutive days.

Although this was of course an exception, it should be noted that Winnipeg regularly has long bouts with cold spells through the winter. This period starts in October and doesn't end until late March, making winter the longest season of all, almost half of the year.

For this reason, Canadians refer to Winnipeg as "Winterpeg".Winnipeg is also known as "Windypeg".

The bone-chilling temperatures and the strong winds come from the city lying on an absolutely flat plain, unprotected by any natural barriers and through which, the cold arctic air flows from the north directly across the Canadian Shield and the Canadian Prairies.

Not your preferred winter vacation spot!

25. Breakfast

Although it wasn't completely restful, Josh did manage to get some sleep. The sun came into the bedroom through the sides of the large bay window and woke him up early. He stared at the view. The sea was calm. Waves came in slowly, tenderly caressing the blond sand at its edge. Seagulls were screening the beach looking for scraps left over by the tide or by sun seekers.

Josh had only seen pictures of such beauty. Now that it was right here where he could have enjoyed it. Somehow the intentions within these walls didn't spur him into contemplation. He longed to get out, leave this place behind, and hopefully forget he ever came here.

He sat on the side of the bed. The clock said six, his body told him noon. The six hours difference between Lakedge and his current location were making the whole situation even harder to handle. He went to the washroom, locked the door behind him, and took a shower. He got dressed in his one spare set of clothing. He certainly had no intention of staying long anyway but now his afternoon flight seemed an eternity away.

It was almost seven when a knock came at his bedroom door. He jumped, his heart suddenly racing.

"Who is it?" he asked.

On the other side the voice came. "It's Teresa. Would like to join me for breakfast?"

The tension must have sounded in his voice when he agreed because Teresa added. "Don't worry; we'll go out for breakfast just the two of us."

He opened the door. Teresa was elegantly dressed in a light blue skirt, a white blouse and a matching light white hat with a blue ribbon.

"You look like you're all ready to go out. Very nice."

"Thank you, I designed it myself. I do wear some of what I design. Not all of what I do gets modeled by Émilie."

She led the way to the courtyard where a silver Volvo was idling. Gilbert was waiting, standing near the rear passenger door. When Teresa came close, he opened it for her. Teresa went in and squeezed to the other side, leaving room for Josh. He sat beside her. Gilbert closed the door and went to take the driver's seat.

They drove out. Josh felt this was a big car for the small streets they were navigating. They didn't speak much on the way except for Teresa pointing some of the sights for which Cannes was known. Through hand gestures and body language she indicated that she didn't want to speak in front of the driver.

They didn't go very far until they found themselves in the centre of the small town. The red shingled roofs, the white walls, and the black fences were everywhere. The street names were fixed to the houses themselves; no post were needed.

Gilbert stopped in an alley and Teresa indicated to Joshua they had arrived. She asked Gilbert to wait for them. He opened the door to let them out. Teresa took Joshua by the arm. They walked on the rough cobblestone sidewalk. At the corner they turned into a small plaza lined with cafés.

Teresa had already selected which one they would go to, probably her favourite place, Josh assumed. There was a terrace but it was a bit too cold for most people to be outside at this time. One brave couple dressed with heavy sweaters was sitting there having coffee.

They walked in the café, and a waiter welcomed her with much enthusiasm. "*Madame Sparks, comme il fait bon de vous voir.*"

Josh didn't get that but it sounded like a friendly welcome.

She replied also in French and the waiter brought them to a table slightly hidden from view and away from the majority of the patrons.

"Now Josh, you must try their *croissant au chocolat*. The owner makes them herself, fresh every morning. It's just heavenly."

Josh didn't dare to disagree. A typical French breakfast sounded nice anyway, so he went along with his hostess' suggestion.

Soon they were savouring the *croissants* with a bowl of strong coffee. The food was wonderful and Josh started to relax a bit and enjoy. He wasn't on vacation but the weather – which to him felt like late spring compared to Lakedge in March – and the surroundings just had to be appreciated.

After they had finished half of the meal, Teresa started.

"I had a long talk with Émilie last night. I went to her room after we came back from the beach. She was getting ready to go out but I managed to keep her long enough to get some concessions. Of course, she was mad at you but that was just the frustrated little girl that didn't get what she wanted. That's why she was going out. She went somewhere else looking for what she didn't get from you." Josh felt awkward but didn't reply.

"So here is what I was able to get her to concede. First, I discussed how the mill workers still had unpaid salaries. I tried to scare her by explaining how the courts would expect her to compensate the employees. The court fees would certainly be expensive."

"Did it work?"

"It took a little prodding, but she agreed. She will ask the lawyer in charge of the estate to release any unpaid salaries immediately. She doesn't want anyone in Lakedge to go in so she will ask the lawyer to assign an auditor to ensure everything is done properly without interference from you or anyone else from Lakedge."

"I appreciate her trust." Josh said sarcastically.

"Well, I actually used the same card to get a little more. I also told her that customers who had agreements might invoke breach of contracts and they could go to court as well. I suggested if she let the mill workers complete any outstanding orders, she would eliminate that risk. She argued for a while on this one, mainly because she didn't want anyone to step onto her property. I finally got her to agree that the appointed auditor would make arrangements to loan any equipment the workers need to do the job and would provide them with access to the customers' list as well as the pending orders and contracts. I explained that you could probably fulfill all the orders from another location but you needed the equipment."

"How come I wasn't able to get any of this last night?" Josh asked, puzzled.

She looked at him with kindness in her eyes. "My poor Josh, you were at a disadvantage right from the start. There was no way you could obtain anything. You're from Lakedge; she hates Lakedge. You're a man; she eats men for breakfast and spits them out when she's done. You wanted something she had; she thrives on people begging her. I should have warned you ahead of time, I just didn't think she would be this cruel with you."

She paused seeing his disappointment in himself. She added "Maybe, I also misjudged you. I thought you would be like other men and give her what she wanted in exchange for what you needed for Lakedge. I'm sorry. I should have seen you were different. It's just that I've seen so many men come to this house before, giving in to anything she wanted, and I guess I thought you were just one more. I know now I was wrong." Josh didn't really know how to take this so he just thanked her for the compliment.

She took a serious look again "So going back to the negotiation, at least the workers can get a bit of money to pay their bills. You should also be able to implement any plans to fill the current orders. I guess it's something. With regards to selling the mill to Lakedge however, I think you may have to forget that option. She already asked the lawyer to examine a proposal made by this company she doesn't want anyone to identify. I guess, she's afraid you might go to them and convince them to change their minds."

Josh sighed. "I'm starting to have doubts I can convince anyone of anything."

"Please. Don't let her get to you this way. Just because she's such an egotistical person, it shouldn't reflect on your abilities. In just a few days I've known you, I've seen a lot of qualities. She does have that effect on people, but don't let it stop your resolve."

She dunked the corner of her croissant into the warm coffee. Josh noticed it was the way everyone around him was savouring the delicacy. He imitated her. It was a bit mushy but quite good.

"I'll have to call Frank and have him get in touch with this auditor. It's been a week already since the mill closed, we can't have this going on much longer." Josh shared his thoughts.

"It's still early and your flight isn't for a few hours yet. You could come back to the house and make the calls you need from there." She calculated quickly and added "It's almost two o'clock in the afternoon in Lakedge. You should make the calls before the end of the day there."

He agreed. She signalled the waiter who came to pick up the empty dishes as she asked for the bill. He came back a minute later and she paid him in cash. They headed back for the car. As they came closer, Gilbert came out of a nearby pub just in time to open the car door for them.

Back at the mansion, Josh called Frank. He had been busy organising a recruitment centre for those who would want to work at the Woodland Mills site. They were still waiting for the final confirmation from the VP but Frank was sure he would agree. With the new information Josh was providing, he knew it was in the bag.

Frank would make a few calls to find out who this auditor was and start making arrangements with him or her to implement their plans. For the first time in weeks, there was an air of optimism in their discussion.

When they were done, Josh went down with his suitcase. He hoped not to encounter Émilie. Teresa was waiting in the living room and saw him come down the steps.

"Come down, Josh. Émilie is still in her room. She went out last night and came back late. I don't expect her to come out for a while."

"Well, I guess there's nothing more I can do here. I'll wait at the airport for my flight. I like to be early anyway. You never know with Customs."

She smiled. "Let me call you a taxi."

They talked a little more about personal things. The taxi arrived and she saw him off. A few hours later he was on his way back home.

26. Surveillance

Even in March, there was at least five degrees difference in the temperature on the Riviera compared to that of Paris. In his heavy suit, all hooked up with shirt and tie, *Lieutenant* Olivier Leroy, in a black surveillance car was feeling the difference.

He was staking out this particular location from which they now were fairly certain the pictures used to blackmail Henri Montelierre were taken. A series of events over the last week had led them to this conclusion.

First they tried the bait. Leroy found the earlier envelope sent by the blackmailer and it gave instructions as to how the delivery was to be made. They placed the money but nobody showed up. They supposed they had missed the deadline or the news of Montelierre's death had gone out quickly. It seemed evident that the blackmailer had been scared by something. It also meant that the culprit would become more difficult to bring out.

In the meantime the lab had been busy. They had scanned every picture at a high-resolution level then digitally recomposed the woman's face from the few parts of it they managed to extract from the pictures. In the process it seemed some other parts of the woman's body had been reconstructed as well, but these weren't included in the investigation file.

With a good composite picture in hand, a good idea of the date of the conference when she had met Montelierre, and a postal origin for the letters to confirm it, Leroy went to Nice for the next stage of the operation. He spoke with many of the people that attended the conference and showed around the pictures of both Montelierre and the mystery woman. Eventually, someone identified her. It was Émilie De L'étincelle a.k.a. Joy Sparks.

They found a lot about her background as a popular fashion model. Originally from Canada, she now resided in Cannes. She had been on the cover of many fashion magazines, paraded at many fashion shows all over Europe, and was a frequent guest at salons and conferences. They assumed she had met Montelierre at one such event.

Now with a name and an address, Leroy was tasked with investigating the place to try and find more clues. *Commandant* Dumont wanted him to take a few days to analyse all the ins and outs of the place before they would take any action.

If the woman was in those pictures, it most likely meant that someone else was taking the picture. They had to be careful not to spook her or any accomplice. She may also be an innocent victim and that could blow their whole case. If she denied the blackmail, they had no proof on her. They did get partial prints on some of the photographs but nothing came up in the registry. If the prints weren't hers, they would be back to square one.

Dumont wanted to know who else lived there and how often gentlemen callers came to the home to get an indication of what was going on. Leroy would need to be accompanied by a local officer who might know more about this.

So together in the car – Leroy in suit and tie, Simonneau in short sleeves and open collar – they watched. Another team came to provide relief so they could go eat, wash up, and get a few hours of sleep between each watch. Leroy enjoyed the company of his new partner, Bernard Simonneau. He was a local policeman from the gendarmerie, jovial, with a deluge of stories filled with humour. The longer they kept each other company in the car, the more Leroy developed Simonneau's typical southern French accent.

They quickly noticed men driving up the alley to see Joy almost every day. They took pictures, hoping to identify someone later. The men would arrive late in the afternoon and leave the next morning.

On the first couple of occasions, Leroy had gone around the house to the side facing the beach. From there he had taken more photos. It had been an awkward adventure, being on the beach in a suit and leather shoes, taking pictures of a house while everyone else around was sporting bathing suit. In the end, he didn't get much. He couldn't get close enough to see anything in the house and nothing suspicious stood out. He looked enough out of place to have people start questioning, so he gave up on that option.

They also identified the servants. A woman usually wearing an apron, which they had to assume was the cook, and a man they supposed was the valet. They took a multitude of pictures of them as well. On one occasion they saw the woman in the picture in the back seat of the car driven by the valet.

They sent the pictures back to Paris to start the identification process of the visitors. They had nothing on the servants, but they did identify a few of the men. All of them were prominent executives from various important firms. Dumont kept a record for each one. If nothing else came up, he may be obligated to confront some of them and maybe even use one or two to set a trap.

The pattern emerged. This woman had somehow attracted the attention of all these men and restrained them into the harness that either by herself or with an accomplice had led to Montelierre's demise.

At one point, another woman had arrived in a taxi with a man they hadn't seen yet. More pictures were taken and the mystery seemed to amplify. This morning, both of them left the house in the car driven by the valet.

The visitors left for a couple of hours, came back, then another half hour later a taxi pulled up and the man left in it. The woman hadn't come out yet. Since Simonneau would go into all sorts of theories every time someone went in or out of the home, many new theories emerged from this visit.

Leroy called Dumont to give more information but they knew they would most likely be investigating for another few days, unless something happened to open new avenues.

A few hours later, a car came out of the driveway with the valet at the wheel. He was alone in the car. Leroy didn't like this; he suspected something. He called for the relief team to take over the watch and told Simonneau to follow the car. They drove for twenty minutes eventually reaching Nice. The car zigzagged through some of the streets and stopped in front of a post office.

Leroy and Simonneau parked a few cars behind him. Simonneau, being less conspicuous, went into the store and started looking at displays of postcards while keeping an eye on the valet. The man gave an envelope, paid the postage fee and left. Immediately, Simonneau flashed his police badge and asked the clerk to see the envelope. He noted the address and gave it back to the clerk. He rushed back to the car and they followed the valet again all the way to Cannes.

Leroy asked Simonneau. "So, where was that envelope going to?"

Simonneau got his notes out. "It is going to someone in Canada, a place called Lakedge."

Leroy remembered the name. "It's *Mademoiselle* De L'Étincelle's town of origin."

"I wonder what's in it."

"I think I have a general idea." Leroy said, pensive.

27. Spy

"Hi Jeff. You here to register?" The young woman addressed him in a cheery mood.

He wasn't quite sure what he was there for. He received a call explaining how there were some arrangements being made to get some work for the employees of the mill. He was told to show up at the Legion Hall to find out more.

He looked at the woman. He knew her; she was one of the office workers from the Sparks Mill. He didn't really know what she did but he recognised her. She seemed to know him well, he didn't really understand why. Then it dawned on him. She was one of the clerks in the personnel division.

"Yeah, I guess I am. What do I have to do?"

She kept on in the same jolly expression. "I just have to put your name on the list and then you go and sit over there. Jim will come out when most of the people are here to explain what's going to happen."

"Oh. Okay then." He noticed some of the guys he usually worked with and went to sit with them. Nobody seemed to know much more than him. They discussed the difficulties they had been experiencing in the last week, their prospect, the decisions some of the other workers had already made, which included leaving Lakedge altogether. None of it was very optimistic but they were all hoping tonight would change some of their outlook.

Finally, Jim Stone arrived. With him were Frank Ellis and a man he had never seen. Once he had taken off his heavy parka, Jeff noticed the man wore a white shirt, a black tie, a black suit and was carrying a briefcase.

He had greyish hair and strong glasses with a wide black frame. He looked like a mix between a lawyer and an undertaker.

Together, the trio went to the front of the room, where a table had been set up with three chairs behind it. They sat, with Jim in the middle and Frank to his right.

"All right guys." Jim started. Then he looked at the crowd and noticed he had just made a mistake. "Oh, sorry. And gals I should say."

There were only five women there but they had just as much right to attend this meeting as the others.

"Everybody knows Frank here, but I want to introduce Mr. Flagstone." Everybody started mumbling. Nobody had ever seen this man and they all wondered why he was there. Their first impression wasn't very good. The man looked stern. They feared he would be more of a bearer of bad news than anything else.

Jim raised his voice a bit to go over the droning of the group. "Mr. Flagstone is an auditor. He is here to help us arrange to provide some work for the workers of the mill."

The mumbling continued with a different pitch. Anticipation seemed to be rising.

"Yes, that's right. With the help of Mr. Flagstone and with Frank here, we are trying to get you some work. Frank will give you the details."

Frank smiled. "Okay. The great news is that Josh Stuart managed to get an agreement from the new owner of the mill to release your pay for the month of February." A shout of approval turned into applause and cheers. "Yes, that's right. All unpaid salaries will be released and cheques will be cut by the end of the day tomorrow. That's one of the reasons Mr. Flagstone is here."

More cheers and yells. This Flagstone guy was starting to sound better. Jim took over. "The other bit of good news is that we have developed a plan with the help of Frank and Mr. Flagstone to take care of some of the orders from our regular customers. We want to explain to you how the plan works and what it means for you."

Each in turn, Jim and Frank explained the plan. Mr. Flagstone remained silent and stoic. There were more applauses but he was unaltered by any of them.

Jeff listened and participated in the ovations. He stayed through the question period and stuck around after the meeting itself was over, laughing and kidding with the rest of the mill employees.

It dawned on him when he walked out. On the way to his truck he reached for his keys in his pocket and found the cell phone Bernie had given him. The touch under his fingers startled him. He quickly sat in the truck, now unsure of his next move.

The meeting had given him hope for the first time since this whole thing started. The pact he made with Bernie might actually jeopardise the whole plan. On the other hand, the plan was only a temporary solution. If things failed, he would be back to where he started. Bernie's money was real. He had received a first payment and was promised more.

He also thought about the guys. If anyone found out he did something to mess their plan, they would all turn on him. That money however would get him the new snowmobile he had been wanting for a long time.

Maybe Bernie would be able to help. He might understand and still give him money for the information but let the guys follow the plan as they discussed it. It can't hurt just to tell Bernie about it. After all, it will become general knowledge soon enough. Jeff felt better. He drove away from the Legion parking. He didn't want anyone to overhear his phone conversation. When he was far enough away and in a more deserted area, he stopped and dialled Bernie.

He told him about Woodland Mills, how they would let them do an evening shift after their normal operating hours. He explained how they would retrieve all the equipment they needed from the Sparks Mill with the supervision of the auditor and use it on the Woodland Mills property. He gave him the details about how they would rent lighting equipment to make sure everyone could work safely even at night. He repeated how Jim would obtain the orders from the regular Sparks Mill customers so they could try to catch up and fill them all.

Bernie was happy to hear all of this. He congratulated Jeff on his excellent work. He said he would have enough for a snowmobile very quickly if he kept this up. In fact, he told him, he would put a couple of hundred dollars in an envelope with his name and drop it at Trucker's Corner in a couple of days. Then he said something Jeff didn't want to hear.

"Are you there? Jeff… I can't hear you. Did we get cut off?"

"No…I'm… I'm here. You can't ask me to do that." Jeff said. Suddenly all his usual bravado had left him.

"What? I'm not asking you to commit murder. I just said you needed to slow them down. That's all. You need to do something to stop the plan for a while until my employer and I can come up with something else. Don't you understand that?"

"Yeah, I heard you. I just can't do it." Jeff replied.

"Oh, I get it. You're trying to get me for more money. Very well, what will it be? I knew you were smart, but not that smart. How much?"

"No…no…" then Jeff stopped. He really wanted that snowmobile. He would never see enough money even working odd hours and overtime. It would take him years for sure. He hesitated "Well…how much do you think this is worth?"

"What's it worth? It could be worth a whole lot, my friend. Why don't we start with a couple of thousand? I'll leave an extra five hundred in the envelope to seal the deal, the rest once the job is complete. What do you say?" Bernie seemed happy and teasing.

"I…two thousand dollars. In cash?"

"In cash"

"Eh… I guess it's good. I… I'll do it."

"Great. I knew you weren't a sissy." Bernie was laughing.

Jeff laughed along although not as sincerely. "Yeah." Then he stopped. "So how do I do this?"

"What do you mean?"

"I mean, how do I stop the plan?" Jeff's voice was concerned again.

"Well, Jeff, you're a smart guy. I'll let you figure it out. I know you'll come up with something, right?"

"Yes, I guess, I will." Jeff said, more unsure than ever.

"Good. So I'll talk to you later." Bernie said indicating he was done.

"Yeah, sure. Later."

He was about to press the end button when Bernie almost yelled out. "Oh Jeff! Wait!"

"What?" Jeff said.

"You remember now. You don't know me and we never had this conversation. Right?"

"Oh, right."

"Good. Bye Jeff. Good luck now." Bernie said and hung up.

"Yeah, bye. Thanks." Bernie never heard his last words. He closed the phone and sat there. He wished he were smarter. He knew he wasn't as smart as Bernie thought he was. Otherwise he would have come up with a plan already. Doubts started gnawing at him. Maybe he shouldn't have accepted the deal. Then the vision of the snowmobile came back. He just had to come up with something. Maybe a drink would help. He headed for Trucker's Corner.

28. Hockey

Robert had agreed to go out with Jasmine that evening only on the condition that he would choose the place. She just wanted to change his mind; to get him out of the house. She was starting to find his constant grumbling, his pet peeves, his ranting against the system somewhat annoying. She felt bad for Robert yet she couldn't really stop her life just because his had been put on hold for a while. She was sure he would eventually find something to keep him busy. Robert's obvious depression was what triggered Jasmine's suggestion to have a night out. He decided it was time enough for Jasmine to learn about sports. In particular, she had to learn about hockey. After all, this was Canada. If Jasmine wanted to become a true Canadian, she had to learn about hockey.

So they ended up at the Winnipeg MTS Centre where they obtained tickets to see the Manitoba Moose play against the Houston Aeros. On their way there, Robert had explained some of the rudiments of the game. They first went to the concession stand. To watch a hockey game you had to have a beer and probably a hot dog; it was part of the tradition just as popcorn went with movies.

They found their seats, third level up, directly in front of the centre line. Robert had chosen that spot to have a good view from all angles. It was a little costly but well worth it.

This wasn't major league NHL hockey; it was the American League. Still they were professional hockey players and Robert enjoyed it.

Jasmine was full of questions. At first she was a bit appalled at the way the players would use body checks and push each other into the boards. She had seen soccer games back home but physical contact in these games was usually accidental and infrequent. The whistle seemed to blow very often and she never knew why. The puck went over the blue line and players were in the other zone; a whistle blew. The goalie caught the puck; a whistle blew. Someone hit someone else a bit hard; a whistle blew. She felt there were a lot of interruptions in this game, in fact, almost more interruptions than game. Every time the whistle blew it would take them almost two minutes to get back into the game.

After a while she started to get the hang of it, and then a loud siren rang. She was startled.

"What's happening? Is it the fire alarm?" she asked. In Afghanistan, sirens usually spelled trouble.

Robert laughed. "No silly, it's the end of the first period. It's the intermission."

As he said it, he got up. "I'm going for another beer. You want anything?"

"No thanks. I'm fine." She replied. This game seemed to be as much about food and refreshments as it was about sports.

It took a while. Jasmine regretted to have let him go by himself. His hands weren't healed yet and the physiotherapy, although helpful, hadn't really brought a lot of changes yet. He may be struggling with the things he was trying to bring back. On the other hand, she didn't want to leave her seat in case she got lost.

A couple of guys sitting next to her started chatting. They asked her if it was her first time here. Then they got into a discussion about sport, about her country, about what she thought of Canada, how she handled the cold, and even more. Jasmine was getting a bit worried that Robert wasn't back yet.

Finally, with the second period already underway, he arrived, his hands full with another beer and another hot-dog.

"Guess what? I got offered a job." he said.

"You were? What is it?" she asked.

"Well I have to tell you the whole story." He sat down and started munching as he talked. "I was in line at the bar when two guys started arguing about twenty feet from me. At first, I tried to ignore them, but they started getting very loud. Then one of them punched the other. That's when I jumped in. I took on the guy who gave the first punch; the other one was just trying to duck. I restrained him, even though it hurt because of my hands, but I managed and I went on to talk to him and try to calm him down. He wasn't letting go so I had to put him down on the floor and hold him there. The security guards arrived and they took over but they asked me to come with them to the office to help with the report, so I did."

He took a gulp of the beer to down some of the food.

"When we got to the office, I saw the supervisor who is a guy I used to know. He is retired from the force and works here in charge of the security guards. When we were finished with the report, he offered to buy me a beer and we started talking. I told him I was just retired and that's when he offered me a job. He said they always need good people who know the law and aren't scared to take a few punches."

Jasmine was listening. She was about to say something when the crowd roared. The local team had just scored. Robert had seen some of the play from the corner of his eyes but not quite enough to get up with the rest. He did cheer a bit, and then sat down again.

Jasmine tried again. "So what did you say?"

"I told him I would think about it."

"Think about it? Robert, what's to think about? This will give you something to do, a bit more money, people to see."

"Well, I am tempted. I would get to see a lot of hockey games with this job, but... I don't know. It's quite a drop to go from homicide detective to security guard. I know a lot of people, I'm not sure what they would think seeing me in a security guard uniform. It's not quite as interesting as what I'm used to."

She understood his dilemma but she insisted. He needed something to keep him occupied. She would rather have him rant with these people than with her. Her parents had also mentioned that they weren't really comfortable with him around. It messed up their routine.

He turned back to the game and tried to concentrate on the play but she asked him again. He got a little unnerved by her persistence. "I said, I'd think about it. Please stop asking. I came here to have a good time watching a game." She dropped the subject.

When the game was over, they got out. She decided to drive since Robert had drunk about five glasses of beer during the whole time. They talked a bit about the game and skating. Jasmine said she found the ability of these people on skates quite amazing. Robert told her that he had been on skates ever since the age of four. Back when he was young and until he finished high school he had played hockey. Then he got an idea.

"I know a place where they rent skates. It's near an outdoor rink. You have to come and try this. You will never call yourself Canadian until you've skated."

She complained. "Robert, are you crazy. It's already late. I work tomorrow, don't you remember?"

"Ah, come on. It's not that bad. You can always call in sick or go in late. You can say your alarm didn't ring."

"I can't do that. It's lying." She was offended by his suggestion.

"You've never lied before, I suppose?" He said with a gentle smile.

"I'm not saying I never did, but I try not to lie."

"All right, I'll tell you what. If you come with me to learn to skate, I will take that security job. What do you say?" he looked at her with a wide smile, sure she couldn't say no.

She didn't like it. "This is blackmail, you should know that. What kind of a policeman are you, using this kind of tactic?"

He kept smiling without a word. "All right. Where is this place?" she said, giving up.

She followed his instructions and soon they were renting two pairs of skates. Robert put his skates on quickly then helped Jasmine with hers. She was shivering on top of feeling unbalanced. He almost carried her to the ice surface then started slowly helping her to skate. She kept her arms outstretched expecting to fall any second. She stood there when he let go and refused to move. So he pushed her gently to start her out. She shrieked and kept wobbling her arms as if trying to fly.

Robert laughed wholeheartedly. The beer and the sight of his wife in such an amusing situation helped bring back a sense of happiness he hadn't felt in quite a long time.

She fell a few times; he helped her up. He went around showing off his own skills on skates while she shrieked and yelped at every slight move of her body. The cold eventually got a hold of her.

"Robert, that's enough. I can't feel my toes anymore and I think my nose is ready to fall off. Let's go."

He agreed and helped her out of her skates.

Back in the car, she started to relax. She warmed herself up, and then admitted. "I have to say this was a bit fun. Thanks."

"Now, you can call yourself a Canadian."

"It didn't say anything about this in the immigration papers, you know."

"Well, that's a mistake. I'll have to call Immigration Canada on it."

They both laughed and headed home. Robert's mood was better. The whole evening had been worth it, although some of Jasmine's muscles already disagreed. She knew that she would regret it when she would get up the next day, but for now she relished Robert's presence and their relationship.

Friday March 3

Town protests Conglomerate Forest Products Closing of Perygonia Mill *Reuters News*

Three months after Conglomerate Forest Products acquired the Perygonia mill, the company announced yesterday it will cease operations at the mill April 1st. Most will be relocated around the country to other mills held by Conglomerate.

For the Town of Perygonia, this represents a loss of close to 300 jobs. Being the largest industry for this small town of 8,000 people, the impact on the local economy is foreseen as a disaster.

A large crowd gathered Thursday in front of the gate to the mill with placards protesting the closing. Mayor John Singleton himself attended the rally. "This despicable manoeuvre by a large company is devastating for us." Singleton said. "We need to raise the attention of the provincial and federal government to this action. We are urging them to stop this closure by enabling a law to protect small municipalities from the impacts of such mergers and acquisitions."

The citizens are determined to block all vehicles entering the compound until they have been heard. Local police are standing by, but they are taking no action to prevent the protest from going on.

A company spokesperson for Conglomerate was reached late Thursday afternoon and issued a statement indicating that the company will relocate workers from Perygonia to other mills. Richard Hemmings, the senior Communications director for Conglomerate said. "Our goal is to solidify the enterprise to make it more competitive in this very aggressive market. However, we will do everything we can to ensure that none of the present personnel of the Perygonia mill will lose employment."

This statement does nothing to comfort Mayor Singleton who now sees it not only as a loss of a major employer but an additional loss of 300 taxpayers for the municipality.

29. Accident

Jeff racked his brains. How could he do his? He thought of many possibilities but there were flaws in every one of them. He had watched a lot of CSI episodes and he could always find a way that someone would nail him if he did it.

He thought he could sabotage the bus that would bring the workers to the other mill. If he cut the brake line then the brakes wouldn't work and the bus would have an accident. The problem was that he had to know which school bus they would be using in advance, and then have access to it in a place where nobody would see him. If he cut the line at the wrong place all the brake fluid would leak and the driver would be alone in the bus when the brakes failed. On the other hand, he didn't mind causing an accident but he wasn't a murderer. If someone on the bus died from this accident, police would investigate and he could be charged for murder, and rot in jail.

At one point, the day before, he felt he had his chance. Jim Stone asked a group of workers including Jeff to meet at the mill. They went into the compound accompanied by Frank Ellis and the auditor, Mr. Flagstone. That's when Jeff thought he could probably cut one of the main belts on the debarker they said they would try to transport over to the other mill. That would delay the operation for a while during the repair time.

When he tried, he found he was never alone. The auditor was always watching. He seemed to have eyes everywhere. Jeff never had an instant to reach the machine, let alone the belt. In the end, he gave up. There would have to be another way. They packed up a lot of the small equipment and identified three larger pieces that would need to be transported by specialised trucks.

So Jeff went back home, still trying to figure out how he would earn his two thousand dollars.

He couldn't access any equipment at this end, he couldn't stop the people from going to work at the Woodland Mill, and he wasn't really sure he could stop the transportation of the equipment either. He would have to wait until they actually got to the other end.

Today, he was on his way to Woodland Mill. He didn't board the bus. He pretended he had an urgent errand to run and would meet them at the site. Actually, he wanted to be sure he had a means of transportation to be able to scout the area where they were going. He had never seen the Woodland Mill.

He followed his map trying to notice anything on the way that could inspire him to create a diversion or cause a slowdown of any kind. The task for today was to move and re-install the equipment at the mill. He was part of the team because of his mechanical skills. He knew those machines very well and had been maintaining them for a long time.

As he drove closer to the site, he noticed that the road narrowed. Here and there he passed a few houses and cottages but they were sparse, separated from each other with large areas of trees and rocks. The road had been ploughed and there were indications of some traffic but he suspected it was mainly for the mill operation. He was alone on the road for a long stretch, not even passing vehicles from the oncoming lane. On one side there were poles with wires and a bit of an escarpment rising from the other side.

Then he passed a transformer station. It was one of those hydro stations where power is fed to reduce the high voltage to a level acceptable for normal household or regular industrial use. From the back of it, he could see the huge feed lines going out through a path in the woods that was gradually filling up with new deciduous trees.

That's when his plan started developing. He felt this would probably be his best chance at the two thousand dollars.

He mulled it over while driving on. He would have to wait for nightfall, probably after the end of the shift. If he could disable the transformer station in a manner that it would take a few days to recover, he would slow down the operations. It might be enough for his new employer to finish what they were working on.

He arrived at the mill and after asking a few people for directions was finally able to hook up with the Sparks Mill team. Jim assigned him to work on the installation of one of the pieces of equipment they had just unloaded. He had to work with a couple of others to ground it properly, stabilise it, oil it, and then run a few tests. It took them all afternoon to accomplish this and repeat it on the two other machines. By the time they were finished, evening was well underway. They had installed special floodlights in various areas to try and provide as much light as possible to ease the installation process.

When the work was complete, Jim gave instructions to go back on the bus and head home. Jeff returned to his truck. He let the bus go so it would be well ahead of him. He drove slowly, way behind, until he couldn't see the vehicle's red lights anymore. He went bit by bit along the road, squinting not to miss the transformer station along the way. A number of times, he thought he had gone too far. He regretted not having measured the distance to the mill on his way there. Apparently, he wasn't a true criminal yet.

Then he saw it. Nobody was in sight. He stopped along the road hoping no vehicles would come by. He realised he was vulnerable so he had to act quickly. He reached in the back of the pick-up for his tools. In there were a bolt cutter and a flashlight. He picked them up and in a few seconds had popped the lock on the gate to the transformer.

He walked in and looked around. The heavy snow made walking a challenge. He saw the signs: "*danger*", "*high voltage*", and "*no trespassing*". He ignored them and went to the point where the main cables hooked up to the station. This was his target.

He knew there would be a lot of dead wood lying around near the tree line. He went out of the small compound and started collecting branches. When he had enough to make a good pile he brought them in and packed them in front of the connecting section of the transformer. He went back to the truck. He always carried a spare canister of gasoline. In these parts, you never wanted to run out. You could be days without anyone coming to find you.

He took the gasoline tank but had to leave the flashlight behind. It was too heavy and with the deep snow, too hard to travel with both at once. The darkness shrouded him but his eyes quickly got used to it. With the glow from the stars reflecting off the snow he was able to feel his way around. He struggled to reach his woodpile.

He splashed the gasoline on the wood. He was reaching for his matches when it dawned on him that if this thing blew up, he might not be able to reach his truck fast enough. He had no real idea how much impact this would have. So he carried the empty gasoline tank back to the truck, put away the bolt cutters and kept only his flashlight to return to the pile. By now he had created a bit of a path for himself and he was able to return much more quickly by walking in the footsteps from his previous trips. For an instant, he remembered the CSI episodes and wanted to erase his traces, but he was too pressed for time and too nervous. He just wanted to get the job finished and leave as soon as possible.

He took out a lighter and this time ignited the pile. The gasoline was quick to react and spread to the whole pile, almost instantly creating a bonfire. Jeff started running back toward his truck. He didn't look back, not wanting to trip. He went quickly although he would have liked to have even more speed. The snow was hindering his running and he heard the crackle at his back seemingly gaining momentum.

He finally reached the gate and the road. He went into the cab, threw the flashlight on the seat and started the ignition. Just as he did he heard the sound. He looked up and saw a huge fireball. The explosion that followed was brief and caused the truck to rock a bit. Jeff figured the sound had probably carried for miles around. The night was now as bright as day at least in the area of the transformer.

He decided not to stay much longer. He drove for a short distance on his way back to Lakedge. He started imagining what was going to happen. He reached a few houses and noticed there were no lights anywhere. He couldn't be sure if it was normal. It was late and people might already be in bed. It seemed to him however that the electricity had been cut off for these people.

He kept going and reached a village. There was a gas station on the side of the main road. It seemed closed. He stopped anyway. As he stepped out of the truck, an older man came out.

"Sorry, son. I got no power, so I can't fill you up."

Jeff feigned surprise. "Oh, what happened?"

"Don't really know. Power just went off about ten minutes ago. It happens here once in a while but we had been pretty lucky recently. It might just be a racoon. You know the pesky critters get into the transformers and get fried trying to chew the wires. Then it takes a few hours before we get the power back."

"So what happens now?" Jeff seemed genuinely interested.

"Well, the utility company will soon find out something is wrong on the grid and send a crew to look into it. It may take them a little while to locate the exact site then once they have it, they will call back for a crew to fix it."

"Oh, I see. Well, I guess, I'll be on my way then."

"Right. See ya. I hope you have enough gas to get to the next station."

Jeff was satisfied. The outage was fairly large and it would take some time to have the power back. Even if the crews did locate this quickly, the damage was most likely going to be extensive enough to translate into a number of days before they recovered.

He still had doubts. What if the mill had a backup generator? He hadn't noticed any while he was there but he didn't have much of a chance to look around. The uncertainty started gnawing at him. He had to be sure. He turned around and headed back towards the mill.

He slowed down when he came closer to the transformer. In the distance he could see how the fire was now only a glow. The woodpile seemed to still be burning but had lost most of its intensity. He couldn't really tell the extent of the damage and didn't dare stop to check. He went by.

He continued to drive until he reached the mill. There were no lights there either. When they had left, the floodlights had been turned off, but a few security and emergency lights were on. Now everything was pitch black. He was happy. His plan had worked. He headed back.

He reached the transformer station again and saw headlights. A truck was there. He slowed down a bit and saw that it was a utility truck. A man was standing outside with a portable radio in his hands. His curiosity was too strong so Jeff stopped a little further away.

He walked to the hydro repairman who was discussing the situation on the radio. Jeff saluted him but received only a wave of acknowledgement in return.

The radio conversation went on for a short time, and then the man hooked it back on his belt.

"Hi." Jeff said. "Need any help?"

"Nah. Thanks. There's not much we can do at this time. We have to wait for police. This is vandalism and police will have to make a report. I'm going to be here for the rest of the night most likely."

"What happened?" Jeff feigned interest.

"Well, someone had a little bonfire behind the main transformer. This is the main feed for the power grid for miles around. We've had something similar once before. The police told us later it was a diversion so a bunch of criminals could break into many places without fear of burglar alarms."

"That's not good. So how long is it going to take to get the power back?"

"It depends in part on how long the police will take for their investigation. If they go quickly at this, we can start work as soon as the crews arrive. At best, we are talking about a couple of days. If the weather holds, that is. With bad weather, we could be out for a week."

Jeff started praying internally for a snowstorm or something similar.

"Well, I guess I'm of no use here. I'll be on my way." he said.

"Right, thanks anyway." The man replied.

Jeff left the area somewhat satisfied. He would have to come back tomorrow to see if they had started repairs yet but for now, the two thousand dollars seemed a lot closer.

He drove on for a few kilometres then decided it was time to call in to Bernie. Bernie was pleased with the news.

30. Backroom deals

Peter Cohen was worried. He had finally managed to pull enough strings to get a name: Timbergreen Wood Products. He'd heard the name before and was now trying to trace the person within the organisation that had made the offer to the real estate broker.

After being transferred a few times, he heard a man's voice on the line.

"Yes, how may I help you?"

Pete needed to be smart about this. His career, his bank, in fact maybe even the whole town depended on this call.

"Am I speaking to the person who made the offer to buy back the Sparks Mill in Lakedge?" he asked already knowing the answer.

"Maybe, who's asking?" the man said.

"Sir, my name is Peter Cohen. I am the manager of the only bank located in Lakedge. I am calling because I was able to find out that your company has made a bid to acquire the Sparks Mill. Is that correct?"

"Well, the amount of the bid is confidential, but the list of bidders isn't so I guess it would be futile to deny. Yes, Timbergreen put in a bid to acquire the Sparks Mill. Now, what would be your interest in this?"

Peter expected this. "My interest isn't really what is important here. I think what can be of importance is how our respective organisations can work together for mutual benefit."

He paused to gauge the interest at the other end. "I'm listening."

"Good." Peter thought, then speaking slowly containing himself not to show eagerness or apprehension. "The way I understand it, you will become the new owners of the mill. As we are the only financial institution around, we are of course, associated with everybody. We have all of Lakedge's financial details, we own all the mortgages and all the loans." He stopped again.

"And you believe this might be useful for us?" The voice at the other end prodded.

"I think it could. On the other hand, the bank will want to see some benefit as well."

"What do you propose, Mr... Sorry, what was your name again?"

"Cohen. But you can call me Pete."

"Very well, Pete. I'm Sam, by the way. What do you have in mind?"

Pete was playing the game. You never showed all your cards at once. You had to make the other player *want* to see them first. You always let the player ask for more.

"I'm sure this purchase of yours is going to require a major investment which means borrowing money. Since you will be moving to our parts, I thought you may want to obtain some of this loan directly from here. I am authorised to give you a mortgage on the property at an extremely low rate for the next fifteen years."

That was only the first card, but he had to drop something on the table to get the game started.

"Pete." The man said his name to gather his thoughts. "Timbergreen has mills all over the country. We already deal with a banking institution that has been providing us with all the mortgages we need at some very good rates. Why would we want to change institutions? Do you really think you can compete with what we have?"

Pete knew this would be part of the negotiation. "I can better any rate that your current institution offers by at least 1%. That's my promise."

"What if I told you such a proposal would bring you under the current prime rate, Pete? Wouldn't you stand to lose a lot of money with such an offer?" The man sounded sarcastic.

"Well, first I doubt that you have such a rate. Secondly, even if you did, the bank has other ways of getting money back to compensate from any losses we would make on this deal."

"Ah, I see. You would bring in conditions that would have us tied so we would have to pay extras in other places."

"Maybe not extras." Pete was cautious. "I would speak more of exclusivity."

"Do you have examples of what you are intending to hold exclusively?"

"For starters, we would want to manage the payroll directly. There would be a competitive fee for this service but it would mean that all the transaction for salaries and benefits would be going through our bank and garnering some interest in the process." That was just a small card to keep the game rolling. The opponent didn't have to give away anything significant and Pete gained a small advantage.

"That might be arranged. I have a feeling you have more ideas."

Pete chuckled gently. "I see you can read minds."

The man laughed. "I may work for Timbergreen, but I'm not green at this kind of discussion. I've had my share of negotiations."

"Yes, I figured you did. Which makes this even more interesting."

Pete knew flattery wasn't going to win the game, but it could ease the tension a bit. He continued with his next card.

"We would also want to manage your credit transactions, and probably your accounts receivable."

"That might be a bit more difficult since we already have contracts with another banking institution for these." Sam wasn't giving an inch to help Pete.

"Ah yes. However, this is a new line of business. Even though Sparks Mill would become part of the Timbergreen family, it could remain as a subsidiary, retain its original name, and be managed independently of the mother company. This would leave the freedom to have transactions managed through a separate banking institution." Pete had thought of this in advance and done some research. He knew he had to add an additional card here to sell the idea. "The way I see it, Sparks Mill already has a well established customer base, and a good, if not great, reputation. Maintaining the name Sparks Mill would mean a seamless transition when it comes to the customers. It would benefit Timbergreen and allow us to have this agreement."

There was silence at the other end for a moment. Pete still didn't have what he wanted. He kept his other cards but they depended very much on what his opponent would drop this time.

"You may have a point there, Pete. Somehow, though, I get the feeling that you are looking for something else."

A lump came in Pete's throat. He was dealing with an astute player; the game may just have gotten more complicated. "What do you mean?"

The man laughed softly. "I mean Pete, everything you've given me so far is really peanuts. You can't make a bundle on payroll and on credit management. You stand to lose on the mortgage. So I am asking myself, why would this bank really want us to deal with them? I think I may have an answer for this. Tell me if I am right, Pete. If we buy the mill and we run it differently from what you have been doing with Sparks, you will lose a lot of business. More importantly, if we decide not to run the mill, all of these mortgages and loans you referred to earlier will then go into default and you will be forced to foreclose on them. With no industry in the area, who will want to buy back the homes? The answer is simple: nobody. So, in the end, your bank will be left owning a ghost town. Did I get this right?"

Pete knew he was right but needed to push this to the limit to get the final play.

"You may be right. I wonder however, why would you even consider buying a mill and not run it. You stand to lose a lot of money. I'm sure buying this place will not be cheap. If there is nothing in return, why buy it in the first place?"

"I'm sure you know the answer to that question. You probably did your research before calling me. If you did, you already know that Sparks is our main competitor. If we get rid of Sparks altogether, we stand to regain every penny we invest in buying the place within a couple of years at the most."

Pete felt he almost had an answer to his main question. "Sam, do you really think this is a good idea? You may get your money back eventually, but in the meantime you will have created, as you said, a ghost town. That's not very good for your reputation, is it?"

Sam laughed again. "Our reputation is the least of our worries. When contractors buy wood to build houses, they don't check the reputation of the supplier, they only want to get the best price for the best quality. That's why we want to close Sparks. We currently have the best prices, but Sparks keeps beating us on the quality. Without Sparks around, we will have the best of everything to offer, regardless of our reputation."

Pete had it. The man had confessed. He had revealed his true intention. He had definitely said they would close the mill. With this in hand, Pete would be ready for the next stage of his plan.

"I guess you have me at a loss there, Sam" Pete said seemingly defeated. "Is there any way I can convince you to change your mind? Could we still be considered for this mortgage? We could offer you 1% over prime. Would that be competitive enough to what you already have?"

"I have to admire your persistence. You are a good negotiator. The simple truth is that we want to have as little as possible to do with Lakedge. Even if you were to offer us the moon, we would still refuse. We have a good relationship with our existing bank and we will maintain it. I hope you understand."

Pete sighed. "I do. I was just trying my best."

"I understand. Thanks for the offer."

"Thank you for taking the time to listen."

"You are welcome. Bye for now." He was about to hang up when he added. "Oh and Pete?"

"Yes?"

"I strongly suggest you find another job and move out of Lakedge… quickly."

"I guess so. Thanks for the tip." They hung up.

31. Package

Lindsey came back from the post office. She called out to Josh as soon as she passed the door. There was much anticipation in her voice.

"Josh, you got a package in the mail! It's marked *private and confidential* and it has a stamp from France." Josh came up the stairs from his basement office.

"From France? It must be from Teresa. I wonder what she is sending me. I would have thought it would have been sent to my office."

Josh took the package, a large brown envelope with only his address and the stamp; no return address. He opened it delicately. He peeked in. There were only what seemed to be a few small documents so he reached in and pulled them out. They were photographs.

He started looking at them with Lindsey right beside him. The pictures were fair quality, a bit grainy and black and white. Immediately Josh recognised Émilie's silhouette. The top picture was of the both of them in Émilie's living room that evening when they were discussing the future of the mill. He flipped to the next picture and it showed Émilie with her hand on his thigh. The next one had her kissing him on the cheek. Another one presented her with her arm around his neck. Lindsey was there, looking on, unsure of what to say. Josh himself was almost in a daze, and then he noticed Lindsey.

"This is not what it looks like. You have to believe me." He looked at her. She still didn't say anything. "Why don't we sit down?" he suggested. She followed him to the living room where he sat on the couch and she sat beside him. As he did, he reached in to the envelope again to see if there was anything else and pulled out a paper. It was a typed note. He read it and Lindsey read over his shoulder.

"This is just beginning. Send money 10,000€ March 15 limit. If no money, more pictures to your wife, pictures to your boss. No police or else."

There was an address of a post-office box in Nice. Someone who evidently had little mastery of the English language had written this.

"This is blackmail and it's not Teresa. It looks more like Émilie's doing" Josh said. Then he turned to Lindsey. "There are no more pictures. I left the room after she tried to kiss me again. I swear to you Lindsey; nothing happened. She came on to me, flirted, tried to get me to have sex with her but I left. You have to believe me." Her eyes were watery. She couldn't say anything.

"I'm so sorry you had to see this Lindsey but you have to trust me. Absolutely nothing happened. This is a plot to make our negotiation go bad. She is more devious than I ever thought. She is trying to discredit me or force me into something I don't want to do."

Lindsey found enough of her voice to question. "But why would she ask for money? Didn't you say she was rich? 10,000€ is probably peanuts to her."

Josh pondered. "You're right. I hadn't thought of that. So maybe someone else is behind this. Or maybe she is just using the money to throw us off track."

Lindsey had regained some of her composure and was now analysing the situation. Although still a bit distraught by the pictures, she did trust her husband. She tried to push any doubts away to concentrate on what should be done next. "What are you going to do about this?"

"One thing I won't do, is give this person any money. I think I should go to the police. This is a crime. Someone is trying to blackmail me, whether it's for money or for something else, I need the police on this. I'll go see Mark right away. He has to see this." Josh got up, putting the pictures and the note back in the envelope.

"I'm coming with you." Lindsey said.

"Are you sure you want to do this?" he asked.

"Someone is attacking my husband. That person is attacking me at the same time. I want to be behind you every step of the way."

Her eyes were still watery. He looked at her. Then he put the envelope down and took her in his arms. She didn't resist.

"I love you Lindsey. You're the only woman in my life. There will never be anyone else. I love you now just as I did the day I fell in love with you. No, actually, I love you more. I love you more each day and I will never stop loving you."

Now the tears were falling. She stayed in his arms. The strength of his protection seemed to wipe away all the threats she had felt minutes before. They stayed there for a long time, just holding each other. He bent to her and kissed her. She returned the kiss passionately.

They released their embrace slowly. Without another word they walked to the front and put their coats and boots on. They hopped in the van and headed to the police station. At the counter, one of the officers greeted them.

"Mr. Stuart, Mrs. Stuart. Good evening, how can I help you?"

"Hi James, I would like to see Mark please. Is he in?" Josh asked

"You're in luck. He just came back from a patrol. I'll get him for you."

The officer went to the office and informed Mark of his visitors. Mark Dexter, even though being only a sergeant, was the senior officer of the detachment and Joshua preferred to deal with him on this matter. Mark came out of his office, greeted them and shook their hands.

"Could we go in your office?" Josh suggested.

Mark agreed and they followed him. They closed the door. The office was actually just big enough for Mark's desk and two visitors' chairs. In small towns, the police stations weren't built for extensive policing.

Josh pulled out the envelope and dropped its content on Mark's desk. "I just received this in the mail."

Mark took one of the pictures delicately by the corner. Josh and Lindsey remained silent as he flipped through all the pictures and finally got to the note.

"Blackmail. Interesting." Then he looked at Josh, a bit uncertain of what to say next. He glanced slightly at Lindsey then back to Josh. "Should I know more about this?"

"There isn't any more." Josh replied "Nothing happened, it's just a bluff to get me to pay up. I swear."

"I believe him." Lindsey added.

"Good. I believe you too. So tell me a bit more about these pictures. Where did this take place?"

Josh explained the trip to Cannes, the discussion, the flirting, his response, and the whole mess this was having on the town. They discussed it at length and Mark took extensive notes of everything Josh told him. Lindsey offered a comment here and there as well. In all, it took them almost an hour to review the situation and make sure Mark had all the elements that were available at this time. In particular, Mark wanted to know more about the mansion and the room where all of this had taken place. Josh hadn't really paid much attention to Émilie's house except for noticing that she was really wealthy. There were servants but Josh had hardly been aware of their presence.

They left the package with Mark and went back home. As soon as their coats were off, Josh took Lindsey in his arms and carried her to their bedroom. She didn't complain.

32. Investigation

Mark looked at the package on his desk. How was he going to handle this? He examined the pictures closely and could see fingerprints on them but he wasn't equipped to analyse them. Anyway, they might be from Josh and Lindsey if this criminal was slightly careful.

There was no return address on the envelope, the mailbox for the money to be sent to was probably not linked to anyone identifiable, and it would probably be closed after the deadline to ensure it couldn't be traced. Mark had no contact with the French police and no budget for going there himself.

If he referred this to his superiors, it would most likely be dismissed as something of insignificant nature. The force wouldn't put any money or investigation time into this.

Mark, however, knew this was important to Josh and Lindsey. It was probably important to the town as well, although he had no way of knowing it.

He needed outside help. Then he remembered someone, the Winnipeg homicide detective who had helped him solve the multiple murder case. He struggled a bit to remember his name.

He got up and peeked out of his office door. "James, what was the name of that homicide detective who worked with us on the multiple murder case last summer? You know, the guy from the Winnipeg Police?"

James strained to force his memory. "Wasn't it a Cluster or something like that? No wait. It was a French name, I recall."

"Cloutier. That's it. Thanks." Mark said.

"Anytime."

Mark went back to his computer and searched in his address book. It took him a few seconds to find the name and phone number. He called and got patched through the Homicide Division of the Winnipeg police. Someone then informed him that Robert Cloutier no longer worked for them; he had retired. It took a bit of convincing and had to go through a few steps to prove his identity but eventually, they gave him Robert's home phone number.

"If he's retired, then he has time to help me. Let's see what he says." Mark said to himself, hoping for the best.

He dialled the number and a lady with a bizarre accent answered. It wasn't a French accent so Mark was a bit worried that he had the wrong number. The lady may have misunderstood him at the other end. He waited, then a new voice came on, which he recognised this time.

"Hello." Robert simply said.

Mark had to be sure. "Is this Inspector Robert Cloutier?"

"Well, it's Robert Cloutier all right, but it's not inspector anymore. I'm retired now. Who is this?"

"Inspec…I mean Mr. Cloutier, this is Sergeant Mark Dexter from the provincial police detachment located in Lakedge. We worked together last summer on a murder case. Do you remember?"

"Oh yes, Sergeant Dexter. How are you?"

For the first minute or two they chatted about how things were in general, about Robert's retirement, about Lakedge, the snow, the cold, and other generalities.

"Robert" Mark addressed him by his first name at Robert's insistence. "I'd love to chat some more but that's not really why I called. I would like to enlist your support on a situation that just popped up here."

"Oh? Tell me more." For the first time in weeks Robert had something that really peeked his interest.

"There's a problem however. I don't think I can pay you for this." Mark went on to explain how he had no budget for this kind of investigation.

"Mark, let's not talk about money. If I can help you I would love to do it; just as a favour. Right now, I have to be honest with you, I'm bored stiff. Any activity you can send my way will be greatly appreciated."

Mark sighed with relief and went on to explain the situation starting with Sparks' death and closing with the blackmail.

"I've never been to France." Robert said after a few seconds of consideration. "A trip would be good for me; particularly if it gets me out of this cold. I'm your man."

They both laughed. The discussion turned to the details of the case. Mark would scan and e-mail the pictures and the note as well as the postage stamp. Robert would leave as soon as possible on a flight to Nice where he would try to find out as much as possible about the situation and then match up with the French authorities to get their support.

Mark would call Josh to inform him of the arrangements and to see if there was any possibility for him to cover the cost of the trip.

They made sure they had all of their respective contact information and started implementing their plan.

Wednesday March 16

The French Riviera, known in French as "Côte d'Azur" or coast of blue skies, is one of the most famous resort areas in the world, along the Mediterranean Sea.

Until the end of the 18th century, the Côte d'Azur was a remote and impoverished region, known mostly for fishing, olive groves and the making of perfume. A new phase began when the coast became a fashionable health resort for the British upper classes in the late 18th century. The first British traveler to describe its benefits was the novelist Tobias Smollett, who visited Nice in 1763, when it was still an Italian city within the Kingdom of Sardinia. Smollett brought Nice and its warm winter temperatures to the attention of the British aristocracy through 'Travels in France and Italy', written in 1765. At about the same time, a Scottish doctor, John Brown, became famous by prescribing what he called climato-therapy, a change to a warm climate, to cure a variety of diseases including tuberculosis, known then as consumption.

In the mid-19th century, with the arrival of railroads, British and French entrepreneurs began to see the potential of tourism in the South of France. At the time, gambling was illegal in France and Italy. In 1856, the Prince of Monaco, Charles III, began constructing a casino in Monaco, which, to avoid criticism by the Church, was called a health spa. The first casino was a failure. Then, in 1863, the Prince signed an agreement with a French businessman, François Blanc, to build a resort and a new casino. Blanc arranged for steamships and carriages to take visitors from Nice to Monaco, built hotels, gardens and a casino in an area called Speluges, which was renamed Monte Carlo, after Charles.

Snow is rare, falling once every ten years. 1956 was exceptional, when 20cm blanketed the coast. Nice has an average of 2694 hours of sunshine, or about 112 days, a year. The average maximum daily temperature in Nice in August is 28°C, while the average minimum daily temperature in January is 6°C.

Excerpt from Wikipedia: French Riviera

33. Stakeout

Although it is French, the language spoken on the South coast of France doesn't sound quite the same as what Robert was used to. The accent was quite particular but the terminology and the local idioms mixed in much of the conversations made for an interesting variation. Coming from Saint-Boniface, Manitoba, Robert had a use of the language that was punctuated with a lot of English. Many of the sentences he used had an English grammatical structure. In fact, his French was even different from that of francophone people from other parts of Canada.

The taxi arrived at the address. Immediately, Robert noticed the black car parked further up the street and instructed the taxi driver to continue. They went up another block before he told him to stop there. He had left his luggage at the hotel back in Nice. He wanted it to be his base of operations, preferring it to be outside of Cannes to give him more flexibility. This first trip was to familiarise himself with the place. He chose a local driver so that he'd learn more details about the area. Later, he would rent a car and do the rest on his own.

He asked the driver to wait for him. He had bought some clothes to help him blend in a bit more with the locals. Coming from the cold of March in Winnipeg, he was now standing in shorts and already sweating even when the temperature was actually mild by Mediterranean standards.

He came from behind the black car. The car was unmarked. Two men were sitting in it. They seemed to be concentrating on the mansion with the address he had been given. They hadn't noticed him. The passenger was dressed in a light coloured short-sleeved shirt with flowery patterns. The driver was in a suit, white shirt and black tie; quite a contrast. Robert wasn't sure what to make of them, except that the first might be a local resident and the other a stranger to the area.

His gut feeling told him these were police officer staking out the place. If they had any information on what was going on here, he needed it.

He approached the car from the passenger side where the window was open. He addressed them in his best possible French.

"*Bonjour messieurs.*"

.Both of the men in the car jumped. He had taken them completely by surprise. They must have been here for quite a while to relax their guard so much.

"What is it?" the driver asked, startled, in a variation of French resembling neither Robert's nor the local accents.

"Sorry, I didn't mean to scare you. I'm just visiting here and I had a few questions." Robert tried to reassure them, grinning internally at the reaction.

The passenger asked him. "How can we help you?" Then he frowned. "What is that accent? You're not a Frenchman, are you?"

"I am a Canadian. I come from Winnipeg, which is in the middle of Canada."

Both policemen's faces lit up. The driver said "Canada, I've always wanted to go on a trip to Canada. It's such a beautiful country."

"Thanks, I love it too." Then looking into the back of the car he noticed a pile of candy wrappers, lunch bags, and empty water bottles. They definitely had been on a stakeout for a few days. "I'm a police officer from the Winnipeg Police Force." He added and waited to see the effect.

The driver was definitely the leader and he responded quickly. "Really? How long have you been a police officer?" he asked.

Robert was leaning on the door of the car with his head slightly bent towards the passenger so he could see both of them. "I've been a police officer for over twenty years now. Actually, I just retired. I now do private investigations."

He didn't have any license to do private investigations, he had no more police badges, yet he had been given a task by the Lakedge Police. He needed these people's help but had to establish his credibility first. Mark had given him a letter to prove he was working on this investigation on behalf of the Provincial Police. The document was on official letterhead and he kept it close so he could pull it out as needed.

He handed over the letter to the driver. "This is what I have been asked to investigate here in Cannes."

The driver read a bit then said. "Maybe we should discuss this. Why don't you come in, have a seat, *Monsieur* Cloutier?"

Robert looked back and remembered the taxi. He explained that his taxi was waiting but the driver insisted. "Send him away. We'll call you another one later."

Robert obeyed. Once the taxi had been paid and left, he got into the back seat of the car pushing a few of the empty bottles to the other side so that he would have a place to sit.

"*Lieutenant* Olivier Leroy, from the *Police Judiciaire*." the driver introduced himself, pulling out his hand in greeting. They shook hands.

Next, the man in the passenger seat introduced himself. *"Constable* Bernard Simonneau, from the *Gendarmerie.* Welcome to Cannes." he said in an animated tone.

"Thank you. Robert Cloutier, retired homicide detective from the Winnipeg Police." All of the strangers built a quick confidence.

They chatted a bit about the French Riviera, the weather and other general topics, and then they moved on to the investigation.

"So tell me more about your reasons to investigate this property." Leroy enquired.

Robert gave them what he knew of the situation in Lakedge and what was relevant to their case. He mentioned Warren Sparks' death, the sale of the mill, the attempt by Lakedge to buy the mill, and Joshua's visit to Émilie. It all made sense to them. When retracing the sequence of events, they remembered Joshua as the unknown visitor with Teresa.

Then they discussed the blackmail. In comparing the events on both side of the ocean, they knew their cases had the same root. Robert was a bit appalled at the suicide and the letters found by the French police, but it triggered his interest. His blood started pumping as if he hadn't really been alive in the last few weeks. Finally, something that could get him back into what he did best.

He asked why they hadn't moved in yet. Couldn't they get a search warrant? Olivier explained that he was awaiting orders because this series of blackmails had implications with high-ranking officials in various powerful arenas of France. This woman went around and her arrest would create waves in many ways. If she was involved in the blackmail, they had to be careful not to implicate her victims and create uproar in the French government.

Robert realised he had no such political agenda. For once he didn't have to report to Inspector Moreno on his approach. He enjoyed the freedom of action.

Together they compared what they had as evidence in the case so far. Robert showed them the photos from the blackmail package. It seemed to point to Émilie, although her face was never clear in any of the pictures. Joshua had confirmed however that it was her. In comparing Robert's pictures with the photos of the Montelierre blackmail, they were now sure it was the same person.

They also compared the two letters in both the typeset and the language used. Again, it seemed a perfect match. They knew the package they had identified at the expedition point was the one Robert now had in his hands.

The problem was to find out who was behind this. Basically, everyone in the mansion was a potentially suspect. They felt fairly sure, however, they could eliminate the cook as a suspect. She was only there a few hours a day, an old woman with very little education, and living in underprivileged conditions. That left Émilie, Teresa, and Gilbert, the valet. They started analysing what they had on each of them. Robert had spent a lot of time with Joshua reviewing everything he could about his visit to Cannes.

Émilie was quickly characterised as a greedy, self-indulging woman, hungry for power and wanting to exert it over men in particular. That in itself, beside the desire for more money, could be considered a motive. She had the means to carry the scam since she could plant cameras anywhere in her own house, and then have the valet deliver the messages in the mail. She also had the opportunity since she decided where her romps with her victims would occur. She could trigger pictures or videos remotely and sort them later to select only the ones where her face could not be identified.

Looking at it even further, they surmised the recent attempt at blackmailing may have actually been triggered by a desire to humiliate Joshua because he refused the advances she had made on him. Leroy and Simonneau were actually surprised that Joshua had refused, but if Joshua was telling the truth, it also meant the blackmail was a bluff. Joshua would know the blackmailer had nothing more on him and the blackmailer knew Joshua wouldn't buy it. Most likely there was more to this than what they had so far.

They wondered about Teresa. She also had access to all parts of the house and the valet did chores for her just as much as he did for Émilie. Suddenly, her trip to Canada took on a whole new meaning. Perhaps she had gone there to stakeout Josh, the situation, or the conditions of the sale of the mill. She had the means and the opportunity. They struggled a bit on the motive, but Robert remembered Josh mentioning how Teresa had repeatedly spoken very critically about her own daughter. She had mentioned how she was ashamed of her. Teresa's financial situation, although not needy, was fairly dependant on her daughter. If she owned the mill and the mansion in Canada, she would be in a much stronger financial position. She could have been trying to discredit Émilie in order to get control over the assets for herself.

Then there was the valet. Gilbert had been the one delivering the package but he may be doing it for someone else in the household. There was no direct proof of his involvement. Leroy did entertain doubts because they had followed the man to Nice. Why didn't he just use a post office in Cannes? If he had been delivering a package for someone else, that would have been the normal way. Going to Nice to mail it seemed to indicate his wanting to hide the delivery. The postal box for the blackmail money payment was in the same post office. True the man had stopped for a drink on his way back and had met with friends there, but that might simply be a measure to ensure he wasn't being followed.

When they mentioned this, Robert had an idea. A plan started to form in his mind. He may be able to help the French police and stop this blackmailing situation at the same time. He also had a secondary objective to help Lakedge in their trouble with the closure of the mill.

He shared his idea with the two police officers and together they refined the plan until they were ready to take action. Leroy had to make one call to get the authorisation. If all went well, by tomorrow their surveillance operation would be over and they could finally return home.

They left the site and headed back to Nice for the next stage of the operation. Since everything would be set-up for the next day, the three decided they would enjoy themselves that evening. So with Simonneau as the guide, they went on a tour of the area. Robert found out a lot about local delicacies and got to taste some fine wines you could only find in these parts of France.

Robert had finally regained his sense of self-worth. For the first time in weeks, he felt excited about what he was doing. He had a lot to tell his wife, but he'd have to wait to call Jasmine since the seven-hour difference meant that most people in Winnipeg were already asleep, and he wouldn't dare wake her up now.

34. Casino

Mayor Vivian Hedgerow was a woman dedicated to her community. Her heart was as large as her whole stature. Her town was as precious as her own family. As a mother wants to lash out when someone tries to hurt her children, she wanted to lash out at those who wanted to hurt Lakedge.

She had been racking her brain to find ideas to help her town survive. So when she received the call from one of the developers owning a lot of land in Greenmeadows, she was interested. This man said he had an idea that would save the town. He had read about the ordeal and had been looking for an opportunity into which he felt Lakedge could participate advantageously.

She invited him into her office. He was a man in his late thirties with a very refined suit giving her an indication that he must have some money. He greeted her with honours, referring to her as your worship. She cut him off right away. "Don't worship me. I'm just another human being doing the job of the mayor. Just call me Vivian and I won't get offended."

Taken aback by this but more interested in his offer than protocols, he agreed. "It's a deal, Vivian. I'm Richard."

"So Richard. What do you have for me?" Vivian asked.

She sat at her desk and he took a chair. He pulled out a folder from his briefcase.

"Your... I mean Vivian, I have a plan for you to turn this town around and make it the capital of tourism for the whole northern parts of this province."

He opened the folder and pulled out a colourful picture representing a modern and fancy building in a beautifully landscaped environment. He put it in front of her and said.

"Here is the Lakedge Casino."

She gasped but contained herself. "Casino?"

"Yes, Vivian. I have been looking for a place where I could develop this project. Then I came to take a look at Lakedge when I heard about your difficulties."

Vivian was staring at the picture. He went on.

"I figured a community with such a predicament would gladly work with me to build the facility knowing it would spur on the economy of the town and solve all the financial problems you are presently facing."

"I'm not sure I'm following you." Vivian said still looking at the picture.

"It's very simple. Every town that has a casino has seen their tourism dollars go straight up. In turn this brings more money to the local economy. The local stores, making more, are ready to expand and it translates into bigger taxes and better municipal services."

Vivian didn't know what to say. It sounded good in principle but something inside her was hesitant. She decided she needed help on this.

"Can I ask you to hold on a bit? I want to ask my town manager to join us if he can."

"Sure" he replied.

She picked up her phone and instructed her secretary to ask if Josh could come to her office.

"Now Richard, do you own the company or what is your role besides having this plan and trying to sell it to us?"

He started explaining how he had his own development company but was a partner in a consortium of developers. He lived and worked in Greenmeadows and the consortium had properties all over the province. He was giving more details on the organisation when a knock sounded at her door.

"Come in" she said. Her voice showed a bit of relief but Richard didn't seem to notice. Josh came in. She introduced him and Richard introduced himself, briefly going over what he had just explained to Vivian about his credentials. Vivian cut in when she felt he was almost finished.

"Richard has a project he wants to share with us."

Josh was sitting beside Richard and listening. Richard handed him the picture of the casino and repeated what he had said to the mayor.

Josh frowned and looked at Vivian. She was observing him intently, trying to read his reaction to the project. Richard, oblivious to the body language, was going on.

"The way I see it, this is going to represent a lot of jobs for people in town. First, there will be construction and later, there will be jobs for people in the casino itself."

"What do you think Josh?" Vivian asked.

Josh hesitated. "I…I think I need to review this a bit more before I can give an opinion."

"Oh, of course." Richard quickly responded. "I understand."

Josh felt impatience in his tone, not understanding. "There are a lot of elements I would like to know more about." He said.

"Please go ahead. I can answer any questions you may have."

"Good. Then, let's start with the location; where do you plan to build this?" Josh asked.

"Oh, I have the perfect spot. I put in a bid to buy the old Sparks mansion."

Josh contained a gasp. Richard pulled out a set of drawings with floor plans. "I know these may not be exact because I haven't gone in yet and all I could find were an old set of drawings. The mansion will be transformed into a restaurant. We will build the casino itself on the East side of the mansion, with an artificial lake just around it, here. The parking lot will be going from the edge of the restaurant all the way to the end of the property on the West side. I estimated we could probably fit 150 cars."

Vivian watched Josh intently trying to decipher his impression. She felt the same apprehension she was entertaining and knew Josh enough to feel he was restraining himself.

She looked at the artwork more closely and seemed to recognise the property but the mansion itself had been completely defaced to render a modern concept. Josh kept his head bent over the drawings. Richard persisted. "We change the gate to have a parking booth – another job by the way – and we change the wall surrounding the property to have a better view of the Casino from further away. The effect upon arriving will be truly impressive."

Josh needed to stop him. "I'm not sure I follow all of this. You haven't bought the place yet and you have all these plans. When did you come up with this?"

"Oh I work fast. When I get an idea, I almost don't sleep until I can accomplish it." he said proudly.

Josh and Vivian looked at each other. Josh saw the uncertainty in her eyes. He wasn't sure if she read the anxiety in his expression so he said to Richard. "Why don't you leave this information with us? We will take a bit of time to review the plan and your suggestions, and then get back to you."

Richard stopped. "Well I was hoping to get at least a bit of feedback from you now. The way I see it, I am throwing this town a buoy. I was wondering what you were ready to offer in return. I need to know because it will make a difference in the financing of the project."

"What do you mean?" Josh asked.

"Well, I was thinking the town could waive some of the normal development charges. I was also hoping we could look into giving me tax immunity for the first couple of years to help the project gain momentum. In a few years, the town will more than double whatever you don't get from us."

Vivian was the one to reply to this. "You understand Richard that this kind of project is going to require a serious review. Anyway, this is not a decision either Josh or I can make. This kind of arrangement needs to be presented to council."

Richard's face dropped slightly. "Oh, I see. I had hoped you could have given me the support on this. Maybe if you would give your blessing, the council would be more apt to approve it."

Josh got up. "As we told you, we need to review this in detail before we make any decisions. You have to agree this is too serious to say yes to the first offer."

Richard rose from his chair as well, somewhat disappointed, yet agreeable. He smiled at the mayor and she thanked him. Josh shook his hand and held the door open for him. He left.

Josh closed the door behind him and returned to his chair while Vivian slumped back in hers. They stayed mute for a minute. Then Vivian broke the silence. "What are you thinking Josh?"

"I'm a bit shaken up. I've gone to the Sparks mansion so many times. I think I was sixteen the first time I went there. I can't imagine it different than what it's always been."

"Good" she said.

Josh looked up questioning "Good?"

"Yes, good. I thought I was the only one feeling this way."

They laughed. It relieved the tension.

"We have to look at this with a clear mind. We need to analyse this project without any misconception. We can't do this based on feelings. We have to examine the pros and cons." Josh offered.

"He seems convinced this project of his is the solution to our problems. Maybe he is right."

"I don't share his conviction. I want to do a bit more research on this and I do seem to remember reading about addiction caused by casinos and gambling."

Vivian chastised him. "Now, make sure it's not only because of your religious beliefs. I know about your principles and I'm pretty sure gambling is something you don't endorse. As you said, however, we need to look at it from a rational point of view. This town needs jobs. The very reason why we are in this difficulty is because we relied on one industry. Bringing in some new source of income and employment may be the chance we need to survive. We made the mistake of overlooking the dependency on the mill and we are suffering the consequences now. Let's not repeat that mistake."

"You're right. At the same time, I want to make sure a casino is truly the only answer to our woes. The concept of bringing in new revenues is good. The idea of bringing in tourists and making Lakedge a destination may be the right way. I'm not so sure gambling should be the way we want to market it though. That's all I'm saying, regardless of my personal religious beliefs." Josh said.

"I was just making sure, Josh. I know how much you care for this town and I trust you will do the right thing."

"Why don't we do a bit of research and reflect upon this for a few days? Maybe we can come up with more information to help us make this decision."

"I like that. I don't know if I'm going to get much sleep, but I like it. Thanks Josh."

He got up nodding and left her office. Sleep was something he hadn't had much since the arrival of the photographs. He was glad she trusted him. If things didn't get straightened out soon with good news from France, he might need every bit of that trust.

35. Council

The small council chamber was filled. Everyone wanted to attend this meeting. The future of Lakedge was at stake.

Jim Stone was one of the first to arrive. He was chatting with Frank Ellis while waiting for the council to walk in.

"I tell you, it's unbelievable all the bad luck we've had since we started at Woodland Mills. First it was the power outage. Police know it was arson but have no suspect. There were a few break-ins in local stores they think may be related. Somehow the arsonist would have caused the blackout to eliminate the alarms and rob the stores. When we finally got the emergency generators hooked up, we had one of the main belts of the sander snap. Rob Sloan was injured, almost got his arm cut off. Jeff Wallis was also there but had stepped out for a cigarette. If he had been there it could have killed him. Then yesterday, one of the trucks lost its full load right in front of the main processing plant. One guy got his leg crushed and another one has broken ribs. So far, that's three injuries in a matter of a few weeks. We can't continue to have these accidents. It's having an impact on the production, on the staff numbers and on morale."

"Do you think it's because you're not used to the place? The guys aren't as careful as they would be if they were here?" Frank asked.

"It could be. Maybe it's because everyone is on edge. We have to travel long distances, work evenings and into the night, we're not in our own environment. Then there is this whole situation of the sale of the mill. It's getting to the guys. The uncertainty is driving us nuts."

Frank nodded. "It's having an impact on me too. I'm not as closely involved as you are, but I am concerned about where we are going with all this. I just hope Josh's plan works."

As he said this, Josh stepped in the room with the town clerk and they took their seats. Next Vivian came in. Everyone in the room stood up as she entered. She maintained a stately posture, wearing the official Mayor's Collar around her neck. Finally, the six municipal councillors, all dressed in their best attire, followed.

The mayor went to her designated seat on the platform. It had been set in such a way that it brought her a bit higher than the others. The seat had been selected especially for her. Her size required a larger than normal chair and because of the load she had to carry the seat was cushioned in order to provide sufficient comfort for long meetings.

Council members took their seats and the mayor struck her gavel to call the meeting to order. They stood at attention while "O Canada" was played on the public address system. Everyone hummed along or sang. When it was completed, Vivian asked the crowd to bow for the reciting of the Lord's Prayer. The majority knew the prayer by rote and said the words almost in unison. A few were grateful that other would keep their eyes closed and their heads bowed, this way nobody would know they didn't memorize the words.

The mayor sat down and rapped the gavel once more. "I declare this council meeting of the Town of Lakedge open."

Vivian went through a few formalities, confirming the agenda, ensuring none of the council members had a conflict of interest for any of the subjects to be discussed. Then she obtained approval for the minutes of the previous meeting. Although there were a few other reports and issues for council to consider, the mayor knew the main reason that the meeting was filled beyond capacity.

Vivian went right to the first item on the main agenda. "Report on the offer to purchase Sparks Mill. Report presented by the town manager, Joshua Stuart."

Josh got up. "Madam Mayor, members of council, distinguished guests, I would like to offer this report on the status of the offer made by the Town of Lakedge for the purchase of the Sparks Mill. I need to inform everyone that for reasons of confidentiality and negotiation, I will not divulge any actual amounts in this report. A previous report was offered to council 'in camera' on March 1st of this year to obtain approval for the initial offer. Council may refer to the amounts provided at the closed agenda session for financial data."

An 'in camera' report was a report presented behind closed doors. In this case, a public discussion on the amounts would have created an advantage for the other bidders against the municipality.

"An offer was provided to the real estate agent on March 2nd according to the amount approved by council. On March 8, we were informed that an offer was presented to the real estate agent from an undisclosed bidder. We were informed this undisclosed bidder had previously made a bid on February 27 and this new bid was a counter offer to the Town of Lakedge bid. On March 8, at an emergency council meeting, approval was given to initiate a counter offer, raising Lakedge's bid by two percent. This decision requires an additional authorisation to borrow the differential amount in order to be in a position to confirm the purchase should the bid be accepted."

"Therefore, I would first like to recommend that council receive this report and I would like to recommend that council approve the additional amount to be borrowed under usual borrowing terms and conditions."

He stopped, gave a copy of the document to the city clerk, and waited for the mayor. Vivian in her usual pompous style when she was in an official

261

function called out "I need a motion to accept the recommendations and I need someone to second it."

One of the council members raised her hand first and was noticed by the clerk, and then a second hand went up. The mayor called out "Moved by Councillor Hansen, seconded by Councillor Johnston. The floor is now open for discussion."

Each member of the council had a question. It was important politically to be seen as interested in such a crucial discussion. None of them wanted to be perceived as uninvolved as this could have dire repercussions in the next municipal election. Each councillor constructed valid, educated questions.

One of the questions was about the financing. Josh responded to explain the Town had arrangements for a loan from the bank and he didn't see any difficulty in obtaining an increase in the amount. Peter Cohen was in the crowd. As the bank director he had a special interest in this meeting, particularly because of what he knew of Timbergreen's intentions. He couldn't say anything publicly about his conversation with them, but he intended on doing everything he could to thwart their plans. When the question came up, he stood and nodded to offer confirmation to council on what Josh was saying. The councillor wanted to hear it and asked that Pete be allowed to address council. A quick show of hand indicated no dissension on the request so Pete was invited to come to the front.

"Your Worship, members of council, I would like to confirm that in my authority as director of the banking institution providing the funding for the Town of Lakedge initiatives, I have no reservations in securing the amounts requested by the Town. In addition, I wish to reiterate how I have already offered a reduced interest rate for the mortgage which will ensure the purchase will not become a burden on the town's operations."

He continued...

"I do this because it is important for the bank to see Lakedge survive this challenge. The bank has too much invested in this town in the form of mortgages and personal loans to citizens to see it all disappear. Having the town run the mill directly will be the best possible solution for the citizens and will ensure the safeguard of jobs."

"On a personal basis," he added, "I care for Lakedge as much as everyone else here. I was born here and raised here and I intend to retire here. To do this, I will do my utmost to help this town succeed in this bid. Thank you, Madam Mayor and members of council."

It was a great impromptu speech. Josh listened and caught more than what had just been said.

More questions went on until finally all details of the transaction — except for the actual price – had been discussed. The motion was voted on and passed with unanimity. The clerk handed the report to the mayor who signed a document to confirm the vote.

The meeting went on to other topics and then the floor was opened to the public for question period. Most of the audience wasn't really familiar with the process and in the end nobody really knew what to ask and how to ask. So the mayor called for a motion to adjourn.

As soon as the gavel went down to close the proceedings, Josh signalled to Frank. "Get Pete Cohen to come to my office in ten minutes, will you?"

Frank agreed. Josh went to the mayor to finalise a few details and action plans emanating from the meeting. It took only a few minutes, and he left the Chamber for his office.

Frank was there with Pete chatting about the meeting.

Josh went to Pete and shook his hand. "Pete, thanks a lot for that speech. It was quite good."

"I meant it, Josh."

"I know you did. Tell me, Pete. Did I sense that there was something in that speech you weren't telling us?" Josh enquired.

Pete reflected on his reply for an instant. "Maybe. Was it that obvious?"

"It was to me. What did you think Frank?"

"Now that you've mentioned it, I did get that sense too." Frank replied.

"So what is it?" Josh asked, looking at Pete.

"Well, I had a private conversation with someone highly placed at Timbergreen. This is your competition, you know?"

"Yes, I did find out, but it's supposed to be undisclosed. How did you find out?"

Pete smiled. "Maybe it's better if you don't know this. Suffice to say that I have a lot of clients in a lot of places. Don't forget, real estate agents need banks to approve mortgages in order to be able to sell property."

"Good enough for me." said Josh. "So what about this conversation?"

"I shouldn't be telling you this because this kind of conversation is sort of private. Banker's oath of confidentiality comes into play. I will tell you however, because my loyalty is much stronger to this town than it is to the bank."

Pete went on to relate his conversation with Timbergreen, his attempt at obtaining concessions from the company, his effort to protect the jobs, and finally the confession that all of this was a bid to actually close down Sparks Mill forever.

Both Frank and Josh were angered but not surprised. It just reaffirmed their desire to secure the bid and buy the mill.

They discussed the situation a bit longer. Then each went his own way but with renewed energy in wanting to save Lakedge.

36. Timbergreen

Bernie was getting impatient. He hated being put on hold. He wasn't too fond of classical music to start with so the wait was even more frustrating.

"Hello."

Bernie recognised the voice at the other end. "Boss, it's me. I have news."

"I hope it's good, I'm not in the mood for bad news."

"I wish I did. I just got a call from my contact in Lakedge. He attended a council meeting. The town voted to up their bid. Then this guy from the bank came and offered some kind of special deal to the town. He offered to loan the Town as much as they needed for their mortgage." Bernie tried to keep a calm voice.

"The bastard. I knew he would be a pain from the first time I spoke with him."

"You know the guy?"

"I don't know him, but somehow he tracked me down and called to try and offer a deal. I turned him down so now he's making trouble for me."

"You want me to do something about it?" Bernie asked.

"Nah. I have other ideas."

"I have to say, our guy in Lakedge has been very active. I think we're investing some good money there."

"Oh, how's that?"

"Well, he's already caused a number of accidents slowing down the operation quite a lot. He didn't even get caught so I think it's going well."

"That's good to hear. Keep feeding him, because who knows how we may need him in the end."

"I am." Bernie laughed "He thinks I'm giving him huge amounts, but compared to some of the other deals we have going on, this one is actually pretty cheap."

"Just make sure it works."

"Sure boss."

"Now, something else just landed on my desk. It will certainly help us."

"Oh, what's that?" Bernie was attentive again.

"I received some anonymous photos in the mail today. Someone send them to me with a request for money. The letter promises more pictures with more explicit content if I submit to the request."

"What kind of pictures?"

"These are somewhat compromising pictures of the town manager with the current owner of the Sparks Mills. Judging from these pictures, there were unethical deals being made. If there is more, it could really become juicy."

Bernie was intrigued. "So are you going to get the rest of the pictures?"

"I don't need to. These ones are good enough. I just want you to feed this to the local media. Once this hits the front page of the local newspaper, I'm sure it will cause enough of an uproar to discredit anything the town is doing. In turn, it will make our bid easier to succeed."

"That sounds interesting. I can't wait to see these pictures."

"Keep your shorts on Bernie. There's not a lot to see. The gal certainly is cute and has a lot to offer but she doesn't show too much in this picture. What most important for us is what you can't see, not what is on the photographs."

"Oh, too bad." Bernie said.

"I'll scan the pictures and have them to you in about an hour. Make sure you get them to the press soon."

"Will do Boss."

They hung up at each end. Bernie turned his computer on and waited for the signal to feed through. Once the pictures arrived he would be able to forward them on to the media under a temporary e-mail address. Once the pictures were gone, he would delete the address and erase all traces of it ever existing.

Thursday, March 17

Gambling

The momentum seems to be on the side of those who want to legalize gambling as a way to supplement state revenues. But these states and their citizens often ignore the costs that are associated with legal gambling.

The economic costs that gamblers themselves incur are significant. Consider just the issue of uncollected debts. The average compulsive gambler has debts exceeding $80,000.

Proponents argue that state lotteries are an effective way to raise taxes painlessly. But the evidence shows that legal gambling often hurts those who are poor and disadvantaged. One New York lottery agent stated, "Seventy percent of those who buy my tickets are poor, black, or Hispanic." And a National Bureau of Economic Research "shows that the poor bet a much larger share of their income."

Studies also indicate that gambling increases when economic times are uncertain and people are concerned about their future. Joseph Dunn (director of the National Council on Compulsive Gambling) says, "People who are worried about the factory closing take a chance on making it big. Once they win anything, they're hooked."

Gambling adversely affects a state economy. Legalized gambling depresses businesses because it diverts money that could have been spent in the capital economy into gambling which does not stimulate the economy. Boarded-up businesses surrounding casinos are a visible reminder of this. Money that could be invested, loaned, and recycled through the economy is instead risked in a legalized gambling scheme. Legalized gambling siphons off a lot of money from the economy. More money is wagered on gambling than is *spent on elementary and secondary education ($286 billion versus $213 billion in 1990).*

Excerpt from http://www.leaderu.com/orgs/probe/docs/gambling.html by Kerby Anderson

37. Heritage

Josh was in Mayor Hedgerow's office. He had spent much of the day researching the pros and cons of casinos. The evidence wasn't very favourable. Everything pointed to casinos being bad for local economies.

He had figures on actual money spent in the local economy from the returns of the establishments and they generally showed it was sent to initiatives and profit centers outside the immediate area.

He had stories about cities that had invested in similar projects thinking it would translate into job creation only to find out the jobs actually went to people who had experience and usually came from outside the city. Instead of creating needed jobs aimed at reducing unemployment, this only served to add to the overall population of the city if they came to live here. In itself a larger population might be seen as a good thing, but for Lakedge the jobs had to be offered to people already in the community.

The gambling itself brought along a long list of woes ranging from personal bankruptcies to suicides, divorce, spousal abuse, robbery, drug use, alcoholism and many more. Vivian was quickly convinced a casino was not the option to help Lakedge bounce back from its economic downfall.

The key still seemed to be linked to the reopening of the mill. They were both praying for this part of the plan to work. They recognised however that they should come up with a plan B in case this didn't turn out the way they had planned. The casino being brushed off meant they now had two problems. First they still didn't have a plan B, but now they also had to find a way to ensure this casino project didn't get off the ground.

271

Josh had been thinking of this as well and felt he might have a solution.

"In your opinion, how important is the Sparks mansion to the Lakedge image?" he asked.

Vivian was unsure of the meaning of the question. "What are you getting at?"

"I mean, where does the mansion fit in our identity as a community?"

"I don't really know. I guess it is important because it belonged to Warren and he was a leader in the development of Lakedge as a community."

"Good" Josh got up and paced the room. "That was my thought as well."

"So?" she frowned.

"So, I looked up the criteria for Heritage buildings. In order for municipalities to declare selected buildings as protected under heritage by-laws, they have to hold a special significance to the community and its history. It usually applies to buildings a hundred years old or more, but it doesn't have to be."

"The Sparks mansion is about fifty years old if you consider the initial parts of the property but Warren made a lot of additions later as his personal wealth grew. I think the last portions of the renovations were made no more than fifteen years ago."

Josh agreed. "You are probably right. The fact is, some of it is at least fifty years old and it has a special meaning within the history of Lakedge."

Vivian still questioned "That's fine, but what does this have to do with the casino?"

"It has everything to do with it." He bent over her desk. "This casino project plans to demolish part of the facility and to redo the landscaping of the grounds. If we turn the property into a heritage building, the new owner will be obligated to maintain the property in its historic state. This means no major renovations, no demolishing, no parking, and no new landscaping. Do you think this Richard will want the property under such conditions?"

She smiled. "I guess not. I see now." She paused and he let it sink in. "I suppose you know how to do this?"

"I did some research on it. The first thing we have to do is set-up a heritage committee. Then we have to submit a by-law to confer the property a heritage designation. Once it is approved by council the owner has to comply with provincial rules on the conservation of heritage properties. We can get all that done in the matter of a week."

Vivian did have a doubt. "Wait. What if Richard appeals? Can he bring us to court or something like that?"

"We will have to notify him of our intent prior to his formalising the purchase although he can always back out of the sales contract based on information unavailable at the time of the signature." Josh replied.

"That doesn't answer my question, Josh. Does he have any legal recourse against us?"

"He does but only up to a point. The intent of the provincial legislation is to provide an avenue for municipalities to stop developers from demolishing properties of particular interest to the community." Josh sat down again. "He would have to go to the Municipal Board to launch an appeal and ask to have the by-law reversed. Even if he does get to that point, you know how the Municipal Board works. It will take the Board a year to come up with a decision. By then we will be in a better position to work through any negative decision we could be faced with. We could even offer compensation to Richard to relocate his project somewhere else. He may even drop it altogether out of frustration from having to go through such aggravation. He didn't seem to be much of a patient man."

Vivian was usually optimistic but lately the turn of events had weighed heavily on her morale. "I hope you are right," she said.

"I hope so too. I will get the work started on the report to council. I want it on next week's agenda. In the meantime, you may want to think about who you would like on the committee."

He got up, picked up his papers and walked out. As he passed in front of the secretary's desk she hailed him "Josh! I have something here you will want to see before you go anywhere else."

He turned and looked at what she was showing him. It was the day's newspaper. The front page had a headline and a picture underneath. He almost fainted. He immediately recognised the picture as the one he had received in the mail a few days ago. It was his picture with Émilie. The headline read: "Town Manager in Cahoots with Rich Heiress."

He regained a bit of composure. "Can I have this please?"

"Sure." She gave him the paper and he started reading the column. The writer clearly implied that Joshua had used his charm to obtain special favours. It quoted an anonymous source who told the writer how a competitor had made a bid for the sale of the mill, but the Lakedge administrator was trying to benefit personally from buying the mill for the town. The text implied as well that unethical negotiations had taken place in order to have the current owner reject the competition's offer and accept what Lakedge presented as the successful bid.

Josh walked back in the mayor's office. "Vivian. You have to see this. I swear. It's not true. It's a set-up."

Vivian looked up from her desk confused. "What set-up?" She saw the headline and the picture, blanched, and looked up at Josh. "What is this?"

Josh put his papers back on her desk and sat again. "Let me explain." he said.

He proceeded to explain the interview with Émilie, his exit, the package with the pictures, the investigation already taking place. Then he assured her someone concocted everything in the article, most likely the competition.

She agreed, although shaken up by the article she had just skimmed. "We certainly didn't need this in the mix." she sighed.

She put the paper down and looked at Josh. She crossed her hand and fingers. "You know I trust you Josh. I believe what you are telling me. However, not everyone in Lakedge will be of the same opinion. On top of this, we will need to do our own investigation to prove this wrong. We need to do some damage control here." He nodded, remaining silent.

"I'm going to have to put you on a temporary leave of absence. I will pull every string possible to get you back as soon as possible, but you understand for the moment, you cannot be seen as associated with anything the town does in this file. As you are the prime suspect in this situation – at least in the eyes of the public – I have to protect the interests of the town. I have to show the people of Lakedge that they come first. Even if it goes against my personal feelings for you."

"I understand." he said with resignation in his voice. He got up. She asked her secretary to come in.

"I have to make a few announcements. I need to get a press release out. You'll have to stay home. I'll call you if I have new developments."

He was at the door. She added. "I'm sorry Josh. We shouldn't have sent you there. You got caught in a harness we hadn't foreseen."

"I guess I did." He left the room, went to his office to get his coat and boots, said a few words to his secretary, and walked quickly to his car, hoping nobody would see him.

He reached his car and drove off. He breathed a sigh of relief. When he got home, he saw a police car parked in front. He left the car in the middle of the street and rushed to the house. As he came closer he noticed a huge hole in the front window. Someone had thrown something and it had smashed right through.

He walked in to meet Mark standing in the living room examining a large rock on the floor surrounded by glass shards. Amanda was in the hallway.

"Amanda, are you all right?" he asked.

"Yes dad. I'm ok. I was just a bit scared when I heard the noise. I came up but I didn't see anyone. I tried to call you but they told me you had left. So I called the police."

"It was a good decision." Mark said. "Do you have any idea why someone would do this to you, Josh?"

"I have a very good idea. Did you read the newspaper this morning?" Josh replied.

"No I didn't."

Josh went to the mailbox and pulled out the newspaper. He unfolded it and showed the front page to Mark.

"I see." he said. "I guess with the current state of mind people in Lakedge are in, I shouldn't be surprised. We have been dealing with so many incidents lately. Tempers flare and arguments turn into fights, people don't have enough money and turn to pilfering and thefts. We can't respond to everything. I've asked for additional help so the head office is sending me a few constables."

Josh pointed at the newspaper. "That's not good. You know we are doing everything we can to solve this situation. I promise you, this article is all wrong. It's a set-up."

"After seeing the pictures in the initial package I believe you. The hard part is to make the residents of Lakedge think the same."

"Mayor Hedgerow is going to try something. In the meantime I am on leave."

Amanda heard. "Dad, did she fire you?"

"No Mandy. She only asked me to take a leave of absence until things calm down."

Mark tried to help reassure both of them. "Well, I hope our man in France can come up with something soon. We need all the help we can get. In the meantime, for your own protection, I suggest you go to a hotel in Greenmeadows for a while. That will keep you and your family safer."

"I know what you are saying and I thank you. On the other hand, it might be perceived as if I was trying to run away. I want to show I have nothing to hide. I will stay here."

"Your choice Josh. I respect what you decide. I'll tell the guys to patrol in front of your house a little more often than usual. Just for safety's sake."

"I appreciate it Mark."

"In the meantime, I don't think we can do much about this particular incident. I will take a few pictures out in front. Maybe we can recognise a boot print. If Amanda didn't see anything, I doubt we will be able to identify anyone."

"Thanks for trying." Josh said.

Mark left. Josh pulled off his coat. Amanda was still standing in the hallway. He noticed she was hesitant. He pulled her in his arms and she readily accepted the hug. He kept her there for a long time.

"What's that picture in the newspaper, Dad?" she asked, hesitant.

Josh seized but quickly recovered. He knew he had to open up to Amanda. She had every right to know why she was targeted along with the rest of the family. He brought her gently to the kitchen and sat at the table to explain the situation.

When he was finished, she gave him another hug. After a few endearing moments the likes of which neither had experienced for quite a while, Josh suggested, "What do you say we clean up this mess before your mother comes home?"

"Yeah. I'll get the broom."

Together they picked-up the glass and vacuumed the floor. Josh called for a window repair shop and went to the shed to get a piece of wood. He nailed it to the window to cover the hole. The window repairman would come by tomorrow.

Better take this in stride. He was now dependant on others to bail him out. The lack of control was difficult to tolerate. He had to convince himself it was best for him to leave it.

"I guess this is the vacation I've been wanting for a while. Maybe I can get to some of those projects I've been meaning to do. Let me see what Lindsey has on the "honey do" list." he thought to himself and smiled.

38. Trap

Robert, Olivier and Bernard were now the three musketeers in this episode. Although not quite matched, they did make a formidable team. Robert was the man with the experience in investigation, Olivier was the man with the connections in the national police force, and Bernard was the local cop who knew the underground as well as the environment.

The three got up early, coordinated their watches and tested their radios. They had typed a letter seemingly from Josh indicating he refused to negotiate. The letter was left in the box as per the instructions provided. Bernard waited near the post office to signal the arrival of the valet and his reaction from the note. Robert sat at the café Gilbert usually frequented and ordered breakfast while Olivier observed from a distance ready to step in at any moment.

Robert was wired to record the conversation and allow Olivier to listen in. They waited a couple of hours. Robert was on his third coffee when Bernard called in to announce the arrival of the valet. Gilbert walked into the post office, went to the mailbox and retrieved the letter. He didn't open it right away, returning instead to his car, where he proceeded to read it.

As expected, he then went to the café. He sat at his usual table, just behind the one Robert had selected. When he had his usual *pastis* in front of him, a yellow liquorice tasting drink very popular in this part of Europe, Robert turned and addressed him.

"Excuse me sir, are you in the employment of *Mademoiselle* De L'Étincelle?"

Gilbert was a bit taken aback. He seemed nervous and Robert noticed it. It took him a couple of seconds to compose himself . "Who wants to know?"

"My apologies, how rude of me. My name is Robert Cloutier. I am from Canada and my employer asked me to look into something for him. From the information I have, you may be just the person to help me."

Gilbert was still uncertain "And who is your … employer?"

"Oh my employer is not what is important. What I am ready to offer for a bit of information may be of much more importance to you."

"What kind of information are you looking for?" Gilbert wasn't relaxed.

Robert got up and changed seats to face him instead of forcing Gilbert to turn around. Once in this position, he leaned towards him and started talking in a quieter tone.

"My employer has made a bid to buy a property owned by your employer. We don't really have a lot of information so far on the status of the transaction but we are aware that there is some competition. My employer would like to ensure his bid is the successful one." Robert stopped to take a sip of his coffee carefully watching the effect of his words. He added "My employer is ready to invest quite a lot to get this deal." Another sip and then "I think you may be in a position to help. In a way, this arrangement may be beneficial to all of us, don't you think?"

Gilbert observed without saying anything for a minute. He drank a bit of his *pastis*. Then he smiled. "You are right in assuming that I work for *Mademoiselle* De L'Étincelle. I am sure you knew this already. You seem to be well informed. You also seem to think I can be of influence on any deals my boss is working on. I assure you, I am only the valet. I take care of the house and I run errands. I don't take care of her business."

Robert persisted. "I understand. I think however that you underestimate your influence over the lady. I would venture to guess that you manage a lot more in that mansion than just the dustpan." Gilbert was a bit flattered but not quite relaxed.

Robert continued. "You can't tell me you don't see the mail coming into the place. You might even be the one to open it and sort out the junk from the important stuff, no?"

"I do handle some of the mail." He paused then had an idea. "In fact, I know who the various bidders are for the Canadian property. So if you tell me the name of your employer, I may be able to judge a bit more on the validity of your claim."

"Very well, but this is private. You have to promise me that you won't tell anyone. If you do, any deal is off. Understood?"

"Understood." Gilbert said, starting to relax now that he felt he was more in control of the conversation.

"In that case, I can tell you that my employer is Timbergreen. I won't give you any names but just the company is sufficient for now. Anyway, very few people in the company are aware of this deal."

Gilbert knew the name well. "So I guess you want to know what the Town of Lakedge is doing about this deal. You want to know what they are offering?"

"Yes, and anything that could offer my employer an edge in the negotiation."

Gilbert moved back in his seat. "Well, I think you are a fraud, *monsieur.*"

Robert wasn't expecting this. Olivier and Bernard, who had just joined him in the car, were ready to jump, fearing their first try was a bad start.

"I don't understand. Why would you say I am a fraud?"

"Because I sent a package to Timbergreen two days ago and if you worked for them you would have known about this."

It was a twist Robert wasn't ready for. He scrambled to quickly change the plan. Used to quick thinking he retorted "Are you sure they received the package already? They would have told me but then you have to remember the time difference. It's early in the morning here so my employer hasn't had a chance to contact me yet today. Also, all the mail is received by the central reception and sometimes my boss doesn't get his mail until early the next morning."

Robert knew he had to move quickly to maintain his credibility. He pulled out a small envelope from his back pocket and dropped it on the table. "I have an incentive here to help justify my claim."

Gilbert peaked into the open end of the envelope and quickly recognised a hefty pile of Euros.

"You carry some convincing arguments." he said.

"Good. Maybe we can make a deal after all."

Robert sighed internally in relief. The bait seemed to work. What Gilbert didn't know was that the money had been dusted with a special powder to stain the fingers of anyone who touched it and that it wouldn't wash off. They had planned this in order to know if anyone other than the valet was involved in on this scam.

"By the way, may I ask what was in this package you sent?" Robert asked.

"You can ask." Gilbert leaned ahead towards Robert. "I sent some interesting pictures."

"Pictures?"

"Yes, I had pictures I felt someone might be interested in buying so I sent them to a couple of places."

Robert felt sweat even in the cool March breeze. They knew about the pictures to Lakedge but somehow they had missed the other set.

"Which places would that be and what pictures are we talking about?" Robert pursued.

"The pictures are those incriminating the negotiator for Lakedge, that place in Canada, with my boss. I sent them to… how should I say… supplement my personal income. After I had sent it, I had a feeling the gentleman wouldn't bite. So I also sent them to your employer. Mind you I only sent a sample of pictures. I asked for a reasonable compensation for my efforts in return for more pictures. I was waiting for the reply but since you are here, maybe we can seal the deal."

"I see." Robert replied. "But what if this person does bite as you say? What if he does come up with the money and pay you for these photos?"

Gilbert laughed. "Who cares? I'll have double the amount for the same job. Anyway, he just answered as I expected, he isn't paying."

"Don't you think that's odd? If he is in a compromising position, isn't he afraid the truth would get out?"

Gilbert must have realised then that he had talked too much already because he just stopped. He finished his drink and started to get up.

"Wait, please. Let me buy you another one of these." Robert said, pointing to his drink. Gilbert hesitated but sat down again.

"So what does your boss think of this?" Robert asked.

"The lady doesn't know a thing. This is all my idea." Gilbert answered in pride. "I have tons of pictures and videos of her with all sorts of people, in all sorts of situation. Let me tell you this: if you ever want a peep show, I'll send you some of the juiciest ones. You can't even find videos like these on the internet."

Something in the way he said it made Robert twitch. "Why do you do this? Is it just for the money?"

"You're pretty observant. You're sure you're not a cop?" Gilbert asked suddenly nervous again.

"No, sir. I'm not a cop, but I'm a good listener." Robert answered. He could say it with a straight face because in fact it was true. He was no longer in the police force even if he was investigating and working with the police. He wasn't sure if it would hold in a court of law, but he was too close to divulge his identity just yet.

"You want to know why I do it? I'll tell you. Yes, there's the money. I do get a bit here and there. The more important aspect, however, is how I get back at her. You see, she took me in. She made me her lover for a time, and then she returned me to my functions as a valet. She started taking other men and ignored me as if I was just a toy. She acts with me as if nothing ever happened."

He stopped as the waiter brought the drink. "All these men think she loves them, until she drops them as well. Then I come in with the pictures and show them what it's really all about. I humiliate them even more than she does. It feels good to have them squirm. They all think they can take my place. I show them how much they are wrong."

Robert waited while Gilbert drank. He still had one more question to ask.

"I was also wondering about this older lady living with your boss. Is she involved in your scheme?"

"Madame Teresa? Never. She is too good. She would never go for anything like this. As I told you, this is all my idea, my doing, no one else."

"Well, then I guess you're the real deal here. You did it."

That was the signal Olivier and Bernard were waiting for. As soon as he said it, they jumped out of the car and crossed over, coming from different sides of the café. They moved in, Bernard blocking the back exit, Olivier going directly to the table.

"Gilbert Pannetier, you are under arrest for blackmail and accessory to homicide." Olivier said.

Gilbert jumped and tried to get out but Robert was too quick and punched him in the stomach causing him to fall back in the chair. Robert wanted to hold him but his hands still didn't have much of a grip.

Gilbert looked at him regaining his breath. "You said you weren't a cop!"

"I'm not. I'm a private investigator." Robert answered laughing.

Bernard had joined them. He showed him the tape. "And we have everything right here."

39. Exodus

The cube van backed up slowly into the driveway. The beeping was loud to alert anybody standing behind the truck. A couple of big guys were standing on each side of the driveway waiting for the truck to stop. When it did they rolled up the back door. The truck was empty except for some tarps, ropes and a couple of dollies. A ramp was pulled out from a hidden compartment underneath the cube and laid out from the back to the stairs.

Children from the neighbourhood, unaccustomed to this kind of entertainment, closed in. Many neighbours were gawking through their windows, some of them on the phone already spreading the gossip.

Moving usually occurred in summertime and the current snow accumulation would hinder the workers. Their boots made the work more difficult. The water in the hallway would make it slippery and dangerous but the mess was the least of their worries.

Dahlia Glendon had red eyes. She had been crying but tried to keep a good front with the movers. The men first went from room to room to assess the workload. John Glendon was showing them around. They figured it wouldn't take long.

They started with the heavy pieces. The fridge, the stove, the washer and dryer, and the freezer were the first to go. Then the rest of the furniture was placed in the truck, carefully packed to protect it from any damage. Last, they brought in the boxes with all the family's belongings. The children were at a friend's house so they wouldn't be in the way. John and Dahlia would pick them up after the house was empty.

They were well underway when a long car came up and parked right in front of the truck. Vivian Hedgerow emerged. She struggled as always to get her enormous body out of the seat. The snow hindered an already difficult manoeuvre. She wore a bulky coat and big boots, which added to the ordeal.

She walked up to the house. A couple of the guys had to move aside to let her go through. She stepped in and called out. "John? Dahlia?"

Dahlia was closest and came to the door. "Yes… Oh it's you Vivian. Hi. How are you?" she said as a polite formality. She wasn't really concerned with the mayor's well being, just being polite.

"The question is, how are you?" Vivian replied. "And most importantly, what are you doing?"

John showed up at that instant. "Oh hi, Vivian."

"John, what's going on?" she asked again.

"We're moving, that's what's going on."

"How come I didn't know about this?"

Dahlia replied. "We didn't want anyone to know. We just wanted to go as quietly as possible."

They were standing in the hallway and the movers were trying to get by with some boxes. Vivian asked "Is there a chair somewhere so we can talk about this?"

Dahlia showed her to the kitchen where a few chairs were still there. Vivian sat down as gently as she could, a bit afraid the small chair would collapse.

"Let's start from the beginning. Why are you moving?"

John answered. "It's simple really. No work, no money, can't pay the bills, can't pay the mortgage."

"So where are you going?" Vivian insisted.

"My brother who lives in Kenora will take us in. He's already trying to get me a job at the factory where he works. Dahlia will do odd jobs to get some more money so we can help my brother and start saving to find our own place."

"What about the house?" Vivian asked.

"The house will go back to the bank." John said, giving the impression he had accepted his fate.

"Can't you try to sell it?"

"Vivian, who's going to buy a house in Lakedge right now? Everybody knows there are no jobs. I'm sure a lot of people are going to be forced to leave just like we are. On top of that, I read the papers too. I know what your town manager does. I knew the guy was crooked. Now I have the proof." His anger was mounting.

"Now calm down John. I know for a fact that what was in that paper was bull. It's a scam and although I can't prove it yet, I will," Vivian brought her tone of voice up a notch too. "You just wait."

"That's just it, I can't wait. The bank will be after me and foreclose in the spring if I can't come up with the mortgage money. I'm getting out now while I still have a bit of dignity."

"Couldn't you have come to me? I could have tried to help you."

He laughed sarcastically. "Ha. Sure you can help. Like you helped last summer. Your pet town manager destroyed our house with everything in it. The insurance gave us peanuts and just as we are starting to rebuild our lives in a new house, I lose my job. Now you want to help. Where were you before?"

She cut him short. "That's not fair John. You know we helped. The whole community got together to help you build this house. Everyone donated something to help you buy new furniture. Even the bank was good enough to give you a low interest mortgage. Yes, I agree, the insurance wasn't very good to you, but there wasn't much we could do about it."

Dahlia was crying again. The memories brought on instant stress. "You have to understand us, Vivian. We lost our house to the fire and we were almost killed by a landslide. Now John lost his job and I don't make enough to cover all our expenses. John's brother is holding his hand out to help. We have to take it. It's our only chance."

John added "We're cursed here in Lakedge. Look at everything that's happened in the last few years. First we have this influenza stuff. Did you ever wonder why it hit Lakedge before any other part of Canada? Then we get the forest fire last summer and we have to evacuate the whole town. Many people lost their home. When we finally think it's over we get the heaviest rains I've ever seen in my life and then the landslides take away all our properties. Isn't that enough to understand this town is doomed? I don't know what we did to God to deserve this, but I'm out. The closing of the mill was the last straw. I can't take any more of this. I'm not waiting until something happens to my family. You can't keep me here any longer. Goodbye." He got up to leave.

"John, please wait." Vivian asked.

He stopped but remained standing. She continued.

"I know Fate or God or Luck, whichever you want to blame, hasn't been very good to you. You have to look at the other side. We did have a lot of incidents thrown at us, but the important thing to remember is that we always pulled through. We stay together as a community and with a lot of imagination, hard work and dedication, we survive. That's the real lesson here."

"But don't you understand. We can't survive this. We already have had too much to deal with. The hard work and dedication, as you call it, has drained everyone. We have no strength left to handle this crisis. I certainly haven't. The Harpers, the Grenvilles and us have been hit the hardest of all. I heard that the Harpers are thinking of moving as well. I tell you, there's going to be many more." John explained.

"John, you can't give up now. We've only started to work on this particular crisis. You have to give us time. The bank can't do anything before the spring anyway. There's legislation preventing them from throwing anyone on the street during winter. In a northern area like us, we can actually get this extended until the snow is melted, which means probably the end of April or even mid-May. By that time, I'm convinced we will have this settled and we will have the mill back in production."

"Wrong. With the shenanigans your town manager is dealing with, I'm convinced we will never see work in this area again. I'm getting out while I still can."

Dahlia tried a more conciliatory tone. "Vivian, all this stress is too much for us. The kids feel it too. They know we are tense. We've had more fights in the last few weeks than we have ever had in all of our fifteen years of marriage. It's causing a toll on all of us. John's brother is kind enough to help us out. We can't refuse this."

Vivian sighed. "I guess I can't change your mind. I must be starting to lose my touch."

"You are getting affected just like everyone in town, Vivian. You need to see it our way." Dahlia said, speaking softly.

"No, I can't see it your way. I won't. I may be able to accept your decision, but I'm not giving up on Lakedge. As long as I have a breath in me, I will continue to fight for this community."

She looked at Dahlia and saw the tears roll on her cheeks. "I'm not saying this to blame you. I'm just sorry it had to come to this." Then she had a thought and turned to John. "Promise me something."

"What?" he replied.

"Promise me that you will keep in touch with me. When we get through this —and I say when not if – I want to be able to contact you and see if you are willing to come back."

John thought about it for a minute but Dahlia was the one to answer. "I'll stay in touch Vivian." She got up and reached for a piece of paper and a pen. She scribbled and handed the paper to Vivian. "Here. This is the phone number for John's brother. His name is Paul. I know the number by heart now. I've been calling so much lately. If something changes here, give us a call and we'll see."

"Don't keep your hopes up." John said. "I know I won't."

"Well, I guess that's where you and I are different John. I'm an eternal optimist. I always keep my hopes up." She turned to Dahlia. "Thanks, Dahlia. I'll contact you as soon as we have something."

She got up and walked slowly in the direction of the door. Halfway there she stopped and turned. She took Dahlia in her arms and gave her a big hug. "You take good care of yourself, right?"

Dahlia couldn't speak but mumbled an agreement. Vivian then turned to John and gave him a hug as well. "I'm not mad at you John, just sad. Maybe a bit disappointed, that's all."

"I'm sorry it had to come to this Vivian, thanks for trying. In a way I guess I do appreciate it." He squeezed her in return.

Vivian walked out trying not to be in the way of the movers who had almost finished. She got back to her car, sending a last wave to the occupants before getting in.

While trying to tie the seatbelt –always a difficult task for a large woman– she started worrying about the other people in Lakedge. She would have to see the Harpers and the Grenvilles soon. The scene she had just encountered was probably the first of many. She dreaded the thought and tried to push it back as she started the engine.

40. Reversal

Émilie leaned on the doorframe. Her face was flushed. Even with her deep suntan she was somewhat paler than normal. Inside Gilbert's room two *gendarmes* were packing row upon row of DVDs from shelves into evidence boxes. Another one was taking pictures of the elaborate installation Gilbert had. On the desk were four monitors, a video recording device with capacity for capturing images from two cameras at a time, and a computer to manage all of the equipment.

Other officers were combing the mansion for cameras. There were wireless cameras transmitting to the controller remotely from various locations within the house. Most of them were hidden in the ventilation shafts and light fixtures. There were some in every room, but the bedroom and bathroom were equipped to ensure full coverage of every corner.

Commandant Dumont had obtained a warrant based on the taped conversation and ordered a full search of the house. *Lieutenant* Leroy was executing the search with a local team. Émilie had stepped aside to let them work. She had almost fainted at the sight of the equipment and the tapes. The *lieutenant* had popped one of the DVDs in the machine and reviewed a portion of its content. Émilie had gasped at the first few images, recognising herself in a sexual position with one of her partners. She had stepped back toward the hallway, trying to grasp what this meant.

Leroy addressed her. "*Mademoiselle*, could we have a talk somewhere else? In the living room perhaps?"

She didn't reply. She led him to the living room. Robert was already waiting there. Dressed in light coloured shirt and shorts, he clashed with the uniformed agents. When she walked into the room, Robert got up.

Having proper etiquette, especially in front of women, was an old habit. He observed her coming in. This woman was especially attractive.

She sat in one of the sofas, subdued. Leroy sat across from her. Robert regained his seat.

Leroy started the conversation. "You need to know that this situation has far-ranging implications. We have already identified a number of key governmental and high-profile businessmen on these tapes."

He looked at her with a mixture of contempt and sympathy. She never looked up from the floor.

"Did you know Monsieur de Montelierre?" Leroy continued.

She just raised her shoulders.

"Then I guess you don't know he committed suicide."

She raised her head. Her face expressed shock. Leroy hoped he would find remorse or compassion in some way, but he couldn't. There just wasn't anything of the sort. All he read was anger at what was happening to her, and fear. Robert believed she was just afraid of being infamous more than anything else.

"*Lieutenant*, may I have a word, please?" Robert asked.

Leroy accepted and they left the room for a couple of minutes speaking in a low voice. They came back and Robert started.

"*Mademoiselle*, my name is Robert Cloutier. I represent the Lakedge police authorities. You do remember Lakedge, where you used to live?"

"*Monsieur*, I don't care to remember the place. I have always lived here. Before this home, there was nothing." she replied without looking at him.

Robert shook his head. "Then why would you care who buys the property you own over there?" His tone denoted a bit of puzzlement.

She raised her shoulders again and gave a quick sigh. She turned to the *lieutenant* and said "Do I have to go through this?"

Leroy raised his eyebrows. "Maybe not." He waited then continued. "I think you might actually be interested in an offer *Monsieur* Cloutier wants to make. It could be worthwhile listening."

She kept her position, her eyes fixed on the *lieutenant* with anger. A rat in a corner would have seemed gentler. Leroy looked at Robert and nodded.

"*Mademoiselle*, with everything that happened in this house, we have enough to tarnish your reputation forever. With a little leak to the press, the whole world could see how many lives you have destroyed, how many marriages you broke, how many people you manipulated. So far, the *lieutenant* has been able to contain this case. Only a few selected people are working on it."

He watched to see a reaction but he felt her retreat even deeper into her shell. Was she trying to protect herself, or was she selecting her weapons to lash at him?

"You were lucky in a way, because we have a taped confession from Gilbert Pannetier, your valet, confirming he acted alone. He told us you knew nothing. At this moment we have nothing to prove it. He could have been trying to protect you. He did say he fell in love with you. So maybe he didn't want to implicate you out of love."

He stopped here again but she still didn't respond, and she refused eye contact.

He went on. "If you were to be accused as an accomplice, you would have to be tried in court. You would need a lawyer, and this lawyer would need to investigate." He grinned. "I love your system in France. Here you are guilty until proven innocent. It means you have the job of proving the police wrong. In Canada, it's the opposite, leaving all the work to the police. I can just look back at the amount of work I could have saved myself if I had been a cop in France."

He sat back in the chair.

"I would like to propose something. *Lieutenant* Leroy and I are in agreement. You give a break to Lakedge, you let the town have the mill for a reasonable price, and in return, we believe Gilbert."

She responded, spitting the words. "You arrest Gilbert for blackmail but you don't hesitate in using it yourself. Is that how police work is done in Canada?"

"Oh, good one! I don't think it can really qualify as blackmail. You already have an offer on the table. It is reasonable. We just want to be careful and protect your reputation. If you aren't interested, why should we care? I'm only asking you to give us an incentive to help you preserve what is most important to you."

"I'll denounce your tactics," she looked at him for the first time. In her eyes Robert could read revulsion.

Leroy responded, "I don't think you want to do this. You'll have to prolong your ordeal even more. It will cost you more in lawyers' fees and in the end, it's your word – that of a suspect, may I remind you

– against the words of a police officer... By the way, Officer Cloutier has just recently been decorated for courage in the course of his duty."

Robert was glad this medal was useful.

Émilie got up to leave, walked a few steps and turned back. "Have it your way. You can have your mill. I just hope every one of you dies in it. I hope you all burn in hell." She left the room.

Leroy looked at Robert. "I guess that solves your end of it."

"I guess it does. Although I am still a little worried."

"Worried?" Leroy asked.

"Yes, Gilbert did say he sent a package of compromising pictures to this Timbergreen company. I would like to know what they plan to do with it."

"I see. You have a point there. Well, maybe you should head back then. There's nothing left for you to do here."

"I'm afraid you're right. I was just starting to enjoy the place. I'll have to come back for a vacation. I'll bring my wife and we'll spend some relaxing time together." Robert laughed.

"You should do that." Leroy laughed with him. "Let me know and I'll bring my wife here too; we'll double date."

Robert got up. "It sounds like a plan," he said while holding out his hand to shake Leroy's.

"Let me get Bernard to bring you back to the hotel and to the airport." Leroy offered.

"Very well, I accept. I'll get his address and he can be our guide when we come here." They laughed again and walked out.

Friday, March 18

The invention of banking

The invention of banking preceded that of coinage. Banking originated in Ancient Mesopotamia where the royal palaces and temples provided secure places for the safe-keeping of grain and other commodities. Receipts came to be used for transfers not only to the original depositors but also to third parties. Eventually private houses in Mesopotamia also got involved in these banking operations and laws regulating them were included in the code of Hammurabi.

In Egypt too the centralization of harvests in state warehouses also led to the development of a system of banking. Written orders for the withdrawal of separate lots of grain by owners whose crops had been deposited there for safety and convenience, or which had been compulsorily deposited to the credit of the king, soon became used as a more general method of payment of debts to other persons including tax gatherers, priests and traders. Even after the introduction of coinage these Egyptian grain banks served to reduce the need for precious metals which tended to be reserved for foreign purchases, particularly in connection with military activities.

Precious metals, in weighed quantities, were a common form of money in ancient times. The transition to quantities that could be counted rather than weighed came gradually. On page 29 of 'A History of Money', Glyn Davies points out that the words "spend", "expenditure", and "pound" (as in the main British monetary unit) all come from the Latin "expendere" meaning "to weigh". On page 74 the author points out that the basic unit of weight in the Greek speaking world was the "drachma" or "handful" of grain, but the precise weight taken to represent this varied considerably, for example from less than 3 grams in Corinth to more than 6 grams in Aegina. Throughout much of the ancient world the basic unit of money was the stater, meaning literally "balancer" or "weigher". The talent is a monetary unit which we are familiar with from the Parable of the Talents in the Bible. The talent was also a Greek unit of weight, about 60 pounds.

Davies, Glyn. A history of money from ancient times to the present day, 3rd ed. Cardiff: University of Wales Press, 2002. 720 pages. Paperback: ISBN 0 7083 1717 0

41. Evidence

Gilbert was a very well organised criminal. Every single DVD was tagged with a label and every label matched an entry in a register. He had been at this for about two years. Initially he only had one camera in the bedroom that shot Émilie mostly by herself.

It was evident that Gilbert became more thorough in his quest as he did more recordings. The DVDs contained less dead air time and more "action" shots. He had expanded his camera to the bathroom, the living room and a few of the other rooms around the mansion.

Leroy and Simonneau had been reviewing the recordings for hours. They were keeping each review of a segment short, trying to hold back their arousal. Gilbert had some names in his register, but more often there was just a date, a time, and a quick note explaining where the man or the men in the video came from.

Émilie chose males from all backgrounds. She wasn't fussy on their origins but seemed to have a preference for men with money, status, or both.

They also found another register where Gilbert had noted the few people of particular interest for him. In it, they found names, addresses, and dates of transaction. These were the targets Gilbert had selected for his blackmailing.

Their main job now was to connect the recordings with the targets. A number of DVDs had the unfortunate Henri Montelierre. The register showed he had been hit three times in the last year and a half. The repetition had been too much and drove the man to suicide.

They selected all of the videos linked to on-going blackmail operations and started identifying the various individuals involved. Some of the men were well known to Leroy who was fairly knowledgeable on the high society of France. He recognised a couple of ministers, a few rich industrialists and a number of people in the "haute couture" circle of Paris. Then there were a few faces he didn't recognise, but some of the names seemed to ring a bell.

"One thing for sure, this lady really got around." Leroy said.

"I guess when you do a good job with one client, you get a referral to others. These people know each other. They probably gave her number to each other in case they were interested."

"It's a form of prostitution in a way. We can't really prove this but I wonder how she got paid for her services."

"Are you sure she got paid? She may simply be a nymphomaniac. We haven't seen her bankbook yet. She might have received a lot of gifts. I wonder if she asked for money or if she just gave herself and waited to get something back voluntarily." Simonneau said, pensive.

"You have a point. I don't think too many of her clients will want to help us. We may get a few of them grateful enough to know that the blackmail operation has ended."

Simonneau scratched his head. "One thing does baffle me?"

"Oh yeah, what?" Leroy asked.

"Well, how come, none of the blackmailed people ever came to us?"

"I'm not surprised. Most people don't trust the police, and the higher they get, the less they talk. What I wonder is how come none of them ever confronted Émilie? Or did they? And she is leading us on?"

"Good point. She's hard to read. Either she really didn't have a clue, or she's a darn good actress." Simonneau pondered. "Maybe she loved being in front of the camera."

They got to the video of Joshua Stuart and his encounter with Émilie. They watched the recording. The interview in the living room, the flirting, the uneasiness demonstrated by Josh was all there. After all they had seen, they expected the next portion to go to the bedroom, but they were surprised when they saw Josh get up and leave the room.

"Now, that's a change." said Simonneau.

"Yeah. Look at her expression. She is fuming."

Émilie had picked up her glass and drank the rest of its content in one gulp. She then walked over to her bedroom and Gilbert had done a cutover of the video to that location. In the room she had thrown a fit, launching pillows and clothing in every direction until she fell exhausted on her bed. The DVD ended there.

"What do you think it means?" Simonneau asked.

"I get the feeling she didn't like to be refused. What does the other register say?"

Simonneau opened the other book, the one arranged by date. "There's another entry for the same date but it wasn't in the blackmail registry."

"Let's have a look."

Simonneau got up and found the right DVD. He plopped it in the machine and they saw Émilie walk in the bedroom with a man they never saw before. She had the same dress as before and the time stamp indicated a delay of a few hours after the previous tape.

"She sure works fast." Simonneau commented.

"When you have her looks, it doesn't take long to get the man you want. She has them eating out of her hand. All of them." Leroy stopped then retracted himself. "Well, except for one I guess."

They stopped the DVD before it became too explicit. They didn't need to see the rest to know what went on. Leroy remembered Robert asking him to follow up in any way possible on the situation with Joshua Stuart.

"So what do you think we should tell our new Canadian friend?" he asked.

"It seems pretty clear to me that Gilbert had no dirt on Mr. Stuart."

"That's probably why he went to the police in the first place. He knew he had nothing to hide. I'll make a call to Robert to inform him of the good news."

"There's still some hope for the human race." Simonneau said, hopeful.

"Yes, it's comforting to see someone with integrity after encountering so many jerks with only one thing on their mind. The poor guy didn't deserve the lady. I better make the call now. The guy must be anxiously waiting to hear from Robert."

Leroy left the room to make the call. Simonneau continued to review the blackmail register, searching for the tape of the next victim. If there wasn't a publication ban on all of this, it would have made the front page news.

"Too bad." he thought "A coup like this would have been good for the police force. It could have been good for my career as well."

42. Deal

"Josh. It's Vivian." The phone crackled a bit.

"Hi Vivian, what's up?" He sounded sleepy.

"I hope I didn't get you out of bed." She laughed.

Josh felt somewhat embarrassed. "Don't worry. I'm sure I had to get up by now anyway. I've been catching up on lost sleep lately. There's not much else I can do, cooped up inside like this."

"Well, this whole thing may be over soon. I have good news and I have bad news. Which one do you want first?"

Josh rubbed his forehead. "I don't think I'm good for riddles right now, why don't you decide what you want to tell me first?"

"Ok then the bad news is the developer for the Sparks Mansion received our notice of intent to designate it as a heritage building. When we sent the request to the Provincial Heritage Board, we had to tell them the property was for sale and we had to give them the name of the real estate broker. They informed the broker and he forwarded the notice to this casino guy, Richard. He called me. He was mad as hell and he threatened to make us pay for this."

"He threatened you? I hope you called the police on this." Josh said, cutting her off.

"Nah. Don't worry, the guy was just angry. I don't think he would do anything to harm me physically. He said he would contest. He may try to cause us some difficulty, but at this point, I'm ready to take anyone on particularly with the good news I also have to tell you."

"Well, I still think you should let Mark know about this. Let him decide if this guy's liable to do something more than just sue us."

"If it makes you happy, I'll call Mark." Vivian agreed.

"Good. So what's the good news? Or do you have more bad news before the good news?"

"No, just good news from now on." she chuckled. Josh felt happy to hear her. Lately, cheeriness had been missing in Lakedge. It seemed as though all that was left was the laughter of children. Adults in town appeared to have given up on amusement and fun.

She went on. "I got a call from the auditor. You know the dark faced white collar worker who seems to shadow us everywhere we go lately?" Vivian asked jokingly.

"I know who you mean. He sort of gives me the creeps. I guess he's very efficient at what he does."

"Well, anyway. He called me to confirm that the mill is ours. This Aymeelee lady agreed to sell it to Lakedge. What do you say to that?"

Josh felt a thousand pounds just lifted off his back. A shiver ran through his whole body. He closed his eyes and clenched his fist. "Thank you Lord." were his only words.

"Amen to that." Vivian added.

A moment of silence passed. Josh felt his breathing slow down and relax as he hadn't for weeks. He looked outside and the sun was bright. The snow was pure and reflecting the light in thousands of microscopic mirrors. It was just a perfect day all around.

"So what happens next?" Josh asked.

"Well, the auditor said he was making sure all the paperwork was drafted. Since we already have the approval, all I have to do is sign the papers. He said we should be able to sign everything by Monday."

"So now we need to decide how we are going to manage this. We have to rehire everyone that used to work at the mill back in their positions but we need to create a new senior administration structure and a board to oversee the management of the enterprise." Josh had now put his administrator's hat back on. He was thinking business administration again. It was in his nature and he was good at it.

"I've given it some thought as well. I think we can create a board composed of various key individuals in town. I already have a few names in mind but we can finalise the list later. As for an administrator, how would you feel with having Frank Ellis as the chief executive officer for the Sparks Mill?"

"Frank?" Josh though for a second. "Yes, that's a good choice. He knows the mill very well; he worked there for years and he's good with finances and administration. We could find someone else to replace him at his current position."

"Good, then I'll let you announce it to him. He's still your best friend, isn't he?"

"Yes." Then a warning light went up in his mind. "Actually, that may be a problem. Frank's my best friend. With everything that's happened lately, plus this whole Émilie scandal, I could be accused of nepotism for choosing him."

"No, no." Vivian quickly cut in. "That's the other good news I haven't had time to tell you about."

"What?" Josh wasn't sure what could be better than the purchase of the mill.

"I got a call from Mark early this morning," she replied quickly.

"About?"

"About the pictures! The police in France, with the help of a private investigator, caught the guy who was doing the blackmailing. A full tape of your interview with Aymeelee was found and they watched the whole thing. Mark assured me that there is nothing controversial on the tape. It was clear she was flirting with you and the tape shows you leaving the room before the situation gets hot."

Josh was somewhat relieved. "I knew that, but it still didn't stop people from making assumptions. How can Mark assure the citizens of Lakedge that nothing went on after I left that room? They could say we went into another room."

"No, you see. They can't. This guy was a maniac. He had cameras in every room in the house. Apparently he'd been blackmailing a lot of other people as well. So they checked all the tapes and he had absolutely nothing on you. It's clear the pictures the guy sent you and the newspaper were just part of a fishing expedition. He was trying to make believe he had more. All this was just to get money and make trouble."

"I see." Josh said. "We are still going to have an uphill battle in convincing the population of this."

"True." It was her turn to do some quick thinking. "Why don't I call a press conference for this afternoon? I can make the announcements for the purchase of the mill and your reinstatement as town manager at the same time."

"It's an idea. You should get Mark there to give the information on the investigation himself. It would have more credibility."

"Right. I can also announce the appointment of Frank as CEO for Sparks Mill."

"You may want to talk to Frank first to make sure he will accept." Josh reminded her.

"Yes, of course. If you are sure it would be better coming from me, I'll call him in my office right away." She paused and reflected. "My, this is exciting. I feel as giddy as when I go shopping in a big mall!"

It was Josh's turn to laugh.

She kept going. "Now that's a lot of things to remember and do. It's usually your job. I'm not good at details, you know that."

"I'll tell you what. Why don't we meet in a couple of hours at Trucker's Corner to prepare the press conference? Talk to Frank about the appointment. Bring him along and call Mark to invite him to join us as well. Ask Communications to send invitations to a press conference."

"Wait, wait!" Vivian stopped him. "You're going too fast. I can't get all this down so quickly. Ok. Frank, then Mark, then Communications. Got it. Anything else?"

"You may want to ask the auditor if he wants to join us to confirm the purchase. It might be good for his image."

"Are you kidding? What image? He's liable to break every television set in town just by having his face on it."

"Vivian," Josh said in a quasi horrified tone, "he's not that bad, come on."

"I'm kidding of course. I just don't like to have him too close to me, that's all."

"Well, I'll let you decide on that one."

"Ok, anything else?"

"Politically, you may want to have all of council attend, even if they don't get a chance to speak. This is huge for Lakedge so they should get some political payoff from it as well."

"Yes, of course. But I don't want the whole troop at Trucker's Corner."

"No, just invite them to the press conference itself." Josh confirmed. He was about to close the conversation when he thought of something else. "Oh, also, Vivian?"

"What is it?"

"Perhaps you should involve Jim Stone in this as well. He's the key person at the mill right now. Everybody respects him and I think he should be part of the press conference with all of us. Bring him to Trucker's Corner."

"Good idea." She knew Jim well and was familiar with his skills. In her mind she had already decided he would be playing a key role in the new Sparks Mill administration. "He's been in my rear view mirror all along. I just forgot to mention it."

"Very well. Call me back when everything is arranged to decide what time we meet."

"I'll do that." She replied. Then she added in a cheery mood. "I told you I had good news didn't I?"

"You sure did. Thanks. Talk to you later. I have to call my wife now."

They both hung up.

43. Editorial

Mike felt the buzz of the cell phone at his belt. He picked it up. He wasn't expecting a call. Ashley only usually called in the evenings; it wasn't even ten. He had just come out of a class and didn't have anything scheduled until two. He flipped the phone open.

"Hello?"

"Hi. Is this Michael Stuart?"

Mike was surprised by a voice he didn't never heard before. "Yes, it is. Who's asking, please?"

"Mr. Stuart, my name is Aaron Feilding. I'm a writer for the Toronto Star. I was handed a copy of the article you submitted recently, you know the one about the resiliency of small towns in Ontario?"

Mike did remember. He had sent the article almost two weeks ago to the newspaper editor. Having heard nothing since, he had given up on anything coming of it. The call caught him unprepared.

"Yeah… I mean, yes. I did send the article."

"Well, I like it and so does the editor. In fact, we were wondering if you would like to work with us on a series on the subject. What this would mean is that we would want you to rewrite the article by expanding on some of the aspects in a format that we could get four or five articles out of this one. Of course you would be paid for each article. We felt you would probably prefer this since it would mean four or five times the pay. What do you think?"

Mike was unable to speak. He had never expected the article to be published, let alone be transformed into a series.

"I…I think we can do this. I mean, I think I can do this." he stuttered.

"Good. When can we meet to discuss this and have you sign a contract?"

Mike wanted to jump and shout "Right away! I'll be there in fifteen minutes!" But he subdued himself, quickly keeping a professional attitude for this by not seeming either too anxious or too laid back.

"Great. We will see you then." The man gave Mike the meeting location.

Mike was thrilled, his heart fluttered. He wanted to review the article right away. He remembered much of his research but didn't quite recall all of what he had included in the final version. He rushed to his residence and hopped on his computer, grumbled through his teeth at the length of time it took to boot up the device.

"Death of a Small Town, by Michael Stuart"

He started reading, keeping a notepad at his side to make observations. He was already considering how he could transform this into five articles.

"Throughout history, humans have congregated in order to survive. Families from the antiquity stayed together establishing themselves as collectives. Groups of families moved to be nearer to the resources they needed the most to survive. Often, bodies of water were the main reason for selecting a particular site. Over time, if the site was suitable, trade would spell prosperity and newcomers would join the existing community. With a bit of luck and some well advised direction, the community would evolve into a

village, then a town, and finally into a city; some of them actually turning into metropolis."

Mike was now concentrating on the text, trying to see if this was good to keep without any editing. He hoped the Star editor would be able to help him on this, but he also worried that if he was seen as too young and inexperienced, he may not get the respect he wished for. His text would be his only fall back. He had to come up with a refined product before even meeting these people.

He continued reading.

"This story would be a fairy tale come true if every community would progress the same way and constantly see prosperity on the rise. The reality is that there are different types of communities. You have small communities, medium communities, and large communities. Each of these have their own set of issues and concerns."

"In exposing the difficulties encountered by small towns in Canada, we find that most of the issues link to the problem of sustaining the economy. Statistics demonstrate that most small towns are dependant on one or two main industries. Towns are usually built around the area where the industry first landed, often even in expanding circles of residential areas suburban to the particular industry."

"Too often however, the dependency of the very industry that created the town in the first place becomes the cause of its downfall. A number of well-documented examples exist. The majority of these cases are related to natural resources exploitation. Industries in the mining, forestry, and to some extent agriculture sectors, are the most vulnerable. Once the primary resource runs out, the company closes and the community soon becomes a ghost town."

That's when the story started to go into the various examples. Some of his selected communities had disappeared, others had found innovative ways to survive. Most likely this would be where the series would expand. The first article would have the introduction to the topic and study one of the towns. The other articles would present case studies from other towns. He would have to use the research he did initially to write more about each of the towns he had selected. For now he read what he had provided.

"One of the examples that comes to mind is Elliot Lake in Ontario. This town was first created from a boom in the local mining industry. A number of mines were opened and a community was built in proximity. Soon after, commercial ventures opened to provide amenities to the miners. Support services moved in eventually generating more jobs and a municipal administration. When uranium became a desirable natural resource, Elliot Lake was suddenly a booming town. Many made their fortune from this expansion. The honeymoon lasted for almost four decades. Then the mine ran out."

"The company exploiting the mines closed its operations leaving not only the miners but the whole community on its own. Most of the residents left town, bankrupt, destitute, but hoping to start a new life elsewhere. The town administration was left with a slew of properties repossessed for unpaid taxes. If the town had bowed under the pressure and resigned, Elliot Lake would be a ghost town today. Instead, the administration came together and brainstormed to find a solution to their dilemma."

"Today, Elliot Lake is a retirement community. Instead of giving up, the Town developed a whole plan to provide services and activities geared towards the aging population. The homes sold at prices much below what they would cost in other communities. Soon, the word was out and the houses started selling. The support services and the commercial ventures pitched in to ensure newcomers to town would find everything they needed right there. The mining industry in Elliot Lake is gone but the community survived because of the will of the leaders to adapt and transform. Not all communities fared so well however."

Here Mike reflected. Maybe this was where he could go into much more details on the history of the place. He could have interviews with people who lived there to make it even more relevant and personal. Maybe, the Star would pay for his travel expenses. He was starting to enjoy the project.

"Another example is Val-d'Or in Quebec. Literally, the town's name means the 'valley of gold'. Somewhat similar to the gold rush in Yukon, Northern parts of Quebec had their own gold rush and Val-d'Or was one of the main communities to experience this."

The article went on to explore the growth and later demise of the town. It explained how, only through the development of alternate sources of employment such as forestry and agriculture, did the town survive. Even today it still has a high rate of unemployment, with much of the work being seasonal, but at least the town exists.

"More recently, the Town of Nipigon in Ontario suffered a major blow when the mill considered one of the major employers in town burned down. The company had been bought by a co-op only a short time earlier and the savings of most of those involved had disappeared in smoke in an instant."

Mike had tried to give a face to the tragedy by relating some of the witness statements he had found on the web. A visit to Nipigon would probably give an even more vivid image of what the loss of the mill represented for the residents of Nipigon.

As he reflected on the article and the opportunity, Mike started seeing himself going places, literally. He would visit new towns and get interviews with people. He would cover the range of emotions from despair to triumph, anger to elation.

The last segment of his article was the most precious to him.

"There is one more example added to the list only weeks ago. The situation in Lakedge has transformed the peaceful community also known for its battling of the Influenza Virus a few years ago. When the owner of the forestry mill passed away recently, he left behind a strong industry in the hands of an heir who wanted nothing to do with it. In the example of the Eaton's demise, the new owner, more concerned about her own way of life, closed the mill and suddenly sent hundreds of people to the unemployment line."

As he read his line, the resentment for the Sparks heir came back to the surface. Although he wanted to suppress it, he felt his anger may actually be what forced his emotions to come out on paper and make it an interesting article.

He was sure this would be a part he would have lots to talk about. In particular because he knew the story was not quite written yet, he would be ready to add material as the situation in Lakedge developed.

In his initial research he had come up with a few more examples he had only touched upon in the conclusion of the article, but he could readily expand them into a larger version to help fill the fifth instalment of the series. With Elliot Lake, Val-d'Or, Nipigon, and Lakedge, he had enough for four articles, then a fifth to tie everything together with a quick overview of a sample of other towns across the country and a solid conclusion on the need for communities to build resiliency before being faced with similar stories.

He sat back in his chair. Now he was anxious for the meeting. He almost regretted he couldn't have met with the Star today. He knew the excitement would leave him sleepless tonight. He looked at his watch. It was almost time for his next class. Just enough time to grab a quick bite on the way.

44. Press Conference

Vivian Hedgerow walked onto the platform light as a schoolgirl notwithstanding her heavy armature. This was probably her happiest day of the year. She went up to the microphone. They had staged everything for maximum impact. It was sunny and not too cold, so Communications had selected the Sparks Mill parking lot as the perfect location for this press conference. With everybody pitching in they had quickly installed a small platform, brought in a portable generator to power a speaker system, and set-up pylons to separate the parking area from the press conference area.

She looked at the crowd; a few hundred people had assembled. Most of them were mill workers and their families, at least the ones who were contacted through a fan out telephone chain. The front of the area had been reserved for the press and for council members.

On the side of the platform the other members of the panel were lined up, each waiting their turn to go up to the microphone.

"Members of council, members of the press, citizens of Lakedge, colleagues and friends," she started the speech her communication expert had helped her write. It was her feelings but with protocol added into it by the experts. "It is with great joy that I am here today as your mayor, to make this extremely important announcement."

She had a flair for the dramatic. She touched on the subject, everybody having some sense of what she was going to announce but she let the suspense hang on by not saying it right out.

"This town has experienced a number of challenges in its existence. In the last few years, we have been particularly hard-hit. We have suffered but survived through epidemics, forest fires, floods, landslides, extreme cold and snowstorms. I am sure each and every citizen of Lakedge has his or her own version of how they coped through all these threats. We probably have enough to write a book or even a whole series of books on this. What keeps me hanging on as your mayor is how every time something is thrown our way, the people of this town stand up and fight it together. Our history is not one of giving up. Many people would look at Lakedge and refuse to come and live here because we seem to constantly be confronted by disaster. I reply that on the contrary, Lakedge is the best place to come and live in because we have passed every test that we were put through with flying colours." She paused to look at her notes.

"Today, I can say again, we have succeeded in the latest test we were faced with. I have full confidence that, just as we have every time before and again today, we will continue to resist any menace we will ever encounter as a town." She gauged the crowd and knew it was time to move on to the crux of the announcement.

"I have asked a few of my colleagues to join me here today for this announcement, so rather than hearing the news from me, I would like to invite Mr. Flagstone to confirm the announcement himself."

She stepped aside, careful not to trip and fall off the platform. The grey and stern Mr. Flagstone, still with the same raincoat covering a white shirt, black tie and black suit, came up to the mike. He wasn't used to public speaking and it had taken a bit of coaxing to get him there.

"I…Thank you… Madam Mayor. I…I want to confirm that my client, Miss Aymeelee Deu L'aytinchelle," it was obvious he had no French in his background. It was a good thing Émilie wasn't present. She may have cut him off at that. Upon hearing the name, a few hoots and hisses came from the crowd. Flagstone continued "My… client has agreed to the sale of Sparks Mill and all attached properties to the Town of Lakedge."

Everybody had anticipated the announcement but huge cheers rose with applause, as if in surprise. Many turned to the people beside them and hugs were exchanged. It took a number of minutes until the noise level was brought down allowing Flagstone to continue. "My client has allowed me to draft all the necessary papers in order for the mayor to sign the official purchase on Monday."

That's all he had to say. He turned and stepped off, glad the ordeal was over. Internally, he was hoping this was the first and last press conference he had to participate in.

The mayor came back to the microphone. "Isn't this the greatest day for Lakedge?!"

Again, a volley of cheers and applause came from the crowd. She waited for it to subside. "In light of this announcement, I would like to immediately inform you of a few of the decisions I have made to ensure the quick reopening of the mill." The sounds died with everyone's attention now on her.

"I decided to name a few people to administrative positions in the mill. These decisions will have to be ratified by council later, but we will be able to temporarily start working on the reopening and get workers back to their jobs quickly."

She checked her notes again. "First, I would like to announce that I have asked Mr. Frank Ellis to take on the newly created position of chief executive officer for the Sparks Mills. Frank has accepted the position and he will be starting to take charge of the company as of Monday morning, right after we sign the paperwork." She turned to Frank who was waiting to the side. "Frank, would you like to say a few words?"

Frank wasn't the greatest speaker but he gladly went up.

"Thank you Viv... I mean Madam Mayor," Ripples of laughter ran through the crowd. Protocol wasn't easy when you were so close to everyone. "I want to say I am honoured to be allowed to serve my community in this position. It will be a challenge for me to step into the very big shoes that Warren Sparks left behind. For this I will count on everyone's help." He paused a second. "I want to give my commitment to everyone that my first priority will be to reinstate every worker into their regular position and to get the mill back in operation within the shortest period of time. Once we are back in business, I want to seriously look into some long-term plans to ensure that Sparks Mill will never again be faced with a similar situation and that no one in Sparks Mill will ever be laid off again. This is my personal promise to all of you and I will do my utmost to fulfill it."

Renewed cheers and applause met this promise. He stepped off and Vivian came back. "In order to assist Frank, I have also named Jim Stone as the chief operating officer. Between Frank and Jim, I have no hesitation that the mill will be just as successful as when Warren Sparks ran it himself."

More cheers. Jim simply waved but had categorically refused to say anything.

She waited a bit then went on. "Now, I have another bit of news for you and I will ask Sergeant Mark Dexter from the Lakedge Detachment of the Provincial Police to come to the mike." Mark walked on the platform in full dress uniform.

"Thank you, Your Worship. Members of council, members of the press, citizens of Lakedge: following an investigation involving the collaboration of our own Provincial Police and the French Judicial Police, as well as some private investigative support, I would like to share our findings concerning allegations of misconduct on the part of Joshua

Stuart, town manager for the Town of Lakedge, in the negotiations for the purchase of Sparks Mill by the said Town."

He read, more than announced anything. It was important for Mark not to go off track in any way. Protocol, chain of command, codes of conduct, and rules were a way of life for police, particularly at his level of responsibility. Although he was only a sergeant in rank, in a small town like Lakedge, he was the top gun for the police organisation and as such had to embody the discipline for which the police were known.

"The combined findings of the French Judicial police and the provincial police have determined that in no way was there ever any misconduct on the part of Joshua Stuart in this situation."

Mumbles and discussions started in the crowd so Mark quickly moved closer to the mike, raised his voice and continued. "Our findings were that an unnamed individual well situated within the surroundings of the owner of the Sparks Mill, took covert pictures of Mr. Stuart and doctored them in a way to indicate wrong doing. These pictures were sent to the press in an effort to gain personal financial advantage for this individual. The individual in question has since been apprehended by the French police and is undergoing proper judicial process according to French law."

He looked up. Josh had been sitting in his car on the road far back so no one had noticed him coming. Mark saw him and went on reading his prepared speech.

"Therefore, on behalf of the Provincial Police, I wish to confirm that any doubts caused by these allegations must immediately be dropped without reservation and further I recommend that any action taken causing prejudice upon Mr. Joshua Stuart be overturned. Thank you."

Some of the press started yelling questions but he stepped off without answering any.

Vivian came back. "Please, I would like to ask you to keep your questions for the end. I still have a few things to say."

The press silenced, she looked at the crowd again. "In conforming with the recommendations from Sergeant Dexter, I want to inform you that I have reinstated Joshua Stuart immediately as the town manager with full authority and full compensation. As a matter of fact, I have asked Joshua Stuart to join us this afternoon and here he is!"

Josh came forward as the crowd turned in the direction Vivian was pointing to. There were mixed emotions. Some cheered, but many still had doubts. He walked to the platform and spoke.

"Thank you Madam Mayor. First, I want to give my apologies to all the citizens of Lakedge for what this whole situation has brought on. I am sorry that through a personal attack on my reputation, every citizen in Lakedge was affected. I am thankful to Sergeant Dexter and his counterparts in the French police as they were able to clear these allegations. I can assure you that I have always had the best intentions for the well-being of Lakedge and I rejoice we now have confirmation of the purchase of the mill. I will continue to do everything I can to manage this town successfully and I will give all my support to Frank and Jim in the administration of the mill. I also want to thank all those who remained convinced of my innocence and for the support you have provided me through this difficult period."

The cheers were louder as he walked off. Vivian addressed the press.

"I will now allow questions from the floor."

Hands were raised and questions were yelled. She pointed to a man with his hand up.

"Madam Mayor. Can you tell us how much this purchase is going to cost the town?"

"I'm afraid until all the paperwork is signed, this is something I can't reveal." As she said this she turned to Flagstone who nodded.

Someone else yelled. "Mr. Stuart, can you tell us what exactly happened when you went to France and how those pictures came about?"

Vivian looked at the group; they had forgotten to address this issue. Too late she realised that as a mayor, she should have thought about it. Josh and Mark were looking at each other, trying to decide who would address this. Mark signalled with his hand to Josh that he would go up.

"I would like to reinstate that there is still an on-going investigation in the criminal activities behind this event and therefore we are limited in what we can tell you about the situation. Suffice to say that these pictures were selected and arranged to influence the viewer into thinking that Mr. Stuart was involved in misconduct. We have yet to find and prove who sent the pictures to the media and if there was any wrong-doing on the part of the news media that printed them."

Vivian jumped on that occasion. She now knew what she wanted to say. "I want to add that this situation would never have occurred if the media would have done their homework and had verified the source of the pictures. I find this extremely irresponsible on the part of the newspaper. Right now, I can assure you that once the police investigation is over, we are going to take legal action against the particular news organisation for defamation of character and attempt to ruin the reputation of an outstanding citizen. I'm not going to let this lie without a fight!"

She moved back from the mike, and then moved forward again. "And most of you know how I am when I get into a fight."

Laughter and cheers came from the crowd. Someone yelled "You show them, Vivian!" Many similar comments erupted. The members of the media in the front suddenly felt a little less confrontational. For a minute, there were no more questions.

Then one of them asked. "Are municipalities allowed to operate profit-making organisations?"

Vivian wasn't sure how to answer so she turned to Josh. He came up. "I want to reassure you it is perfectly acceptable for municipalities to operate money-making activities. If you think about it, transit is a moneymaking operation. Many municipalities operate the electrical distribution. Certainly, the majority operate the water distribution. I'm sure if you examine other municipalities around the province you will find many examples."

He continued. "I do want to remind you that there will be a transition period. Our first concern is to get the mill back in operation. The mill has been closed for almost a month now. Although we have taken some measures to alleviate this, we fear we may have lost a number of key customers and we need to rebuild the relationship with all the past customers. Frank Ellis was selected as CEO mainly because of his background as a director of purchasing. His skills make him a good negotiator and we hope he will be in a position to revive some, if not all, of the contracts the mill had before the closure. We are going to institute a board of directors for the mill and this group will look into the long-term management of the mill. We may, at some point down the road, return the mill to a private enterprise model, but we want to have assurance before we do this, that never again will the mill be at risk of closing."

The person asking the question seemed satisfied with the answer so he stepped down. A few more questions, more general in nature came up.

Finally Vivian thanked everyone for coming and finished by saying. "I have one last announcement. In order to celebrate this great news, we will be holding a party in the community centre tomorrow evening. The whole town is invited. It's time we had some fun here. The last month has been much too gloomy to my liking. Come one, come all!"

More cheers and shouts of joy followed her as she stepped down and joined the group. Some media members asked for one-on-one interviews with different people. A few congregated around the mayor in what quickly became a scrum. She declined to say any more.

"Guys; we told you enough already. Now, I'm tired. When you carry my kind of load…" she put her hands to her thighs to indicate the weight she was referring to, "you can't stay standing too long in one place. I need to go sit down. Then, these people and I have a party to attend."

The scrum dispersed. Josh offered a few words to confirm much of what had been said and then left with the others. The crowd hung on in small groups discussing the news all over the parking area. It took a while but eventually everyone went back home. A public works crew dismantled the platform and loaded the sound system and generator in a truck. A few clouds had gradually formed in the sky over them and the snow started to fall very gently, eventually hiding the footsteps as if nothing had ever happened in the lot.

Saturday, March 19

"I don't like this," he said.

"No, me neither," she replied.

"This guy thwarted you first but I thought you were just too weak. Then when he got me, I saw how I had misjudged him," He turned to the little one, "Now he's having the upper hand on you as well. I don't know how we can get to him."

The little one looked at both of them. "Sure he fought your disease." While saying this he pointed at the lady. "That was something their science has been able to handle for decades now."

"It wasn't their science that did it, it was their unorthodox way of looking at the issue that controlled the influenza," the lady replied, offended, her Spanish accent heavily audible.

"Whatever. You weren't up to the task" The little one went on. The lady turned her back on him but listened. "You weren't more effective because you brought physical hazards on them." This time he was speaking to the big guy. His name, El Niño, meant the child, but his looks were anything but childish. The only thing immature about him was his attitude.

"I still caused them a lot of pain." the big guy said, whining.

"Sure, but you forgot that humans are extremely resilient. They get back up when they are attacked and they keep going. That's why you failed as well."

"You're not doing much better." the big guy replied.

"Oh, but I'm not done yet. When I bring it all together, I, the little Demon of Greed can accomplish a lot more than what the two of you together ever could. Because it's their heart I attack, not their body or their possessions. That will get them every time."

45. Party

Giddiness was in the air. Even the loud music couldn't drown the exuberance swelling in the room. As indicated by the bulging coat racks, the hall was already full. An extra table even had to be brought out near the entrance on which to pile more coats.

The line-up near the bar was long with the waiters doing their best to keep up. Although it had been put together in haste, many had pitched in to make it a success. People had started arriving as early as three o'clock in the afternoon. The bar opened at six and the first arrivals were already starting to show signs of intoxication. The sound level had inched up gradually and moved to a high pitch once the d-jay turned on the music.

At about mid-way through the evening, and hoping it wasn't too late to be heard, yet too early to disrupt the mood, Vivian Hedgerow and Josh Stuart went on stage and made a few short speeches to boost morale. They were mostly thank you to the people who had contributed in various ways to sustaining Lakedge through the difficult times they had experienced.

Vivian went on to reiterate how the community would take its survival very seriously from now on. She hinted they needed to look at other economic sustainability avenues. That's when Richard, the casino developer jumped on stage. He grabbed the microphone from Vivian's hand.

"That's a lie. Don't listen to her," He said angrily to the crowd. Vivian was so surprised by his sudden appearance from the midst of the crowd, she hadn't resisted. Josh didn't see him coming either. Richard evidently had a few drinks in him, but wasn't quite inebriated. The drinks were probably more to give him the courage to interrupt as he was doing. "What they are not telling you is how I came up with a plan to help this town and they turned it down. These people are feeding you with bull and you can't even see it."

Josh had now recovered and tapped him on the shoulder. "Hey! It's enough! I think you should regain your place now." He was firm in his tone yet not confrontational. Richard swore at him then turned back to the crowd. "You see? They don't want you to know the truth. They don't want me to tell you. Well I will anyway."

The hall was now very quiet. Even the people at the bar had stopped and the bartenders quit serving anyone.

"I made an offer to buy the Sparks mansion and turn it into a casino. If anybody wants to see it I have all the plans. A casino would have brought tourism and ensured that a lot of money came to Lakedge."

Josh insisted. "You need to get off this stage right away." He glanced and noticed Mark Dexter coming to the front with one of his officers. They were in civilian garbs, but they still represented the law. Richard didn't give up. "I'm going to stay right here until everyone knows. You see folks, they knew I had a good plan and they couldn't stop me. I came to your mayor to get help in making it happen and I was ready to offer some of the profits back to the town if I had the support in the first place. I need the permit from the municipality to make it happen."

Mark was nearing the platform. "What your mayor did instead is to request that the Sparks mansion be declared a heritage property. If this is approved, then I can't renovate and I can't turn in into a casino. This means no jobs for you people, no money for your stores, and no additional revenue for the town. Is that what you want?"

Mark was now on stage, and together with his partner they took him by the arms and gently pulled him away and tried to get the microphone out of his hand. Mark informed him. "Sir, I am Sergeant Mark Dexter of the Lakedge Detachment of the Provincial Police. I am asking you now to get down or I'll have to arrest you for disturbing the peace."

Richard took a last chance to yell in the microphone. "Even the police are on their side! I tell you, someone is going to pay for this! You can't stop…" Mark got the microphone. Richard tried to wiggle away but both officers now had a firm grip on him. They escorted him down and made their way to the door. They helped him find his coat and stayed at the door until they were sure he was gone.

Vivian and Josh confided a few minutes. The crowd was now mumbling, the noise level almost as high as before they had started. There were questions on everyone's face. Josh read them and knew they had to say something.

After a few moments, both Vivian and Josh turned to the crowd and gave explanations for their decision. They gave details on what happened in other places where casinos were opened. They provided a lot of information based on the research Josh had done. They even answered a couple of questions yelled from the crowd. In the end, Vivian promised this would be discussed again at council and everyone was welcome to share in the discussion. She promised a public meeting on the subject. She wanted to get back to the party. The initial happiness that had engrossed the party had been dimmed by Richard's outburst. The music came on again but no one went up to dance for a while. The conversation had turned to casinos and the Sparks' mansion.

Jeff Wallis was in the crowd with his wife. His cell phone buzzed. He had forgotten all about it. He excused himself from the table and headed for the door, meanwhile answering and asking the caller to wait a second.

Once outside he went to the side of the building. There was a group of smokers there, chatting and discussing the situation just as seriously as everyone else inside. Jeff looked around for a place where he would be alone.

A few of the guys from the mill noticed him and chided. "Wow, Jeff, a cell phone? I never thought you'd become so high-tech." It drew laughter and Jeff smiled uncomfortably, still trying to get some privacy.

He did find a spot where he felt fairly sure his conversation wouldn't be overheard. The guys weren't paying much attention to him otherwise they would have noticed the happiness had left him the second the phone rang. He seemed to argue for a while but gradually calmed down and in the end had an air of resignation to him. He went back in and told his wife he was going out for a breath of fresh air. It was too stuffy for him in here. When she inquired about it, he reassured her he would be back soon.

He tried to be as subtle as possible, not wanting to draw attention to his departure. He was gone for less than an hour, then returned, got a beer, and sat with his wife. She was so involved in conversations with her friends that she had hardly noticed his absence.

46. Escapade

The snow was twirling around swiftly, slapping her face. She clung tightly to her boyfriend's chest, the speed of the snowmobile creating a force threatening to throw her off at every turn. She loved it.

Amanda knew there would be consequences for her escapade. She knew she shouldn't be here but she brushed it off. For now she felt   more alive than ever. This was freedom, exhilaration, adventure; everything life should be about. She wasn't going to let any guilt spoil the moment. She wanted to experience this to the fullest.

The full moon was flashing through the top of the pine trees like a strobe light. The sky was clear and the snow on the ground was light. The vehicle kept speeding through paths already dug up by other snowmobiles.

Their vehicle was somewhat slow according to Tim's concept of speed. He had wanted to use his father's new snowmobile, but his dad had refused. The treads on the belts were a shredded in spots and the skis were slightly warped but the old one still worked. Tim had to constantly fight to correct the course and keep the vehicle centered but he was used to it.

They went into places she didn't even know existed. Tim seemed to know his way around the area. Then he slowed down and came to a road crossing. She recognised it as the top end of Industrial Avenue, the road that led to Sparks Mill.

"I have an idea," Tim said, "Let's go to Sparks Mill."

Amanda was a bit surprised at the suggestion. "Why would we want to go there?"

"There's all sorts of machines. I'll show you."

Her conscience seemed to kick back in gear. "Are we allowed?"

"Nobody's been there in over a week since it was closed down. Don't worry, there's no guards, or dogs, just a fence that's easy to go over. I've done it many times."

She still hesitated a bit but her desire for adventure was stronger so she agreed. They sped along the road towards Sparks Mill.

As Tim had predicted there was nobody around. The place was deserted. There weren't even any lights. Only the full moon illuminated the piles of wood, now abandoned and snow-covered. The gate was closed and locked. A "*No Trespassing*" sign had been installed in front but they ignored it. The gate was almost ten feet high.

"You want us to climb over that?" Amanda enquired.

"Wait, I know a spot in the back where it's not as high. We'll go around." He went through the empty parking lot and then slowly crawled over the embankment and into the fresh snow. There were no paths here. The snow gave in under the weight of the vehicle and he had to manoeuvre bit by bit until he rounded the gate to the north end. There was a small hill on that side which brought the gate to about seven feet. Tim brought the snowmobile close to the fence and turned it off.

"We'll use the snowmobile to give us a boost." Tim explained. "Here, I'll lift you part way then you climb the rest and jump over."

Amanda followed the instructions and was soon dangling over the fence trying to get down on the other side. Tim reached her, went down and jumped faster than she did, then grabbed her legs to help her down the rest of the way.

Her body was tingling from the excitement. She was doing something she shouldn't and it was thrilling. She wondered if it was a sensation criminals experienced when breaking the law.

They walked slowly around various piles of wood and Tim led them to the small vehicles' compound. In a corner of the lot three and four-wheeled off-road vehicles sat, parked in a line. He went to a three-wheeler and started it.

Amanda came close and whispered. "What are you doing? What if somebody hears us?"

Tim laughed. "Silly, nobody can hear us from this far. The closest home is kilometres away. Here, take this one, I'll start another one."

"Tim, I've never driven one of these."

"It's simple, let me show you. Hop on."

She climbed on and he demonstrated the basic controls. Then he let her try it. She moved forward in jerking motions at first but soon got the feel of it and started driving the vehicle down the main path. He caught up to her and they started racing up and down the yard.

Amanda was laughing and screaming in enjoyment. After almost an hour, her trike ran out of gas. Tim came to get her. They abandoned Amanda's three-wheeler there and she hopped behind Tim. They drove around one more time then Tim suggested they go into the main building.

The doors weren't locked. Who would want to steal any of this equipment anyway? They fumbled around in the dark. Tim tried to turn on some lights but the switches didn't respond. The electricity to the whole compound seemed to have been turned off.

They went into a lounge. Amanda went to sit on a sofa, exhausted but thrilled with her adventure. Tim came next to her. He started snuggling close suggesting that it would help them conserve their heat in this cold. Amanda didn't resist and soon they were kissing.

The excitement of the ride, the escapade, the danger of getting caught, all created an added ecstasy that both of them felt deeply. They were getting into heavy petting when they heard a noise. They both stopped abruptly.

The sound of an engine was coming their way. They stood and went to the window looking out towards the parking lot. It confirmed their fear. A snowmobile approached the compound. It stopped and a large man came off. He took out some sort of tool and went to the gate. He snapped the chain blocking the gate and walked into the compound in seconds.

Tim watched, frozen. Amanda tried to pull him down. "We have to hide. What if this man sees us?"

Tim seemed to come out of his daze. They crouched and watched the man go toward one of the sheds. He kicked the door open. He went in and came out with gasoline cans. He transported two of them near the building where Tim and Amanda were hiding. This was the building where all of the main machinery for the mill was housed.

They lost sight of him. They kept down and out of view.

The man came back and got more gasoline. He did this four more times. Then they waited quite a long time. Suddenly they saw the man running away towards the main gate. He went out, jumped on his snowmobile and sped away.

All of this seemed very strange and they couldn't figure out what had happened until they heard the explosion. Immediately after, they saw the flames. The whole side of the building was engulfed in them. More explosions occurred as the fire reached the other gas cans. The smoke started to spread. Amanda panicked and started screaming. Tim looked around. He couldn't distinguish much behind them. There were no exits in sight.

He saw the window. "Here, the window, we have to leave through here!"

Amanda was still transfixed by the glow. She couldn't move. Her body refused to respond. Tim pulled her violently to get her to react. She coughed from the smoke and finally followed Tim. He started banging on the window to break it. He never imagined windows were this tough. He didn't have anything hard to break it with. Amanda joined in and both of them knocked on the glass in unison. Then the glass broke and shards flew all over them. Amanda fell towards the outside. She stabbed her wrist on a sharp piece of glass still hooked to the frame. The blood started squirting. She screamed, this time in pain. Tim began removing glass pieces from his face. He looked at Amanda and saw blood everywhere. She was holding on to her wrist.

Neither of them knew first-aid but Tim remembered having seen how they applied pressure to a wound in movies, so he took off his mittens and put one of them on her cut, trying to do the same.

Now the smoke was heavy and dark. They started to feel the heat radiating from the fire. Tim pulled the couch closer to the window and helped Amanda on it. He removed the largest pieces of glass still on the window frame. Then he pushed Amanda up and over the window. She fell into the snow outside. Tim quickly joined her.

"This way!" He pointed to a path around the compound to the location of their snowmobile.

"Wait!" Amanda mumbled amidst her tears. "I can't climb over the fence like this." Tim hadn't thought of it. He looked around for an answer.

"Then we have to go through the front gate and run to the snowmobile."

It seemed the right thing to do but it would be a long path in deep soft snow. He pulled her arm in the direction he was aiming for. She followed. They ran through the parking lot and followed the fresh path they had made just an hour earlier. But the snowmobile hadn't really compacted the snow that much. So, at every step they took, their boots dug deep in the snow. They had to lift their legs way up out of the snow each time only to find the next step just as deeply entrenched as the previous. Tim was half carrying Amanda. She was using one arm to hold the one she had injured and keep pressure on the wound. She was loosing blood and her balance wasn't very good.

Every four or five steps Amanda wanted to stop and stay there. Tim had to coax her. Sometimes he would plead with her, other times he would yell at her and then going back to coaxing. Finally she gave up and lay down in the snow, unable to move forward. He yelled, screamed, pleaded and prayed but to no avail. She had given up.

Tim decided to leave her there and get the snowmobile. Already near exhaustion he struggled but finally reached the vehicle. He took a moment to catch his breath then started the motor. He retraced his steps and soon was beside Amanda. She wasn't moving and her breathing was shallow. He carried her onto the snowmobile. He put her helmet and goggles on, then strapped her as best he could. He would have to go slowly since she wasn't able to hang on anymore.

He eventually rejoined Industrial Avenue. That's when he realised he didn't know what to do next. He stopped and turned to her. "Where do we go now?"

Amanda was gradually loosing consciousness. "I need to go to the hospital," she replied faintly.

Tim was shaking. "We can't. If we go there, they will ask questions. They will ask us where we were. They'll think we started the fire."

Amanda replied. "Tim, I don't want to die. I don't care what they ask. I just want to go to the hospital."

Tim still resisted. "Can't your mother help you with this? She knows first-aid, doesn't she?"

Amanda was losing strength but still had more sense than Tim. "My mother will ask even more questions than the hospital, you know that. I'm not ready to see her looking like this. Go to the hospital!"

Tim couldn't argue any longer. He went down Industrial Avenue and headed for the hospital.

47. Fire

Someone had seen the glow rising above the trees. At first, they thought it was the northern lights but quickly dismissed it. The colours and shades had nothing in common with the phenomena. Eventually, a couple of people hopped into a car and went in the direction of the light. They arrived near Sparks Mill only to be confronted with an inferno. A 9-1-1 call was made, and crews were on their way. When they arrived, there was nothing they could do. With no fire hydrants and no major source of water the firefighters quickly knew that the place was doomed.

The one tanker they had was aimed towards the nearest edge of the forest on the side closest to the parking lot. There was no way to reach the opposite side without going through the compound, and with the intensity of the fire, that option was inconceivable.

Chief Grossman was at the community centre attending the party when his pager vibrated. It took him a few seconds to realise what was the feeling on his belt. With the loud music creating a vibration of its own, he wasn't sure he could distinguish between the two. He pulled it out and saw the number for the dispatch. He went outside to call and as he looked up noticed that the sky was brighter than usual for this hour. He soon got the news and understood. He ran back inside and found Joshua.

"Josh, we have a major problem. There's a fire at Sparks Mill. It's bad."

Josh's face changed from the joy and laughter of a few seconds ago to a total surprise and dismay. He jumped up from his seat, looked around the room and noticed Jim Stone and Frank Ellis chatting at a table.

He ran to them, Chief Grossman right behind him. He repeated the news his fire chief had just given him and provoked a similar reaction from the two.

They all headed for the exit and crammed into the fire chief's pickup. He put on the siren and lights and sped out of the parking. Many people had noticed the commotion and came out to see what was going on. Some of them saw the glow and got in their cars. In a matter of minutes there were people on cell phones and the news went around. The music died, the community centre emptied and most of the town rushed towards Industrial Avenue.

When they arrived, Josh and the others felt their heart constrict upon viewing the scene. A police cruiser was already blocking the access at about 500 meters from the parking lot entrance. Seeing the fire chief's red truck with lights and siren on, he opened the barricade for it, and closed the barrier behind the truck right away.

The smoke was dense and rising in a white and grey plume in the dark night. It danced and was swept by a light wind, taking on some of the colour of the fire underneath it. The flames rose high from the two main buildings and had now reached the wood piles to continue the damage.

They parked at a safe distance from the scene. Chief Grossman handed gortex coats to the other people in his truck and walked towards a fire captain who seemed to be the onsite commander. He addressed him and soon was briefed as to the situation. He let the captain retain command and came back to Josh.

"I'm afraid there's nothing we can do. It is too far gone and we don't have any way of combating it. All we can do is limit the spread. Luckily with all the snow we have had, the trees are wet and it shouldn't turn into a forest fire. Once the bulk of the wood supply stocked in the compound has burned, we will be able to contain it."

Many people were starting to converge on the location. Some started crying, other started hugging each other. The smoke rising over what used to be their place of employment suddenly robbed the happiness and hilarity that had engulfed the community for the last twenty-four hours.

Vivian Hedgerow arrived to where Josh and the others were observing in silence. She was panting. John Grossman took her aside and repeated his rundown of the situation.

She seemed ready to cry. Her face was as white as a ghost except for rays of orange reflecting in her eyes. It was a scene she couldn't bear to see, yet from which she couldn't tear herself away.

Mark Dexter joined them once he was assured his personnel had control over the crowd and traffic flow. Chief Grossman asked him what he thought.

"I can't really say right now, but I don't like the looks of it. I would like to think that it was accidental, but apparently the power had been turned off weeks ago so it couldn't be electrical. The place was locked when we came for the press conference yesterday so without any activity inside the compound the risk of accident is literally impossible. On top of this, one of your guys told me the front gate was opened and the lock had been cut."

"So this is a crime scene." Chief Grossman suggested.

"At this point we have to consider it as such." Sergeant Dexter confirmed.

"All right, I'll ask the guys to try and preserve as much evidence as possible."

"I'm going to look for witnesses. I wonder if anyone saw something. With most of the town at the community centre, I doubt we are going to get much. Whoever did this felt safe."

Josh was nearby, listening in. "Do you suspect anyone?"

"It's still early for this but right now there are a lot of suspects. First on my list is this casino developer. His outburst tonight was a bit too emotional."

Josh agreed. "Could be, but I don't know him enough to know if he would go to that extent."

"That's why I said, it's still too early. We have to do background checks on a number of people. I think I'm going to enlist the help of the private investigator who went to France. I got the feeling he was looking for something to keep him busy anyway." Mark said, hopeful.

They stayed there for a while, just watching, unable to express anything. Many thoughts went through each of their minds. The future of Lakedge seemed once more in peril. Then Josh felt his cell phone vibrate. He answered. It was Lindsey. She had gone home to wait for the news and received a call from the hospital. Amanda was there and was hurt. Lindsey was frantic.

He assured her he was on his way then turned to the group. "Amanda's been hurt. She's at the hospital. I need a ride from someone."

Vivian pulled her keys out and handed them to Josh. "Here, take my car. It's on the road about a block from the police gate. I hope Amanda's fine. Call me when you have more information."

Josh grabbed the keys and promised he would call. He ran to her car, found it and was on his way in a matter of minutes.

48. Hospital

Lindsey arrived first at the emergency room. There were people in the waiting room, a couple lying down on the chairs, others sitting. Tim Wallis was one of them. He was sitting alone, his snowsuit half open, the bottom part completely soaked. She saw him and wanted to go and ask him where Amanda was and what had happened but the nurse at the desk recognised her and called "Lindsey, Amanda is over here!"

She followed the nurse, thanking her. She took one last glance at Tim with his eyes down to the floor, not daring to look at anyone. His face revealed guilt and fear all over. She filed it in the back of her mind for future reference. She also noticed the scrapes on his face. The sight didn't reassure her on Amanda's fate.

They walked through a short hallway. Amanda was in one of the cubicles in the observation room. She was lying on the bed, the bottom half of her body under a white sheet, with a hospital gown covering the rest. A pile of wet clothes lay on the floor in the corner. Immediately, Lindsey noticed heavy bandages around her wrist.

Amanda was pale. She had her eyes closed and seemed to rest. She had a small bandage on her cheek and a few minor scrapes on her forehead. An IV drip with a blood transfusion ran down from a pole to her left arm. Lindsey's heart stopped as she saw her.

Just as they reached the bed she tapped the nurse on the shoulder and asked "How is she? What happened?"

The nurse smiled at her. "She'll be fine. I'll let Doctor Francis give you the whole story. Why don't you wait at her side? As soon as he's available he will come to speak with you."

Lindsey thanked her again as she went back to the front desk. Lindsey came closer to the bed. Her little girl was hurting. She felt guilt going through her soul. She knew she had been neglecting Amanda lately. With the stress of the situation the town was in, her attention had been turned to Joshua. The scandal had put additional strain on the whole family. Amanda was somewhat left on her own the last few weeks. Looking at her, ashen and bruised, Lindsey felt she hadn't been the mother her little girl needed.

Amanda seemed to notice her presence and opened her eyes. Immediately seeing her mother, she tensed. "Mom, I'm sorry. I didn't mean for this to happen." She tried to get up but Lindsey stopped her.

"Stay down. Take it easy. I'm not mad at you. I just want you to get well. We will talk about this later."

At that moment, Josh arrived, also escorted by the nurse. He joined Lindsey. "How is she?" he asked.

"I haven't seen the doctor yet. I don't know," Lindsey replied.

Again, Amanda tried to get up. "I'm okay Dad. I'm sorry."

Josh calmed her this time. Doctor Francis was on duty as the emergency room physician. Josh remembered him from the time of Margaret's illness. He had treated her for the Guillain-Barré syndrome when she first arrived. He knew Joshua both from reputation and from that event.

"Hi Josh, Mrs. Stuart," he greeted them.

"It's Lindsey," she replied.

"So this is your daughter?"

"Yes. How is she doctor?" Lindsey was quick to ask.

"She has a nasty cut on her left wrist, which required a few stitches. Because it was deep and into some major veins, it bled a lot. The loss of blood made her weak. The young boy brought her here just in time. She went into shock but we were able to bring her back and now she is doing better. I want to keep her here overnight for observation. She should be well enough in the morning to go back home. Apart from a few cuts and bruises, she may have a small scar on that cheek but nothing serious."

Lindsey let out a breath of relief. "Thank you doctor."

"No problem. That's why we're here," he smiled.

"So what happened?" Josh asked.

"Well I think you'll have to ask the young lady here for the details. I just patched up the results. From what I gather the wound came from a piece of glass slashing her wrist. She did get into a bit of smoke but there are no complications on that part. The exhaustion of the trip and the loss of blood is what caused her to faint and go into shock."

Josh frowned. "The smoke. What smoke?"

"As I said, you need to ask her. One thing is for sure, the smell of smoke is all over her clothing."

Lindsey was already over Amanda, prepared to ask for more. She needed to know. The doctor left them.

"Amanda dear, I won't get mad at you I promise, but I want you to tell me everything." Lindsey started.

"We didn't do it, Mom. It wasn't us."

"You didn't do what?" she asked, puzzled.

Amanda explained how they had gone on a ride and ended up at Sparks Mill. She related some of the events leading up to the fire, their escape, and her injury. Josh asked questions along the way to clarify the story. He was concerned. His daughter was his main priority right now, but knowing she would recover reminded him of the fire and the impact this would have on the town. A small weight was being lifted from his shoulders as Amanda was now out of danger, but a much larger weight had been added.

They talked a bit about Tim and his condition. Amanda asked if she could see him. At first, both parents resisted. Then she insisted "He saved my life. He's the one who brought me here. He had to carry me part of the way."

"He's the one who brought you out there in the first place. If he hadn't, all of this wouldn't have happened," Josh retorted.

"He didn't bring me anywhere I didn't want to go. It's not his fault. He did save my life and that's what's important." Although she was still weak, her insistence forced Josh and Lindsey to agree.

"I'll go get him." Josh said.

"Dad…" Amanda stopped him. He turned. "Please be nice to him," she pleaded. He frowned, took a deep breath, and agreed.

It took a few minutes and he came back with Tim at his side. The young boy still didn't dare look anyone in the face. His eyes were glued to the floor.

Lindsey tried to greet him in the best possible tone she could muster through her remnant of anger. "Hi Tim. Are you hurt?"

"No, Mrs. Stuart. I'm fine." He replied, still not looking up.

"Do you want me to call your parents?" she suggested.

Immediately his expression changed, he looked at her with intense fear and quickly replied, "No. Please don't."

She was taken by surprise and didn't insist. "Oh… Well, I see." Then remembering why he was there, she added. "Amanda wanted to speak to you."

His eyes went back to the floor. Josh opened the curtain a bit so that all three of them could get to the cubicle.

"Tim. Are you okay?" Amanda asked, with legitimate concern in her voice. Lindsey couldn't help read something into this. She had been so inattentive to her daughter's needs that she hadn't seen how involved Amanda had become with the boy. Now, seeing him as a hero would have an even more profound impact on her and the budding relationship.

Tim wasn't quite the person Lindsey had hoped Amanda would connect with. She wanted a respectable man from a well-to-do family as most mothers want for their daughters. Tim was the son of a lumberjack, living in what she would rank as substandard conditions. The little she knew of the family didn't make much of an impression on her. It seemed to her the Wallis family spent more of their income on beer than on food and clothing.

Josh and Lindsey walked away from the bed to give a bit of privacy to their daughter.

"What are you thinking about Josh?" Lindsey asked reading concern and stress in his face.

"I'm a bit overwhelmed right now. The mill is almost burned down. I'm not sure exactly what she saw but it's clear that she was there when the fire was set. She just confirmed to me that this was a criminal event. I'm going to have to speak to Mark Dexter."

"I'm just relieved Amanda is not badly hurt. At this time, I can't take much more." Lindsey had tears stuck to the corners of her eyes.

Josh took her in his arms and tried to console her a bit. The hug actually did some good to him as well. They stayed there hanging on to each other for a while. The world around them was falling apart.

Tim came out of the cubicle. "I'm going home now. I'm sorry for what happened to Amanda. I'm just glad she's okay."

He said all this without looking at them. Josh took out his hand and presented it to Tim. Tim looked up, uncertain, and accepted Josh's hand. Josh shook it saying "I have to thank you Tim. Amanda told us how you carried her and brought her here. If it wasn't for you she might be dead. Thank you for saving my daughter's life."

Tim didn't know what to reply. Lindsey wanted to emphasize the moment. Although this wasn't her choice for her daughter, she knew that she may have to build a relationship with this young man. Now might be the best time to start. She held out her hand as well. "I also want to thank you Tim. I understand that this was a brave act you did." Tim shook her hand still unable to answer. He left and they returned to Amanda's bedside.

They discussed plans for the night. Josh would have to go back to speak with Mark Dexter so Lindsey would stay with her for the night.

Anyway, Josh had to return Vivian's car. They kissed each other in turn, and then he left. Lindsey started to make herself comfortable.

Monday, March 21

Fire Destroys Lakedge Icon

Only a few charred log piles and the foundation of a few structures remain on the site of Sparks Mill in Lakedge after a huge fire engulfed the wood product factory during Saturday night.

The fire raged on throughout the night and most of the day on Sunday with firefighters only able to stand and watch. Having no hydrants on site and only minimal access to water, they had to wait until the wood was almost completely burned to go in for a final attack and smother it.

No one was hurt but the damage is estimated at over one hundred million dollars. It is too early yet to identify the cause of the blaze according to fire officials. The fire comes right on the heel of an announcement Friday afternoon from Mayor Vivian Hedgerow that the town was coming into possession of the mill. According to the mayor, the town had acquired the mill, and papers were going to be signed on Monday morning.

When reached, the mayor was unable to confirm the impact of the fire. "I can't get my head around it right now. The town is going to need a bit of time to sort this out and decide where we go from here." Hedgerow told the press.

Lakedge had been struggling in the last few weeks since the death of the owner of the mill, Warren Sparks. His heir, afraid that the mill would be mismanaged in her absence, had shut down operations temporarily and arranged to sell the company. Much debate had arisen about the way the transaction was handled and the town manager himself, Joshua Stuart, was identified in some compromising pictures, which were apparently forged to discredit the administration of the Town.

The next chapter in the Lakedge soap opera has yet to be written, but controversy seems to be right in the middle of every page.

49. Arson

Mark Dexter, Nathan Makwa, and Robert Cloutier walked carefully around the property. The fire was out although there were still embers in many places and wisps of smoke rising from piles of ashes and logs. The air was thick with a smell of burnt wood and a faint cloud of ashes shrouded the evergreens.

This was now considered a crime scene. Once the fire was out, the police took over. Mark was a good policeman, but the expert in fires was Nathan. A native from the Ojibwa nation, a volunteer firefighter, and a long-standing resident of Lakedge, he was the best person for the job. He could read signs in the snow no one else could see. He easily recognised elements conducive to fire and he could read the path of the fire as if it was a book.

Through the reeking smell of ash and smoke, Nathan was able to distinguish a faint smell of gasoline. He identified the starting point and determined the progression the fire took. There was an accelerant to ensure the fire would grow quickly. Nobody lived nearby so the fire was only noticed when it was too late to do anything to stop it. There were no water sources nearby and tanker trucks were insufficient to enable any kind of fire suppression. All the factors played against the survival of the mill.

The place was a total loss. The task at hand for the three was to identify all the possible evidence so they could track the culprit and ensure they could use this in court. Mark knew he needed help and he had called Robert Cloutier. The retired detective had driven in the middle of the night to get there. Anything to get him out of the house was good. Mark suspected Lakedge or even the police wouldn't be in much of a position to pay for Robert's services but the change in environment and the action was payment enough for Robert.

Mark spoke with Joshua and confirmed the suspicions of arson. The little bit of information that Nathan had given Mark had been enough to help him finding clues. They had picked up the remains of the broken lock, and they had found the snowmobile tracks at the spot at the back of the fence where Amanda and Tim had jumped over. Nathan had also noticed the blood trail where Amanda had walked with her slashed wrist.

Trucks and firefighters had trampled the parking lot, leaving very little possibility of noticing snowmobile tracks there. They searched for entry points around the parking but most of them were from heavily travelled areas. Snowmobiling was a popular leisure activity in the area, with many enthusiasts travelling over the trails leaving minimal evidence to identify a single vehicle amongst the others.

They were despairing of finding any evidence. Trying to identify one snowmobile in Lakedge was like finding a needle in the proverbial haystack. They worked around the property for over an hour coming up almost empty-handed. In the end, they sat in Mark's cruiser to discuss what they had.

Robert was the investigation expert and led the way. "Well, we don't have much from this end. We will need to have a long chat with the two kids. So far, I think they are the only solid lead we have."

Mark agreed. "I also want to ask the population to help in this. I will send out a request for people who know something to come forward."

"Good idea." Robert said. "In the meantime, do you have any suspects?"

"I guess we have a few but it's so vague, I can't really be sure."

"Try me." Robert suggested.

"Well there's the whole real estate deal that didn't necessarily please everyone. I don't have all the information on the amount of the sale but maybe this lady wanted to collect insurance. If she was geared to get more money from insurance rather than selling the mansion, it could be a motive."

Robert disagreed "I've met her. She's tough and inconsiderate but I don't think she's a criminal. It seemed to me that she just wanted to get rid of any ties with Lakedge as fast as possible. Wouldn't she have guessed this would have brought her right back in the midst of it instead? A sale would have been a much faster way out. I saw where she lives. I don't think money was a factor for her."

The others nodded then Robert added. "But I'll keep an open mind. I've been surprised before. Come to think of it, she did say we could burn in hell when I saw her last." He paused, then added, "Who else? Anyone local?"

Nathan intervened. "Possibly. There may be somebody else somewhere giving the orders but the person who did this knew the place. The gasoline was sprayed at the point where it was likely to cause the most damages to the mill. He, or she for that matter, didn't go for the logs or the administration building first. Whoever it was knew the mill couldn't operate if the main wood transformation unit was destroyed."

"So somebody local might be disillusioned by the purchase of the mill. Who would benefit from it? Doesn't most of the town depend on the mill to survive?" Robert wondered aloud.

Mark replied. "That's what gets me. Why would anyone from Lakedge want to destroy their main source of income?"

"I've seen people do strange things in my career. Usually it all boils down to one thing: money." Robert replied.

"That may be the reason. If someone wanted this place destroyed and paid enough for it, then who could resist?" Mark paused a second then had a thought. "I think I'll have a talk with Peter Cohen. He's the local bank manager. I'll ask him to be on the lookout for any unusual transactions."

"That might work, but if this person was smart, they would deal in cash alone and they wouldn't hide it in the bank. What you may want to look for is someone suddenly spending a lot of money; maybe making major renovations to the house, buying a new car or some luxury items." Robert suggested.

"Well, that gives us a few avenues on the local side. Who do you think would pay to have this done? And why?" Mark said.

"Well for starters, who else wanted to buy the mill? For what reason did they want to buy it?" Robert answered.

"Right. There's also that guy who interrupted the party, the developer. He talked about a casino. He said the mayor was misleading the citizens. He also said the town would pay for this. We had to escort him out."

"When did this happen?" Robert asked, taking notes about their discussion.

"Oh, a few hours before the fire."

"We'll add this guy to the list. I'll find out more about him and maybe pay him a visit. In the meantime, if you can round up those kids, we'll have an interview with them. Let me know when you're ready." They shared phone numbers and Mark drew a map of the town with the location of the main points of interest: the town hall, the hospital, and Trucker's Corner. They each went to their car and headed into town.

50. Litigation

Robert looked at the drawings on the wall. The framed illustrations were architectural representations of all sorts, but mainly of multi-storey buildings. A lot of modern elements of glass and steel were nested in beautifully landscaped environments.

Although he did appreciate the modern style of the facilities including the one he was waiting in, he had a preference for older homes and buildings. He wasn't a heritage buff but he felt the intricacies of the design, the attention to details and the artistry that used to be part of the construction business had been lost.

The door opened and Richard, the man with the casino idea, popped his head out. He had been told Robert wanted to see him but he didn't know why.

"Good morning sir, how can I help you?"

Robert looked at the receptionist and said. "Could I have a bit of your time to chat... in private?"

Richard noticed his look. "Sure, sure, come on in."

"Thanks." Robert walked into the office. He saw two seats in front of a desk. The room was wide. In one corner, a small table held a model building under a glass cover. The building was half modern, half older style resembling a Spanish mansion. It actually reminded him of some of the houses he had seen while on the Riviera. Immediately, he assumed this was the model for transforming the Sparks mansion into a casino.

He sat in one of the chairs as Richard closed the door behind them.

By the time Richard reached his chair on the other side of the desk, Robert got up again to shake his hand. "My name is Robert Cloutier."

He sat down again.

"Pleased to meet you Mr. Cloutier. How may I help you?"

"I heard about a plan for a casino. I wanted to know more about it."

Richard was pleased and surprised at the same time. "The casino? Of course. Have you seen the model?" He pointed proudly at the glass-covered design like a father showing his newborn baby.

Robert got up and looked at it. Richard started to give a description of all the amenities planned for the facility. Robert nodded and asked a few questions, helping to enhance Richard's enthusiasm about the project.

They sat down again. Richard asked "So in what manner are you interested in this project?" Then a doubt came. His tone changed. "You're not from the ministry, are you?"

Robert smiled. "I'm not sure which ministry you are talking about, but no I'm not from any ministry."

Richard relaxed. "Oh good. I was afraid someone was looking into this heritage affair. I haven't had a lot of time yet to prepare my defence on this."

"Funny you should mention it. I heard you had some difficulties and ran into some kind of a stumbling block. This is where I come in. I might be able to help you here…for the right price of course."

Richard's eyes widened. "What do you mean?" He stopped for a second and asked "Who are you anyway? Who do you work for?"

Robert gave a wide smile. "I work for myself. I'm really nobody. I just have some skills you could put to use. Let's just say I'm in the investigation business and I am good for all kinds of jobs most people wouldn't do."

Richard started to tense. "I'm not sure of what jobs you are talking about but I don't really think I want that kind of help."

"Now, now. Don't worry. I'm very good at what I do; I am a professional. You have nothing to worry about when it comes to my abilities. Let me give you a few ideas. You see, everyone has a skeleton in their closet. You need to search a few closets to show off the skeletons some of your adversaries are hiding. I can do that for you."

Richard was unsure but curious. "What adversaries are we talking about?"

"Well, for one, I think the mayor in Lakedge is trying to stop your project. I heard you had a run-in with her last week."

"I did. It wasn't very smart but I had just heard about her submission to designate Sparks mansion as a heritage. If that goes through, I can't make any renovations in the facility maybe not even on the grounds either. My whole project dies with this. I was mad. I knew I would find her at the party so I went there to confront her. I wanted the whole town to know. Unfortunately, the whole town thinks of her as a goddess. Nobody will challenge anything she says."

Robert bent closer to the desk. "That's just it. Everybody thinks she's a goddess. My question is: do they really know who she is? You don't think of her as a goddess, but you have nothing to back it. What if I unearthed a bit of dirt on her you could use to discredit her. Then you campaign the citizens for the casino. Get them to decide. Call for a referendum. What do you think?"

"You would do this? Why?"

"I told you. I do it for money. You see, I'm recently retired and I'm looking for new sources of revenue. I have all the time in the world and nothing to keep me busy." Robert explained with his hands widespread.

Richard scratched his forehead. "I like the idea, but I'm not sure I'm ready to go to this extent."

Robert felt the bait was taken. Now he had to make sure the hook was set. "Are you squeamish, Richard? I'm sure you've done other things in your life not quite legal but necessary for the advancement of your dreams."

"You don't really know me, Mr. Cloutier. I may have pushed the limit here and there, but I have never broken any laws. I may consider a campaign to promote the casino concept but I'm not sure I want to resort to the kind of services you are suggesting."

Robert looked at him intently. "You want me to believe you have always followed all the rules. You have never done anything to get a deal through no matter what?"

Richard was getting indignant. "No sir. I don't like where this conversation is leading. I'm an honest man. People may not like all my ideas and I may be a bit pushy when I want something, but that's called sales. There's nothing illegal in my approach. I think this discussion is over."

He got up to indicate he wanted Robert to leave. Robert sat upright in the chair. "Very good Richard. I think you have passed the test. I believe you. Now, let me tell you a bit more about myself. I am a private investigator and recently retired from the Winnipeg Police Force. I also have some friends in Lakedge that asked me to help them investigate the whole Sparks affair."

"What do you mean? The fire?"

"Yes, the fire. I see you are already informed."

Richard grinned but stayed standing. "This is a small place Mr. Cloutier, if that is your real name. Word gets around fast."

"Yes, that's my real name. As I said, I am investigating the fire at the mill. I thought I would give you a bit of a test to see if you might be the one who caused this fire in the first place."

Richard was indignant, turning red in the face. "That's preposterous! I had absolutely nothing to do with this!"

Robert tried a calm tone. "I understand but I had to do it. You have to admit things don't look too good for you. You have an idea. It gets rejected and blocked. You threaten those people in front of half the town, the police escort you out, and then the mill which has just been bought by the people you threatened, burns to the ground. Who do you think the police see as the primary suspect?"

Richard sat down as though a weight were pressing on him. "But I didn't do it."

"You know that, and I am inclined to believe you, but with the incident at the party, until we find who actually did it and we can clear your name, you are at the top of the suspect list."

Richard sighed heavily. "So what do I do to convince the police of my innocence in this?"

"Well, there's not a lot you can do, but you could lay low for now on the whole project. Let the Town present their case for a heritage and work with the system to present your case. Don't do anything to give to the police or the citizens of Lakedge a reason to suspect you."

"I can't drop this! It's a chance of a lifetime! The mayor and the citizens of Lakedge don't see the opportunity to save the community, they are missing the boat."

Robert shook his head. "I don't agree with you on this. I've seen the results of gambling as a police officer. I don't think this is the solution."

He rubbed his hand still a bit stiff from the burns, not quite healed yet. "I'll tell you what I think might be a better plan. Take it or leave it. Basically you want to make some money and you think this is the deal that will do it for you."

Richard objected. "Stop right there! You make it sound as if I'm a devious real estate mogul ready to do anything to get rich. That's not true. Sure I want to make money, like everyone else. I also care about these people if you can believe it. I saw their plight and I thought my idea would be a way to get them out of their misery. With the mill burned down, they need the help even more now," he stopped than quickly added, "And no, I didn't burn it down so they would need my help."

"I see. You have ambition and I can read it. So if it's not money, what is it?"

"I'll be honest with you. I thought this casino would become a marvel of mixing new and old design. You may have noticed that I am very much interested in architecture. I have an architectural degree but I was never good enough to become a full-time architect. I want to design the next architectural wonder and get recognition in a field I always loved. That's my real goal. The Sparks mansion casino would have helped me reach it."

Robert nodded in understanding. "Interesting." They didn't speak for a few moments. Robert started again, "I have an idea. If you are meeting so much resistance on one project in Lakedge, why not try something else? With the mill burned, the town will have to raise money to rebuild and I'm not on the inside to tell you their plans. At some point down the road however, they will be ready to rebuild. Would your architectural skills be of any use there? If you dropped your attempt at transforming the mansion into a casino in exchange for exclusive rights to design the new mill, you may have a deal with the town."

Richard moved forward in his chair. "I don't know. It's an idea I hadn't thought of."

Robert could see that the man was thinking deeply. "I think I'll leave now. You have some design work to do."

Richard lifted his head. "I do? I mean, yes, I do. Thank you. Mr. Cloutier."

He started escorting Robert to the door. "Oh by the way, if the police wants my help in any way regarding this investigation, please tell them I have nothing to hide. I will be most happy to cooperate."

Robert thanked him shaking his hand. "I think you've already done quite a lot."

They walked out. As Robert was leaving he heard Richard telling his secretary. "Hold my calls, no visitors! I have a lot of work to do!"

51. Questions

The police station was small but sufficient for a community the size of Lakedge. Of course Robert had been used to more amenities than this with the Winnipeg Police. He was a bit familiar with the place after his visit the previous summer to investigate the murder of four students in a nearby cottage. That case had landed him the ire of Inspector Moreno. He still shivered at the thought.

Today, he didn't report to Inspector Moreno. He was here on a volunteer basis. He knew this community wouldn't be able to pay for his work but he didn't care. He was doing what he always wanted to loved: police investigation. Having one more chance to do what he loved was remuneration enough. His pension would pay the bills.

Mark arrived with the two teenagers. Lindsey Stuart and Jeff Wallis, Tim's dad, were following. They all walked in and Mark pointed them to the small boardroom serving as an interview room. He introduced Robert as a private investigator helping on the case of the Sparks Mill fire.

Both teenagers seemed afraid. A police station for a young person can already be intimidating, being questioned by Mark whom they knew very well would have made things easier, but having a stranger and their parents in the room enhanced the anxiety in Amanda and Tim. Robert noticed a bruise on the young boy's cheek. There was a red blotch starting to turn blue just below his left-eye, it appeared recent. Someone had hit Tim earlier today.

Amanda's hand was bandaged but she would be fine. Her eyes were a bit puffed from crying.

Mark started, looking directly at the teens. "So here is what we know. We know you were at the mill the night of the fire. We found the traces of your snowmobile and we identified the tracks positively to the vehicle. We know from your footsteps you were both there and we followed your tracks around the compound. We also followed the blood trace and we can most likely link it to your injuries. The hospital staff corroborated your story. What we don't know is what you were doing there and how did this fire start. So why don't you help us out here?"

Amanda started first, very defensive. "It wasn't us. We saw this man. He got some gasoline cans and the next thing we knew there was a fire going all over."

Robert intervened. "Tell me more about this man."

Amanda replied. "He was huge…"

Tim quickly interrupted her. "No, he was small."

Amanda looked at him astonished. "What do you mean 'small'? He was big. He took two full cans of gasoline and carried them as if they didn't weigh anything."

Robert asked. "What else can you tell me about him? What was he wearing?"

Amanda replied obligingly. "He had a snowsuit. It was black with red stripes."

Tim interrupted again. "No, it was blue." He hesitated, and then added, "no stripes, just blue."

Amanda was dumbfounded. "Tim, what are you talking about? You saw him just like I did. The suit was black with red stripes!"

Robert stopped them both. He pulled Mark outside the room and whispered. "It's obvious these kids haven't had time to rehearse their story. So why don't we ask this young man to step out with his dad for a few minutes while we discuss the situation with the young lady."

Mark nodded in agreement and went back in. "Tim, Jeff, would you please follow me?" Tim gave a last glance at Amanda as he left the room. There was fear written all over his face. All three walked out and Mark gave instructions to the officer at the desk then came back in the room.

Robert asked again. "Why don't we start fresh? Give me a description of this man."

Lindsey was nervously wringing her hands together watching Amanda silently.

Amanda didn't seem so sure of herself anymore. Robert had noticed the exchange of looks and it seemed that something in Tim's eyes had scared her. She hesitated a bit. After a moment she must have made up her mind to stick to what she knew to be the truth. The stress of being so deep in trouble must have convinced her she didn't need any more.

She willingly offered the description. "He was a tall and big man. He wore a black skidoo suit with red stripes. He had a ski mask on so I couldn't tell who he was. He seemed to know the place because he went directly to the gate. He cut the chain and walked right to the shed. He got the gasoline cans out and I guess he lit the fire. Then he ran away on his snowmobile."

"Why did you say I guess? You're not sure?"

"By then he was out of sight."

Mark intervened. "Okay. Do you know what kind of snowmobile it was?"

Amanda bashfully admitted. "I don't know much about snowmobiles. I only rode on a couple. This one seemed new. It didn't make as much noise as Tim's. It had two lights instead of the one that Tim has on his."

Mark continued. "Did he wear a helmet?"

"No he didn't." She looked at her mother. "I was a bit surprised at this because I always wear a helmet when I'm on the snowmobile."

Lindsey nodded in agreement. Amanda was trying to show she followed at least some of the rules, wanting to get back in the good graces of her mother.

They tried to get more details and Amanda gave them everything she remembered. Robert was satisfied. This was just a typical teenager looking for excitement, maybe even a quiet place to make out, not an incendiary criminal.

"Mrs. Stuart, Amanda, we thank you for coming down here. We may have to call on you again if we find anything else that requires more questions."

Lindsey was ready to comply. "Yes sir. Please don't hesitate to call. We will do everything we can to help."

Amanda stayed silent. She had said enough for today.

As they walked out Robert observed her intently. Her eyes connected with Tim's and he lowered his look. She raised her eyes at the boy, clearly expressing her incomprehension at his attitude. He stayed numb and inexpressive. She walked past him without saying a word. Robert read a whole story here, beyond what words would have conveyed.

They invited Tim and Jeff in the room. The same questioning started. Tim hesitated at each question. The description he gave was completely the opposite of Amanda's. Robert knew he was lying. This boy was protecting someone, trying to throw them off course. He was a mere amateur and not a good liar at that.

So Robert prodded him further. "Tim, have you ever heard of being an accessory to the fact?"

Tim shrugged. Robert went on. "How about abetting a criminal? Do you know what that means?"

Tim stayed mute. Jeff moved in. "What is this questioning leading to, officer?"

"Mr. Wallis, I just want Tim to understand that if he tries to hide something from us in any way, he can be charged. So I want to be sure he understands and we can be certain he tells us all the truth. Right Tim?"

"So maybe we need a lawyer here, don't we?" Jeff asked.

"Tim isn't charged, so you don't need a lawyer. I'm just making sure he understands the importance of what he's saying here." Mark explained.

Neither Tim nor Jeff answered.

Mark and Robert tried a few more questions but quickly realised they were getting nowhere. They concluded the interview with instructions to remain available. After the two had left, Mark and Robert compared notes.

"So what do you think?" Mark asked.

"It's clear the boy is trying to protect someone. The girl was direct, she had her facts straight, she spoke without hesitation. He contradicted everything she said. I think she wasn't able to identify the person but he was. He knows who it is. It's probably someone close for whom he cares a lot. Otherwise he would have told us."

"Or maybe it's someone he's scared of." Mark suggested.

"That too. How much do you know about the kid and his father?" Robert inquired.

Mark thought quickly. "Tim is just your average teenager. He has a strong sense of adventure and likes to play pranks, but nothing unusual. Jeff works at the mill. He's been there most of his life. He's not very educated and not very smart so he has never really gone up in the ranks. I think he works on the shop floor but he's mostly there for his muscles, not as a skilled worker. He does have a bit of a knack for mechanical maintenance."

Robert pondered. "He fits the description. Big, strong, knew the place very well. It would make sense that Tim would be afraid to denounce his own father. The snowsuit with the red stripes was familiar to him, which is why he tried to change the description. He is either afraid his father will get back at him for telling or he cares for him and doesn't want him arrested."

"Knowing Jeff, I think Tim is probably more afraid than anything else. Now his father knows he was at the mill. If Jeff did this, he may actually be threatening Tim."

Robert agreed. "Did you notice the bruise on his face? That kid got a bad punch no later than this morning."

"I wouldn't be surprised if his father did this to him when he found out Tim was at the mill that night."

Robert looked at his notes. "What about the snowmobile? Do you know what kind Jeff has?"

Mark frowned, searching in his memory. "Now that you mention it, he does have a new model. I noticed it when I went out to his place. We didn't pay much attention to it because we quickly identified the older version as the one matching the tracks near the mill."

"Do you remember how many headlights it had?"

"Yeah. It was a double-header. It had a headlight on each side of the front cover."

Robert smiled. "So another hit there. It looks like we have a primary suspect. What we would need is that snowsuit. It may even have some gasoline on it. It would seal the case."

Mark agreed but was annoyed. "What I don't get is why. Jeff worked at the mill all his life. He knew there were plans to reopen it. It would have meant work for him."

"Well that's what we need to find out. I don't think this Jeff is much of a brain from what you tell me. It probably means someone paid him to do it. If we get a warrant to search, we might find the snowsuit, but we may also find something else; like money."

"I could ask to have his bank account reviewed." Mark proposed.

Robert agreed, but he struggled with doubt. It seemed too easy. This case was getting solved much too quickly. Somehow, Robert wasn't quite convinced they had the whole story yet and a lot more investigating would be required.

Maybe that was the way with small communities in remote places.

52. Despair

"I understand, Harry. I did notice that people were cancelling their appointments. So how are you going to split the work?"

She sensed hesitation at the other end of the line. Harry, the dentist and owner of the clinic where Lindsey worked, had called to tell her she didn't need to come in today and to ask her to take some time off for a while.

He hesitated on his response "Well, I'm afraid, I... I only asked you Lindsey. The other girls don't have someone at home to bring in a second salary so I have to keep them on, otherwise they'll go broke. You, on the other hand, have Josh to rely on. I hope you can understand my dilemma."

Lindsey tensed. She did understand but it still hurt to be the one selected to take a cut when everyone else would continue as if nothing happened. "If it's the money, I'll volunteer for a while until things get better."

Again, the response was slow to come. "There's not a whole lot for you to do here anyway. We have enough people already. Why don't you take it as a vacation?"

Lindsey didn't see March as a time for vacation particularly with the events of the last month; she needed to keep active.

"Harry, let me come and help, I'll go crazy here if I don't have something to take my mind off the situation my husband is having to deal with. I need to do things that have nothing in common with his responsibilities so I can be a good wife and be ready to support him when he comes home. I'm sure you can relate to this."

Once more the line went quiet. This time, she couldn't wait for Harry to give an answer. She knew the man enough to feel there was something else he wasn't telling her.

"Harry, what is it? Please talk to me! What's really going on?"

"Well, Lindsey, I don't know how to say this. You know I like you a lot. You know I have confidence in you... and in Josh for that matter, but..."

"Cut the bull, Harry. Spell it out. I don't need any patronising."

He hesitated. "It's just... people are talking, Lindsey. A couple of clients have asked not to have you as their hygienist anymore. They want me to switch them to someone else. Your presence in the clinic is having an impact on business. I'm sorry."

"What do you mean, people are talking? What are people talking about?" Lindsey was really angry now; a characteristic Harry wasn't used to. The sleeping lioness was awake.

"Well, people are hinting that maybe Josh, and the pictures and all that, weren't quite impossible. Add the fact that your daughter was connected with this fire, many think it's a plot planned by Josh involving your whole family."

His tone was apologetic but it didn't calm Lindsey down. "That's preposterous! Josh had nothing to hide! He went out there to try and save Lakedge! He got into a wasps' nest and got stung. In return, that's what the people of Lakedge are saying? And don't drag my daughter into this! She was just a witness! She had nothing to do with this fire!"

Harry quickly tried to undo the harm. "Don't get me wrong Lindsey. I know none of this is true. It's not me; it's what the people think. This is a small town, so people have opinions and they share them quickly. When a rumour goes out the next thing you know it becomes a fact."

She didn't buy it. "So if you really think it's not true, why are you sending me home? You're a coward Harry! You can't stand up to these people and tell them what you really think. It's easier to get rid of me so you can keep a good face in front of the others, right?"

She was out of control but he gave it a last try. "Lindsey, please calm down. It's not that. I have a business to run. If I try too much to go against what people say, I stand to lose everything I've worked so hard to build. I can't do that. You also need to think of the other employees working here. I have to make sure they still have a job."

"You don't seem too worried to make sure I have a job. It's my career. You're the only dentist in town. Where are people going to go if you fold? You're still a coward in my mind Harry."

"I'm sorry you feel that way. I can't do anything about it. I had to make a choice. I'm not happy about the choice I made but I have to stick with it. I'm really sorry."

"Sure you are. I'll remember it, Harry. Have a nice day!" She hung up violently hoping he heard her anger in the thump of the phone on the receptacle.

She went into the living room. She quickly went through a range of emotions. She shifted from fury to confusion, back to fury, and gradually broke down in tears of frustration and despair. Inside she felt hurt, broken. The pride she had always had to be part of the community and accepted by her peers not as a stranger now turned to hate. The hypocrisy of people was overwhelming. When things go well, people love you, but they turn on you as soon as the situation gets tense.

Now she had a decision to make. Would she tell Josh about the discussion she just had? He would have to know she wasn't going to work for a while, maybe never again. A thread of doubt suddenly came to her. After the way she had just addressed her boss, her chances of ever working there again were slim, even if everything else was resolved. How could she explain it to Josh?

She spent the next hour just sitting there pondering her situation, examining what she would tell her husband, what she would do with herself unemployed, how they would cope without her salary.

She used to think Lakedge had adopted her but today the feeling was gone. She felt empty, unloved, abandoned. It took her a long time to get up and find enough energy to get to some of the household chores. For the first time in her life, she had lost hope.

Wednesday March 23

The Book of Joshua, Chapter 1

1. *After the death of Moses the servant of the Lord, it came to pass that the Lord spoke to Joshua, the son of Nun, Moses' assistant saying:*

2. *"Moses My servant is dead. Now therefore, arise, go over this Jordan, you and all this people, to the land which I am giving to them – the children of Israel.*

3. *"Every place that the sole of your foot will tread upon I have given you, as I said to Moses.*

4. *"From the wilderness and this Lebanon as far as the great river, the River Euphrates, all the land of the Hittites, and to the Great Sea towards the going down of the sun, shall be your territory.*

5. *"No man shall be able to stand before you all the days of your life; as I was with Moses, so I will be with you. I will not leave you nor forsake you.*

6. *"Be strong and of good courage, for to this people you shall divide as an inheritance the land which I swore to their fathers to give them.*

7. *"Only be strong and very courageous, that you may observe to do according to all the law which Moses My servant commanded you; do not turn from it to the right hand or to the left hand, that you may prosper wherever you go.*

8. *"This Book of the Law shall not depart from your mouth, but you shall meditate in it day and night, that you may observe to do according to*

all that is written in it. For then you will make your way prosperous, and then you will have good success.

9. *"Have I not commanded you? Be strong and of good courage; do not be afraid, nor dismayed, for the Lord your God is with you wherever you go."*

The Holy Bible, New King James version

53. Insurance

Émilie had been trying to get information for three days now. She had questions. Although she had wished to never hear of Lakedge again, she suddenly was inundated with reasons to continue to maintain contact overseas.

The real estate broker had called with the news of the fire. Her first reaction had been to want to fire the guy for his inefficiency. Why didn't these people put more security to protect her property? The change in her point of view was somewhat astonishing. As much as she had hated the place and never wanted to have anything to do with it, now it was her property and she blamed everyone for not guarding it.

She had been on the phone back and forth all week. First, she needed to know if the deed had been signed and the property transferred to the Town. When she found out the papers had not been signed, she wanted to know if the offer and commitment from the town made them owners. She was disappointed to hear the simple commitment did not count as an official sale. The mill was still hers. Actually, the ruins and the land were still hers.

Next, she wanted to find out about the insurance. Would she be able to collect? How much? She soon found out that although there was insurance on the property, it would never come close to the value the town had offered to buy the mill. Maybe she could sell the land but, even including the insurance money, she would never get as much as she would have received had the fire not occurred.

She tried to find out more about the investigation, but since it was still under way she wasn't told anything.

Now, feeling helpless to handle a situation thousands of kilometres away, she was desperate.

The appointed auditor gave her an estimate of what she could get in the end. If she sold the land, collected the insurance and received some compensation from a possible lawsuit against those who started the fire in the first place she may be able to regain about two-thirds of what she would have made from the sale.

Teresa reminded her that if her father hadn't left her anything, she wouldn't have had the money. In the end, maybe two-thirds was better than nothing. Émilie's frustration had more to do with the amount of time spent, the energy involved, the irritation of having to deal with Lakedge, and the anticipation of this newfound treasure, than the final amount she would be left with.

Her concern was also that if the town itself wasn't able to rebuild, or if she couldn't find another interested party, there would be nobody to buy the land. She had made a few calls to Timbergreen as well to try and get a new offer for the land. Her calls were never returned. Her fears grew. The harness she had woven to restrain this town was breaking apart.

For the first time in her life, she had something in common with Lakedge. For the first time in her life, she felt the despair just as it was experienced by everyone in Lakedge. Only, no one saw this ironic twist of fate.

54. Community

Lindsey walked into the Legion Hall with her head high. She had taken a stance and nothing anyone said would affect her spirits. She felt as if she was wearing an invisible shield. She had heard that the Legion had opened a relief centre for people out of work or in difficulty following the closure of the mill.

It had taken her the whole previous day to gather her courage and pray about her decision. Now, she was firmly convinced that if people had something to say about her and her family, they would have to say it in her face. She was going to take every occasion out there to show how she was a member of this community. Even if the community rejected her, she would fight to maintain her position. She would fight to erase the rumours and the lies.

She walked up to one of the ladies and asked, using as gentle a tone as she could muster. "Who's in charge here, please?"

The lady looked up, a bit shy and pointed to another women giving instruction to a group.

Lindsey went over, waited until the woman had finished addressing the group, and then asked. "How can I help? I would like to volunteer."

The woman knew the Stuarts and had heard the rumours; she had a slight hesitation. "Oh, thank you. We can certainly use more volunteers."

She took her over to the various stations spread around the main hall. There was a reception desk at the entrance where people could register and indicate the nature of the help they required. There was a station where people who donated food could drop off their goods. It was sorted and put into bags so others could pick them up. There was a different table for baked goods. Many citizens had taken the time to prepare their best pastries, bread, or cakes. Near the counter usually serving beer to the legion members, pre-cooked meals were packaged and handed out. The meals included bowls of home-made soup, chilli or rice casseroles, all kinds of meat and vegetables the ladies in the community had taken time to prepare and bring over.

Lindsey was somehow reassured to see this. Her feelings of the last few days towards the community were mellowing.

In a further corner of the room, people were sorting through bags of donated goods. They had a number of tables where people in need could come and select items. Near the front was a final table for financial donations. When she arrived close to it, Lindsey stopped and took out her chequebook from her purse.

"To whom do I make the cheque out to?" she asked the lady behind the table.

"You can make it out to the Lakedge Disaster Relief Fund. We have an arrangement with the bank and we will be able to get charitable organisation status soon so you will be able to get a receipt for income tax purpose." The lady answered.

Lindsey proceeded to write the cheque. When she turned it in the lady's eyes popped. "That's so generous of you! Thank you so very much!"

"I want to do something for Lakedge and the people who are in difficulty. This is just a little bit, but at this time, I can't give much more. I'm without a job myself you know?" She felt a bit of satisfaction in letting the words out on how this was affecting her, yet she was still giving.

She turned to the lady showing her around. "It's actually why I'm here. I don't have any work right now, so I have a lot of time on my hands."

"I'm sorry to hear that but we certainly appreciate the help. Would you have a preference in where you would like to work?"

Lindsey considered the options. She quickly realised she would have more exposure if she was stationed at the reception desk. In such a position, everyone coming in would notice her. This was the best place to send her message: I care.

She confirmed her preference and soon was being shown how to manage the reception desk.

She knew most of the people coming in and maintained a gracious smile. Throughout the day, she stayed at her position, occasionally taking a break and spending time with other volunteers. She quickly developed a rapport with many of them. Her initial anxiety in coming in eventually disappeared and she let down her guard. She realised she may have been a bit artificial at first but now she was volunteering because she wanted to help, not just to prove a point.

She was at the desk when she heard the supervisor speaking loudly with a man she. Lindsey knew the face but couldn't place a name. The man pointed at the table and at Lindsey in particular a couple of times and she started to wonder what this was all about. She strained to listen and heard a few words here and there; enough to get the gist of the discussion.

The man seemed to be indicating that he didn't want to have to sign in at the reception desk with Lindsey there. He hinted she was only there to judge people in need like him. Lindsey tensed, already starting to relive some of the feelings she had gone through in the last two days. The supervisor, on the other hand, dismissed the man's claims. It quickly became evident she was taking Lindsey's side.

The supervisor seemed to notice that Lindsey was listening and raised her voice to make sure Lindsey and the rest of the people in the room heard.

"She is here to volunteer. She also lost her job because of this. She's just as much a part of Lakedge as you are. Just because she wasn't born here doesn't mean she isn't one of us. If you're not happy with this, I suggest you go somewhere else. As long as Lindsey wants to help, she's welcome here and I will be the first one to greet her in the morning. She is doing a great job and everybody else in this room is happy to have her around."

She turned to the room and yelled. "Right people?"

The whole room turned to a cheer, almost in unison. "Right!" and "Hear, hear!" and "You bet!"

Lindsey was quickly overwhelmed and tears came to her eyes. She needed this more than she needed air. She felt utterly humbled by it and although she wanted to express her gratitude, the tears only choked her. The woman at the desk beside her, put her arm around her shoulder; Lindsey didn't resist. She took the hug and gave it back.

The man just left. She didn't even feel any resentment towards him. His action had made it possible for her to receive this blessing. Now she truly felt part of Lakedge again.

55. Arrest

It took Mark and Robert two days to gather the facts but Amanda and Tim's conflicting testimonies had been the key. The casino broker wasn't a strong suspect, so they went to work on the other options. They had requisitioned records of bank transactions but those had led nowhere. They had snooped around and found out that Jeff Wallis had just bought a brand new snowmobile along with all the trimmings and a new black snowsuit with red stripes. When everyone else in town is saving, especially those who used to be employed at the mill, how could a guy like Jeff Wallis afford that kind of a luxury?

So, they had followed the leads. The cruiser arrived at the Wallis' home. The house was more of a shack than a house. It was small by anyone's standard. The driveway was a mix of mud and slush. Jeff's pickup truck was parked, with lots of scrap metal and car parts in the back. There were a couple of dirt bikes lined up along the side of the house. Mark remembered Jeff was a mechanic in his off time.

They stepped out of the cruiser and walked towards the back. Right in the middle of the yard with the snow packed by numerous tread marks, were two snowmobiles. One was old, a bit rusty, with lots of usage evident, the other was new, shiny, without a scratch on it.

From Amanda's description, it seemed to Mark that this was the vehicle they were looking for. Mark started to walk to the front door but Robert stopped him.

"You may want to disable this thing. If he knows we are on to him, he might want to jump on it and escape."

"Good call." Mark reached under the dashboard and grabbed the key. He went to the other snowmobile, an older model equipped with a simple push button starter. He looked around and found a wire he pulled on to disconnect the starter.

"There, these vehicles aren't going anywhere for a while."

They both headed for the front door. Mark knocked and waited. There was no answer. He repeated the knock.

"I'll go around the back door." Robert suggested.

He reached the door and waited. It opened suddenly with a huge man trying to get out quietly.

Robert called to him. "Going somewhere?"

Startled, Jeff yelled at him. "What's it to you? What are you doing on my property?"

Mark heard the voices and came running.

"Jeff, why didn't you answer the front door?" he asked.

"I… I didn't hear it. What do you want?" Jeff replied in an aggressive tone.

"Right now we just have a few questions to ask you. How would you like to come to the station with us?" Mark asked.

"Why should I? I have nothing to say. Who's this guy, anyway?" Jeff replied.

"He's just a friend helping me out. Now come on, I'm sure we have a lot to talk about." Mark said.

"I told you I have nothing to say to you!" Jeff yelled at him.

"That's really too bad Jeff, because we have a lot to ask you."

Jeff, aware that he was in trouble, looked for a way out. Robert saw his look and knew he would make a run for it. He braced himself, ready to jump. Jeff darted to his right aiming for the yard. Robert ran but Jeff was surprisingly quick. Robert missed and Jeff quickly reached the snowmobile. He tried to find the key but Mark called to him. He turned. Mark had the key in his hand and was showing it to Jeff.

"Jeff, get off the vehicle and lie down on the ground."

Jeff looked at him, then at Robert. He knew he couldn't escape. "I didn't do anything, I swear."

Robert smiled. "Then why were you running away if you didn't do anything?"

"I don't know. You guys scared me." he replied.

Mark laughed. "A big guy like you, scared? That's a good one. Now do what I said."

Jeff slowly got off the snowmobile and laid down on his belly in the snow. Mark took out his handcuffs, locked them in place, and helped him up.

As they walked to the cruiser, Robert noticed a small face in the window. It looked like Tim was crying but it could have been the reflection in the window.

They pushed Jeff in the back of the cruiser and went back to the house. They knocked and Audrey Wallis, in tears, opened the door. Mark tried to be gentle with her. "Hi Audrey. This is Mr. Cloutier. He's an investigator helping us on the Sparks Mill fire case. Can we come in, please?"

"Sure" she said, sniffling.

"Now Audrey, you're going to have to be strong." Mark told her. "We are going to ask Jeff some questions but he may be in trouble."

She started weeping again. Mark waited and continued. "I would like to know if you have anything you would like to tell us."

"I don't know," she said in between sniffles. "Jeff's been acting strange lately but he doesn't tell me anything. Then last Friday he came home with the new snowmobile. When I asked him how he got the money for it, he told me it was none of my business."

"I see," Mark replied.

"Did he buy a new snowsuit as well?" Robert asked.

"Yes he did. A very expensive one," she sobbed between almost every word.

"Can we see it?" Mark added.

She went to a small closet. Robert noticed the house was full of electronic equipment but the furniture was decrepit. There was a brand new television and a DVD player, but the sofa had duct tape in a number of places to hold the fabric in place.

She brought the garment out. It fit Amanda's description, red stripes and all. Mark took it. He smelled it and it had a faint scent of smoke. He lifted one of the sleeves and brought it to his nose.

"Wow." He moved it back immediately. "This reeks of gasoline."

Robert smelled it as well but didn't get as close to it as Mark. "We'll have to take this with us as evidence." Then turning to Audrey he added. "If it's all right with you."

"I guess," she whimpered.

"Thank you Audrey." Mark said. "We will come back a bit later. I'll let you know what happens as soon as we find out more. In the meantime, I want to ask you to stay in town with Tim. Okay?"

"Okay" she replied softly.

They left with the suit. Mark opened the trunk, pulled out a large plastic bag and put the suit in it. He closed it and tagged it as evidence then threw it in the trunk.

They went to the back of the pick-up truck. They immediately noticed a heavy set of bolt cutters. "I bet this is what he used to cut the chains." Robert said.

"If we bring them back we might be able to compare the grooves with the marks made on the chains themselves." Mark said picking up the tool. "I think we have enough for now. I'll come back with a warrant if we need more."

As soon as they got in the car, Jeff addressed them pleading. "Please don't do this. I didn't mean it. I didn't want to hurt anybody. They made me do it."

Mark immediately read him his rights. "Jeff, you are under arrest for arson in the case of the fire of Sparks Mill. You have the right to remain silent..."

Jeff interrupted him. "I don't care about it. I'll tell you everything I know but you got to let me go. I can't have my son see me like this."

Mark insisted. "I have to finish this, Jeff. Then we can talk as much as you want."

Jeff complied and let him finish.

"So now, what do you want to tell us Jeff?"

"I did it. I started the fire; it's true. They told me to do it. They paid me a lot of money for it; more money than I can make in a year; maybe two years. You have to understand, I needed that snowmobile. The other one is dying on me. I couldn't go on for very long with it. I needed the new one."

Mark looked at him. "Who is 'they'?"

"That Bernie guy. I don't remember his last name. He gave me some money to call him and give him information at first. He wanted to know everything about the mill. So I told him. Every time I gave him some information, he paid me."

"Where did you meet this Bernie?" Robert asked.

"I met him at Trucker's Corner. The first time, at least. Then I called him. He showed up at Trucker's Corner a couple of times after I called to deliver the money and get more details. He always paid cash."

"You have his phone number?" Mark asked.

"No, I don't. I just have this cell phone he gave me and it's on a speed dial. It's in my pocket. You can take it if you want."

Robert was suspicious. "If this is a trick, I'll punch you out right here."

"No trick, I swear." he said quickly.

Robert snickered as he opened the door. "Right. You also swore you hadn't done anything wrong just a short while ago."

"No trick, please believe me." Jeff repeated.

Robert slowly opened the door to the back and reached into Jeff's pocket. He found the cell phone.

"What's his speed dial?" Robert asked.

"It's B, like in Bernie."

Robert tried it. Almost instantly, an electronic voice came on. "I'm sorry. There is no service at the number you have dialled. Please check the number and try again."

Robert laughed. "I expected that much. I think your friend Bernie left you out to dry."

Mark added. "So when did you see this Bernie last?"

"I didn't see him for a while but he left me envelopes with money in it at Trucker's Corner, and then called me to say it was there. The last time I spoke to him was at the party on Saturday. He said he had left a large sum for me but I had to burn down the mill. I tried to argue with him. I told him the mill was going to reopen. I told him I wanted to get my old job back. That's when he said that if I did the job right, there would be another ten thousand dollars waiting for me. He hung up and I went to Trucker's where I found five thousand in the envelope. I've never seen so much money. I had to do it."

Mark shook his head. "Jeff, you've been had. Now they left you all alone to fend for yourself. Did you get that ten thousand?"

"No, when I called on Sunday, Bernie told me he had to make sure the job was complete before he could pay me. He would get back to me on Friday. I was just waiting."

Robert was calculating and a bit perplexed. "If you had the snowmobile to go and start the fire, why did you need the money?"

Jeff considered the question sheepishly. "I bought the snowmobile with the money I had received for the other jobs. Now I wanted to do some major renovations to the house. I also figured I could get a new truck. I wanted a new television and one of those newfangled DVD players." His tone suddenly changed. He sounded like a kid on Christmas morning. "I just got those yesterday. It's amazing how clear the picture is on those things."

Robert and Mark looked at each other, unsure what to add.

"All right, let's go to the station. We have a lot to write on the report."

56. Help!

Vivian turned the speakerphone on so they could have a three-way conversation. Joshua was sitting close to the desk to hear and be heard. The Deputy Minister of Agriculture, Mines and Resources was on the line.

"I want to thank you for returning my call so quickly. I know you must be very busy but we desperately need help."

"Madam Mayor, I've heard about the situation in Lakedge and I've read a report on the recent fire. Let me first offer my regrets on my part and that of Minister McConnelly."

"Thank you Mr. Lorenz, I appreciate your concerns."

"So, Madam Mayor…"

She interrupted him politely. "Please call me Vivian. I also have Joshua Stuart, my town manager in the room with me."

Josh bent a bit closer to the phone. "Good day Mr. Lorenz, you can call me Josh."

"Great. Vivian, Josh, I'm Carl." the voice on the phone said. "So tell me more about the situation so I can understand what you are dealing with there. Then I can brief the minister on it. He may also make a call to the Premier later this afternoon, so we have to be sure we get a clear picture of what you are dealing with."

Vivian and Josh went through the sequence of events, from the death of Sparks, glossing over some of the less important issues such as the scandal and ending with the Sparks mill destruction by fire, but taking time to explain the economic impact on each of the incidents.

Carl Lorenz gave a review of some of the options available.

Most financial aid programs existed to help individuals rebuild homes or to help municipalities rebuild infrastructure destroyed during disasters. Their situation didn't count as a disaster per se since it wasn't an act of God. The mill was not considered an infrastructure of the Town so the normal programs didn't apply. In the end, they would have to count on the provincial government to use other means to help.

One of the avenues they examined was the employment support programs and the welfare programs. They discussed the options for a long time to determine what was involved for each of them.

Concerning the rebuilding, they set out a plan of action where the Town had to buy the land on their own. They had to fundraise, getting contributions towards the rebuilding of the mill. The rest would come partly from a government grant, partly from government interest free loans, and partly from a private loan the bank would provide.

Then they spoke of the minister's visit to Lakedge. He would arrive at the Lakedge Town Hall Friday morning to meet with the mayor first, then the council in a private session. They would go to the mill site, where the minister would announce the support offered to them. They may not have the exact amounts figured out by that time, but the minister would be in a position to promise help for the reconstruction.

A separate call had been made to the police to escort and protect the minister during his visit. The local elected member of the provincial parliament, more commonly known as the MPP, would also join them and a number of government attachés would come along.

They settled on the details, and concluded by exchanging cell phone numbers in case urgent developments required adjustments.

Vivian looked at Josh once the phone was offline. "What do you think? Can we pull this off?"

Josh sighed. "I hope so. We need to start fundraising right away. I'll get a team together to initiate this. Next, I'll talk with Peter Cohen about a bank loan. Let's see what he can come up with. You may want to call again with regards to the purchase of the land. If we don't get it, then we have to rebuild from a different site and it can mean additional delays to get the land, clear it and prep it for construction."

"Add to this the Sparks mansion arrangements."

Josh jumped on the statement, "Speaking of which. I've been thinking. We can't ever let ourselves be caught in this type of situation. We need to develop other sources of income. Our commercial ventures are basically dependant on the mill. If we bring in a few other industries, then at least if we hit hard times with one, the rest of the population can still continue to function normally."

"Sounds great in principle but how do you do this? The casino idea certainly isn't on my list."

"No, but the concept of enhancing our tourism is an avenue I would like to explore. I want to put together a committee made up of citizens to look into initiatives fostering new business."

Vivian shook her head "We have the marina, we have a lot of cottages but it's not much of a tourism industry."

"I agree. I was thinking we could possibly do something with the Sparks mansion. If we keep the building as it is to maintain its heritage designation, nothing stops us from turning it into some kind of a tourist attraction."

"I like the thought. Go ahead, get your committee together."

Josh expressed enthusiasm for the first time in the last few days "I will. I want to include a few commercial people and a few tourism people."

"Don't forget Trucker's Corner."

"I wasn't going to. I think it can be the central connection point for our marketing campaign."

Vivian pondered for a minute. "You know. I've been having some thoughts myself. I might give a call to Teresa Sparks. She seemed like a different woman the last time she was here. I wonder if we couldn't get her to help us in some of this, especially about the mansion and the mill's land."

Josh agreed. "If she can convince her daughter to let us have the land, it would be a great step."

"Yes, let me run a few ideas by her."

Josh got up and stepped towards the door.

"Josh. I'm sure glad we have you to count on."

"Thanks Vivian. I'll always be here for you and for Lakedge."

He left as she was looking through her phone book.

Monday March 28

Minister Promises Help to Rebuild Lakedge Community

Provincial News Review

Following the huge fire that devastated the Lakedge mill last weekend, Andrew McConnelly, the Minister of Agriculture, Mines and Resources visited the people and the site of the fire, where he made an announcement to the effect that the province would provide support to help rebuild the mill.

The mill was the main employer in Lakedge and following the death of the owner, Warren Sparks, had closed earlier this year. It was in the process of being bought by the Town of Lakedge when the fire completely destroyed the building. The fire itself is still under investigation and the police spokesperson was unable to provide more details.

McConnelly said he had been approached by the Town's administration for provincial help and had quickly put together a committee to review the needs of the community. "In times like these, we come together with the people of Lakedge to show how this province is a large community in itself. When a few of us are affected, the whole province grieves."

It is unclear yet what form of help and how much the province will contribute, but with this commitment in hand, Vivian Hedgerow, the mayor of Lakedge, explained they were in a position to get back in business. "We are thankful to the province for its help. I can assure you we will make every penny we receive work for the citizens of Lakedge. This community isn't ready to give up, just watch us!"

The loss of the mill has affected the economy of Lakedge. The mayor also hinted that a number of other initiatives are under way to enhance the economic resiliency of the town, but wouldn't give details on what these included.

61. Recovery

People filed into the council chambers. There wasn't enough room for everyone, many stood leaning on the wall at the back and on the sides. People were asked to have only one person per family inside so as many people as possible could be present. A lot of people sat on the floor and in the stairs of the Town Hall because they couldn't fit. Mayor Hedgerow had announced the unveiling of the Town's recovery plan; nobody in Lakedge wanted to miss this. Their personal survival was closely linked to that of their town.

The meeting was called to order, a few formalities were registered, and the agenda was presented with only one item, a presentation by the town manager on the Lakedge economic recovery plan.

Josh made sure the microphone was working. The sound system had been quickly connected to the building public address system so people in the hallway and the stairs would hear.

"Madam Mayor, members of council, citizens of Lakedge, I would like to present today the foundation for the revival of Lakedge! In the last few years we have been pounded by disasters. If we survived every one of them, it is a testament to our endurance as people and as a town. We feel, however, that survival is not a way to enjoy life. We feel the people of Lakedge deserve a whole lot more than just surviving. Therefore what we want to offer this afternoon is not a survival plan but a *revival* plan!"

He looked around; everyone was anxiously waiting.

"One of the reasons we are in our current predicament is the fact that we relied on a single source of income for Lakedge, Sparks Mill. Too long, the mill has been our only economic drive. The answer to our predicament comes from a new way of thinking called 'diversification'."

"Yes, we will rebuild the mill. Forestry is what we know best. Lumber is our most precious product. We will continue the tradition because Lakedge was built on the lumber trade. We have devised a plan for this purpose and I will explain this plan in a minute. It is important for the economic well-being and growth of this town that we never again rely on the mill only. "

"We asked ourselves what other skills we have, what else do we know how to do. After an extensive brainstorming session with key staff and prominent members of the community, we now have a few options to propose."

"One of our best qualities as people of Lakedge is our hospitality. We know how to welcome people. We greet strangers with open arms. We open our doors, we share our food, and we give of ourselves readily. All the truckers going through this town has felt it when they stepped into Trucker's Corner. Many have stayed over for a night or two in some of the cottages and motels we have along the highway. Others have come for a week in the summer with their family, or for hunting season with their buddies."

"We feel this is one of our strengths we must expand on. I have proposed to council a tourism plan involving a number of actions and requiring involvement of the community in various ways. We will establish a tourism council made up from Lakedge citizens. This council will oversee the marketing of Lakedge as a tourist destination. It will create and oversee a special municipal fund to provide low interest loans for entrepreneurs with projects having a link to enhancing tourism. Any initiative to make Lakedge more attractive to tourists will be evaluated. I have a vision of a time when the lake from which we obtained our name will be a northern beach picture in travel books. I see Main Street lined with cafés and Bed & Breakfasts where people come to enjoy the fresh air of the great North."

As he paused slightly to prepare his next sentence, someone shouted: "They'll enjoy the black flies as well!" A roar of laughter came from the crowd. The joke was passed down to the hallway and the laughter continued as a wave all the way to the outside.

Josh waited for the laughter to subside. "True, my vision isn't perfect. Certainly our stores will make some money selling bug repellent."

The laughs took up again. Josh paused then started where he had left off.

"Right from the start we have prepared two initiatives with a tourism goal in mind. We have enlisted the help of a few key people to make it happen. The first project is the transformation of the Sparks mansion into a museum." Whispers and soft comments came from the crowd.

"I am pleased to announce the return of Mrs. Teresa Sparks to Lakedge permanently. For those who don't remember her, Mrs. Sparks was Warren's wife and although she left a number of years ago to pursue a different career, she has now retired and decided to stay in Lakedge for her retirement years. She bought the mansion from her daughter and is ready to invest her own money into the project."

"Mrs. Sparks has agreed to work with Brent, whom everyone knows, in order to transform the mansion into a museum to highlight and illustrate the history of the North and that of Lakedge. To help her redesign the mansion while maintaining its heritage value, we have hired Mr. Richard Hillman, a real estate broker by trade and an architect by education. We are aiming, with the help of the tourism council, for the mansion to become a select destination for people from across the province and beyond."

Josh took a sip from a glass of water placed on the podium for him.

"The second project is to reopen the gold mine as an educational, recreational and tourist destination. The gold mine was closed almost sixty years ago when it ran dry, but we can transform it into a testimony of the work accomplished there, the conditions the miners lived in and a memorial to the role the mine played in developing Lakedge. With a little help from the province, this will become a summer entertainment with speleological and mining expeditions led by local people, probably a source of income for summer students as well, and a possible educational program for schools."

"We hope these two initiatives will spur many of our citizens to come up with ideas of their own. Together we will forge a new economy."

"As I mentioned earlier, we will rebuild the mill. We have acquired the land from Miss Joy Sparks after she gave up all claims and was assured she would get the insurance money. We were able to buy the site for a very reasonable price. The money we had planned to invest to buy the mill in the first place will now go to rebuild it. We plan to begin the first phase of construction as soon as the ground thaws."

"Police are still investigating the source of the arson and if the people behind this act are found, there may be compensation, but we won't count on it at this time. Anyway, it could take years to resolve and we don't have years to wait."

"We are thankful to the provincial government who has agreed to match every dollar we raise for the rebuilding of the mill. For this purpose, Mayor Hedgerow will be creating a special fund-raising committee in the days to come, and will call on a number of you to help. This committee will be responsible for special events, fairs, contests and draws."

"We are also proud to announce how Peter Cohen, our friendly neighbourhood banker, is ready to put up the amount needed to make up the difference and allow the mill to be rebuilt with a very low interest loan. With this in mind and with the participation of every citizen in Lakedge, we know our mill will be rebuilt one day."

Cheers and applauds came from the crowd. Josh pointed at Peter sitting in the first row and asked him to stand. He did and turned back towards the audience to bow and salute.

"Yes, thank you Peter for helping this community. In the meantime, Frank Ellis and Jim Stone will continue to manage the mill operations with the help of the Woodland mill. We want to keep our customers and ensure that when we open our production, we can quickly deliver the quality goods our customers are used to from the Sparks Mill."

"In order to have the best possible equipment available, the design of the new mill will involve a modest structure to start with. In the years to come, as the mill starts to rebuild its business and aims at maintaining its reputation for quality, all profits will be invested into an expansion plan."

"The plan also calls for us to open a second site. We will then never be completely reliant on a single site. If for some reason the primary site needs to shut down operations for a time, we will be able to shift operations to our backup facility so our customers will never be adversely affected."

"Because of the fire, the province has also announced it will provide special funding to help our residents who are currently unemployed. This special fund will be managed by the local Social Services division and will be available until the reopening of the mill."

"In closing, I want to thank the mayor, the members of council and every citizen of Lakedge for sticking it out while we worked to come up with this plan and negotiated with the various authorities. A lot of discussions went on, many rumours were spread and I can say we all struggled through these hard times. A week ago, we thought we had the solution and we were wrong. We partied but Fate had other plans for us. Today, I know we are being tested, but as we have always done in the past, it's by working together for the same goal that we will succeed in this test as we have in all of the previous ones. I also believe we now have a plan geared to the long-term."

"There is a saying which goes 'A vision without a plan is just a dream and a plan without a vision is a nightmare'. Today, we are offering you a vision with a plan. We are asking you to share in the vision and we are asking council to approve the plan. Thank you."

As Josh returned to his seat, applause rang from the audience. The sound kept coming on and gradually people started standing up until everyone in the crowd was up. Mayor Hedgerow and the council members were standing as well and clapping their hands along with everyone. It took a while until the noise died down and people took their seats again.

Mayor Hedgerow asked for a motion to approve the plan and it received unanimous consent. More applause met the decision. The meeting was concluded and people dismissed.

Josh was walking on a cloud. He had worked on his speech all day, with the help of his staff and had even asked Lindsey for some advice. As he pondered the reaction, he knew this was only a first step. A lot of work was still to come. Writing a plan is one thing, making it happen can be a whole different story.

62. Proof

Robert walked into the station and was greeted by the officer at his desk behind the counter. In a way, Robert was now part of the team. The officer didn't even get up. Robert proceeded beyond the small gate door towards Mark's office, who was at his computer working on some reports.

"Afternoon Mark. Anything new?" Robert asked.

"Good afternoon Robert; hum, no, nothing yet. I have the financial crimes division looking into our case, but they are overloaded so it may take weeks before we get anywhere."

"Yeah, there's just too many criminals out there and not enough cops. I knew you might have some difficulties so I made a call to a friend of mine in Winnipeg. She's a financial forensics expert. She made a few calls and some searches for me. She was able to review Jeff's accounts and all the transactions. Unfortunately, they were all cash deposits, no transfers were made from any outside source. These people are good."

"The difficult part comes from being almost certain we know who orchestrated all of this but having no proof."

Robert sat in the chair across from the desk. It squeaked in pain from Robert's weight but he ignored it. "I can feel it in my bones that Timbergreen is behind all of this."

"We have the description of this Bernie character and everyone is looking for him. Some of the guys at Trucker's Corner said they saw him before. He drives a rig and comes this way once in a while. Odds are we won't see him with all this heat on the case."

"Even if we do catch the guy, he's probably only a middle man. He may not know very much and I doubt he could provide us enough to prosecute anyone."

A knock at the door interrupted them. "Sorry to bother you Mark, Pete Cohen is here and he would like to talk to you."

Mark excused himself and proceeded to the counter. Robert looked around the office. It wasn't much of an office, so small and cramped. It reminded him of his little desk in the homicide squad room in Winnipeg. He had been thinking of his own career. This detective work was interesting. He had fewer restrictions than he used to when he was on the regular force. He enjoyed some of this freedom. Maybe there was a possibility for him in private investigation. He would enjoy a bit of extra money beyond the pension and he would particularly appreciate having something to take his mind off the boredom of retirement. The arena security guard position was the last choice. Ideas seemed to emerge in his mind about how to go about creating his own investigation service when Mark came back in the room with Peter Cohen.

"Robert, this is Pete Cohen. Pete is our local bank manager. He had something he wanted to share with us but since it concerns the investigation we are working on, I felt you should be in on the conversation."

Mark introduced Robert and explained to Pete what role Robert was playing in this case. He asked Pete to start again from the beginning.

"Well, as I mentioned to Mark, I owed him one for a situation he pulled me out of a few weeks ago and I remembered something this morning that might be of help."

Robert sat up in the chair.

"I had a chat with a gentleman earlier this month and it left me with a bad taste in my mouth. His name was Sam and he was a top official from Timbergreen Wood Products. We spoke for quite a while. I was trying to convince him to let my bank do the banking for his company if they were to take over the mill. You probably know by now they are the ones who were trying to buy the mill and they are the main competitor to Sparks Mill."

Mark confirmed. "Yes, we have this information. We are actually watching them very closely but we have no proof of anything."

"Well, I don't know if it qualifies as a proof but in this conversation the man was very straight with me in explaining he wouldn't do banking with us because he had no plans of running the mill. The whole bid was in order to close the mill and reduce the competition."

Robert was showing interest. "Would you be able to testify to this?"

"I certainly would. I have my notes recorded on the discussion. I can provide you with a complete rundown."

"It's not much but it may allow us to get a warrant to search their books. With the name of a contact within the organisation, we could also trace back anyone on the payroll who could be this Bernie."

The sparkle in Robert's eyes was coming back. This investigation was truly reviving him.

Mark continued. "We can trace calls made by this Sam. If we can corroborate your call and we can link him to some of the other calls he made we may be able to show the link between this Sam, Bernie and Jeff. If we catch Bernie, we will have no problem in getting Jeff to confirm his identity."

Robert added. "We can do a timeline of the events to show how each call was linked to an action Jeff took. If we can also get into some of the money transactions, we could be able to show payments."

Pete was listening and seeing a level of energy rise as the two police officers were brainstorming, throwing ideas at each other, and improving on the case as they discussed.

"I think I need to go on a trip down to Toronto where the head office for Timbergreen is." Robert said to no one in particular.

"Yes, the phone number I used was a 416 area code." Peter confirmed.

"Good. Meanwhile, we will continue from here. I have someone following up on the newspaper article, the one with the pictures of Joshua Stuart. From what your colleagues in the French police have ascertained, the pictures were sent to Timbergreen. We are trying to trace back from the newspaper to see if Timbergreen forwarded the pictures. It may not be much, but it could help make the case against Timbergreen. If we can't get them on the arson side, we might get them on a fraud charge or something of the sort."

"The way I see it, we still have a lot of leads to follow. This case is far from over." Robert concluded.

"Well then, I guess I'm sorry and I'm glad at the same time. I'm sorry for giving you more work, and I'm glad this is helpful for your case."

"Yes, it's helpful. Thank you Peter." Mark said. Pete saluted Robert who thanked him as well, and Mark accompanied him back to the front.

"I guess my private investigator company is already doing well" he thought, looking at this as his first private case, and having the potential to keep him busy for quite a while.

63. Freelance

Mike had put in some extra efforts and many long hours to polish the last article in his series on the struggles of small towns. This had to be the best. He felt he owed it to Lakedge. Now, it was real. He could read his name at the top of the page: Michael Stuart, Freelance Correspondent.

Sure it wasn't page one of the newspaper, but it was page one of the Tourism section. It was the best page to help Lakedge. The only time people had heard of Lakedge was from the influenza virus. The first case in Canada had landed in his hometown and this had caused the virus to be dubbed the Lakedge Influenza. It wasn't something to attract tourism in itself, but turning this and the survival of the town into a success story might create some interest.

He started reading, as though seeing it now in print, the story would different than when he wrote it.

"Your house probably comes from Lakedge"

"Have you ever wondered where you would live if it wasn't for wood? What if trees didn't exist or if humans didn't know how to transform the wood into building material? So, where does the wood used to build your home come from?"

"The answer probably lies somewhere in the Canadian North. The Boreal Forest is the largest source of wood products in the country. Almost three of every five homes in North America are built using Canadian forest wood; certainly most homes in Canada use northern trees."

He was hoping a start like this would grab the attention of the readers. The editor had made a few changes to the flow of the story from the original submission Mike had forwarded. The opening had stayed as he had written it.

He read on. His story moved to the history of the development of the North and in particular the role people like Warren Sparks had played. He remembered the long afternoon discussion with his grandmother and Teresa Sparks. A lot of his material came from there.

He kept on reading the article to where it turned to modern days. He started lashing out at the large corporations, deciding on the future of people, villages and towns all for the sake of making money. He accused the forestry giants of taking everything they could, then moving on to new forests without any regard for those whose livelihood depended on the industry.

Mike recalled how angry he was when he heard of the fire and the possible link with Timbergreen. He had wanted to get back at someone or something. He had written most of the section of the article in such a mood. The editor had softened it somewhat but had mentioned how he liked the passion in the writing.

Maybe it's what Mike was to be. As with his guide, he was the messenger. The message shouldn't however be limited to mere words. The message was one of passion, one of survival.

The article continued by attacking the government for not stepping in to help under such circumstances. He linked back to the previous articles on other small communities having barely survived through similar situations and demonstrated how every time there had been token involvements on their part. He demonstrated how the government plays on people when announcing help to communities.

"What most people fail to see is how ten million dollars handed out to help with the municipal infrastructure of northern municipalities once

divided into a hundred communities becomes a mere one hundred thousand dollars for each one. You can't even buy a house today with that amount. Government officials play on the gullibility of people and make big news announcements to get their photo in the paper and get re-elected when, in fact, they are handing out peanuts."

He felt as if he was a warrior, lashing out at the enemy to protect his people.

In the bottom corner of his computer screen, a little box indicated people logging on or off the messaging system. The little tune played every time someone new joined. Mike was used to this and it didn't disturb him in his reading. He just quickly glanced at it. This time a new user logged in; it was Ashley. Mike opened the small screen to the main area of the monitor. Ashley had just sent him a message.

"hey paparazzi whts new ☒"

Mike had sent her the links to his articles. Ashley had made sure all of Mike's friends had read them. The latest one was the last of the series and had garnered a lot of attention. Ashley had been feeding the comments back to Mike. He had quickly become a celebrity in Lakedge. So now she teased him with the "paparazzi" nickname.

"lol hey movie star hows the show"

Ashley had joined a local drama club and was enjoying it. He kidded with her about becoming a great movie star some day. They messaged each other about things important and trivial. The talk was good for Mike. It was a cheap way to maintain a long-distance relationship as they shared their feelings on just about anything.

She did convey the sad mood the town was under. Mike could feel it not only in the actual words but also in the tone of the writing. He tried to comfort her and in fact was trying to cheer himself up as well.

Apparently, his articles had had the same effect for many people in Lakedge. They needed someone to voice their pain and he was it.

After he had ended the discussion with Ashley he pondered on this. The vision quest had told him he would be the messenger. He would tell the message of his people to others and he would help his people convey their feelings, their joys and their pains.

Ideas floated in his head about other aspects of the North he could write about: human interest stories, lives of great people, lives of little people. He finally felt good about himself.

64. Museum

"Well Brent, I guess this means we have a lot of work on our hands." Teresa said.

They were sitting in the dining room, at the end of the table that Warren had always left empty for Teresa in case she came back. She had some papers in front of her where she had started to write some plans. Brent was looking on.

"Yes, Mrs. Sparks. I guess we do." he answered.

"No, no, no. From now on, you must call me Teresa. We are partners on this project and I won't have it any other way." she chided him.

"Yes, Mrs… I mean Teresa."

She insisted on the same theme. "Brent, I would like us to have a relationship as equals here. You are not my servant. I know you had such a position with my husband and both of you were probably comfortable with this. He is no longer here and in my opinion this relieves you of any duty you may feel you owed him. You owe me nothing. Don't you agree?"

Brent hesitated. "I understand. It may take me a bit of time to get used to it. This is your home now. I'm just someone to help around."

"Well I think we need to change this. I may be the landlord but this is your home as well. You cared for it all these years, and invested in time, energy and muscle what I invested in money. So, in my mind, you own a good part of this place. Do you see what I mean?" she looked him with softness in her eyes.

"You are very kind to say this about me. I do care for the place. It holds a lot of memories."

"And together we are going to make sure these memories are treasured by the two of us and by all those who will come to visit."

Teresa had a rough plan of the house on two separate sheets, one for each floor of the two-storey mansion. On a separate piece of paper she had a list of topics. In it were items such as forestry and logging, wood products and mill, Lakedge and Warren Sparks. They discussed the list and added a few names like Trans-Canada Highway, hunting and fishing. Next they had to build a logical use for each of the rooms. They knew that Richard, the architect-developer, would be joining them in the planning, but they wanted a head start on the themes. He would help them mainly on the aesthetic and decorative elements, as well as the configuration of the landscape and parking arrangements. They were in active debate when the doorbell rang.

Brent instinctively got up to answer. Teresa said "I'll go." She smiled. He smiled back, a bit shy. They walked together in the wide hallway.

She let Brent open the door and they found Margaret Stuart standing at the door. "Hello. Did I come at a wrong time?" she asked.

"Absolutely not." Teresa answered. "Come on in."

Margaret just waved at Lindsey who was in the car waiting to see if Margaret would be all right. With the signal, Lindsey drove off.

"What brings you here?" Teresa asked.

"I guess I'm the welcome wagon lady." As she said this, Margaret pulled a bag she had with her and handed it over. Seeing the bag was a bit heavy, Brent reached and helped.

"You shouldn't have." Teresa chided, touched by the gesture. "Now come on in from the cold." They moved inside and Margaret was helped out of her winter coat.

"Come down to the kitchen. Brent and I were just chatting about how we were going to turn the mansion into a museum. You may have some ideas to share." Teresa encouraged, inviting Margaret.

"That sounds like fun." Margaret agreed.

"Would you like a cup of tea or coffee, Mrs. Stuart?" Brent offered.

"Tea would be fine, Brent, thank you. But don't put yourself to any trouble over me." Margaret replied.

"Nonsense. We could all do with a cup of tea." Teresa said.

They walked together to the kitchen; Brent carried the bag of goodies Margaret had brought. He laid it on the kitchen table and Teresa started unpacking. Margaret had made a point of choosing items Teresa had probably not seen in a while, maple syrup being at the top of the list.

While Brent made tea, they chatted about the weather and the trip from France amongst other things. When they sat with their cup of tea in front of them, Margaret asked about the floor plans.

"Brent and I are trying to come up with a plan for the layout of the museum. We have a few ideas of themes we want to use. Maybe you can help us with these. You probably know more about the history of Lakedge than either of us." Teresa explained.

"I guess it's a nice way to say that I've been around for a while." Margaret said laughing.

"Don't be offended; I really meant I respect your experience and knowledge. You still look young to me."

"No offence taken, don't worry." Margaret replied putting her hand on Teresa's softly. "So what are some of those ideas?"

They shared the list, Teresa leading the conversation, Brent offering a comment or a suggestion here and there.

They worked on the plan most of the afternoon. It was getting late when Brent suggested "Would you like me to get dinner started, Mrs…I mean Teresa?"

"That's a good idea. Margaret, you'll stay with us, won't you?" Teresa added.

"Oh, I don't know. I told Lindsey I would call when I was ready for her to pick me up," Margaret explained.

"Nonsense. You can call Lindsey and tell her we still need you here. You're staying with us. What do you say, Brent?"

"There's plenty of food in the fridge. It will be no problem making an extra portion. Please stay, Mrs. Stuart." Brent said

"Well, if it's two against one, I guess I can't refuse," Margaret smiled, "Let me call Lindsey."

Brent pointed her to the phone. She made the call and came back to join Brent and Teresa already active in the kitchen, cutting vegetables and garnering chicken breasts with herbs.

"Let me help." Margaret offered. Soon all three were preparing a feast. They pulled a bottle of white wine from Warren's cellar, and sat down to a delicious meal and friendly conversations.

Teresa highlighted how they made a great team. They seemed to get along very well. The energy from the discussion had been revitalizing.

As the meal progressed, Teresa had an idea.

"Margaret, I was thinking. I haven't had a chance to discuss this with Brent but I'm pretty sure he will agree with me. How would you like to partner with Brent and me on this museum project? With your help we can make it happen. We will need your input in the set-up during the initial stages. When people start to visit, you would have so many stories to tell, it will make the tour so much more interesting. What do say?"

Margaret hesitated. Brent saw this and offered "I think it's a great idea. You would make a great tour guide. I agree."

Margaret looked at both of them, "You are so kind, but I'm an old gal. I don't know if I can stand and walk around all day for this kind of job."

"We'll find a way to relieve you so you don't have to stand all the time. Maybe we can record your stories so Brent and I can tell some of them when you're tired." Teresa was charged up on the concept.

Margaret agreed to give it a thought. She did have a concern. "I don't drive anymore and anyway I don't have a car. I'm not sure I could make it here every day, I can't really ask Lindsey or Joshua to drive me all the time. I would love to help, but I don't really have a mode of transportation to rely on."

"Yes, that could be a problem." Teresa took her chin in her hand, thinking.

"Well, maybe Mrs. Stuart could move in with us." Brent suggested.

"My! That's a great idea! Margaret, there's enough room in this house for all of us and for the museum. What do you say?" Teresa was all fired up again.

Margaret wasn't quite sure what to say. She had been living mostly with Joshua and Lindsey since her illness, but she was spending more time in her own home as her recovery was almost complete. The home itself was much to take care of and she really only kept it for her grandchildren. She wanted Michael or Amanda to have the house if they elected to stay in Lakedge. Joshua had his own home and wasn't ready to come back to the old family home. She had been considering renting the home for a while but with the conditions in Lakedge she didn't see much chance of renting to anyone.

"I would have to find someone to take care of my home if I were to move in." she confided.

"I know someone. I was just talking to Richard, our architect partner. He's working on the plans to rebuild the mill in addition to planning the retrofit of the mansion for the museum. He wants to move to Lakedge temporarily to be closer to the construction site. Maybe he would be willing to rent your home until he's finished. Once the mill reopens there may be more people moving in to Lakedge and you could rent to them." Brent suggested.

"It's possible." Margaret said hesitantly.

"I can make some phone calls for you tomorrow morning to arrange this rental for you." Brent offered.

"You two are very convincing. You don't give me much chance to back out." Margaret laughed.

"You bet. When we see a deal we go for it. Right Brent?"

"You bet, Teresa. In fact, I can set-up a room for you tonight so there will be no need to call your daughter-in-law to come and get you, Mrs. Stuart."

Margaret was overwhelmed by the hospitality both of them expressed.

"Here I was coming to offer the welcome wagon and show the Lakedge hospitality, but I'm the one receiving it. That's unexpected!"

"I'll take it as a yes, then. I'll go up to prepare a bed for you as soon as we are finished, Mrs. Stuart." Brent was always ready to serve.

"I'll accept all of this under one condition." Margaret said, faking firmness in her tone.

They both looked at her, waiting for the condition. She looked at Brent.

"If I'm going to be a partner in this, I want you to call me Margaret. No more of this 'Mrs. Stuart' between us."

It was twice on the same day that Brent received the same request. He would have to get used to it but he agreed.

"Very well Margaret. It's a deal." Brent said as he raised his wine glass. The three glasses clinked together to seal the agreement.

The evening continued with a pleasant mix of business and reminiscing. They discussed the museum; planning an opening ceremony for the late spring, once the snow was gone. They talked about a dedication of the mansion to the memory of Warren Sparks and an annual memorial event.

Not only had a new era just begun for the three, but for Lakedge as well.

Epilogue

"I think I've had enough of this. It makes me sick to my stomach." the Lady said.

"I guess you're right. There's plenty of other cats to be skinned. We've wasted enough time on these ones." the little demon replied.

"It was worth a try." the kid added. "We did have some fun for a while."

"True, and we did leave them with a lot on their hands. This rebuilding is going to take a long time. Some of those people will persist but a number of them are already giving up." the Demon of Greed continued almost gloating.

"You guys are pathetic. You gloat over small victories because you can't admit you were ultimately beaten; typical macho attitude." the Spanish Lady said with disgust.

"Hey, where's your victory? You had the perfect tool with this pandemic. What did you do with it?" El Niño taunted her.

"I didn't stick to one target. I hit a lot of places at the same time. What I wasn't able to do in Lakedge, I succeeded in doing in other parts of the world." she responded.

"You think I stuck to this place alone. Can't you see what I'm doing all over the globe?" El Niño thought for a moment and added "By the way, I'm on this all the time. You take ten, twenty, sometime fifty years to prepare your attack. I guess we won't see much action from you for the next fifty years or so, eh?"

"What are you bragging about?" the demon interrupted. "You're just a kid. You've only been around for a few decades. I've been here forever. In fact, you wouldn't be here if it wasn't for me."

"What do you mean?" Now El Niño was offended. The Spanish Lady looked on with interest.

"What I mean is, mankind wanted more all the time because I spurred them in that direction. With development came the industrial revolution and with it came pollution. Ultimately, you were born from the results of all this."

"He got you there!" the Lady laughed.

"You're no better." The kid lashed out. "If it hadn't been for him…" he said pointing at the little demon. "…you wouldn't be as powerful. You'd just be a weakling local disease."

"What are you getting at?" she snarled.

"I'm saying, it's only because of mankind wanting to expand their reach, go farther and faster that you are able to spread so quickly across the globe." he explained.

"Guys, guys, don't fight over this. You're both right. I am the one who makes all this possible. I've been around forever and I will be around for as long as there are humans on this planet."

"Okay wise guy, if you're so good, where should we go to next?" the Lady asked.

"Ah, good question. I have to say that my preferred target is North America. The response to my inspiration is phenomenal. Greed is truly a work of art in most of this part of the globe. However, I see development in new parts *of the world. There are major changes in East Asia that show promising results. I don't know about you, but I'm heading that way."*

"Sounds like a plan. Let's see how you do it." El Niño said.

"Sure, I'm game. I've done a lot of damage myself in that area in the past." the Spanish Lady added.

"Good, what are we waiting for, then. Let's go." the last words were spoken by the demon of Greed.

65. Peace

The drive was silent. Neither knew how to break the awkward silence. Luckily, the drive to the other side of town took just five minutes. Amanda sat in the back looking at the road but not really seeing it. She seemed eager and anxious at the same time.

The snow had fallen lightly. Although spring was supposed to be around the corner, in these parts spring didn't mean absence of snow. Josh was going slowly because the new snow was making the road a bit slippery.

They drove into the driveway of the old home. The worn out pickup truck was still there. It hadn't moved from the entrance since the day Mark and Robert had come to take Jeff Wallis away. Josh parked the car and turned off the motor.

"Do you want to go in alone?" he asked Amanda.

"No, please Dad," she replied quickly.

"Okay, okay. I'll come with you," Josh tried to calm her.

They stepped out of the car slowly. Amanda was distraught. She had anticipation and fear in her face. She hadn't seen Tim since the interview at the police station. He had tried to call her a couple of times, leaving messages on the home voice-mail but she never returned them. She was hurt yet still had feelings for him. He had saved her life, yet he had lied to her. She was mad and at the same time now understood how he tried to protect his father. Did he choose his family over her? Should she have expected him to tell the truth even if it meant sending his father to prison? All these questions floated in her head. Until now she had wanted to find her own answers before seeing him again.

The previous night, she had discussed all of this with her parents; a rare moment of confidence and soul searching. Although Lindsey didn't approve of the relationship, she maintained control of her thoughts; her daughter was reaching out for help. Teenagers didn't take such a chance very often; it might be the last chance Amanda would give her, so she was very careful.

In the end, the three had agreed to arrange for this visit. Joshua had called Audrey Wallis to ask if they could come around to see her, making sure Tim would be around also. Audrey had agreed and here they were.

They walked up the three stairs to the front porch and knocked on the door. A short moment later, Audrey opened the door. Josh said "Hello" Amanda just raised a hand in a short wave while Lindsey said nothing.

They walked in when Audrey invited them into the living room. The home was modest except for a large screen television and a very expensive sound system. The sofa and couch themselves were patched up and in terrible state of disrepair. The walls were painted light blue but the surface was yellow with age and smoke. They were a bit afraid to sit down but Josh took the lead. He also started the conversation.

"So. How have you been?"

"Well, Joshua, I have to say it's not easy. I try to make ends meet but I don't have much money to go around. I can't sell any of this stuff yet until the police tell me I can. Depending on what they decide, I could lose all of it. It's considered part of the crime evidence." As she said it, the words choked in her throat. Tears rose in her eyes.

Silence fell on all of them. Tim wasn't in the room but they all heard the stairs creak to indicate he had come down a few steps. Amanda froze. Lindsey looked at her. She felt she had to do something.

"How's Tim?" she asked.

Audrey looked up at her. "Oh, he's pretty shaky right now. This whole thing with the fire, he was so confused when he realised it was his own father lighting it. He hasn't said much in the last while." She saw Amanda and remembered the events.

"Oh, how are your hands, dear? I understand you had some bad cuts."

Amanda, shy but polite, answered. "I'm fine now. It's almost all healed. Thank you."

"Oh, I'm so glad. I was so worried. I'm sorry this happened to you. I know Tim is sorry as well." She looked up at Lindsey. "He's not a bad boy, you know. He's just a bit adventurous. There's not a whole lot to do in Lakedge for an active teenager you know. So he's often looking for something new to try and it gets him in trouble."

"I know what you're saying." Lindsey said "I think it's why Amanda gets along with him so well. She's an avid adventure seeker herself. I think, however, that she may have had a bit of a lesson from all of this."

Audrey smiled at Amanda. "They're young. They have their whole life in front of them. I just hope Tim turns out better than his father." As she said this, the tears broke out. Nobody said anything.

She regained a bit of her composure. "I'm sorry, you didn't come here to see me cry."

She looked at Amanda again. "Would you like to see Tim?" she asked.

Amanda didn't answer. She'd frozen up again. Lindsey gently intervened. "It's partly why we are here. I just think Amanda isn't sure how to go about it."

"I understand." Audrey answered. "Let me see if I can get him to come down."

As she said it and started to stand, Tim appeared at the doorway to the living room. "I'm here Ma." His eyes were on Amanda.

Amanda turned to him, remaining silent. "Hey" was all he said. She replied with the same.

He raised his shoulder and asked gently "You wanna talk?"

She shook her shoulders in the same way "Sure." As if this were just a normal chat between them, he left the room and she followed him. Audrey looked at them go, smiling. "Pretty girl you have there, Lindsey."

"Thanks, she's growing up to be a fine young woman. Not always the way we imagined but I guess we never are quite what our parents imagined we would be." Lindsey said.

They chatted a while. Audrey explained how she had filed for divorce. The relationship had gone downhill for over five years already, but she had stayed and endured the hardship all this time just for the sake of Tim. Now, she felt it couldn't get any worse and Tim would probably be better off if Jeff wasn't as prominent in his life. Maybe it wasn't too late to stop the damage caused by the bad influence.

They were still talking when Amanda came down the stairs and appeared in the doorway. "Mom, could I stay here for a while? Tim and I have a lot of catching-up to do."

Lindsey couldn't quite believe how quickly the make-up had been resolved. Amanda had turned from shy and anxious, to eager and cheerful in less than five minutes. In her mind, however, she knew teenagers acted like that all the time, under any circumstances. She looked at Audrey for a sign.

"It's fine with me if you want to leave Amanda with us. I was going to start dinner anyway. She can stay, there's enough for her."

"Are you sure?" Lindsey asked with genuine concern, "You probably don't have very much to spare. I wouldn't want to put you through any trouble."

"Oh, don't worry. It's not one more plate on the table that will push us over. I'll cope. Thanks." Audrey replied.

Amanda turned to her father. "Please Dad? I'll call you when I'm ready to come home." Amanda had always been 'Daddy's little girl' so she knew the look to use to get her father to agree to almost anything she asked for. Josh hesitated and looked in Lindsey's direction. He saw her smile. "Very well. If it's no trouble? We'll come back after dinner. Don't forget to call."

"No trouble at all."

Amanda raced back upstairs. Josh and Lindsey said their goodbyes to Audrey and left.

Once in the car, Lindsey asked Josh. "So, what do you think?"

"I think our little girl isn't very little anymore. She's growing too fast. I guess there's not much we can do about it."

Lindsey sat back and fastened her seat belt. Josh started the car. "Face it Josh. With Mike away most of the year and Amanda soon to follow, we have to start preparing for an empty nest."

Josh pondered on the idea. "That certainly doesn't make me any younger."

Lindsey smiled and added another idea. "It won't be long now before you become a grandfather."

"Oh, please, don't! I'm not ready to be a grandfather. Don't scare me. Grandfathers are considered old. I'm not old."

They both laughed. Lindsey remembered "There's a saying that goes like this 'the only disadvantage to being a grandfather is that you have to sleep with a grandmother!'" They both laughed some more.

As they did Josh moved the car out of the driveway and started down the road. He slowed down. "I don't feel like going home right away. What do you say we go for a ride?"

Lindsey twisted her head. "There's nobody home waiting for us. I'll follow you wherever you want to go."

"Good."

He took the turn towards the main highway and drove North. The next built up area was the Ojibwa Falls first nation reserve. After that, there was nothing but forest for kilometres.

They drove silently for the first while. Josh admired the trees. The evergreens were draped in snow but the end of the branches pointed out in vivid green, slightly dimmed only by the fog created from the melting snow rising above the pavement. The sky was grey but not menacing. It was just a cover blanketing the boreal forest to keep some of the warm air from escaping to the atmosphere. The peace seemed a dramatic contrast to all he had been living through recently.

"I do feel as if the last few years were actually decades. All of this strain and stress has been quite a burden." Josh said.

"I feel the same. I just pray this is over. I don't know if I would have the strength to take anything else on."

"Nor I."

They returned to their silence. The road swerved gently to go around large rock formations here and there. Josh drove slowly to have enough time to take in all the view. Once in a while they arrived in lower areas where a river had created a marsh. In it you could see the beaver huts, probably having played a major role in the creation of the marsh in the first place. The water was frozen and reeds stuck out of the ice, bending in the direction of the wind.

Josh felt as one of reeds. He had been pushed by forces trying to get him to break but every time he had simply bent and regained his posture once the wind had gone by. After a while the reeds seemed to take on a permanent bend. He felt worried about how much harder he would have to bend. Would he look like those reeds?

They came to a sign indicating a logging route. He had seen it before. It led to one of the areas where trucks would access the lands selected for harvesting trees. He pointed it out to Lindsey.

"You know, when I think of Lakedge, I believe we can dispel a myth."

"Oh, yeah. What myth is that?" Lindsey asked.

"Well, the way I see it, for us money actually does grow on trees."

"Well said."

They both smiled and drove on, leaving tire tread marks in the new snow. The marks didn't remain for long, snow covering them quickly. All was peaceful around them. Almost a religious experience, they felt the peace of the forest.

Final thoughts

The following is an original article written on February 18, 2007 by LESLIE SCRIVENER reproduced here in homage to the courage of the people of Nipigon, an inspiration for completing this book.

It should be noted that over a period of about three months, I made numerous unsuccessful attempts at reaching the author and left e-mails and voice mails to the Toronto Star to ask permission to reproduce this text. None of my calls and e-mails were returned so I took it upon myself to reproduce the article here verbatim.

A Town Called Hope

When locals bought the Nipigon mill, things looked brighter. Then came the fire.

NIPIGON - Richard Harvey, the new mayor of Nipigon, drives a visitor down Front St. This was the town's main drag during his childhood, he recalls, with cars drifting slowly up and down. It was exciting and enticing.

Things are different today. Some call Front St. an eyesore. The Plaza theatre – closed. Taxi stand, pizza joint, barbershop – closed. The International Hotel, known as the Nash, once the place to go for a drink, is being demolished. The Normandie Hotel closed last month. The Ovilio Hotel is now a parking lot.

Yet Harvey, a guitar maker by trade, says that, for a couple of months this winter, it looked like everything would change for the better in Nipigon. The mayor, sporting a ponytail, an earring, rimless glasses and a suit but no tie, recalls the excitement over the takeover of a local mill by people in the community.

In December 2005, plywood manufacturing giant Columbia Forest Products, based in Portland, Ore., announced it was selling the Multiply Forest Products plant, the biggest employer in the town of 1,600, and would close the mill if no buyers came forward. No one did until a group of managers from the mill, all people from Nipigon, contributed their life savings to rescue the company.

It was a huge struggle to get financing. "We tried 23 different financial institutions and were turned down by every single one of them," recalls Gilles Boucher, Multiply's new president and a 20-year veteran of the company. In the end, the new team got a line of credit from the local Royal Bank of Canada. "They had an interest in the community," Boucher says.

The deal closed on Dec. 22, 2006. The new owners had bucked globalization and seized control of their destiny.

But management couldn't do it alone. They wanted the employees to have a stake in the company. So they asked the hourly employees – 120 tradesmen and labourers – to contribute 7 per cent of their salaries for one year – to a maximum of $3,000 each – toward modernizing the 50-year-old plant. The workers voted to accept that plan, reasoning a loan was better than a pay cut. "It showed our commitment and looked good to the bank and to the province," says millwright Chris Willan.

Meanwhile, more financing for the mill's renewal came from the province, which kicked in a $400,000 grant.

The first month of the mill's new ownership was a joy. "Things were going extremely well," says Boucher, who's wearing a heavy wool plaid shirt and greets you with a handshake that would crush granite. "Record productivity. Definitely the right attitude by the employees and very good sales – 10 per cent higher than December."

And Multiply placed an order for new equipment, a $3.2-million automated veneer repair line from Finland. It was expected in September. "Everything was uplifted then," says Billy Willan, 41, a debarker operator and 22-year mill employee who's having a coffee with brother Chris in the Nipigon Café. "Things were looking good, and we thought this community will survive."

But then disaster struck this month with a spectacular fire that burned the mill to the ground. The blaze roared all day, and flames shot into the sky at night; firefighters drained the reservoir trying to extinguish it. Mill workers, whose houses are on a hill overlooking the town, could sit in their living rooms and watch the inferno. Some closed their curtains; it was too terrible a scene.

The community is still waiting for the fire marshal's report. But foul play is not suspected, and Boucher says it's believed the cause was a faulty hydraulic hose.

Most crushing for the employees is the possibility that, if the mill can't be rebuilt, they'll have to leave a place where they have deep roots. "For me, this is all about the community," says Chris Willan, 39, who's been at Multiply for 20 years. "We hate to see this community become a ghost town, wiped off the map, with no one to stay. ... It's tough to think of moving somewhere you don't have family to count on."

"I don't know what to think," says Billy Willan. "Everything is so confusing. If you think of the future – will they rebuild? Can we stay?"

Local ownership, which the plant managers and workers saw as protection against the whims of owners more attentive to global competition than the livelihood of the workers in a small Ontario town, was the great hope for Multiply. The mill made highly specialized plywood underlay for vinyl floors. It's a niche market, and most of its sales were in the U.S.

"People making decisions are here, not in Oregon state," says Mayor Harvey, who adds that the local managers would be accountable to "their employees walking down the street and in the coffee shop."

And he adds: "If Columbia, an American company, was still the owner, (after the fire) they would have sent their corporate PR person, held a wine and cheese party and never be seen again."

The plant was insured, though it's unclear for how much.

Since the fire, the latest in a series of calamities for the forestry industry in northwestern Ontario, politicians have been beating a path to Nipigon. Liberal MP Joe Comuzzi (Thunder Bay-Superior North) came back for lunch Thursday to meet with the town council. He's set up a constituency office to help mill workers apply for employment insurance and Grade 12 upgrades. NDP leader Howard Hampton held a meeting in the Legion's Bingo Hall on Thursday night. Premier Dalton McGuinty has been on the phone. Liberal MPP Michael Gravelle (Thunder Bay-Superior North) was in and out of town for a week. Tony Martin, the NDP MP from Sault Ste. Marie, came by.

The mill losses in the region have been staggering. In November 2005, the Norampac pulp and paper mill in nearby Red Rock cut 90 jobs. In March 2006, Sturgeon Timber in Dorion closed, with 85 jobs lost. Norampac shut down in October 2006, for a loss of 300 jobs. Harvey estimates that 20 per cent of Nipigon's work force is now out of work.

Against this background, there was a grim urgency to the town meeting with Hampton.

"How do we get money here and fast?" a woman asked. "That's why we're here. Tell us what we can do. Write letters?"

"We can't wait two years for a new mill to be built," another woman said. "Half of us will move or go on UI for a year and then go on welfare. And there are going to be layoffs in other businesses; people can't afford groceries. We need some commitment now."

"What is the community going to do? Is everyone going to go to Alberta?" asked another.

Ken Oja, a union steward, broke the tension in the room when he said to Hampton: "The next time you're in a meeting sitting across from Dalton McGuinty, there's a favour I think you can do for me. Tell him this isn't a recession. This isn't a depression. It's a disaster. Then show him a map where Northern Ontario is."

The theme of northerners ignored while car manufacturers in Southern Ontario benefit from subsidies had considerable traction in the room. "Some of the largest cities have forgotten about the rest of the country," said Hampton. "I talk to some people in Toronto and they have no idea what's going on once they get 30 to 40 miles out of Toronto. They have no idea of the reality of the rest of us in the province. That's worrisome."

Hampton urged the crowd not to give up hope. "Don't be pessimistic; organize to take them on."

And what, precisely, did organize mean, several asked. The woman who wondered if letter writing would be effective asked about it again.

He told them to make use of the natural leadership in their community and to keep asking questions. "You might need a community protest," he added.

At this point, Glena Clearwater's voice rang out. "Just block the Nipigon Bridge!"

That's a blockade that would halt trans-Canada traffic. It's estimated 5.2 million people pass through Nipigon on Highway 17 every year.

At 68, white-haired and wearing a jaunty orange John Lennon cap, Clearwater is a former school teacher and now writes for the local paper, the Nipigon-Red Rock Gazette, and the Thunder Bay Chronicle Journal. She has three sons who have lost jobs at local mills. "So it's hit hard," she says on her way out of the meeting.

There's another thing that worries her – mounting debt among young people and middle-aged mill workers who didn't finish high school and have few options other than labouring in a mill. House prices have fallen so low that people are buying houses on their credit cards, Clearwater says, giving the example of a house in Red Rock, 20 kilometres south of Nipigon, which sold for $8,000 and was purchased on a credit card.

Surprisingly, in the face of misfortune, the optimism that Hampton urged is circulating through the town.

The new mayor, who was elected in November with a mostly new council, is boosterish on the community and hopeful for the future.

"We're going to be okay," he says, over a coffee in the Nipigon Café. There's a For Sale sign in the window.

"When?" asks John Stavropoulos, the café's 69-year-old owner. His wife, Georgina, described the week after the fire as "a giant funeral – everybody was numb, it happened so fast."

Her husband continues: "Listen, Mr. Mayor, if two years pass or three, nobody's going to be here."

Harvey, 45, the son of the local doctor, returned to his birthplace after years away in which he was a chaplain at Dalhousie University in Halifax and a missionary for an evangelical church in Niger. He is also a professional dog sled racer, and a supply teacher.

"I've travelled the world and I look at the potential here," he says, pointing out that, while a year ago "you couldn't buy a pair of socks or underwear or pantyhose," a department store, computer shop and dollar store have since opened up. Several labour training and re-employment programs are being set up for the unemployed mill workers. Harvey is thinking ahead to the kind of training workers will need for the new mill, if it's built, though most are saying it will happen. Some, like the Willan brothers, are hoping that they can find work in the reconstruction.

Last week, Boucher and other owners went to Longlac, about a two-hour drive from Nipigon, to see if Multiply could operate on a temporary basis in a mill that's been closed.

While workers still turn their hopes to what is familiar, others in Nipigon are thinking of new kinds of employment to keep young people from fleeing – all four of the Stavropoulos offspring have left – and to attract tourists.

"We're losing our greatest resource, our youth," says Hoss Pelletier, a city councillor with Ojibwa roots who owns the local jewellery and flower shop. His sister, Louise Dupuis, is one of the new owner/managers of Multiply.

"We have deeply rooted families and neighbours who have grown up together and, if they have to leave, it's the breakup of the true Northern Ontario."

Yet he says he feels upbeat. The governments appear to be paying attention, though he is also aware it is an election year.

"I keep on feeling we're going to come back and be stronger. We were destined to be the jewel of the north and we could be. We have a new council with a lot of plans, we're canvassing for assistance to revitalize the community, we're building a new library, we have plans to diversify."

Ecotourism comes to mind. The land is wild and beautiful. Fishing and hunting abound. An ice climb festival is held each March. But there are no outfitters in town.

Parks Canada is proposing a National Marine Conservation Area for Lake Superior, Pelletier notes. Perhaps Nipigon could be the administrative head.

Over on Highway 17, Levina Collins works in Nipigon's economic development office. She's pinning her hopes for the town's revitalization on a children's classic storybook, Paddle to the Sea. It's about a wooden canoe carved by a native boy, which he sets on the frozen Nipigon River one winter with the hope that with spring thaw it will make its way through the Great Lakes to the Atlantic Ocean. And it does.

For about seven years, she's been working on the Paddle to Sea Park, two acres in the centre of Nipigon with a reflecting pool, in effect a miniature of Paddle's route, and a series of interactive wading stations related to the book, which was written by the American Holling Clancy Holling in 1941. So far, $3.8 million has been raised from various government sources for the downtown renewal. "We're very close to going ahead," she says.

But she's also aware that people who lost their jobs a week ago aren't much interested in the development of a park sometime in the future. "People are grieving. They're thinking, `Where are we going next? What's my house worth? How am I going to feed my family?'"

She forecasts 69 jobs will come with downtown revitalization and, once it's finished, 123 full-time jobs. "There will be a demand for this," she says. "This is not pie in the sky."

In the meantime, some of the mill workers are moving ahead. A 44-year-old man at the bingo hall meeting says he has already started his Grade 12 equivalency. "This is the part when it comes back that you should have finished high school," he says wryly.

And a fund has been started for the employees of Multiply, whose health benefits run out next month. Bank manager and chamber of commerce president Michael Nitz, formerly of Scarborough, estimates the account will reach $15,000 by next week. Donations have come from across Canada and New York. Some Columbia employees in the U.S. have started a fund as well.

This caring from people outside the north has come as a surprise to the mill workers. "Nobody expected this," says Chris Willan. "But then, we wouldn't have been asking."

—————————————————

The End

About the Author

Alain Normand is a graduate of University of Ottawa, Canada, in Public Administration and Political Science. After fifteen years in various Public Administration positions in the Ottawa and Gatineau area, he embraced a second career in Emergency Management. Involved in many relief operations such as the 1996 Saguenay Floods, the 1998 Ice Storm, September 11, the Blackout of 2003, and other local emergencies, past-president of the Ontario Association of Emergency Managers, he is a much sought-after speaker on topics related to Emergency Management, Business Continuity, and Pandemic Planning. He teaches Emergency Management at Sheridan College and York University.

Employed since 1999 as the Municipal Emergency Manager for the City of Brampton in Ontario, a municipality of 452,000 people, he lives there with his wife Nicole, and his children Nathanaelle and Gabriel. An older son, Philemon, is presently living in Toronto, with his dog Basil.

The Harness of the Riviera is his third published work.

Please visit Alain's website at:

http://ca.geocities.com/alainnormand@rogers.com

Don't miss Book One of the Lakedge Disaster Series:

The Return of the Spanish Lady:

The 1918 Influenza Virus is Back.

Josh Stuart is a family man with firm principles and strong values. But when a stranger rides into the quiet Town of Lakedge bringing fear, division and death, Josh, his family, indeed the whole town are forever changed.

They eventually realise that this Spanish Lady has remained hidden for almost a century. The last time she was out in 1918, she rampaged through the world taking more than 20 million lives. Now she is out of hibernation, she is on the hunt, she is hungry for blood. Her next stop just happened to be…

Lakedge.

Here is what people have said about "The Return of the Spanish Lady":

-It's so realistic, it's scary. S.H.
-Fascinating, I couldn't put it down. M.W.
-My wife is a nurse and when I told her about the book she wanted to read it; she loved it and wants to know more on homeopathy in particular. B.M
-I was scared you were going to give us a fairy tale ending, but you stayed real until the last page. K.R.
-What a great book. I can't wait for the sequel to be out. I.P.
-At 8:30 this morning I sat down and opened the cover of "The Return of the Spanish Lady". I looked up after finishing it and was surprised that it was 4:00 pm. You've written a captivating story! I enjoyed reading it and will encourage my family, friends, & students to read it as well. L.B.

Winner of the
2007 Arts Acclaim Award
Creative Writing, Fiction Category

The Curse of El Ninõ:
Global Warming is Here to Stay.

Lakedge, a quiet forestry hamlet at the border of the boreal belt of northern Canada, is once again facing doom. El Ninõ, using the elements and a strong dose of greed from humans that feed it in the first place, is trying to accomplish what its big sister The Spanish Lady couldn't achieve during the influenza pandemic.

Joshua Stuart, the town manager, is forced to use all his willpower and energy to maintain order and survive. His family, his friends, indeed his whole community is threatened by fire, drought and storms. As the Ojibwa story goes, the evil monsters that are under the earth have been freed and they come to devour the inhabitants of the earth. Someone has to stop them before they succeed.

The critics are unanimous.

"Realistic, an eye opener" S.G.

"Enthralling story, good suspense elements, realistic." M.H.

"I just loved the story. I had a hard time putting it down." K.G.

Printed in the United States
143434LV00003B/1/P

9 781438 924618